Daniel's
Around H... W9-AZI-308

His hand slid across Mercy's back beneath her hair and he wrapped her in his arms. He gathered her to him as gently, carefully, as if she were the most fragile thing in the world.

In a daze of joy Mercy clung to him. She wondered if he loved her as a woman or if he was fond of her because she was his foster sister. Did she only imagine she felt his lips nuzzling her ear? In the warmth of his embrace, she longed to whisper that the love she felt for him was the all-consuming love of a woman for her man. She wanted to tell him to please take her as his mate, to join his body with hers, to plant seeds of his children in her womb. What would he say? Would he be shocked? Disgusted by her boldness?

Her words came in a quivering voice. "I can't imagine life without you..."

Also by
Dorothy Garlock

Annie Lash
Restless Wind
Wayward Wind
Wild Sweet Wilderness
Wind of Promise
Lonesome River
Dream River

Published by
POPULAR LIBRARY

RIVER OF TOMORROW

Dorothy Garlock

POPULAR LIBRARY

An Imprint of Warner Books, Inc.

A Warner Communications Company

POPULAR LIBRARY EDITION

Popular Library ® and the fanciful P design are registered trademarks
of Warner Books, Inc.

Cover illustration by Sharon Spiak

Popular Library books are published by
Warner Books, Inc.
666 Fifth Avenue
New York, N.Y. 10103

W A Warner Communications Company

Printed in the United States of America

First Printing: December, 1988

10 9 8 7 6 5 4 3 2 1

To special people—
Candace Camp,
Pete Hopcus,
and Stacy—
  with special love.

CHAPTER ONE

Mercy cast an uneasy glance over her shoulder. It was silly, she knew, to be so jumpy about going home to an empty house, but the two men who had loitered across the road from the school for a good part of the afternoon bothered her. When at first she had glanced out the window and seen them there, she hadn't thought much about them. Then later, in the middle of the afternoon, she noticed they had moved to the edge of the woods across from the school and had built a fire. Were they camping there? It was far too early to build a supper fire. The men were still sitting by the fire when the school day ended and Mercy dismissed the children, but when she left the school to walk the mile home, they were gone.

Travelers constantly passed through Quill's Station on their way to or from Vincennes, the city that had been established by the French almost a hundred years ago in 1732. Quill's Station, on the banks of the Wabash, sat astride the direct route to the city. The village of more than one hundred people, surrounded by rich timber and grassland, stretched along the river road.

With her shawl hugged to her, Mercy walked briskly down the well-packed dirt road. She called a greeting to Mike Hartman when he came out onto the porch of the store, owned by Mike and Mercy's father, with several coils of rope over his shoulder. She nodded to the father of one of her students who was passing in a two-wheeled cart.

As she passed Granny Halpen's rooming house, she waved to the elderly woman, who sat in her rocking chair on the porch, a quilt across her knees to ward off the chill, a snuff stick in the corner of her mouth. Granny knew everyone and everything that went on in Quill's Station. Farrway Quill had once said that the village had no need for a newspaper when it had Granny.

The houses in the town, no more than two dozen, were hewn timber set upright in the ground and chinked with stone and mortar. Except for the Quill house, none was more than one story high. All had porches on at least two sides, some on three. Surrounding each was a garden and fruit trees. Most of the houses were evenly spaced on long, narrow tracts of land and were set close to the road.

The Quill house, the largest and by far the grandest house in town, was on the bend of the road at the far end of town. As Mercy walked up the path from the road to the white, two-storied house with its massive stone chimneys, she thought how empty and desolate it seemed without lamplight shining from its windows. A sudden yearning to see Mary Elizabeth and Zack running to meet her, and her mother waiting for her in the doorway, sliced through Mercy so acutely that tears filled her eyes.

Inside the house, she lit the lamps to disperse the gloom. It looked different somehow—big, lonely. The fire in the fireplace had been banked. All Mercy had to do was rake aside the ashes and add kindling from the wood box, then a larger piece of wood. She did this now, squatting, holding her skirts up over her knees to keep them from being soiled. Soon the cheery blaze was sending warmth into the room. She removed her shawl and hung it over the back of the chair.

Darkness had brought a lively wind from the northwest. Mercy listened to it scurrying around the corner of the house, worrying a limb of the walnut tree and causing it to rub against the roof, making a scratching sound she easily identified. Now the brisk March wind was beginning to find its way down the chimney of the huge cobblestoned fireplace, teasing the flames, flattening them so that sparks came out of the burning wood, then dancing back up the chimney.

Curled up in the big chair where Papa Farr usually sat in the evenings, Mercy watched the flames and wondered what her life would have been like if he had not found her in the cellar of a burned-out homestead down in Kentucky and brought her here. She remembered someone saying that Farrway Quill had a habit of gathering up orphans. On the same trip he had found Liberty and her family stranded on the river road, and Daniel Phelps, the only survivor of a train of settlers who had been ambushed by river pirates. He had fetched them home, married Liberty, and together they had become a family. Daniel and Mercy had been as much a part of the family as Farr and Liberty's own children, Zack and Mary Elizabeth. Mercy liked to think that her real parents would have been people just like Farr and Liberty Quill.

"I'll be all right, Mamma," Mercy had said only that morning when Liberty and the children were preparing to leave Quill's Station to join Farrway, who was serving as a congressman in Vandalia, the capital of Illinois. He had been chosen in the fall election to represent his district, and he wanted his family with him.

"Eleanor and Tennessee will be back from Vincennes

in a couple of days, and Tennessee will stay with you until school is out. Then you're to come on to Vandalia," Liberty had told Mercy as she gave her a parting hug.

Tennessee Hoffman, the daughter of the French postmaster of Davidsonville in Arkansas Territory had been brought to Quill's Station by Gavin McCourtney and his wife, Eleanor, when they came to buy the sawmill from Farrway Quill. The childless couple were very fond of the French-and-Indian girl who was a few years older than Mercy.

Although Mercy was half a head taller than the woman who had raised her, Liberty and she could be taken for real mother and daughter. Both were blond and blue-eyed. They were not tall, but they were slender and graceful, and each had a beautiful mouth, whether laughing, talking, or in repose. They were totally feminine women, fragile to look upon, but with wills of iron.

"Did Daniel say he would take me?" Mercy had asked.

"He said that he would make sure you had a reliable escort. I'll not worry about you one bit as long as Daniel is here to look after you. He always has, you know."

"Too much!" Mercy had retorted spiritedly, because she was afraid she would cry. "He finds something wrong with every man who comes courting me and reports it to Papa. If he doesn't let up, I'll soon be an old maid."

"An old maid at nineteen?" Liberty had scoffed. "It's 1830, dear. Girls don't marry as young as they did in my day. And besides, I don't think you've really liked any of the men who have come calling."

"I haven't," Mercy admitted with a shy smile. "But, Mamma, I told you what Daniel did at the Humphrey barn dance. He hit Walt Cash because his hand slipped down to my bottom while we were dancing. Walt meant no harm. He had been drinking. Daniel should control his temper."

"His temper? He said Walt was acting improperly."

"Walt is only a boy of eighteen, even if he is big as an ox, and Daniel is a twenty-five-year-old man. Since he built his own house, he hardly ever talks to me. He just stands around, silent as a tree stump, then he orders me to do this or do that."

Liberty laughed. "He's been doing that since he was a boy. Now he has all that wheat land west of us, and with Farr being busy in Vandalia, he has the responsibility of the farm and the mill, not to mention our most valuable asset —you."

"Oh, damn, Mamma! I'm just being cranky. I'll miss you!"

"Don't swear, dear. I'll miss you too!"

Above the ticking of the mantel clock, Mercy heard another noise. It was not the tree scraping on the roof or the creaking of timbers. It came from outside the door. She sat quietly, her ears alerted anxiously for a repetition of the sound. Daniel was going to stop by on his way home, but it was too early for him. He would be busy at the mill for another hour. Old Jeems would have done the outside chores and gone back to his cabin in the woods hours ago. The freed Negro hated to be out after dark.

The sound came again, a barely audible scratching at the door. Mercy came to her feet and reached for the pistol that lay on the mantel. She stood holding her breath, her eyes fastened on the door.

The sound was repeated, followed by a throaty "Me-oow!"

It sounded like a cat. The only cat that had been in the house was Mary Elizabeth's cat, Blackbird, and he had disappeared months ago.

Mercy's mind went wild. Robbers had learned from the Indians to imitate a turkey or some other fowl to decoy a victim. She had never heard of one imitating a cat. Yet was it a cat on the other side of the door, or someone who knew she was here alone, using a trick to get her to open the door? She had to know. Her feet felt like lead. This is stupid, she thought, and willed her legs to move. Why in tarnation was she so jumpy? Was it because she had never before been alone in the house at night?

By the time she reached the door, her fingers were sweating on the pistol. Silently she lifted the door bar and lowered it into the holder. There was no sound. She could hear her heartbeat vibrate into the wood where she pressed her ear. Another "Me-oow" came from the other side of the thick panel. As she cautiously eased the door open an inch, a loud purring began. She pulled the door open wider and looked down. Out of the darkness came the eerie glint of eyes. Relief made her feel foolishly weak.

"Blackbird!" Mercy swung the door back. "Blackbird, where in the world have you been all this time?"

The cat seemed larger than she remembered. She could see that even in the shadows where he paused, taking his time about entering. He purred, moved, tilted his head to look at her, sweeping the floor with his majestic tail.

"Are you coming in or not?" Mercy asked with a laugh. "Oh, I wish you had come yesterday. Mary Elizabeth would have been so glad to see you. She cried, you know, when you couldn't be found."

The huge animal finally moved across the threshold, and Mercy closed the door. He walked to the hearth, seated himself, and stared up at her with his slanting, yellow eyes, then lifted a paw and flicked it daintily with a pink tongue. He was as black as night, tall and rangy, with ears ragged from many battles. When he had been little more than a kitten, Mary Elizabeth had caught him with a small blackbird in his mouth. She had named him Blackbird to remind him of the dastardly deed.

"Me-oow," he said, and began washing his face in earnest.

"I suppose you're hungry."

The cat stopped licking and looked at her.

Mercy placed the pistol on the mantel and went to the kitchen, knowing the big tom followed her. She put a biscuit in a wooden trencher and spooned meat drippings over it, set it on the floor, and looked at the cat. He looked back at her, made his way to it leisurely, smelled it, then began to eat daintily.

"Don't think I'm bribing you to get you to stay," Mercy said sternly. "You'll work for your keep, or else you'll—"

The loud, determined rap on the door cut off her threat to the cat. The knocking came again before she could take a breath. Who would knock like that? Not Daniel. He would open the door and call out her name. Open the door! She remembered she had neglected to drop the bar in place when she let in the cat.

The heavy oak door shook from the force of the pounding as Mercy hurried from the kitchen. She had almost reached the door when it was flung open with such force that it bounced back against the wall. The cold wind swept past her to the hearth, sending a shower of sparks up the chimney. Two men stood before her, blurred against the darkness. Her first thought was that they meant to harm her; otherwise they would have waited for her to come to the door. Her second thought was the pistol on the mantel. She ran toward it but was caught from behind by arms that pulled her tightly up against a man's chest.

She heard the door slam shut.

"We ain't goin' ta hurt ya none, if'n ya behave. We want ta look at ya, is all." The man spoke close to her ear, then turned her around and pushed her up against the wall.

Mercy could smell their unwashed bodies before her eyes focused so that she could see them. They wore round-brimmed, peaked leather hats pulled down over shaggy, straw-colored hair, that contrasted sharply with the black beards on their faces. Over homespun shirts that were dirty and ragged, with sleeves much too short for their long arms, they wore sleeveless vests of cowhide. Powder horns and shot bags hung from their shoulders by leather straps. The younger man, the one with the short fuzzy beard, held both the muskets. As Mercy's frightened eyes met his, his wide mouth twisted into a grin, showing large square teeth.

"By granny, Lenny! She's sightly. I do be swearin' it."

"Who . . . are . . . you?" Mercy's voice came out heavily, and she spaced the words because she was breathless with fright.

"She's purty as a button."

Mercy's eyes moved from one man to the other. "You'd better get out of here. My brother will be here any minute. He'll shoot you—"

"She got the mole, Len. I'll be dogfetched if'n we ain't done gone 'n' found 'er."

The man called Len said nothing. His eyes narrowed as he thrust his face close to Mercy's, scanning her every feature from the soft blond hair held in a loose knot at the back of her neck to the delicate oval of her face, her wide-spaced, sky-blue eyes beneath curved brows, and her generous mouth. He pinched her chin with rough fingers and turned her face to the light, so that he could see the small mole among the thick fringe of gold-tipped lashes on her lower eyelid.

Mercy jerked her chin from his grasp. Fear pounded over her, making her tongue thick in her mouth and her stomach feel like a slab of rock.

"Get out of here!" she choked. "Daniel will tear you apart if he catches you here!"

"Hush yore blabberin'." Lenny spoke sharply, the words coming through tobacco-stained lips.

"Ya ain't ort to rile Len," the second man told her. "He kin be meaner 'n a ruttin' moose when he gets his dander up." He looked about the room. "Lordy! Ain't this a fancy place? Lookit them shiny floors 'n' them glass lamps. Hit's light as day in here, Lenny. I'd shore like Maw ta see it." He sidled over to the kitchen doorway and looked in. "By jinks, damn! They got one a them cook stoves like we seen in the picture—"

"We ain't here ta sightsee, Bernie. Let's get on with what we come fer."

Bernie stood in front of Mercy, the twisted grin distorting his face. He fingered a strand of her hair. She glared at him, refusing to jerk her head away.

"Yep, she's purty as a speckled pup."

"Air ya the schoolmarm what's called . . . Mercy?" Len asked.

"You know I am. I saw you camped across from the school today. What do you want with me?"

"Have ya got a brown spot on yore butt 'bout this big?" He made a circle with his thumb and forefinger and held it up in front of Mercy's face.

She drew in a deep, shocked breath as her eyes shot to the door. Her mind raced frantically with ways to escape. But her common sense told her it was useless. *Daniel*! *Please come*!

"She'd not know, Len. How'd she see it lessen she put her head 'tween her legs 'n' looked up? Haw; haw, haw!" Bernie's laugh was loud and coarse. He leaned the muskets against the wall. "She ain't goin' ta tell us, 'n' we ain't goin' to know 'less we take us a look."

Mercy's mind was blotted with a heavy cloud of fear, but in a back-of-mind way a thought raced to her brain. They knew who she was—or thought they did. *Oh, God*! she prayed, *don't let them be my real kin*!

Almost before she could complete the thought, Len grabbed her, knelt down, and bent her over his knee. The surprise attack held Mercy dumb and motionless. Her skirts were thrown up over her head, and she felt rough hands pawing at her underdrawers. Panic forced a scream from her throat. She screamed again before a hand clamped over her mouth. Almost mad with fear, she kicked and bucked with all her strength.

"Be still!" A heavy hand came down on her bottom with a sharp slap. "By Jehoshaphat! I'll be hornswoggled if she ain't a Baxter! She got the Baxter mark on her ass like Ma said. Lenny, we done found little Hester!"

"I knowed it! She's sightly, like Maw's side, 'n' she got the mark, like on Paw's side."

Mercy was not aware of the reason the hand was suddenly torn from her mouth and she was thrown to the floor, or why the table went crashing, or the cat screeched and ran over her back to get out of the way. For a second she was stunned; then, in desperation, she rolled away from the tramping of heavy boots and righted herself so she could see.

Daniel had hit Lenny in the mouth with a rock-hard fist, sending him sprawling against the table. Blood sprayed down over Lenny's shirt. Bernie, screeching like a wildcat, jumped on Daniel's back, wrapped his legs around his middle, and threw his arms about his head.

"I got 'em! I got 'em! Hit 'em, Lenny," he yelled.

Lenny got to his feet on unsteady legs, shaking his shaggy head to clear it.

Daniel, taking a step back toward the heavy oak door, reached up and grabbed a handful of Bernie's hair. Using it as a handle, he whacked his head sharply against the edge of the door. Bernie immediately went limp and fell to the floor in time for Daniel to meet Lenny's charge, that carried them both out the door.

Mercy scrambled to her feet and ran to the mantel for the pistol. On the way she stumbled over the cat, who screeched and hissed and ran with tail straight in the air.

By the time her frantic fingers found the pistol, Bernie was on his knees, his head hanging between his arms. When he attempted to get to his feet, Mercy moved over and whacked him on the back of the head with the gun barrel. He sprawled facedown on the floor. She waited a moment, and when he remained still, she ran to the doorway.

With the tip of his knife in Lenny's back, Daniel was urging him up the steps of the porch. Mercy stepped back out of the doorway, and the two men came into the light. Daniel's eyes went to the man on the floor, then to Mercy.

"You all right?" He had a cut on his cheek, his shirt was torn, and he had a look of cold fury on his face.

Mercy nodded. She was trembling from head to foot. The pistol she held out at arm's length wavered as if she hadn't the strength to hold it. Daniel put his knife in his belt and gently lowered her arm until the barrel pointed to the floor, never taking his cold eyes from Lenny's face.

"I ought to blow your goddamn head off!" His voice was quiet and deadly, his face dark with a fury Mercy had never seen.

"We warn't hurtin' 'er. We came ta fetch 'er home."

"Fetch her . . . home?" Daniel's eyes went to Mercy's white face, then back to the man who had spoken the shocking words. "What the hell are you talking about?"

"She's little Hester, what was took from us down on the Green in Kaintuck."

"How do you know that? You stupid son of a bitch! Stay away from her if you want to keep that mangy hide in place."

"We ain't goin' ta do that. Maw said fetch her if'n she had the Baxter mark on her butt. It's thar, right where Maw said it was. She's got the mole too. Me 'n' Bernie got ta take her home."

Daniel grabbed the front of Lenny's shirt and shook him. "I should kill you for putting your hands on her!"

"How else was we gonna know? She warn't goin' ta tell us if'n she had the mark."

"She's not the woman you're looking for, damn you! Her people were all killed. Farrway Quill found her. Now get the hell out of here and take that dog meat with you." Daniel jerked his head toward the man groaning on the floor.

"Hester'd been stayin' with kinfolk while Maw had another youngun," Lenny said stubbornly. "When Paw went to fetch her, he found all our kin thar was dead, but Hester warn't among 'em. We heard 'bout this here light-headed woman livin' here with the high mucks. Peddler man said she come here 'bout the time Hester was took by them what killed our kin."

"Are you accusing Farr Quill of killing your kin and taking your sister?" Daniel asked quietly.

Lenny put his hands on his hips and jutted his chin forward. "Wal, it shore do look like he done it, 'cause *she's* Hester."

Daniel struck out suddenly and viciously. A knotted fist flattened Lenny's lips against his teeth, and at the same time another fist grabbed him and slammed him back against the door. While his legs were melting under him, another fist connected with his nose, and Lenny slumped to the floor.

Mercy could see murder in Daniel's eyes.

"Get up, you bastard! I'll not kill you while you're lying on the floor!"

"Daniel!" Mercy grabbed his arm. "Don't! Just make them go!"

Daniel looked down into her tear-filled eyes. His hand moved to her shoulder, gripped hard, then slid across her back and pulled her to him. Mercy leaned against him, and just for an instant he stroked the top of her shining head with his chin before he moved her away from him.

Daniel picked up Lenny's hat and sailed it out the

doorway and into the night. Then he fastened one hand in Lenny's shirt, the other in his crotch, and threw him out after the hat as if he were no more than a bundle of straw.

Bernie was getting to his feet.

"I'm a-goin'," he murmured as he staggered to the door, his hand on the back of his head where Mercy had hit him with the gun barrel. At the door he turned and reeled back toward the muskets propped against the wall.

"Leave them," Daniel said sharply. "You can get them in the morning . . . at the mill. Then if I see you near Mercy again, you'll wish I'd killed you tonight. Understand?"

Bernie staggered out the door and Daniel followed.

"Daniel! Don't go!"

Daniel turned, and his eyes caught her pleading ones. The pain in her voice knifed into him.

"I'm not going." His voice was deep and warm, confident, and . . . safe. It smoothed over her like a tender hand across a bruise.

"Mister?" Bernie's voice came out of the darkness. "Air ya sister's man?"

"I'm the man who's going to tear you up if you come near *Miss Quill* again."

"We ain't meanin' ta do 'er no hurt. Our Maw's been holdin' off the dark angel o' death so she could see little Hester once more. The Lord's been callin' her to come, but Maw's been shuttin' 'em out. Says she ain't goin' till sister comes home. We done swore to find 'er fer Maw."

"Mercy's not your sister," Daniel grated out harshly. "Even if she was, you're strangers to her. She's lived here all her life with a family who loved her . . . looked after her."

"She's Hester," Bernie said stubbornly. "I can't be helpin' it if'n she don't claim kin ta us. She's Hester Baxter. The Lord knows she's Hester too."

Standing just inside the door, Mercy closed her eyes and put her hands over her ears to keep from hearing any more of what was being said. Now a new fear invaded her, and a slow freeze of new horror and humiliation settled over her. She forced herself to breathe evenly, to marshal her thoughts. After all the years of wondering who she *really* was, did she know at last? Did the same blood run in her veins that ran in the veins of those two disgusting creatures? Oh, God! she cried silently. Please don't let it be so.

Mercy opened her eyes to see Daniel close the door and drop the bar across it. When he turned, she lifted eyes filled with anguish to his face. He had always been there when she needed him, just as he was tonight. Mercy's earliest memories were of Daniel, a boy with serious brown eyes and thick brown hair, holding her hand, taking care of her.

"Look at the tadpoles, Mercy, but keep out of the water.

"Put that down! You'll cut yourself.

"Get out of that pen, you silly girl, before you're stepped on.

"No, you can't see the bull put to the cow! It's not a sight for girls."

Mercy realized that she had not looked at Daniel, really looked at him, for a long time. Now he was a man with a quiet clean-shaven face, deep-set mahogany-brown eyes, thick chestnut hair that curled over his ears and drooped down on his broad forehead. He had a large frame, but life had given him a lean trimness. Constant hard work had built a powerful body with a vast supply of vitality. He was self-assured and confident, a man who knew who and what he was, and who was comfortable with himself.

He was all that was dear and familiar in Mercy's world, and now that world had suddenly been split apart. Her eyes fastened on his face in mute appeal.

"Oh, Daniel!" Her voice choked on the cry, and her face crumbled helplessly. Great tearing sobs shook her, and with a soft cry she ran to him and threw herself into his arms, crying hysterically.

"Don't cry. Don't cry," he said against the top of her head. He held her close against his chest, one hand at the nape of her neck, the other soothing her back, waiting for the storm of tears to spend itself. "Shhhh . . . don't cry. You'll make yourself sick."

No sound was as comforting to Mercy's ears as Daniel's voice, deep and warm, with a strange, intimate tone he used when speaking only to her. It had always been so. She had not been close to him like this since they were children. He was like a rock, a fort; she felt safe and cherished. She needed the closeness and security that lay within his arms. Her crying eased a little, though she still trembled under his caressing hands.

"Are you through now?" he asked as gently as if he were soothing a child. Firm fingers raised her chin, and a soft handkerchief wiped her eyes and nose. Slowly her lashes fanned up, and her enormous blue eyes, all shiny with tears, looked up into Daniel's. "Where's that sassy spirit you've had all these years?" he asked her. "Didn't you tell Mamma you could stay here by yourself for a few nights? Didn't you say that you didn't need me to stay with you because it would give old Granny Halpen talk to spread up and down the river?"

"Yes, I said . . . that." She gulped back the tears. "Please stay, Daniel. I don't care about old Granny Halpen. Let her talk." She leaned back and grasped his arm so she could look into his face. Her mouth trembled. "Do . . . you think I'm *their* sister? I've always thought of myself as *your* sister, yours and Zack's and Mary Elizabeth's." A teardrop rolled down her smooth cheek and settled into the corner of her mouth. Her fingers clutched Daniel's forearms as if she were about to slide off a cliff. "I don't think I can stand it if I'm who they think I am."

His arms tightened, and she clung to him as if only within his arms there was safety.

"Of course, you can stand it." His voice was husky with emotion. "It wouldn't make any difference to us here. You would still be Mercy Quill, daughter of Liberty and Farr Quill." He nuzzled his face into the cloud of golden hair beneath his chin.

"But my blood would be the same as . . . theirs! Oh, Daniel, they had lice in their hair, they were filthy dirty, and they smelled like . . . like they'd been sleeping in a hog pen!" She looked up at him again, her eyes filled with the misery that was tearing her apart.

"We're what our upbringing makes us," Daniel said earnestly. "Maybe if they'd had the examples of Farrway and Liberty Quill to follow, they would be like you and me."

"And if Papa hadn't found me, I'd be like *them*. Is that it?" she demanded tearfully.

"You wouldn't have minded, because you wouldn't have known anything different."

"But I do now! I'll not go with them. I don't know the woman who's . . . dying. I feel sorry for her, but I don't know her!"

"Of course, you won't go with them!" he said sternly. His hands moved to her shoulders and gripped them. "You're not to worry about that. This is your home. You'll stay right here."

Mercy wrapped her arms about his waist and buried her face against his chest. When she spoke again, it was in a low, muffled voice, and Daniel had to lower his head and press his cheek to hers to hear what she was saying.

"They knew about the mole on my eyelid and the brown spot. I didn't think anyone knew about the brown spot but Mamma."

"I knew about it," he said with an attempt at lightness in his voice. "I remember seeing it when we were children.

I had forgotten about it until now." He wrapped her more firmly in his arms and held her against his long length as if he wanted to take her hurt inside himself. "Won't you try to accept that you may have been born Hester Baxter, but now you're Mercy Quill, then forget about it?"

"I can't forget about it, Danny." The name came naturally to her lips, though she hadn't called him that in years. "You've always known who you are. I've wondered for a long time about the people I came from. When I was a little girl, I'd watch a family come into town and wonder if they were my kin coming to get me. I never dreamed I would be kin to people like the ones who came here tonight." She began to cry again.

"Mercy, Mercy, don't take on about it," he whispered with infinite gentleness. His fingers stroked the silky strands of hair back over her ear. "It's true that I've always known who I was, but at times I wished that I didn't. The man who sired me was a mean, cruel old man. I was only a small boy when we left Ohio, but I remember the whippings he gave me every night after he had read to me out of the Bible. 'Spare the rod and spoil the child', he'd say. And most of all I remember how my mother would cry while he was whipping me. Then she and I would sneak away and she would hold and cuddle me. It may have been good in a way to know about him, because it made me determined not to be like him."

Mercy looked up at him with a world of sorrow in her eyes. "You never told me that."

"I never told anyone. I'm not proud of who I came from, but it doesn't bother me."

"Oh, Daniel, I wish I'd known that." Mercy took his face between her hands and searched his eyes for traces of bitterness and hurt. His facial expression was unreadable, but there was a warm fondness in the eyes that looked deeply into hers. She stood on tiptoe, and her lips brushed his chin. He moved back as if she had touched him with fire. The muscle in his jaw was jumping, but she didn't notice.

"If Granny Halpen is looking in the window, Quill's Station may be looking for a new schoolmarm tomorrow," he said, his voice wavering slightly. "Let's have some supper. You are going to give me supper?"

"I'll make some hot biscuits, but I warn you, they're not as good as Mamma's. But first I'll wash that cut on your cheek." Her hands moved down his arms to his hands. She held them up and looked at them. "Oh, your poor hands! They're all cut."

"Not as bad as that Baxter fellow's mouth and nose. He'll not be eating or smelling much for a while." His brown eyes twinkled into hers.

Mercy smiled through her tears. "The younger one will have a headache he'll remember. After you cracked his head against the door, I hit him with the barrel of the gun when he started to get up. I was afraid I'd kill him, so I didn't hit him hard. But it flattened him out."

"Good. I was going to teach you to defend yourself, but you already know how to bash heads. How are you with the pistol?"

When Daniel smiled down into her eyes, the creases in his cheeks appeared. She had forgotten them and his even white teeth. Daniel was a handsome man. It was no wonder he was invited to so many get-togethers.

"I know how to point and pull the trigger."

"That would be enough most of the time."

Daniel moved away from her as if it were important to take the long iron from the holder and poke at the fire. He added a stout log from the wood box and glanced at the cat that came to sit on the hearth and clean his paws.

"Is that old Blackbird, Mary Elizabeth's cat?"

"It's Blackbird. He came scratching at the door tonight. I let him in and forgot to put the bar across. That's how *they* got in."

"He's making himself at home. I was thinking about bringing my old wolf dog down here to stay with you at night. He'd let you know if anyone was prowling about. If I do, the cat will have to go. Andy would tear the house up to get to him."

"I thought you were going to stay with me till Tennessee gets back," Mercy said quickly.

His eyes twinkled at her. "I *am* staying until Tennessee gets back. We might as well give Granny Halpen something to really talk about."

"I'm glad. I mean I'm glad you're staying, not glad we'll be giving Granny something to talk about." They stood for a moment, smiling at each other. "Being here like this is like it was when we were kids, isn't it?"

"Not quite," he said with a shake of his head.

Mercy lifted her shoulders. "I'll fix a pan of warm vinegar water," she said when she saw him flex his fingers. "Then I'll cook supper while you sit at the table and soak your hands. It'll take the soreness out."

They ate in companionable silence at the same table where they had eaten as children. Mercy looked at Daniel across the table and realized how much she had missed being with him the last few years. She wondered if he had missed looking out for her or if he was glad to be away from the family and on his own.

Daniel had spent a few years down in Arkansas with Rain and Amy Tallman. When he came back, Gavin McCourtney and his wife Eleanor came with him. Gavin bought the sawmill from Farrway, and Daniel took over much of the business of running the gristmill when friends began to pressure Farrway Quill to run for state office.

A couple of years ago Daniel had purchased the old Luscomb place, a mile down the road from the Quills, rebuilt the house, and moved in. He had acres and acres he put into wheat. It was ground at the mill, and sacks of flour were shipped down the river to places like Memphis and

New Orleans. He employed three families of freed Negroes to work his farm. Each family had their own house and a patch of ground for a garden, besides the yearly wage he paid them. Daniel was known as a man who was fair, generous, and hardworking, but not a man to be pushed. He was a listening man who spoke his views only when someone asked him for his opinion.

Mercy remembered hearing Liberty ask Farr if Daniel was planning to take a wife. He had smiled at her and told her that he was sure Daniel would wed when the time was right. Mercy had never heard of Daniel seriously courting a woman unless it was Belinda Martin, a widow who lived with her elderly mother and father. He had danced with her at the Humphrey barn dance, and she had seen him going into the store with her little boy perched on his shoulder. The thought of Daniel and Belinda together made Mercy's heart plunge. She wasn't half good enough for him.

"Daniel, have you ever been sorry Mamma and Papa didn't move to Arkansas Territory with Aunt Amy and Rain?" she asked to get her mind off Daniel with Belinda.

"No, and I think Papa is glad, too, now. Mary Elizabeth was too sick to move, and besides that, Colby Carroll couldn't come to take over here. It put a quick stop to moving plans. As Farr says, sometimes fate steps in and takes decisions out of a man's hands. He came here when he was just a stripling, with old Juicy Deverell. They knew men like Tecumseh and Zachary Taylor, and they inspired him to want to do something for this country now. Illinois is his home, and he wants to keep it from becoming a slave state."

"Is Arkansas going to adopt slavery?"

"It's anyone's guess right now. In the southeastern part of the territory there are cotton plantations, and where there are cotton plantations there are slaves. It will be sometime before Arkansas is admitted to the union. The western part is still such a wild and dangerous country with its mountains and fast streams. The land seems to suit Rain and Amy, though. And, in a way, I liked it too."

"If you liked living there, why did you come back?" Mercy asked quietly.

"I guess I got homesick," he said with an unashamed grin on his face.

CHAPTER TWO

“ **M** orning.”

Daniel called a greeting to Granny Halpen the following day as he and Mercy passed the rooming house on their way to the school. Granny's thin, black-draped figure looked fragile, but she declared she was strong as a horse. She had come out onto the porch to sweep the steps as Mercy and Daniel came down the road. Daniel's hand was firmly attached to Mercy's elbow, something Granny's sharp eyes noted immediately.

“Mornin' to ya. How be ya, Mercy? I'm a thinkin' yore missing yore ma.”

“Yes, I am.”

“I 'spect ya'll be leavin' soon.”

“As soon as school is out.” Mercy called, then murmured to Daniel, “We're in trouble now. Before mid-morning everyone in town will know you walked me to the school and that you spent the night at the house.”

“Does that bother you?”

“Yes, in a way. I'd hate it if scandal reflected on Mamma and Papa.”

"Our schoolteacher is a fallen woman! She spent the night alone with a man." He grinned down at her cheerfully.

"Be serious, Daniel!" Mercy looked up at the tall man beside her with worried eyes. "Not all the people here wanted to be represented by Papa. The ones who voted against him, like Glenn Knibee for instance, will be quick to put a bad light on anything that we do."

"We can't spend our entire lives worrying about what other folk think of us. Papa would be the first to tell us to do what we thought was right, and to hell with what people think."

"Yes. He would say that, and Mamma would agree. She would have wanted you to stay with me. Do you think the Baxters have gone?"

"No. They're still here. I've still got their muskets. They'll not leave without them. Don't worry about it. As soon as I get you to the school, I'll go hunt them up and send them on their way."

Mercy loosened her elbow from his grasp and hugged his arm with both hands. She could feel the muscles ripple under the cloth of his coat. For an instant she pressed her cheek to his upper arm.

"It was comforting to know you were downstairs last night. Thank you for staying with me."

Daniel moved his hand over the one on his arm and patted it gently. "Since when have you started being so polite, Miss Quill? You know there's no need for thanks between us."

They had reached the school. Several students were standing beside the door.

"'Lo, Mr. Phelps." The girl who spoke to Daniel was Mary Knibee, a brazen fourteen-year-old who was too pretty for her own good. Her hair was black, her skin a clear white. She had enormous blue eyes and long silky lashes she used with great effect. The dress she wore showed off her small waist and well-rounded bosom.

"Hello, Mary."

Encouraged, Mary sidled over close to Daniel while he waited for Mercy to open the door.

"I'm comin' to the mill to wait for Pa tonight. Will I see you there?" She tossed her curls back from her face and smiled what she considered her most fetching smile.

"No, I'll not be there."

"Ah . . . shoot! I thought *you'd* be there. I don't like to wait around by myself." She licked her red lips, then stuck the lower one out in a pout.

"You won't be by yourself. George and Turley Blaine will be there. Turley might even make you a reed whistle or some other pretty thing to play with while you're waiting."

"A whistle?"

"Would you rather have a doll? He made a doll for the little Kelsey girl. She's made clothes for it and plays with it when she comes to the mill to wait for her pa."

"I ain't wantin' no doll or no whistle to play with! And I ain't waitin' around with no nigger and no old fool like Turley Blaine." Mary flounced into the school, her back straight and her face red.

Mercy could almost feel sorry for Mary but not quite. The girl could speak correctly when she wanted to, but when she was angry, she reverted to her parents' way of speaking. Mercy kept her head turned so that the other girls didn't see the smile she couldn't suppress. She heard a muffled giggle come from one of them. Mary's flirtatious ways had not earned her many friends among the female students. It was not going to be a pleasant day. Mary would find fault with everything and everybody, and use any excuse to disrupt the class.

"Go on in, girls." Mercy swung open the door. "Arabella, you may write the morning Bible verse on the slate."

After the girls filed into the schoolroom, she smiled up at Daniel. "You've just made sure that Mary will not learn anything today. She'll be as cross as a bear with a sore tail."

"She needs her bottom spanked. Glen Knibee better watch that one, or she'll drop a babe on his doorstep before he knows it," Daniel said with a boyish grin that made him suddenly very handsome.

Mercy laughed. "Why, Daniel! I didn't know men talked of such things."

Daniel's heart lightened at the sound of her laughter. It was like the song of a meadow lark, and he had heard it far too seldom of late. Mercy was an extremely pretty woman. He had heard comments about her beauty from the men who loafed at the mill. None had been disrespectful. It was a well-known fact that Daniel was protective of his foster sister.

"Granny Halpen doesn't have an exclusive on gossip. Men gossip too."

"Even you?" She laughed again.

"I don't gossip, but I listen. You wouldn't expect me to close my ears to all the interesting tidbits I hear at the mill, would you? Here's your dinner." He handed her the small, cloth-wrapped bundle he'd been carrying for her. "Send one of the boys to the well for water when you need it. I'll be here when school is out."

"I hope the Baxters are discouraged enough to leave. I don't know if I can bear the shame if they go around telling people that I'm their . . . sister."

"There'll be shame only if you let it be," he said quickly and sharply. "You've nothing to be ashamed of. Hold your head up. You'll be stepped on if you're lying down but not if you're standing up looking folks in the eye."

"You're right as always, Danny. I'll make out as long as you're here with me." More students arrived, and Mercy asked one of the boys to build a fire in the hearth to take the chill off the room. As she stood at the door waiting for him and the other boys to pass into the schoolroom, she worried aloud. "The Baxters wouldn't come here to the school, would they?"

"Not if I find them first. Calm down."

"You'll be back?"

"I'll be back before school is out."

Mercy watched him leave. She had a strong desire to run after him, to take his hand as she had when she was a small, barefoot girl. It had been a happy time with Daniel, Mamma, Papa, Amy, Rain, Grandpa Juicy, and, of course, Colby Carroll and Willa. The family was scattered now. She and Daniel were the only ones left at Quill's Station. Even Grandpa Elija and Grandma Maude were gone; they had died last year after eating tainted meat.

Mercy heard a commotion in the schoolroom. A bench had been turned over, a girl screeched, and there was a babble of excited voices. Without supervision her pupils were a rowdy group. It was time to bring the class to order, and she went inside, grateful for the work that would keep her mind occupied.

In the middle of the morning the reader was passed around to the older students so that each could read a passage aloud. Mercy was standing behind one of the boys who was having trouble with the words when the door behind her opened and the room suddenly became quiet.

She turned slowly, almost knowing what she would see. Her hand went to her throat, and the blood flowed from her face, leaving it deathly white. Lenny and Bernie Baxter crowded through the doorway and stood at the back of the room.

The men were even rougher looking in the daylight.

Their faces and hands were filthy with ground-in dirt and soot. Their ill-fitting, bedraggled clothes were blackened with smoke and grease stains.

"Get out!" The words exploded from a throat tight with fear.

"We gotter talk ta ya, Hester." Lenny's nose was swollen and his lips cut, making his face lopsided.

"You've no right to come here. Get out!" she croaked.

"We ain't goin'. If'n ya want ta talk in front a the young-uns, so be it!"

"No! I'll talk to you . . . later."

"That big fellow what stayed the night with ya ain't goin' ta let us get in spittin' range of ya, and that's gospel." The silly grin Bernie had had on his face the night before was gone, and in its place was an expression of intense dislike.

The import of Bernie's words sank into Mercy's mind slowly. When it did, she realized that fourteen sets of ears had heard them, and the words would be repeated to eight different farm and town families that night. Tomorrow her reputation would be in shreds.

"I must spend this time with my students. Please leave." She felt cold and hot by turns, and she was not sure her legs would hold her. "I'll speak to you tonight . . . after school."

"We ain't got time ta be pussyfootin' 'round til ya can jaw with us. Maw's ailin' 'n' we got ter be gettin' back ta Mud Creek." Lenny stared at her with hard, bitter eyes.

"I'm sorry about your mother—"

"Ya can't've done forgot Maw, Hester!" Bernie spat out. Sparks of anger danced in his eyes.

"Why are you calling her Hester?" The voice that came from behind Mercy was Mary Knibee's.

"Hush up, Mary. This isn't any of your business."

"It would be my pa's business if you're calling yourself Mercy and your name is Hester." There was unconcealed pleasure in her voice.

"Shut your mouth, Mary," Arabella said sharply. "Or I'll shut it for you."

"You just try!"

The children began to talk excitedly to each other, and Mercy smothered the urge to scream.

"Go on out," she said to Lenny and Bernie, her voice as calm as she could make it. "I'll talk to you outside."

Somehow she managed to move the feet that seemed glued to the floor, and holding her hand, palm out, in front of her and making little pushing movements, she followed them out the door and closed it behind her. Through the door Mercy heard the shrill voice of her students discussing the disruption. Her face burning and her knees quivering with humiliation, Mercy pressed her back against the door. Bernie and Lenny stood in front of her as if they were afraid she would run. "Hold your head up," Daniel had said. She lifted her chin and looked first Bernie, and then Lenny square in the eye.

"You had no right to come to my school and speak to me about a private matter in front of my students. It was an ill-mannered thing to do."

"Ill mannered! Hell! Did ya hear that, Lenny?"

"I heared. Ya've got uppity livin' with the high mucks, ain't ya? Air ya thinkin' ye're too good ta be a Baxter?" Lenny sneered.

"It's what she's thinkin'," Bernie said nastily. "She ain't fit ta be no Baxter nohow, but a Baxter she be as sure as shootin'."

"All right. It may very well be that I'm . . . your sister. If what you say about the . . . Baxter brown spot is true." Mercy almost choked on the words, but she spoke evenly, without a sign of what the words cost her to say.

"I ain't no liar!" Bernie's mouth twisted into a sneer.

"If'n I'd had my rathers, ya wouldn't be Hester. Not a cold bitch what don't care 'bout folks."

"That's what I'm trying to tell you," Mercy said patiently. "My first memories are of being here with the Quills. As soon as I was old enough to understand, they explained that I was not their child and how I came to be with them. I love them. They are my family. I don't feel kinship with any of . . . you. Can't you understand that?"

"Quills ain't yore folks. Yore folks, what's left of 'em, is down in Kaintuck on Mud Creek. Yore paw met his maker a time back when a tree fell on him. He be buried alongside four young-uns Maw lost afore they was knee-high. Yore Maw's flat on her back a-waitin' fer the dark angel 'n' grievin' ta see her little lost girl young-un."

"But surely she has other children." Mercy tensed her body as she tried to stop trembling.

"Three boys aside us. Ain't no more girl young-uns," Bernie said through tight lips and then spit a stream of brown tobacco juice into the dirt at his feet. "Gid, the youngest boy, ain't dry behind the ears yet."

"I'm sorry. Go back and tell her you didn't find . . . Hester. I can't—"

"I said I ain't no liar!" Bernie's hand shot out and gripped her wrist so viciously that she could scarcely keep from crying out. The bitterness of his stare made the color rise to flood her face, but her lips were white, compressed.

"What do you want of me?" Mercy's voice was raw.

She looked from one to the other for her answer, but Lenny and Bernie were staring past her up the road. She heard the sound of a running horse and turned to see Daniel on his big buckskin galloping toward the school. Daniel's hard-boned face was taut with rage. At once her mind jerked awake. *Daniel was angry enough to kill them!*

Bernie dropped Mercy's wrist, and the Baxter brothers moved apart, ready for the attack from the man whose anger rode high in his face. Daniel saw Mercy's fear, and it was enough. He jumped from the horse and smashed his fist into Bernie's face. One moment Bernie was on his feet, and the next he was flying through the air and landing with a thud on the bare ground. Lenny backed away, shaking his head, his hands held out in front of him.

"We ain't wantin' no fight. You ain't got no right steppin' inta a family conflab!" He moved over to Bernie, his eyes never leaving Daniel's face, and extended a hand to help his brother get to his feet. "You ain't got no right!" His voice echoed shrilly.

Mercy held tightly to Daniel's arm, scarcely aware that the door had been flung open and that her students were trooping out into the yard.

"Get back in there and shut the door. Right now!" Daniel roared over Mercy's head. His voice was as harsh and powerful as the jaw that jutted in angry determination and the mouth that was straight and very hard. The children never questioned the order. They scurried back inside.

Mercy hesitated as if to follow them. Then she looked up and met Daniel's piercing brown eyes. When his hand covered hers, she felt calm and reassured. Together Mercy and Daniel faced the Baxter brothers.

"When I gave you your muskets, I told you to stay away from her. Go on back to Kentucky and leave her alone." Daniel's powerful body was tense, ready to fight again.

"Air ya a-lettin' him do yore talkin'?" Lenny's angry eyes stared into Mercy's. "We ain't goin'." He shook his head slowly. "We ain't goin' till ya come with us ta see Maw."

"You're just about this far from getting yourselves killed." Daniel held his thumb and forefinger an inch apart.

"Ya ain't Hester's kin, mister. 'Nother thing, down on Mud Creek no decent woman'd be spendin' the night with a feller if'n they ain't wedded or blood kin. You'd be horsewhipped if 'n brothers Wyatt and Hod heard of it. Me 'n' Bernie done thought on it. We ain't sayin' nothin' 'bout it to Maw or nobody, or it'll get out 'n' the Baxters will be looked down on."

"You'd better get the hell out of here while you can walk because I'm about to shoot your legs out from under you."

The raw violence in Daniel's voice made Mercy tremble. She glanced up and saw the muscles in his jaws jerk nervously as he fought to contain his anger. His whole body was like a tight coil, ready to spring; his fists clenched and unclenched. His face was twisted with smoldering rage. In all the years she had known him, she had never seen him so angry. She was suddenly afraid he would lose control and kill the two men who faced him. Her hands gripped his arm tightly.

"We'll go, fer now." Anger and resentment blazed in Lenny's eyes when he looked at Mercy. "Ya ain't fit to be no Baxter nohow. Ain't no Baxter I heared of what wouldn't go 'n' ease the pain of a dyin' maw what went down in the valley a death to birth 'em. Ya've done been ruint, sure as sin."

Mercy stood close to Daniel's tall, powerful body, her two hands clasped about his arm. They watched the Baxters until they disappeared into the woods. When she looked up at the tall man beside her, her blue eyes were strained and overbright.

"I don't know what to do," she whispered.

"About them? Leave them to me."

"No. I keep wondering if I should . . . go see her."

"Is that what you want to do?" he asked gently.

"I don't know what I want to do."

"I could take you to Vandalia. Tennessee can take over the school."

"No! I couldn't do that. They'd follow me. I know

they would, and I . . . couldn't bear to have Mamma and Papa mixed up in this."

"You don't have to decide anything now. We'll talk about it tonight. Do you want to dismiss school for the day?"

"No. I've got to face my students sooner or later. It may as well be now. Things won't be any different tomorrow."

"I'll come in with you if you want me to."

"No. But make sure *they* don't come back." Mercy cast a fearful look over her shoulder.

"I'll make sure of it. Go on in." He squeezed the hand on his arm and opened the door.

Daniel mounted his horse, his eyes searching along the road for a sign of the Baxters. Neither was in sight, but that didn't mean they were not lurking in the woods. He walked his horse along the road, his eyes scanning the edge of the forest for any movement. From up ahead he heard a dog bark, and then another chimed in. He urged his horse into a trot, and when he rounded the bend in the road, he could see two riders ahead. The Baxters were heading south. Old man Gordon's dogs were nipping at the heels of the mules they were riding.

Daniel pulled his mount to a stop. As he watched them, one turned and looked back. *They want me to think they're leaving,* Daniel thought. He wished to hell they would, but there was only a small chance of it. He had seen the determination in Lenny Baxter's eyes. He might be able to buy or scare off the younger Baxter, but not Lenny.

He turned his horse and rode toward the mill, trying to figure out what to do about the men who claimed kin to Mercy. The only wrong they had done so far was to burst into the house and manhandle her. Although that made Danny want to kill them, it was not enough reason to call in the law. Besides, Mercy would hate the fuss that would stir up. Daniel decided that whatever was to be done, he would have to do it himself.

The wind was coming up and driving rain clouds toward him from the northwest. Daniel pulled up the collar of his coat and wondered how Mercy was going to hold up under the pressure of dealing with her *real* brothers. He and Mercy had not been as close the last few years as when they were children. He had spent a couple of years in Arkansas; she had lived for a year with the Colby Carrolls in Carrolltown. He had been busy with the mill and the farm; she with the school. They had been together only for occasional Sunday dinners and on holidays.

All these years he had been as fiercely protective of Mercy as any brother would be of a sister, but he had not touched her for years, not until last night. What a lovely, soft woman she had grown up to be. It had been such a jolt to his senses to feel her small, firm breasts against his chest, her soft arms about his neck, that he had remained awake the better part of the night thinking about it.

Daniel thought about the women he had held and had kissed. Belinda Martin, for one. She was a pretty woman and would have fallen in bed with him in a minute if he had made the right moves. He had thought about it. At times he wanted a woman so badly that he got out of bed and walked the floor. But bedding Belinda would mean marriage, and he wanted to feel that the woman he married was something more to him than a vessel to ease his aching loins. Whores were available to do that.

It suddenly occurred to Daniel, as he rode up to the mill and dismounted, why casual kisses and New Orleans whores had been so disappointing. He wanted to love his woman as Farrway Quill loved his, and he wanted her to love him back equally as much.

Nothing he had experienced before had been like holding the long, soft length of Mercy against him, feeling her heartbeat against his chest, her warm breath on his neck, and smelling the sweet scent of her body.

The secret that had been wrapped up and hidden away in the back of his mind for as long as he could remember suddenly came forth and unfolded. *Mercy was his woman, his alone, to love and cherish, as it was meant to be.*

It was the most miserable day of Mercy's life. The children were too excited and curious about what had happened to settle down and concentrate on anything. Mary Knibbe was delighted with what had taken place. She watched Mercy with a smug smile on her face and made numerous remarks about "teacher" and Mr. Phelps. One time she called her Miss Hester, then corrected it quickly to Miss Quill. Mercy tried to ignore her, but it was hard to do. She was sure that Mary was counting the minutes until she could leave the school and spread the news about Daniel's spending the night at the Quill house.

The day dragged slowly by. The sky darkened with rain clouds, and Mercy had to light the lamp. She gathered her younger children, three boys and one girl, around her and held up the cards with the alphabet on them.

"Charles, what is this letter?"

"*W* for . . . warthog!" The boy laughed and looked over his shoulder at the older students to see if they appreciated his answer.

Mercy ignored him and flashed another card. "Jason?"

"*P* for . . . poot, what Pa does after supper."

Mercy closed her eyes tightly, then slammed them open when she heard the loud snickering.

"That's enough!" She snapped out another card. "Agnes?"

"*B* for baby, what Ma says a girl'll get if she don't keep her legs together."

Mercy looked at Agnes's sweet little face in stunned, openmouthed silence, before panic set in. The child gave her an impish grin. The room was deathly quiet as the students waited to see what teacher would do. Mercy quickly flipped another card.

"Robert?"

"*T* for . . . turd, horse turd, cow turd . . ."

Gales of laughter erupted. Mercy slammed her hand down on the desk.

"Quiet!" she shouted. She was losing control of the class. For the first time in three years she was losing control. "Go stand in the corner, all four of you. No, not the *same* corner, Robert. This room has four corners for four naughty children."

By the time the afternoon ended and it came time to dismiss school, Mercy's nerves were at the breaking point and she had a throbbing headache. Nevertheless, she pasted a smile on her face and stood beside the door while the children put on their wraps before going out into the light rain, pushed by a cold March wind.

"'Bye, Miss Quill."

"Good-bye, Timmy. Put your hat on before you go out."

"'Bye, Miss Quill. See you tomorrow."

"Good-bye, Arabella."

"I doubt if you see me here again after I tell Pa what happened today . . . or rather last night," Mary said with a sly, knowing smile as she crowded out the door.

Mercy caught her breath sharply, and her mouth went dry. Mary's words stabbed at her, their implication sending a quiver through her body. Because she was determined not to let the spiteful girl know she was on the verge of crying, she steadied her voice when she called after her.

"If your father doesn't want you to come to school,

Mary, it's all right with me. It's a pity. But there isn't a law against being ignorant."

Mercy battled the storm that pounded inside her, threatening to accelerate beyond her control while she waited for the last student to leave. Finally a small boy trudged out the door, and Daniel came in. Water dripped from the brim of his hat and from his cowhide coat.

Nothing would stop the tears that came to Mercy's eyes when she saw him. She turned swiftly and went to get her shawl. She knew it was stupid to cry, but there was nothing she could do about the tears that rolled down her cheeks.

Daniel followed her. He placed his hands on her shoulders and turned her around to face him. He wiped the tears from her cheeks with his thumbs.

"That bad, huh?" His face was full of concern.

"I'm just mad, that's all."

"That's all?" he teased. The soft, caring light in the brown eyes that twinkled down at her made the tears come again.

"Mad and scared. I'm mad because those Baxters came to Quill's Station looking for me, and madder that they came here to the school. Within an hour everything that was said will be all over town. Mary Knibee caught what Bernie said about you spending the night at the house. She said she doubts she'll be back to school after her pa hears about it."

"I'd think you'd be glad of that. Isn't she more trouble than all the others put together?"

"She's trouble, but I wouldn't be glad! Mary can't read. She'll go through life not being able to read if she doesn't come back to school." Heavy, wet lashes lifted from tormented eyes that shone brightly.

"But you can't teach her if she doesn't want to learn. As for me being there at the house with you, those who want to think the worst will think it regardless of whether I spent the night or not."

"Damned old busybodies!"

"Don't swear, love. I've heard Mamma say that a hundred times. Dry your eyes. I'm going to take you to the store. You can stay with Mike while I do a few things; then I'll come back for you."

"Oh, Daniel! I've cried more in the last two days than I've cried in a long time. You used to tell me to dry up. You hated for me to cry. Remember?"

"I remember, and I still hate for you to cry," he told her quietly. He pulled a piece of oiled cloth out from under his coat and draped it around her shoulders. "I didn't think you had anything to keep you dry, so I got this from Mike at the store. Put your shawl over your head and let's go. I think it's set in to rain all night."

"Daniel." Mercy placed her hand on his arm to stop him when he went toward the door. "I've got to know . . . something. This finding out about my . . . folks has been such a shock to me. I keep thinking . . . things."

Daniel watched her struggle to speak calmly.

"Of course it's a shock." His eyes held hers and he touched her cheek with his fingertips. "What *things* are you thinking about? And what do you need to know that's so important it makes you look like a frightened little rabbit?" Daniel spoke gently, but inside he had bitter thoughts. Those sonofabitches! He could kill them for what they had done to her.

"Do you . . . feel different about me now that you know the kind of people I came from?" Her voice reflected the misery in her soul.

"Do I feel *different* about you? No, dammit, no! Why would I? Do you feel different? Is that what's bothering you?"

"I feel as if I don't know where I belong anymore. It's

like I don't belong to *anyone*!" A sob caught in the back of her throat.

"Mercy, Mercy..." His arms were a safe haven around her. She leaned against him and hid her face in the warm flesh of his throat. He hugged her tightly, and his voice came from close to her ear. "I don't want you to feel that way. You *do* belong to someone. Believe me, you do."

Mercy wanted to tell him how much his words meant to her, but the flood of emotion she had held in check all day broke loose. She cried as if her heart would break. Never before had he seen her let down her barriers like this. Daniel held her tightly to him and stroked her hair until she was quiet. Then he put his fingers beneath her chin and raised her face so he could look down into her tear-wet eyes.

"Are you all right now?" he asked anxiously.

Mercy took a deep breath. "Yes. I'm sorry."

"You've nothing to be sorry for. You deserved a good cry after all you've been through last night and today. I'll bank the fire so the place won't burn down during the night, and we'll go home."

CHAPTER THREE

*I*t was still raining when Mercy and Daniel stepped up onto the board porch fronting the store. Daniel opened the door and they went inside. It was dark and gloomy, but toward the back a lamp cast a circle of light. The store was like a second home to Mercy. She had grown up among the kegs of salt, stacks of pelts, bolts of cloth, tools, harnesses, guns, and gunpowder. The smells of leather, spices, and oil-brushed iron tools were nothing new to her. She didn't even notice them anymore.

Mercy went into the store feeling as if she were wrung out. She was tired and sleepy, and her hands were icy. She longed to go home to her attic room, crawl into her warm soft bed, and find oblivion in sleep.

Weaving his way between stacks of goods, Mike came to meet Mercy and Daniel with a worried look on his face. A few years older than Daniel, he had come to Quill's Station ten years ago without family or friends and had been made welcome by Farrway and Liberty Quill. He was now considered one of the family.

"What went on down at the schoolhouse, Dan? Mary

Knibee came in when she saw her pa's wagon out front. That girl's got a nasty mouth."

"It's a long story. I'll tell you later unless Mercy wants to. I want her to stay here with you for a while, Mike. I've got to go down to the mill. I'll come back and take her home."

"Well . . . sure." Mike hesitated, his eyes going from Mercy to Daniel. "But there's someone in the back room that wants to talk to you."

"Who is it?"

"He says he's Levi Coffin."

"The Quaker from Newport?"

"The same."

Mike was not as tall or as heavy as Daniel, but he was broad-shouldered and had a head of thick russet hair combed back from his forehead. His brown eyes were clear and anxious as he looked closely at Mercy. Mike usually had a smile on his pleasant, if not handsome, face, but the smile was missing now as he turned to meet Daniel's level gaze.

Daniel took his time in replying, first lifting the wet cloth from around Mercy's shoulders and hanging it over a stack of coiled rope, then removing his hat and his wet coat.

"I guess I'd better go talk to him."

"There's something else, Dan. He's got a Negro girl and an infant with him."

Mercy looked quickly at Daniel to see how he reacted to this news. Daniel's dark brows went up a fraction; other than that, his expression was as unconcerned as before.

"Stay here with Mike."

Mike moved close to Mercy and placed his hand on her arm as if to hold her there. Daniel's dark eyes swept slowly over the two of them before he walked away, the heels of his heavy boots making a hollow sound on the plank floor. He went into Mike's room and closed the door.

"Come on over to the stove, Mercy," Mike said when he saw her shiver. "It's the last of March, and it's colder than it was in January."

"It's because it's so damp."

"When are you letting school out?"

"I had planned on the first week in April. The children have to help put the crops in. I don't dare try to hold them longer than that. It seems the school year gets shorter every year for the boys and older girls. I can't start in the fall until the crops are harvested, and I have to close in early spring."

"How long will the McCourtneys be gone?"

Mercy held her hands toward the heat coming from the stove. "I thought you knew. Eleanor said a couple of weeks. Gavin said ten days."

"It'll be a couple of weeks, then."

The words were spoken without sarcasm. It was a well-known fact that Eleanor could persuade her husband to do most anything up to a point. But when the big Scot put his foot down, Eleanor toed the line.

Mercy rubbed her palms together and watched as Mike lifted a lid from the stove and inserted a short piece of wood. When a murmur of voices reached them, she saw Mike glance toward the back room. He filled the stove, then went to the door to look out. He stood there for a long while with his hands clasped behind his back as if in heavy thought.

It wasn't like Mike to ignore her, and after a while Mercy began to feel uncomfortable. She wanted to ask him what Mary Knibee had said, but he was plainly avoiding any further conversation with her.

"Mercy." Daniel's voice broke the silence. "Will you come back here?"

Mike whirled around when Daniel spoke, and Mercy was almost sure he was going to say something. But he didn't. He turned back to look out into the dreary, wet, late afternoon.

Daniel stood in the doorway of Mike's living quarters, and when Mercy reached him, he stepped aside to let her enter the room. She was not as familiar with Mike's room as she was with the store, but she had been here before. It was a big square room with a bed built into the corner, a table, a bench, a washstand, and a large chair beside the fireplace. Mike had made it a comfortable and attractive place with a curtain on the window and a colorful patchwork quilt on the bed. Mercy, however, did not notice any of these things. Her eyes went to the woman huddled on the bench with a babe in her arms, then to the tall man with the hawklike features who stood beside her.

"This is Mr. Levi Coffin," Daniel said. "Miss Mercy Quill, sir."

"Farrway Quill's daughter?" The sharp eyes bored into Mercy's.

"Foster daughter," Mercy replied evenly. "It's a pleasure to meet you, Mr. Coffin. Do you know my father?"

"I've not had the pleasure, but I'm hoping to in the near future."

"We need your help, Mercy." Since Mercy's head came to a little above Daniel's shoulder, she had to tilt her head to look up at him. "Mr. Coffin has been honest with me. The woman is a runaway slave. He's trying to get her up into the Iowa Territory. Her man is there working in the lead mines. She's been whipped, and her back's a mass of welts. I didn't want to get you involved in this, but we need to get her into good enough shape so that she can travel tomorrow."

Mercy turned sympathetically to the thin black girl hunched on the bench. She had not taken her eyes from Levi Coffin's face. She looked at him as if he were her savior. The babe in her arms was wrapped in a piece of dirty blanket, and from the odor she could tell the child had messed and the mother had been unable to clean it. Its little head seemed too heavy for its neck, and Mercy could see the veins throbbing in its temples. The tall, hawk-faced man was silent. He watched Mercy closely to gauge her reactions.

"What do you want me to do?" Mercy asked in breathless pity for the poor creature huddled before her.

"Tend to her back and do what you can for the baby.

She doesn't have enough milk for it. There's something else. The man she ran from, the one that whipped her and is after her, is Hammond Perry."

Mercy looked up at Daniel quickly. "Hammond Perry? Papa's old enemy?"

"The same. He'd like nothing better than to find her here. He could accuse Farr of hiding a runaway slave before the state legislature to try to ruin him."

"Papa wouldn't turn her away because he was afraid of *that*!" Mercy said angrily. "You know how Papa feels about slavery."

"I know. And I know how he feels about Hammond Perry, and Perry about him. Perry hasn't forgotten that he tried to get Papa hung for treason twenty years ago, failed, and lost face with old Zachary Taylor."

"The last we heard, Hammond Perry was in the keelboat business over at Kaskaskia."

"He's in the slave-breeding business now, miss," the Quaker said, his voice stiff with indignation. "He and a fellow named John Crenshaw have leased the salt lands down near Shawneetown. They rent slaves from across the line to labor in the mines. Ah, miss, those slaves belong to landowners who rent them out in the winter months when crops have been harvested. That way the owners can keep from feeding them in the slack season. Crenshaw and Perry hope to develop a breed of Negroes of exceptional strength to stand the arduous labor in the mines."

"That's the most horrible thing I ever heard!" Mercy gasped.

"I agree. They have a system of selling the offspring as soon as they are weaned. This woman refused to be put to another man when her child reached the age of two months. She was beaten unmercifully. I don't know how she managed to get to Evansville, but she did. A friend of mine found her there. She was heading up the Ohio, going in the wrong direction."

"Good heavens!" Mercy exclaimed. "Oh, you poor thing." She went to the woman who cringed away from her. "Don't be afraid. Let me help you. Let me take your baby. I will clean it and feed it." Mercy held out her arms. The woman's frightened eyes continued to remain on Levi Coffin.

"She's a kind lady, Dovie." Levi Coffin's voice was deep, as if he used it a lot, and it was gentle when he spoke to the woman. "Let her take the babe. It must be cared for, or it will die."

The dark eyes moved down to Mercy's face. In their depths was such a helpless, hopeless look that it tore at Mercy's heart. Mercy's hands slid beneath the blanket, and she lifted the baby up into her arms. It scarcely weighed more than a kitten. She cuddled the child to her while the mother watched anxiously. The baby let out a soft mewing sound of protest at being moved, but Mercy swung her arms from side to side in a rocking motion and crooned to it.

"Hush, baby. Oh, you poor little thing! We'll clean you, and soon you'll feel better."

Mercy looked up to find Daniel watching her. Her eyes held his for a long while. A bond existed between her and this big, quiet man. It had always been there, but somehow it was different now—stronger and warmer. The Quills had always acted as a buffer between them. Now it was just the two of them. Daniel was depending on her that day, as she had depended on him the night before.

"What do you need, Mercy?" Daniel's voice came from close behind her, and she felt his hand on her back.

"I need milk and pap for this baby, and good solid food for the mother so she can nurse it. I want a clean, warm dress, a petticoat, and a shawl for her. Go to my room and get the heavy, dark brown dress hanging beside a blue one. There's a dark shawl there too. And . . . find something for her feet. Get two warm blankets from the store and a tin of salve. There's some clean rags in the kitchen we can use on the baby's bottom. And . . . I want a big hunk of meat put on to cook in that iron kettle of Mike's right away. I need those things now, Daniel! What are you waiting for?"

"Yes, ma'am." Daniel's face broke into one of his rare, brilliant smiles. "I'll swear, Mercy, you get to be more like your mamma every day."

Levi Coffin and Daniel set on kegs in the storage room behind the store, and Levi told Daniel how an abolitionist friend of his had found the girl, Dovie, under a turned-over boat in Evansville, half starved and shaking with fever. They had taken care of her the best they could, then turned her over to Levi. He had brought her, covered with carpet samples, to Quill's Station in the back of his wagon.

As a devout Quaker, Levi hated slavery in spite of his Southern birth and upbringing. Raised on a farm in South Carolina with little opportunity for formal education, he nevertheless had become a teacher. He had opened a Sunday school for slaves in South Carolina. His school was soon closed, however, when masters forbade their slaves' attendance.

He told Daniel how he had followed the kidnapers of a free Negro woman, employed by his family, halfway across the state of Pennsylvania. During that ride the horror of slavery had grown so intense that he seemed to hear a voice telling him that he must devote his life to the persecuted and enslaved.

When he moved to Newport, Indiana, Levi said, he discovered he was on a route of the Underground Railway by which fugitive slaves made their way from the South to Northern Territories and Canada. Coffin had made his home into a depot, and he used much of the money he earned as a merchant to hide and convey "passengers" on their northern journey. He had come to Quill's Station to plead for yet another depot for his Underground Railway.

"I'm only part owner of the mill, Levi. And the store here is owned by Mike and my foster father, Farrway Quill. I do, however, have a place about a mile north on the river road. To my way of thinking, it would be more suitable for a depot than here in town."

"Praise the Lord!"

"I send out a freight wagon every few weeks. We go north to Vincennes and northwest to Springfield."

"I'll give thee a list of contacts that can be made along the way. Thee realize what will happen if thee should be caught?"

"I'd lose my farm, my mill. What are those things, compared to a man's life? With the help of George Washington, Turley and I have passed a few men through here." Daniel paused when the Quaker gave him a startled look. "Yes, that's the name of a man who works for me at the mill. His father was a Negro, his mother a Shawnee. The father named himself Mr. Washington because he admired the man. His son's name is George. He's a loyal employee and a good friend."

"That's the lad that met me at the mill?"

"Did he give you any lip?" Daniel was smiling.

"None. So this is the place that's called Sugar Tree. I've heard of thee."

Daniel laughed. "I hope that not too many more have heard what we do here. George finds people, or people find George. I haven't discovered which. Sugar Tree was George's mother's name. We use it as a password."

"Many people have heard about Sugar Tree, but they don't know where it is."

"Let's hope it stays that way. I'm not at liberty to leave here at this time, so I'll send Turley Blaine, a completely reliable man, north to Springfield with the woman and child as soon as she's able to travel."

The Quaker lifted his quiet face to the ceiling and clasped his hands in front of him. "Thank thee, God!"

After Dovie's back had been washed with vinegar water and coated with healing salve, she put on Mercy's dress. Before Mercy diapered the baby, she covered his little bottom, chapped and covered with sores, with the same salve she had used on his mother's back. Now, his little stomach full of milk and pap, he lay sleeping on Mike's bed.

The black woman dozed beside the fire after Mercy forced her to drink a hot rum toddy. Mercy looked at her. Even in her sleep her hands twitched nervously, and periodically her eyelids flew open. How terrible it must be to be a slave at the beck and call of a master like Hammond Perry. The woman had been given a terrible beating, but whoever had whipped her had made sure the scars were on her back, where they wouldn't be seen when she was put on the auction block.

She had been separated from the man she considered her husband after she became pregnant. The father of her child had been too "willful" and had been sold to another master, but he had managed to escape and had sent word back to Dovie to tell her where he was. All of this was told them by Mr. Coffin. Dovie was still too weary and too scared to talk.

Mercy stirred the kettle of cubed meat she had cooking on the stove. Her own troubles seemed as nothing compared to those of this poor creature. When the meat was tender, Mercy stirred up a batch of dumplings and dropped the dough by the spoonfuls into the hot broth. The meat and dumplings would make a nourishing meal for the black woman.

They heard a soft knock on the door. The woman jumped to her feet and looked wildly around for her child. She grabbed him up from the bed into her arms and cowered back against the wall. The door opened, and Daniel and Levi Coffin came in.

"It's all right, Dovie," Levi said. "Put the baby down and sit down. You're safe here."

The woman's shoulders slumped in relief. Placing the baby back on the bed, she sat poised on the edge beside him. Daniel held out a pair of moccasins he had found in the storage room. Dovie looked at them but didn't make a move to take them from his hand. Finally Levi took them out of Daniel's hand and placed them in hers. She looked at the moccasins and then up into Daniel's face. He smiled and pointed to her feet. Continuing to look at him with puzzlement in her eyes, she hugged the warm shoes to her breast.

She doesn't know how to respond to kindness, Mercy thought sadly. She went to Dovie, knelt down, gently took one of the moccasins from her hand, and put it on her foot. She tied it, then looked up into the woman's puzzled face and smiled.

"They fit just fine, and they'll be warm too." She stood and looked first at Daniel, then back at the woman. "Where did you find them?"

Daniel grinned. "In the storage room. I think they're Mike's. Yours were not near big enough, and mine were too big."

"You'd better tell him he's missing a pair of shoes." Mercy tossed a saucy grin over her shoulder and went to move the teakettle to the back of the stove.

"We've got to be going." Daniel had followed her, and now stood behind her, speaking in low tones. "It's still light enough for Granny Halpen to see us leave. We don't want her thinking you spent the night here with Mike, and she's sure to think that, if we don't leave soon."

"You'd rather she think I spent the night with you?"

"Why, sure," Daniel said in a teasing tone. "Unless you want her to think you have two lovers instead of one."

"Daniel! You're being ridiculous." She looked at him over her shoulder with blue eyes that came alight with sparkles. A small giggle bubbled from her lips.

"Yes, but it made you laugh. Get your shawl. Mike and Levi can take care of things here."

"But what about getting Dovie and the baby away from here? Hammond Perry is sure to show up sooner or later."

"Don't worry about it. The arrangements are made."

Mercy tied her scarf over her head. She leaned over the bed to stroke the baby's satin ebony cheek with her fingertips and rubbed his woolly head.

"'Bye, little boy," she whispered. "Oh, I hope that when you grow up, you can be free and happy." She straightened and placed her hand on Dovie's shoulder. "Good luck to you, Dovie. I think your baby will be all right now. I pray you find your husband and that he's all right."

The Negro woman fell to her knees, and being careful not to touch Mercy, kissed the hem of her dress. Tears sprang into Mercy's eyes.

"Oh, no! You needn't do that."

Mercy reached down and lifted the woman to her feet. They were almost the same height and age. Tears rolled down Dovie's smooth, dark cheeks. This was the first time Mercy had seen her cry. Not even when her back was treated, did she cry out or shed a tear.

Except for the grace of God, Mercy thought, her throat clogged with tears, *this could be me standing here, black-skinned and enslaved like an animal.*

"Missy . . . Missy?"

"It's all right. It's all right," Mercy crooned to the black girl. "I know you want to thank me, but thanks aren't necessary. I wish I could do more. Just take care of yourself and your baby."

Mercy grabbed up her shawl and, almost blinded with tears, went to the door. Daniel followed, closing the door behind him. He waited a moment for her to dry her eyes, then took her elbow and urged her toward the front of the store.

"Shhh . . ." he said softly to Mercy before he spoke to Mike. "We're going, Mike. Turley will be here early in the morning. I told him to pull up out back and load up some hides we're sending along with the flour up to Springfield. It looks like rain, so make sure his cover is on good and tight. Oh, hello, Samuel. I didn't see you there."

"Howdy, Daniel. Howdy, Miss Mercy."

"Hello, Mr. Brown."

"Let me help you load up, Samuel." The elderly man was straining to lift a heavy sack. Daniel swung it easily to his shoulder.

"Mercy." Mike came from behind the counter as soon as the men were out the door. He came close and spoke in low tones. "I hate it that you got mixed up in . . . this."

"Why? I'm a grown woman. You and Daniel don't have to shield me from unpleasant things. That poor woman was so pitiful."

"Don't worry about her. Coffin and I will take care of her. There's something else. There's talk about Daniel's staying at the house last night. If you don't want to stay alone, go down to Granny Halpen's."

"Granny Halpen? That old gossip? Oh, no! I couldn't stay with Granny Halpen! How could anyone think . . . dirty thoughts about me and Daniel? He's like a brother to me, even if we're not blood kin."

"I know that. It's you I'm thinking about. Mary Knibee is a spiteful little baggage, and she's spreading around all sorts of things about you and Daniel."

"What can she say that will hurt me and Daniel?"

"She's talking about the two men who came to the school and called you Hester."

His words brought back the living horror still facing her. The needs of Dovie and the baby had pushed her problem to the back of her mind for a short while. She started to turn away from Mike.

"What is it?" He placed his hands on her shoulders and turned her back to face him. "What's happened to make you look so frightened? Goddammit! If they hurt you—"

"They didn't hurt me." Mercy placed her hand on his arm and looked into his worried face. "They didn't hurt me," she repeated.

Daniel paused in the doorway when he saw Mercy and Mike standing close together; Mike's brow beetled, Mercy looking anxiously up at him. Something uncomfortable happened to Daniel's heart—something that would not have happened at this time last week. He stood there thinking, wondering if Mercy had feelings other than brotherly ones, for Mike? The thought caused the muscles in his stomach to jump and his heart to ache beneath his ribs.

"Let's go, Mercy."

Mike walked with her toward the door. "Is it still raining?" she asked.

"No. It's stopped. See you tomorrow, Mike." Daniel gripped Mercy's elbow and ushered her out into the early night.

"Coming back?" Mike followed them out onto the porch.

"No. I'm staying at the house tonight. I'll be by in the morning."

"Dan, do you think that's wise? There's already talk going around."

"Talk? Talk about me staying at the Quill house?" Daniel spat out the words angrily.

"Yes. About you . . . staying last night."

"I'm staying again tonight, so they'll have twice as much to talk about, won't they? Does my spending the night in the house with Mercy bother you, Mike?"

"You know better than that."

"Then say whatever it is that's bothering you, so we can get going before it starts raining again."

"What's got into you, for God's sake? Stop trying to cut me down! I'm thinking about what the talk will do to Mercy, and so should you."

"Don't worry, Mike." Mercy looked pleadingly from one man to the other.

"Come on, Mercy. We don't have to explain our actions to anyone." With his hand on her elbow, Daniel urged her on down the road. "I should have brought my horse and left it at the store," he said when she stumbled on a rut in the road.

"I don't mind walking as long as you're with me. Why were you so angry at Mike?"

"I wasn't angry."

"You acted as if you were."

"I've got a lot on my mind. I didn't want to ask your help with the woman, but there was nothing else I could do. Levi and I certainly didn't know how to tend to the baby."

"I wanted to help. Have you ever seen anything as pitiful as that poor starved creature trying to protect her child?"

"Yes. I've seen worse. But I don't want to tell you about it. I want you to forget you saw her or Levi Coffin. Can you do that?"

"I can't do that, Daniel. I'll never forget the hopeless look in that woman's eyes. But I'll not mention it to anyone. Will that do?"

"That'll do fine."

Mercy cooked a supper of eggs and smoked meat for herself and Daniel while he brought in firewood and the milk Jeems had left in the cellar. He strained the milk into the churn and poured some of it into a pan for Blackbird, who meowed and rubbed against his legs.

"You can have some milk, cat. There seems to be plenty." He set the pan on the floor. The cat licked his paws daintily, then leisurely made his way to the pan, hunkered down, and began lapping up the milk.

"You'll spoil that cat," Mercy said, her smiling eyes catching his.

"I didn't want to throw out the milk." His eyes teased her. "I'll put him in the barn in the morning. If he works, he'll be so full by tomorrow night, he'll not be able to waddle to the house to beg for milk."

They ate in almost complete silence. The few words that passed between them were of no consequence. When they finished, Mercy hurried through her dishwashing chores, then carried the churn to the chair beside the hearth. Daniel was smoking his pipe, just sitting there staring unseeingly at the fire with one hand on the arm of the chair, his long fingers tapping.

Mercy worked the dasher up and down while she studied the side of Daniel's face. His lashes were long, his brows straight, beginning at the inside corners of his eyes. The dark tuft of hair on the right side of his brow grew back in a different direction than the rest of his hair so that a lock of hair folded over onto his forehead in spite of the way he tried to brush it down.

Mamma had said the cowlick and the small indentation in the middle of Daniel's chin were a double sign of admirable qualities. Of course, she had said that one time when Mercy was angry at Daniel. Mercy had tried to climb up in the hayloft so that she could watch the men castrate the pigs. Daniel had caught her and sent her to the house. "It's not a sight for you," he had said. Mercy remembered being so angry that she had run all the way to the house to tell her mother how she hated him.

Mercy thought now of all the memories she shared with

Daniel. She didn't think that real brothers and sisters were any closer than she and Daniel, Zack and Mary Elizabeth.

Brother. That thought tripped her mind into another channel. What was she going to do about Lenny and Bernie Baxter? What was she going to do about the woman down in Kentucky? If what Lenny and Bernie said were true, the woman was her real mother, and she was dying. What was she like? Had she had felt as protective of Mercy as Dovie was of her baby? Had she grieved when she lost her little girl? She looked up to see Daniel's eyes on her.

"Daniel." His name came from her lips on a long, soft sigh. She looked into the fire and said nothing more while the clock ticked the time away.

He stretched his legs out in front of him, folding his hands over his stomach. His eyelids lowered as he waited and watched her. Images flashed across his mind. He saw a small, chubby girl lifting her skirt and squatting in the yard and laughing when he scolded her. He saw her as a six-year-old and heard her shout, "You're not the boss of me, Daniel Phelps." He recalled the time he came back with Rain from Louisville, his first trip away from home, when he bought her a blue ribbon with the money he had earned. When she was fifteen, old man Finnigan had caught her behind the barn and tried to kiss her. Daniel was so angry that he had knocked him down, even though the man outweighed him by forty pounds.

Where has the time gone? he thought. *The chubby little girl has grown into a beautiful, sweet woman, and I love her, love her. Not as a sister, but—*

"Do you think that woman down in Kentucky grieved when they couldn't find me?" Mercy's voice broke into his thoughts, and it took a full minute before he could answer.

"Yes. I'm sure she did."

"Dovie's baby was so helpless. I was like that when I was first born. That woman took care of me, fed me, cleaned me, kept me warm."

"What are you trying to say?"

Mercy's heart lunged into a terrific pounding that forced her to take short little breaths. It took every ounce of effort to bring her voice out evenly.

"I'm feeling guilty because I hate the thought of admitting that Lenny and Bernie are my brothers. I don't want to go see that . . . woman they say is my mother, yet a part of me wants to comfort her. Somehow I feel I should let her know I've been taken care of all these years, that I've had a family who loved me." She worked the dasher up and down in the churn automatically.

His eyes held hers for seconds, and his heart thumped in his neck. "I understand how you feel, but the tie is broken. It may be best to leave it that way."

"I guess so, but I'm afraid that later, when I have my own children, I'll be sorry that I didn't go to see her."

"Then you've no doubt about being a Baxter?"

"It would be a miracle if I'm *not*. A small girl was lost on the Green River with a mole under her left eyelid and a brown spot on her bottom. That's where I was found. I want to think that I'm not a Baxter, but the evidence points to the fact that I am. Lenny and Bernie could have made up the story of the mole after they saw mine, but they couldn't have known about the brown spot."

"What do you want to do?"

"I don't know. I'm thinking about it." Her eyes were troubled and her mouth trembled.

Daniel got to his feet and knocked the ashes from his pipe into the fireplace.

"If the butter is made, why don't you go to bed, Mercy. You can dip it out in the morning. You look worn-out."

"I guess I will."

"I'll take a look around outside, then I'll check the fires and bed down in my old room."

Mercy was in bed when she heard Daniel come in, shut the door, and drop the crossbar. Thank you for being here,

Daniel, she thought, and swallowed her tears. Worn and disturbed, she drifted into a fitful sleep, waking repeatedly as her mind, filled with angry resentment, refused to rest.

Downstairs, Daniel lay on his back with his hands clasped behind his head. Lord God Almighty! What was he going to do if she insisted on going to Kentucky to see the woman who had birthed her? The thought made him twist over in bed. Then, with a sudden, violent curse, he swung his feet out onto the floor and planted his elbows on his knees, his hands cupping his chin. If she decided to go, the only thing he could do would be to try to get things squared off here so that he could go with her and then bring her back home where she belonged.

The image of Mercy standing close to Mike filled his mind. Was Mike in love with her? Of course he was! How could Mike not be in love with a woman as pretty as Mercy? He had seen Belinda Miller eyeing Mike and trying to cozy up to him, the same as she had done to him, but Mike had ignored her. Since unattached women were not all that plentiful here in at Quill's Station, it must be that Mike had feelings for someone else. He was a normal man and must want a woman of his own.

Mike was a good man, but the thought of him and Mercy together caused Daniel to search his mind for a reason to find fault with him. Mercy needed a stronger hand than Mike would provide. Thunderation! If Mercy told Mike to jump in the fire, he'd do it, then she'd lose respect for him and her life would be miserable.

What a hell of a mess, he thought. He was in love with a woman who had considered him a brother for eighteen years. He should have stayed in the Arkansas Territory with Amy and Rain Tallman and saved himself all this heartache. Daniel understood now how deep Farrway Quill's feeling's were for Liberty. He loved Mercy. He wanted to be with her, make sweet and gentle love to her, build his life around her and their children.

The acceptance of that fact made Daniel's heart ache. He sat on the edge of the bed until his feet were so cold, they were numb. He lay back down, rolled over on his stomach, buried his face in his pillow, and wished for sleep to wipe the troubled thoughts from his mind.

In the hotel in Vincennes, Eleanor McCourtney rubbed the bottoms of her slender feet against the tops of her husband's and snuggled into the warmth of his embrace.

"Gavin? Are you asleep?"

"Nay, lassie. How can a mon sleep with ye a-wiggling yer tail against him and pesterin' him with yer soft kisses?"

"Pesterin', ye say? Mon, ye don't know what pesterin' is." She mocked his Scottish accent and brought her leg up over his rough thighs until her knee nudged at his maleness.

"Nora, lassie," he growled. "Ye best not bait the bear lest ye find yerself pinned to the bed."

"Gavin, darling, you know you don't scare me with your threats. I'm so happy."

"Sure, 'n' ye ought to be. Ye got the best man this side of the Allegheny."

"You puffed-up Scot." She laughed happily and leaned over him, her elbows on his chest. She placed small kisses on the face that bore the traces of a hundred barroom brawls. "I've got something to tell you."

"Tell it afore ye bust, lassie." He drew her over on top of him and settled her between his thighs. His huge hands cupped her buttocks and pulled her tightly against him. "Tennessee done told ye she's got eyes for Mike," he said with a deep chuckle, sure that he knew her secret.

"She's got eyes for him and he's got eyes for her, but that's not it, smarty."

"How do ye be thinkin' so much 'bout Tennessee and Mike? Ye got a husband to be thinkin' about."

"I'm not blind. He makes excuses to be near her, and she blushes and gets all tongue-tied when he's around, but that's not what I want to tell you."

"Ye got my attention, love, but . . . not for long," he added when she moved up so that the tip of his maleness nestled against her soft down.

"What is it you've wanted more than anything?" she whispered.

"I be wantin' nothin' more than havin' ye where ye are, sweet wife," he growled, and moved her rhythmically against the hardness that lay between them.

"I love you. Have I told you that today?"

"Aye, but ye can tell me again."

"We've been wed ten years, Gavin. I love you more now than I did when you and Rain were taking me to Belle Point to be wed to Will Bradford."

"Aye. Ye be more than I dreamed a havin'."

"I know you've been disappointed we haven't had children," she said in a small, tight voice.

"'Tis God's will. I not be blamin' the mon. I got more'n my share, right here."

"Gavin . . . I think we are."

"Ye be thinkin' we are what, love?"

"I be thinkin' we're going to have a baby."

Gavin was silent for the space of a dozen quick breaths, then the air exploded from his lungs.

"B'gorry! B'God! What'er ye sayin'?"

"I think we're going to have a baby," she said slowly, spacing out the words. "I haven't bled in two months. Haven't you noticed, you big ox?"

"Aye . . . nay . . . I thought, I thought . . . I dunno what I thought! Air ye sure?"

"Reasonably. I waited until I could talk to a midwife before I told you."

"Ah, lassie! Ah, love! 'Tis grand, but will ye be all right?" he asked anxiously.

"I'm only thirty-three, silly. Some women have babies when they're forty or more."

"But I been . . . lovin' ye somethin' fierce. I could've hurt ye!"

"No. I asked the midwife about that too. She said I could pleasure you right up to the last month." Eleanor giggled. "I should have asked her if I could pleasure myself on you. She would have been shocked speechless."

Gavin put his arms around his wife's small body and held her tenderly. "It's almost more'n a mon is due, havin' ye and a bairn too. I love ye so, lassie. Ye be my heart and soul."

"And I love you, my big wonderful man. Come Christmas we may have a wee laddie. What was your papa's name?"

"Charles."

"Charley McCourtney," Eleanor said against his throat. "How does that sound?" She leaned up to look into his eyes. The moonlight coming in through the window shone on his face. She could see the sparkle of tears in his eyes. "I want to go home, sweet man, and wait for our son to arrive. But tonight you're going to get loving better than any you could get in bed with one of those high-priced floozies down in New Orleans."

CHAPTER FOUR

D aniel spent a restless night. He was up before daylight and down at the barn, where he curried his buckskin and a mare that was kept for pulling the light wagon. Blackbird sat watching. Jeems came to the barn to milk the cow.

"How's things going, Jeems?"

"Only fair ta middlin', Mistah Dan. Ya want that I start the plowin'?"

"If that piece out beyond the rock fence is dried out, you can start. Did the corn you saved for seed winter all right?"

"Yessah. Mistah Farr got wire ta string it on. It's tied high up in da barn so da rats can't get ta it."

"I'll send Jasper and his boys over to help you when they get their plowing done. Meanwhile, you can grease the wheels on that light wagon. We may be wanting to use it."

"Dey all be greased, Mistah Dan. I 'bout ta start spadin' da garden spot. Miz Quill be back ta see 'bout dat garden. She set store by dat garden."

"Yes, she does."

"Miz Quill be mighty put out if'n they ain't no garden."

"She'll not be here to see it, Jeems."

"It make no never mind. Missy see it growin' 'n' tell Miz Quill."

"Have you seen any strangers hanging around?"

"Days ago I seed two good-fer-nothin's lookin' 'round. Dey jist look, didn't do no hurt ta nothin'."

"You keep close, hear? There'll be some fellows up looking for runaways in a day or two, and they're not above snatching you and taking you back over the line. Are you still keeping Gerrit tied up?"

"Yessah. I got ta, 'cause he go off if'n he ain't tied up. He gettin' more crazy in his head. He pay no 'tention to nothin'. He eat, he sleep, he get mean sometime."

Daniel placed a hand on the Negro's bent shoulder. "I know it's hard for you to see him like that. Does he talk sense at all anymore?"

"Sometime he look at me 'n' know I'm him's papa. Sometime he think I'm him's mama. It bears down hard on da mind, Mistah Dan."

"I'm sure it does. But I'm afraid that if he gets loose, someone will get scared of him and shoot him."

"Yassah. I know dat. He might hurt somebody too. He donno no bettah."

"I've thought of boarding off a corner of your cabin for him so you wouldn't have to keep that iron on his leg. He's big and strong, and if he got his hands on you while he was in one of his rages, he could kill you."

"I watchin' for that. I watchin' real good. When I see it comin' on, I stay 'way."

"You do that, and be careful. And if he gets to be more than you can handle, let me know, and we'll try to figure out something."

"Gerrit is me boy, Mistah Dan." The old man's

shoulders sagged even more. "I ain't goin' ta let him kill me; den he have nobody."

"How about a chicken tonight for supper? Dress one for you and Gerrit and one for Miss Mercy. Maybe she'll make some dumplings to go with it."

A pleasured grin split the old man's face. "I do dat, Mistah Dan."

Daniel shut Blackbird up in the barn and thought about the old black man and his devotion to his son. He had come up the river six or seven years ago with a woman and the boy who hadn't been right from birth. His former owner had been going to knock the boy in the head because he said Gerrit wasn't worth feeding. Farr had taken in the runaways, paid off the owner when he came for them, and let them build a cabin out in the woods behind his place in exchange for work. The woman had died the year after Farr had bought their freedom, but the boy, big and healthy except for his mind, lived on. The last time Daniel had seen Gerrit, he was a big man, standing head and shoulders over the father who took care of him.

Mercy greeted Daniel cheerfully when he came in to breakfast, but there were dark shadows beneath her eyes, proof of a sleepless night. During breakfast he told her of Jeems's concern for his son, Gerrit. Mercy had seen Gerrit only one time, and that had been several years ago. She told Daniel about it and said she never wanted to see him again.

"He was awfully big and his mouth hung open. He was more like an animal than a man." She shuddered. "I'm sure he's grown since then. I don't know how Jeems handles him. But Gerrit is his son, and he must love him. That, right there, is proof that Negroes are human just like us. It makes me so damn mad when I hear some smarty spouting off about the African race being part animal and that they don't think, feel, love, and hate like the rest of us. They are people under that black skin, the same as we are."

"You don't have to convince me." Daniel had been watching the color come up in her face, and her eyes began to glitter with sparks of anger. "Mr. Washington was one of Papa's best friends. I remember how Papa grieved for him when he was killed during the war."

"Are you sending Dovie to Springfield with Turley? Is that why you were telling Mike that Turley would be by the store? You said that for Mr. Brown's benefit, didn't you?" Mercy began to clear the dishes from the table.

"You ask more questions than a four-year-old. I'll say what Mamma used to say when you asked things you had no business knowing. She would say that what a woman didn't know she couldn't tell."

"I'm not a blabbermouth, and you know it, Daniel Phelps!" She stood beside his chair, glaring down at him. He tilted his head to look up at her, and she could see the teasing glint in his eyes. "Sometimes you make me so mad. I'm not a child, you know," she said impudently, but she was smiling.

A lovely, leaping flame of desire flickered through Daniel as his gaze followed her about the kitchen. She was so much a woman, he could never think of her as a child. He felt the urge, when she passed him, to seize her arm and pull her down onto his lap, bury his face against the warm, scented flesh of her neck, and tell her he had waited all his life for her to grow up. But he knew to do so would be disastrous. She was not ready to think of him as a man who wanted her in all the ways a man wanted the woman he loved. He stood. For a long moment he stared at the nape of her neck while she worked at the stove. He had an almost overwhelming desire to touch her. Why didn't he? She was his woman, wasn't she? What if he went to her, put his arms around her, and drew her back against his chest?

Don't be stupid, Phelps, an inner voice cautioned. He must bide his time. This was new to him. He must think of what a shock it would be to her. In order to hide the feelings that had sprung up restlessly within him, he picked up the teakettle and went to the washbench to shave.

They met on the porch for the walk to the schoolhouse. Although they were unaware of it, they were a handsome couple. Rich morning sunlight filtered through Mercy's hair, turning it to the color of ripe wheat. The head that rode proudly on her slender neck came to just inches above his shoulder. Her dark skirt and white shirtwaist were covered with a long, dark shawl, folded across her breasts and held in place by her crossed arms.

Daniel's dark hair was still wet from the morning combing. On his jaw, the small cut oozing a drop of blood was evidence of his inner turmoil as he attempted to rid his face of several days' growth of dark beard. The front-lacing leather shirt hugged his broad shoulders and hung down over duck breeches that were tucked into calf-high boots. Always aware of what was going on around him, his dark eyes saw everything that moved; his ears were alert for any foreign sound.

They walked easily, step matching step, and turned the bend in the road. The sun behind them cast two long shadows before them. As they neared the settlement, the tall shadow moved closer to the slender one, blending into one.

"Jeems is going to dress out a chicken today," Daniel said, his hand cupping her elbow and holding her close to his side. "Do you suppose I can have chicken and dumplings for supper?"

"I suppose so,'" she said absently. Then, "I wonder why so many wagons are at the store this time in the morning. Is that Glenn Knibee's?"

"Looks like it."

"Could it be because of . . . Dovie?"

"Not likely. It's time to start planting. Mike is always busy this time of year."

When Daniel glanced down to see if Mercy had accepted his explanation, he saw her lips pressed so tightly together that they made a crease beside her mouth. As they passed the store, they heard the sound of male voices raised in a heated argument and Mike's voice telling someone to watch his mouth or he would close it for him.

Granny Halpen came out onto the porch of the rooming house as they approached. She let the door slam behind her, leaned on her broom, and watched the couple coming down the road.

"Morning, Mrs. Halpen," Daniel called.

Granny turned her back, and the stiff straw broom swished vigorously back and forth across the steps. After Daniel and Mercy passed, they heard a loud, "Humph!"

Daniel looked down at Mercy's face. It was a dull red, but blanched to white as he watched. He moved his hand down her arm, grasped her bare wrist with strong fingers, and drew her even closer to him. They walked smoothly together, his stride matching hers.

"Don't let one gossipy old woman bother you."

"I . . . can't help it."

They were silent until they reached the schoolhouse. Daniel shoved open the door.

"It's early. I'll build a fire."

Mercy whipped the shawl from her head and let it settle on her shoulders. Taking the broom that leaned in the corner, she began to sweep around the table that was her desk, and the two long tables and benches where the younger students sat. Against each of the side walls was a table and bench, one side for boys, one for girls. The hearth had a brick chimney that went straight up through the roof.

As she swept, Mercy thought about how she had prevailed upon her father to make the extra tables, to place the hooks in the walls for coats and shawls, and to build the necessary building out back. She had paid for the lamp from her first earnings, even though her father had said he and Mike would donate one. It wasn't a fancy school like the ones in Vincennes, but it was her school, and she alone was responsible for the education the children in and around Quill's Station would receive. When she finished sweeping, she stood the broom back in the corner.

Daniel had the fire going in the hearth and opened the door a crack to make the draft take the smoke up the chimney.

"You don't need to wait," Mercy said when Daniel sat down on one of the benches. "I don't mind being here alone. The children will be along soon."

"I'll wait a few minutes."

Ten minutes passed, then twenty. At the ten-minute mark Mercy knew that the children were not coming, but she said nothing. She sat at her desk with her hands clasped tightly in front of her, staring at the door. Daniel sat on the bench against the wall with his elbows on his knees, his hands clasped and dangling between them.

The soft knock on the back door caused both their heads to swivel around toward it. Mercy glanced at Daniel, then, with a quivering smile, got up to lift the bar and open the door. Arabella, with tears streaming down her face, beckoned to Mercy and ran to the outhouse. Mercy turned to Daniel with mute appeal in her eyes.

"I'll be right back."

He nodded, wishing for a way to wash the hurt from her face and wanting to strangle a dozen fools.

Inside the outhouse there was scarcely enough room

for Mercy and Arabella. Arabella was sobbing, her head buried in an arm as she leaned against the wall. Mercy held the door closed with one hand and drew the girl to her with the other.

"What in the world is the matter?"

"We can't come to school no more, Miss Quill. That piss-ant Mary Knibee and her pa came by last night and told Ma and Pa...bad things about you. They said... they said...They won't let me come. Oh, I hate Mary! I hate her!"

"What did they say?" Mercy asked quietly.

"They said your name is Hester. That...your people are...trash. They said you didn't come from...good stock, that it's showin' up now. They said you're pretending to be somebody."

"If all of that were true, it's no reason to keep you from coming to school. I can still teach."

"And they said you...you was forn...forncate. I can't say it. But you were doin' it with Mr. Phelps while the Quills were gone."

The teacher in Mercy caused her to say. "The word is *fornicate*, Arabella. The word means to...mate with someone you're not married to. Mr. Phelps and I have not done that. He's like a brother to me. I was afraid to stay alone because of the men who came here to the school yesterday. I asked him to stay with me. Tell your parents that."

"I can't, Miss Quill, they won't listen. Mary and her pa have got everybody all riled up. Pa says when school starts up again, they'll get a new teacher. He says even a Indian'd be better. I've got to go. I slipped off to come tell you. If Pa finds out I've been here, I'll get a whippin'."

"Thank you for telling me, Arabella. I'm sorry your parents feel the way they do. Go on home now, before someone sees you here."

Mercy walked slowly back to the schoolhouse after

the girl left. Her thoughts spiraled to the only woman she had ever known who had been thoroughly disgraced. It had happened right here at Quill's Station. Her husband had caught her in bed with her lover. He had killed the French and Indian trapper and had beaten his wife unmercifully. He turned her out, denying her the right even to see her children. Later, after she had been found hanging from a tree down by the river, the man took his children and moved away.

Now she, Mercy Quill, was in disgrace and was perfectly innocent of any wrongdoing. She might be Hester Baxter posing as Mercy Quill, but she hadn't known about it until two days ago. After seeing Lenny and Bernie, they had judged her as coming from inferior stock, unfit to teach their children. They assumed that she and Daniel had slept in the same bed because he was at the house all night. The unfairness of it was beyond her understanding.

She walked through the back door of the schoolhouse and straight into Daniel's arms. He stood there in the middle of the room beside her table with his arms open, his brows beetled with concern. She went to him. He wrapped his arms around her. She turned her cheek to his chest and leaned against him, huddled close in his arms, too numb to cry.

She was like a small, sweet-smelling, boneless kitten; so vulnerable, so damned defenseless. He desperately wished for a way to shield her from hurt. He pressed his cheek to the top of her head. What the hell was the matter with people? Why didn't they realize how fortunate they were to have her teaching their kids? Holding her tightly against him, Daniel vowed he would do something to make it right. He would, by God, or he would crack some heads.

It was a long time before she spoke, and when she did, it was in a low, husky voice that sounded as if she needed to clear her throat.

"I'm in disgrace, Danny."

He said nothing.

"They don't think I'm fit to teach their children."

He said a curse word against the top of her head.

"They think I'm sleeping with you. You, my brother! How could they think that of me?"

"Goddamn!" The word he murmured was for two different reasons.

"It's because the Baxters came looking for me."

He grunted agreement, his heart hurting for her.

"Maybe it isn't their fault. They love their mother and are trying to ease her dying. I can't hate them for that."

His crossed arms tightened, and his hands stroked her arms, which hung at her sides. Her voice was so full of sadness and defeat that he wanted to hurt someone, anyone. At that moment Daniel wished he had shot the Baxters and dragged their bodies off to the river that first night he'd found them with her. The thought shocked him. Lord Almighty! He'd never wished anyone dead before. Is *that* what love did to a man?

"There's no point in staying here," he said softly to the top of her head.

"Where can I go?" Her voice was wooden.

"You can go home or to the mill with me until I can take you out to my place. This will blow over. It needs a little time. I'll go speak to the families and explain what happened."

"No! We've done nothing we have to explain." She placed her hands on his arms and moved back to look up into his face. The spirit seemed to flow back into her with the uttered words. Her chin came up, her body stiffened, and she turned away from him to cross her arms over her chest and look out the door. When she turned back, her jaw was set stubbornly, her lips pressed into an angry slash. "Damn them! Damn them to hell and back for not knowing or caring what they are doing to their own children!" She poked at his chest with her forefinger to give emphasis to the words. "And don't tell me not to swear. I feel like swearing. It feels good to swear! Damn! Goddammit! Hell! Hellfire! Shitfire!" she added defiantly.

"Mercy Quill! I may have to wash your mouth out with soap," Daniel said sternly, but he was smiling.

"I'm just so mad! The fools are depriving their children of an education because of their narrow-mindedness."

"That's true."

"They don't want me to teach their children because they think—they *think*—I'm a fallen woman. They didn't want Tennessee to teach because she's part Indian. I'm *not* a fallen woman, and Tennessee is smarter than all of those ignorant, narrow-minded, wooden-headed farmers put together."

"You're right about that."

"Not two parents among the eight families can read and write. Oscar Walker didn't want Robert to come to school, but Nettie Walker insisted. Oscar said Robert didn't need to know how to read in order to plow." Anger had loosened Mercy's tongue. "They are so stubborn, they want their kids to be stupid too. Glenn Knibee's fourteen-year-old daughter can twist him right around her little finger." Mercy held up her finger and circled it with the forefinger of her other hand.

Their gazes locked; his was proud, hers angry.

"If Glenn Knibee thinks I'm going to shut down the school, he's shouting down the rain barrel, Daniel." She shook her finger beneath his nose before she sat down at her desk. "I'll be right here in case one of the families come to their senses. I'll sit here until time for school to be over and . . . to hell with the Baxters!"

"Now hold on. There's no point in staying here alone."

She looked at him steadily, then got to her feet.

"You're right!" Her sudden about-face surprised him.

"I'm glad you agree."

"I'll not stay here. And it isn't because of the Baxters. It's because I'm going down to the store to tell Glenn Knibee what a . . . a horse's ass he is!" She pulled her shawl up, lapped it across her bosom, and headed for the door.

"Wait a minute. That's my job."

"Education is not your job. It's mine." Mercy walked right out the door.

"Anything that concerns you is my business."

She stopped on the step, turned and looked into Daniel's concerned brown eyes while her mind groped for something to say.

"Oh, Danny! You've been my friend, my brother, my childhood playmate. All my life I've been willing to hang back and let you take care of me."

"I'm not stopping now," he said evenly, although her words about his being her friend and brother had hit him like a fist in the stomach.

"I think it's time to stand on my own two feet and not depend on you to make things right for me. I'm not going to lie down and let people like Glenn Knibee walk on me! If I have to leave Quill's Station in disgrace, it will be with my head up, not crawling on my knees."

"Leave Quill's Station? What the hell are you talking about?"

She sucked in her breath. "I . . . don't know why I said that. I've no place to go except to Vandalia, and I'll not take my troubles to Mamma and Papa. They've done enough for me."

"You'll come out to my place. Minnie and Rose will take care of you. I want you there."

She was unaware of the intensity of his last words.

"I'm not running with my tail between my legs. I'm going up to that store, then I'm going home. You don't have to stay with me. I'm no longer afraid of the Baxters or what they'll say about me being their sister. They won't harm me. I'm sure of that."

"They sure as hell won't, because they won't get the chance." Daniel closed the door to the school and took her arm. "If you're determined to go bait the bear, let's go."

As they retraced their steps up the road, Mercy could see that Glenn Knibee's wagon, as well as two others were still in front of the store and that Granny Halpen sat in her rocking chair on the porch of the rooming house. The inevitable snuff stick was firmly embedded in the corner of the old woman's mouth, her birdlike eyes taking in everything in sight. Granny's imaginative mind always conceived its own distorted images of what went on in Quill's Station. As they neared the rooming house, Mercy deliberately veered toward the side of the road that passed within a few feet of the porch.

"You'd better come on up to the store, Granny," Mercy called cheerfully, but Daniel heard the strain in her voice. "I'm going to tell Glenn Knibee just what a stupid, narrow-minded jackass he is. You should hear it straight from the harlot's mouth. It'll give you enough to talk about all summer."

Granny's mouth fell open. The snuff stick slipped out, and a dark stain trickled from the corner of her mouth. Mercy Quill admitting she was a harlot was more than Granny's mind could absorb all at one time.

Daniel couldn't hold back the deep chuckle that rumbled up from his chest. "You could have caused Granny to swallow that snuff stick by giving her news like that. You've really got your dander up, haven't you, honey?"

"Yes, I have. I'm dandered up good, and I mean to have my say. Oh . . . Mr. Knibee," she called when a burly man came out and stepped off the porch of the store and headed for the wagon. "I'd like a word with you."

The man turned, grabbed the porch post, and hauled himself back up onto the porch. He waited, his hands resting on the pouches of fat on his sides. Mercy walked up to within a few feet of him and looked him straight in the eye.

"I understand you've been busy carrying gossip to the parents of my students. You would do well to mind your own business and take care of your daughter instead of spreading tales that prevent other children from getting an education."

"If'n a teacher ain't fit ta teach our young-uns, 'tis my duty ta tell it." He stuck his chin out belligerently and turned to go to his wagon. Mercy wanted to slap him but held her hands firmly against her sides.

"And who says I'm not fit to teach?" Her sharp words brought him back around to face her.

"I say it!"

Mercy was enraged, her face crimson with anger.

"You stupid jackass! What do you know about being fit? You can't read or write, you've got the manners of a hog, and you're standing there telling me I'm not fit to teach."

"I ain't a-talkin' 'bout book learnin'. 'Tis other thin's." He crossed his arms stubbornly.

"What other things?" Mercy demanded. "What gossip have you spread around that has caused the parents to keep the children out of school?"

"Wal, if ya don't know, missy—"

"My name is Miss Quill to you, Mr. Knibee, and I'll thank you to use it."

Knibee made a sound of ridicule in his throat. "Air ya sure that's yore name? Ain't yore name . . . Hester?"

"Hester may be my *real* name. I'm not sure yet," Mercy answered without hesitation, and Daniel was never more proud of her. "But I've been Mercy Quill since I was two years old. But what has my name got to do with my ability to teach children to read and write?"

"That name business ain't all what's been goin' on, 'n' ya know it." Knibee uncrossed his arms, and his huge fists hung at his sides. His small, deepset eyes went past her to the men who had crowded out the door when she had first called out to him. They stood silently on the porch. Damn fools! Why didn't they speak up and say something?

Mercy stood stiff and prim and waited. "Well," she snapped after a lengthy silence, "it seems you've got more to say, so say it. Spit out the gossip you've been so anxious to spread."

Knibee's eyes went to the tall, lean man who stood with a shoulder against the porch post. He had never liked Daniel Phelps. He was too quiet. His way of doing business at the mill irritated him, too—his way of letting a nigger take a turn the same as a white man. Knibee hitched up his breeches. He had been backed into a corner, and now he'd say his piece. He wasn't going to be backed down by a chit who was no better than he was, even if she had been raised by the Quills.

"It's been talked of . . . We heard . . . ah, my Mary heard some fellers say that you'd spent the night alone in the house with Phelps."

"I did. What about it?'" Mercy refused to look away.

"What . . . about it?" Knibee sputtered. "Why, no *decent* unwedded woman'd stay the night alone with a man."

"Are you saying I'm not decent because I spent the night alone in the house with a man who is like a brother to me?"

"But he ain't yore brother! Ever'body knows it. And, yeah . . . I'm sayin' ya ain't a decent, God-fearin' woman. Yore tainted, is what ya are. Ya ain't fit ta be—"

Daniel's fist shot out. The blow was so quick, so vicious, that it would have staggered a horse. It landed square on Knibee's nose. He took two stumbling steps backward and fell off the end of the porch, landing on his back in the dirt. His nose was a spouting fountain of blood. There was no sound except for the thud when Daniel's fist connected with Knibee's nose, and the plop when Knibee hit the ground.

The men behind Mercy crowded to the edge of the porch and looked down.

Mercy frowned up into Daniel's face. It was as calm as if nothing had happened. He was holding his cut knuckles.

"Why did you do that?"

"Because I wanted to."

"But I was going to slap him, and you didn't give me the chance."

"Next time you'd better hurry if you want to get your lick in. I'm not waiting."

Mercy's eyes moved slowly over the men watching, confronting each directly until they turned their eyes away. At one time or another all of them had told her how pleased they were that their children were receiving the education they'd never had.

"You must agree with the 'gentlemen' on his back in the dirt, or you wouldn't have kept your children home from school. If you want them to go through life unable to read or write, to be ignorant, as you are, there is little I can do about it. If you reconsider and want me to teach them, I'll be at home. And by the way, Daniel will stay with me tonight and every night until the McCourtneys get back from Vincennes. If you choose to consider me a fallen woman because of it, it only proves that you are a group of narrow-minded, muddleheads!"

With her head high, Mercy stepped off the porch and started up the road toward home. Behind her, she heard Daniel's voice.

"Get on your feet, Knibee. If one more word about Miss Quill comes out of your dirty mouth, I'll smash it all over your face." The words were spoken in a way that left no doubt that he would do exactly as he said.

"See here! Ya ain't got no right ta hit me. 'Cause Farr Quill's gone ta the State House, 'n' makin' the laws don't make you no better'n the rest a us." Knibee pushed himself up into a sitting position.

"What you said about Miss Quill made me want to break your dammed neck! If you want to keep teeth in your mouth, keep it shut about her." Daniel bit out the words sharply.

The rage that boiled up in Daniel was ready to erupt again. Knibee sensed it; the men on the porch sensed it. Knowing he was no match for the big angry man, Knibee rolled over onto his knees and got to his feet. He pulled a cloth from his pocket and held it to his nose. On his way to his wagon he paused and spoke to the men on the porch. "Ya comin'?"

Daniel glanced at Mercy's retreating back, held stiff as a poker, as she walked briskly down the road toward home. He stepped upon the porch beside Mike, and the two of them watched the wagons leave town.

"I guess that's that," Daniel said, "It appears that school let out a little early this year."

"How'd she take it?"

"Hard at first. Then she got mad."

"She told Glenn Knibee how the cow ate the cabbage. Ignorant jackass, she called him. It takes a while to get her riled up, but when she is, she don't back down." Mike smiled broadly.

"It wasn't easy for her." Daniel's stern words wiped the smile from Mike's face.

"What's this business about her name being Hester?"

"Have you seen the two fellows in peaked hats hanging around?"

"Leather peaked hats? Riding the mules?"

"Yeah. Have you seen them this morning?"

"About an hour ago. They were heading for the mill."

Daniel muttered a curse and glared toward the mill. "What time did Turley leave?"

"Long before daylight. I sent food for the woman.

Pap and milk for the babe. Coffin gave Turley a letter to a man in Springfield and left shortly after. I wish we could have kept Mercy out of this."

"So do I."

"About those fellows . . . what've they got to do with Mercy? Why were they at the school? By God, if they hurt her, I'll fill their hide with buckshot!"

"They didn't hurt her."

Daniel studied his friend for a moment, seeing him once again standing close to Mercy with his hand on her arm, Mercy earnestly looking up into his face. He choked down the jealousy the vision evoked. Whether Mike was in love with Mercy or not, he was like one of the family and had the right to know what was going on.

Daniel told him in as few words as possible about the Baxters coming to the house, upending Mercy to see if she had the "Baxter spot."

"They . . . what?" Mike asked as if he couldn't believe his ears. "They looked . . . under her clothes?"

"She said they didn't hurt her. The mole beneath her eyelid, the brown spot, and the fact that Farr found her on the Green River at the time the Baxter child was taken, are evidence that she is Hester Baxter."

"Can it be true after all this time?" Mike murmured with a worried frown on his face.

"She thinks it is. That's all that matters."

"She's ashamed to be kin to them, is that it?"

"Not all of it. They want her to go back to Kentucky with them. Their mother is on her deathbed, and her dying wish is to see her little lost girl. That's the way they put it."

"That's a bunch of horseshit if I ever heard any! Why, hell! We're not letting her go off alone with those two buzzard-eaters, even if she wants to!"

"Hell, no!"

"Get her away from here. Take her to Vandalia."

"I suggested that. She won't go. She's afraid the

Baxters will follow and be an embarrassment to the Quills. She thinks this is something she has to work out herself."

"What can we do?"

"We're going to wait and see what Mercy wants to do. It'll take a little time for her to get used to the idea that she's got blood kin. Then she'll decide if she wants to see them or not. I'll not tell her to do something that she may regret later."

"If she decides to go, then, by God, I'll go with her!" Mike's jaws clamped shut, and he pounded his knotted fist into his palm.

The thought of anyone other than himself taking Mercy anywhere caused Daniel's brows to draw together in a frown. The pulse jerked in his throat, and he cursed himself for being a jealous fool.

"If Mercy wants to go to Kentucky, *I'll* take her. And I'll make sure she comes back."

"How can you leave here right now with Coffin sending runaways through? I look for this to be one of the main lines of the Underground Railway."

"You and George and Turley will have to handle anything that happens while I'm gone."

"What about Hammond Perry? That man hates everything about Quill's Station. If he even suspects that the mill is the place known as Sugar Tree, he'll watch it like a hawk watches a chicken."

"I'm thinking he'll show up in a day or two. He's a mean bastard. It would be like him to grab some of the people out on the farm, just to show us he can, and to get back at Farr for the year he had to spend at Fort Dearborne after his attempt to have Farr hung for treason."

"He'd be sure to get the legislators riled up if he kidnaps free folk in Illinois. Most of the Negroes here are second-generation freedmen like George. The rest, like the people out on your place and old Jeems and his boy, have papers," Mike protested.

"Ha!" Daniel snorted. "Papers wouldn't make any difference to Hammond Perry. He'd see Jasper's boys as good breeding stallions, and Birdie, Gus's daughter, as a brood mare. They'd be a nice addition to his breeding farm. Damn him to hell!"

"Breeding farm? My God! That's the worst thing I ever heard of. It's like he was raising cattle or horses."

"That's it. To Hammond Perry a Negro is no more than a dumb animal to work in the field. Hell! I don't know the answer. I realize they can't all be turned loose to fend for themselves. They don't know how. But, by God, they shouldn't be treated like animals."

With that comment he stepped off the porch and headed for the mill.

CHAPTER FIVE

~≈—≈~

The rhythmic thump of the mill wheel was a familiar sound to Daniel. The high whine of the saw told him that the mill wheel was being used to rip boards for Gavin McCourtney's lumber business. It had become profitable to both Daniel and Gavin to share the mill. After George opened the flume gate and set the wheel to moving, he would leave the sawing to Gavin's men. George knew as much about operating the mechanism of the mill and keeping it repaired as Daniel or Turley Blaine.

The Baxters' mules were tied beneath the trees behind the mill. Daniel walked rapidly up the stone ramp to the room above where the millstones and the saw were operated by the wheel. If the Kentuckians mistreated George, there would be trouble.

"I ain't ne'er heard such a racket in all my born days." Bernie Baxter's voice rose above the whine of the saw.

Daniel paused in the doorway. George, a heavy sack of flour on his shoulder, turned to face the Baxters. He had worked at the mill since age twelve, and at seventeen he was as tall as Daniel and almost as muscular.

"Then get the hell out," George said as he eyed the two with taunting amusement. "You ain't tied in here."

George was a handsome youth with straight black hair and fine features. His skin was more like that of his Shawnee mother, a light reddish-brown, not black like his Negro father.

"Ya just better watch out who ye'r talkin' to, boy. I ain't a man ta take back talk."

"Is that right? I'm just plumb scared!"

Bernie took a threatening step forward. "I ain't taking sass from a—"

"From a what? A nigger? A Injun? I'm half of each, *white man*." There was a hesitation in his voice when he said the words. "Take your choice, but be careful how you say it."

George Washington was extremely proud. He knew what he was, and took pride in his heritage. To be sneered at raised his anger to the boiling point. He was smart enough, however, to know that if he engaged in a fistfight with a white man, even one such as stood before him now, could get him into serious trouble. But there were other ways to even a score with a white man who ill-used him. One had been known to step on a loose board and break a leg; the axle on another man's wagon had broken despite a light load. The gates at one farm had been left open. It took the farmer a week to gather up his livestock after they had wandered miles from home. But these mysterious "accidents" were few; and Daniel, aware of the circumstances, considered them so well deserved that he never mentioned them to George.

"What are you doing here?" Daniel demanded from the doorway, thinking it time he intervened. The Baxters swung around to face him. "I thought I had made myself clear enough to you that I don't want you hanging around."

"Ya ain't ownin' the whole town," Bernie said nastily.

"No, but I own this mill."

"Well now, ain't ya the high muck!"

"Hush up," his brother ordered sharply. Then to Daniel, "We're a-wantin' a word with ya."

"Go ahead."

"Here?"

"Here. I've got work to do."

"I'd jist as soon walk off a piece. That noise plumb hurts my ears."

"That's the sound of good, honest work. But if it offends your ears, come on."

Daniel left the room. The Baxters followed. They walked back down the stone ramp to the ground level and on to stand beneath the tree where the mules were tied.

"Say what you came to say. I've wasted enough time on you the last few days." Daniel eyes were stormy, his voice full of irritation.

Lenny spat before he spoke. "Nobody ask ya to put yore bill in, mister. What we got to say is 'bout Hester. Jist what air ya aimin' to do 'bout our sister?"

"I'm aiming to keep Mercy Quill as far away from you two as I can. It's for her to decide if she wants to claim kin to you. You've already caused her to lose her school. Did you know that?"

Lenny ignored the question and spat again. "She knows she's Hester. And me 'n' Bernie know ya ain't wantin' us 'round. I ain't a-meanin' that."

"Then what the hell *do* you mean?"

"The Baxters is decent, God-fearing folks. They is looked up to down on Mud Creek. Me 'n' Bernie, bein' Hester's kin, ain't likin' what's goin' on here, a-tall."

"No, we ain't," Bernie said. "If'n ya was down on Mud Creek, ya'd be strung up 'n' feelin' the lash on yore back fer what ya've done to Hester."

Daniel was losing patience. He swore, using words he

reserved for extreme occasions. Of the two Baxters, Bernie was the one who aggravated him the most. The force of his voice, as much as his words, betrayed his irritation.

"What the hell are you two muddleheads talking about? Get to the point."

"I ain't takin' no name-callin' from the likes a you." Bernie's heated tone matched Daniel's.

"Hush up, Bernie. Me bein' older'n ya are, 'n' next to Hod 'n' Wyatt at headin' up the Baxters, I'll be doin' the talkin'." Lenny planted his heavy boots far apart and crossed his arms over his chest. "We knowed ya stayed with Hester all night long with nary a soul around ta be knowin' what ya done. Ya didn't come out till mornin'."

"What of it? I stayed last night, the night before, and I'll stay again tonight."

"See there! See there!" Bernie's voice squeaked. He jumped up and down, his arms flopping at his side like the wings of a chicken who had just been beheaded. "I told ya he'd be braggin' it up. Hester ain't never goin' ta get a decent man ta wed up with her if'n this gets out."

"Mister, if'n Hod and Wyatt gets wind a this, ya'd better look out. We knows what goes on when a feller gets a sightly woman off to hisself. Bernie seen ya huggin' up to Hester. Huggin' leads ta kissin', kissin' leads ta begettin' younguns. Ya better be knowin' there ain't no feller ruint a Baxter woman 'n' lived ta brag on it."

A look of intense anger came over Daniel's face. His eyes, filled with rage, were astonishingly bright with it.

"You dirty, spying, low-lifed, mangy, stupid, mule-headed idiots!" he shouted. "I've taken about all I'm going to take from you. I advise you to get on those mules and head for Kentucky, or by God, you may not leave here at all."

"Warn't make no difference at-tall." Lenny spoke calmly. "Hod and Wyatt knowed where we was comin' 'n' what fer. They'd be right up here to see 'bout us. Hod 'n'

Wyatt'll get Hester if'n they come. They'd not mess around askin' her nothin', like we done. They know 'bout the mole 'n' they'd see the Baxter spot on her butt. Me 'n' Bernie figger Wyatt 'n' Hod got plowin' ta do 'n' their women 'n' younguns to do fer. We be already here 'n' we're goin' to handle thin's the best we know how."

"The best you know how isn't good enough. You're making me want to break your scrawny necks," Daniel said angrily. "I'll tell you this, if it will ease your mind. There's not a woman in the world I respect more than Mercy Quill, and I would die before I dishonored her."

"Ha!" The word exploded from Bernie. "Then why warn't thar but one light on?"

Daniel looked so furious that Bernie backed around to the other side of the mules. Daniel took a deep breath. He didn't want to draw any more attention to the Kentuckians, but if they didn't get out of his sight, he was going to split their heads. If he did that, he reasoned, it would be cause for more talk. Mercy would be the one to take the brunt of it. When he spoke, he directed his words to Lenny.

"I stayed the night with Miss Quill because she was afraid you would break into the house again. She needs time to consider the things you've said about her being your sister. All these years she had thought of herself as Mercy Quill." Daniel tried to speak calmly and in terms they would understand. "We were raised together in that house. The Quills have been parents to both of us. Now get this through your thick heads. I'm going to stand between Mercy and anyone who will try to hurt her. If I have to break your legs, crack your heads, or shoot you, I'll do it. The best thing you can do is back off and give her time to decide what she wants to do. If she wants to go to Kentucky, I'll abide by her decision."

"We ain't got no time, mister. We done swore ta Maw we'd find Hester 'n' brin' her so she can see her little girl afore she passes on."

"I understand that. But give Miss Quill a few days to get used to the idea."

"What's he talkin' 'bout, Lenny? What's he mean abide? Abide what?" Bernie came out from behind the mule scratching his head.

"It means I'll not stand in her way if she wants to go to Kentucky," Daniel said.

"Ya ain't got no right to be standin' in the way, nohow. Ya ain't got nothin' to say 'bout Hester! Ya ain't wedded, 'n' ya ain't no blood kin."

"I've got more right than you have, but I'll not argue the point. I'm telling you, stay away from her and give her time to decide what she wants to do."

"I ain't never heared of the like." Bernie snorted. "Women does what their menfolk tell 'em or they get a switchin'. It'd put a heap a shame on the Baxters if'n folks got wind we was waitin' fer a *woman* to be decidin' what ta do. One mornin' after the next, we're headin' home. We ain't got no time to dally no more'n that."

"Bernie's right, mister. One dawn after this'n we're headin' out."

"That's fine with me. Go. I'll be glad to see the last of you."

"Hester goes with us." Lenny sucked in his cheeks and looked Daniel straight in the eye.

"No." Daniel's eyes locked with Lenny's.

"She goes or we ain't."

"In that case I'll meet you downriver at that place where you've camped the last few nights. Knives or muskets. Take your choice."

"Ya'd take on both of us at oncet?"

"I don't figure that even the two of you are equal to one of me."

"We'd aim ta kill ya."

"You can try. But I'll tell you this: both of you won't leave that clearing."

"Dawn, day after tomorry. Come with Hester, or come by yoreself."

"One way or the other, I'll be there."

Daniel watched them mount up and ride away. He had to admire their persistence and their devotion to their mother's wishes. He would hate to kill them, but he would. He knew he would do just that before he'd allow them to ride away with Mercy against her will.

It wasn't until the middle of the afternoon, after George had climbed down the ladder and closed the flume gate stopping the wheel, that Daniel mentioned something that had been worrying him.

"George, were the Kentuckians hanging around when Levi Coffin came in yesterday?"

"Didn't see nothin' of them. I went down to the wagon when I seen who it was. Mr. Coffin said the woman was beat down and the babe sickly. I knowed that cellar room'd be too cold. I tell him to go to livery, then slip into the back of the store. Turley went too. They took the woman to Mr. Mike's rooms."

"I know all that. I'm wondering if the Baxters saw anything. They were hanging around watching the Quill house last night. They might have been watching the store too."

"Why'd they do that?"

"They've got it into their heads Miss Mercy is their long-lost sister."

"Miss Mercy kin to them?" George rolled his eyes upward. "They can't be no kin to Miss Mercy."

"They think they are. I may be having to—" Daniel stopped speaking abruptly and went to the window. The loud clanking of shod horse's hooves on the cobblestone paving at the foot of the ramp had reached his ears. "The devil himself," he murmured. "Hammond Perry!"

"Lordy! That devil man here a'ready?"

"He didn't waste any time. Someone in Evansville must have seen Levi heading north and passed the word. It wouldn't be hard to trail a peddler."

"Lordy!" George said again. He moved back away from the window after viewing the man who reminded him of a strutting bantam rooster and the six armed men who accompanied him. The sight of Hammond Perry, widely known for his cruelty and his unrelenting pursuit of runaways, sent a shiver of apprehension through George. "What you want me to do, Mr. Dan?"

"Stay here, George. I don't want them to catch you off by yourself. Stay over there by that buffalo gun. But if it has to be fired, I'll fire it."

Daniel reached for a heavy coach pistol, checked the load, and slipped the weapon into his belt behind him. When he could hear the men coming up the stone ramp, he went to lean against the doorjamb.

"That's far enough, Perry. What brings you to Quill's Station?"

Hammond Perry, a short man, hated having to look up at a man towering over him. He motioned for his men to stay and moved on up the ramp to where the slope leveled. Almost a head shorter than Daniel he backed away so he didn't have to tilt his head quite so far back to look at him.

"I'm searching for my runaways, as you well know," Perry sneered. His chinless face was shaped like a turned-over bowl, and reddish-gray whiskers covered the lower part of his face in an attempt to hide the receding chin and weak jaw. He was dressed in a fine linen coat, tight breeches, and shiny black boots. A black beaver hat sat on his head, and a coiled whip was looped over his shoulder.

"Illinois is a free state."

"I own that runaway wench. She was leased out."

"To Crenshaw to breed a superior strain of Negroes? You've no authority here."

"Oh, but I do. I've got friends in high places the same as Farr Quill does. His objection to my searching for my legal property was overruled by the Illinois court. I'm within my rights."

"Not here. This *property* is mine. It will not be searched by anyone other than the Illinois State Militia. I believe one of the conditions attached to your permit was that you be accompanied by a militiaman."

"Bah! I'm not waiting around for a militiaman. By the time I get one, my niggers are long gone."

"It's a shame that a few poor souls escaped your hellhole."

"I know about you, Phelps. Quill is supposed to have found you in a massacred train of settlers, but more than likely you're one of his by-blows."

If Perry thought to rile Daniel by the accusation, he was disappointed.

"If that were the case, I'd be honored," Daniel said. "But my parentage has nothing to do with you being here. So state your business or leave. It makes me sick to look at you."

"Levi Coffin, the Quaker preacher from over around Newport, was seen coming this way. He's got my niggers. A wench and her get. I intend to get them back."

"How do you know he's got them? He came through here, but as far as I could see, he had a wagonful of rug samples and dress goods."

"He's got them, all right. Every planter south of the line knows he transports nigger runaways. He's one of those abolitionists who thinks he's going to change things. It's fools like him that get the niggers all riled up. He's a goddamn thief is what he is."

"A thief is no worse than a goddamn kidnaper. How

many free Negroes have you stolen, taken back over the line, or to that hellhole of a salt mine of Crenshaw's?"

"You'd not be talking so smart if you were down in my territory." Perry looked at Daniel as if he were something that had crawled out from under a rock. His nostrils flared angrily when Daniel grinned.

"What territory is that? Not everyone in the South is as much of a bastard as you are, Perry. I bet you give Rain Tallman a wide berth. You'd better get the hell out of here before Gavin McCourtney gets back. If he sets eyes on you, he'll chew you up and spit you out. He hasn't forgotten you tried to steal the woman who is now his wife. My God, Perry! It's beyond me how you've managed to live this long."

"McCourtney can have the chit. If I had really wanted her, I would have taken her. Now move out of my way. I mean to look around." Hammond squared his shoulders, motioned his men forward, and stepped closer to the door. He stopped abruptly when the barrel of Daniel's pistol poked his belly. "You stupid fool," he sputtered. "Do you think you can hold off all of us?"

"You're the fool. A bigger one than I thought you were! What difference will it make to you what your men do after I blow you to hell?" Daniel looked over Perry's head to the men on the ramp. "Does this little weasel pay you enough to risk getting your heads blown off? This is my property. Come a step farther up that ramp and I'll shoot this worthless piece of horseshit, and the man behind me will open up on you with a buffalo gun." As he spoke, George thrust the barrel of the gun out the side of the doorway. "Make up your minds. Back down that ramp and live, or come ahead and die."

Without hesitation the men turned as one and went back down the ramp.

"You'll pay for this, Phelps!" Perry's face was red,

and his chin trembled. "You're putting yourself above the law."

"Above the law? Hell! When did you ever pay any attention to the law? I'd be doing the world a favor if I pulled this trigger." With the end of the gun barrel deep in Perry's belly, Daniel pushed the man away from him. "I've got a word of warning for you, Perry. If one of the *free* Negroes in this community comes up missing, I'm coming looking for you, and I'll not be hampered by any rules of fair play. I don't believe in giving a snake a chance to bite me. I'll blow you to hell as soon as I get you in my sights."

"You may have the upper hand now, but I'm not a man who gives up. If you're running niggers through here, I'll find out about it and I'll be back with the militia."

"You'd better bring the militia to protect you, or you might find yourself tied to the mill wheel slapping water."

"Goddamn that Quaker," Perry sputtered, needing to direct his anger at someone other than the hard-eyed man facing him. "When I catch up with him, I'll strip the hide off that wench's back."

Daniel followed Perry down the ramp. "That sounds like something you'd do. The only thing you could whip is a woman," Daniel said sarcastically. He saw one of Perry's men hiding a grin behind his hand. Daniel couldn't help throwing a few more barbs. "You're a real blood-and-guts man, Perry. I bet you eat alligators for breakfast, drink buffalo milk, and catch bullets with your teeth."

The ridicule turned Perry's face livid with rage. He mounted his own horse and cruelly jerked on the reins until the animal spun around. He looked down at Daniel. "You're nothing but a two-bit miller. I could buy and sell you a hundred times."

"You may be rich, but you're the ugliest son of a bitch I ever laid eyes on." Daniel laughed when he saw the rage in Perry's eyes. His words had touched a raw spot just as he thought they would. He knew it was foolish to goad

Perry, but he couldn't resist one last jibe. "The poor woman probably got a look at your face, and that's why she run off."

"I'll run that damn Quaker into the ground and have that nigger before nightfall."

"Wrong again, Perry. Coffin's halfway over to Sprin—" Daniel clamped his lips shut and looked down at the ground.

A knowing expression settled on Perry's face. He wheeled his horse and headed south toward the ferry. His men followed. Daniel watched them leave, then sprinted up the ramp.

"He took it, George. He thought I was trying to throw him off the track. Levi was going to take the ferry at New Harmony. He'll leave a trail, hoping Perry will follow him east."

"Turley'll be pert nigh to Springfield by night. Do you want me to follow Perry, see if he crosses over?"

"I'd sure like to know if he goes east. But don't let them catch you, for God's sake!"

"Ain't no white trash like him goin' to catch me." George's handsome face split with a confident grin.

"Don't get too cocky. I'll worry until you get back. Perry knows you're the son of Mr. Washington and that the Quills are very fond of you. He'd love to get his hands on you just to spite them." Daniel placed his hand on George's shoulder and gripped hard. "Be careful, you clabberhead. I couldn't run this mill without you. Remember, just watch and see if he boards the ferry. Don't do anything foolish."

George's eyes shone with pleasure. "You ain't got no need to fret, Mister Dan. My mama's folks teach me to trail when I be ass-high to a grasshopper. It'll be a Shawnee brave trailin' that nigger chaser."

* * *

It was a long, quiet afternoon. With Turley gone and George away on his mission, Daniel tried to concentrate on the ledger where he kept his accounts, but his thoughts gathered and splintered, going in a dozen directions. After several large drops of ink fell from the pen to stain the ledger sheet, he closed the book and sat with his feet on the windowsill and allowed his mind to dwell on Mercy.

His earliest memories of her was as a child of two or three years. Her hair was very light, he remembered, long and tangled. She wore a single garment that came down past her knees. It was something Farr had rigged up to cover her nakedness. Daniel smiled, remembered what a time Liberty had had of breaking her from squatting in the yard to relieve herself regardless of who was near. The grin stayed on his face as he thought of the time he and Mercy hid under the table. Mercy had grabbed Mrs. Thompson's skirt and almost scared her to death.

Mercy had readily accepted her new family, screeching with laughter, planting wet kisses on the cheeks of anyone who held her. From the first he had appointed himself her protector. He had dragged her out of the hog pen, boosted her up onto the rail fence when the angry geese pecked her bare legs, picked her up when she fell on slick rocks in the creek, scolded her for not wearing her mittens. His life had been entwined with hers since the day Farr had found him.

The question that was constantly in the back of his mind came forward to haunt him. Would she ever see him as a man who loved her, not as a brother loves a sister but as a man who loves his wife? The thought nagged at him until he got to his feet and paced the room.

By the time Daniel was ready to leave the mill, a dark rain cloud hovered in the southwest. He went up the steep steps to the attic room where George lived to check the shutters on the windows. The furnishings in the room were sparse, but it was neat and clean. Daniel had not been there for a while, and the walls held even more pictures than when he had seen them last. Some were painted on canvas stretched over frames, others on smooth boards or flattened pieces of bark. The subject matter was the same in all the paintings. George painted happy Negroes in various settings.

One painting was that of a young Negro woman in a bright red dress, reaching up to pluck an apple from a tree. Her body was well rounded, her eyes bright and shining, and a smile curved her lips. On her feet were black slippers tied with ribbons. The young woman looked amazingly like Birdie, Gus and Rosie's daughter. Daniel wondered if George was in love with Birdie.

He moved on to study a larger painting of a Negro family in front of a neat cottage with glass windows and flowers around the door. The mother sat in a rocking chair with a small child at her breast. The father, with several children around him, seemed to be telling a story. All the characters in the painting were smiling. It was a happy scene.

George seldom painted a white person or allowed anyone other than Daniel and Liberty Quill to see his pictures. Liberty had discovered his talent by accident and had encouraged him by taking him to Vincennes to see the paintings at Grouseland, the home of Governor and Mrs. Harrison. She had bought canvas, brushes, and paints and challenged him to see what he could do with them.

Eight years ago Liberty and Farr had heard that Sugar Tree and George were in a village north and west of Vincennes and that Sugar Tree was ill. They loaded a wagon with supplies and went in search of them. Sugar Tree's father and brothers were dead, and she had George, a lad of nine years, to hunt for her. Liberty and Farr brought George and his mother back to Quill's Station where Liberty cared for her Indian friend who died a few months later.

Daniel went around to stand in front of the unfinished painting that faced the window. It was a picture of an angel with a cloud of white hair, rosy cheeks and lips, and startling blue eyes. It was Liberty's face. The body of the angel was in a swirl of clouds, but her arms reached down toward a group of children standing on green grass. The Negro and white children were dressed in fine clothes, and each wore a pair of shiny black shoes. Indian children were dressed in elaborately beaded and fringed buckskins. All the children wore happy smiles on their faces.

The image of the hauntingly lovely picture stayed in Daniel's mind after he had closed the door to George's room and had gone back downstairs. He had no doubt that if George had been born white, he would someday be recognized for his talent. It was grossly unfair that the boy felt the need to hide his paintings rather than have them ridiculed because of the color of his skin.

A low rumble of thunder came from the southwest as Daniel took the path through the woods to the Quill house. His mind was active with the problems Mercy faced, and he wondered how she had managed to fill the day. As he neared the house, his ever watchful eyes noted at once that it was in total darkness, that not a light shone from the windows. He quickly scanned the area, then broke into a hard run.

Daniel leaped upon the porch, pausing at the front door to listen. When he heard nothing except the rumble of the thunder, he opened the door and slipped inside to stand with his back to the wall. The house was as quiet as a tomb except for the ticking of the mantel clock.

Something was wrong! Mercy would not have gone away and not told him.

Daniel could almost hear the pounding of his heart as

his fingers fumbled with the chimney of the lamp. He lit it and looked around. Nothing was out of place that he could see in a brief glance. Taking the lamp with him, he went through the rooms, then to the kitchen. Everything was in order. The cold cook stove told him Mercy had not prepared a meal all day. He flung open the door to the room off the kitchen where he had slept as a child and where he had slept the last few nights. Nothing was disturbed there.

Dread lay heavy around his heart as he took the stairs two at a time to search the loft. He would have staked his life that the Baxters would have kept their word about not bothering her and would have waited until the time he said he would meet them. His fear almost crowded out the thoughts of what he was going to do with them if they had forced Mercy to leave with them.

Daniel shoved open the door to the room Mercy had shared first with Amy, and later with Mary Elizabeth. He entered, and relief washed over him like a warm summer rain.

Mercy lay in her bed, asleep.

Daniel was so relieved, he was shaking. He set the lamp on the table and stood looking at her, letting the fear drain away, letting his heart slow to a normal beat.

Her dress was hung over the back of the chair; her shoes were on the floor beside the bed. One shoe stood upright, the other lay on its side, the laces trailing. Daniel leaned down, picked up the shoes, and held them for a moment in his two hands before he placed them on the floor beside the chair that held her dress. He stood beside the bed. It had been a long time since he had looked at her while she slept.

Mercy lay on her side, her palm tucked beneath her cheek. Thick waves of honey-blond hair spread out over the pillow. Lashes, long and tear-spiked, lay on her wet cheeks. Her lips were parted, and a tear hung in the corner of her mouth. As Daniel watched, she sucked in her upper lip and her brows came together in a frown. A whimper at the back of her throat tore loose.

Daniel squatted down beside the bed. He covered the small hand that lay on the quilt with his. His arm curved up above her head, and his fingers soothed the hair back from her forehead. He could feel the warmth of her breath on his face and smell the womanly scent of her body.

"Shhhh... don't cry," he whispered. "You're not alone." His lips followed his fingers to her forehead. "You've worn yourself out crying."

"Danny." She murmured his name before she opened her eyes, fully accepting his presence. "Oh, Danny. It's been the longest, most miserable day of my life." Her fingers moved against his palm and tightened around his thumb.

"I'm here now. You don't have to be miserable alone."

She caught her lower lip between her teeth. She looked as if she would burst into tears. "I'm... glad you're here. I wanted you to come."

"Did you eat anything today? You can't lie here and grieve over a bunch of ignorant people who didn't realize what a good teacher they had for their children." He smoothed the long hair back from her face, wiping at her tears with the ball of his thumb.

"I feel badly for the children, but it's the... other." Tears blurred the eyes that looked up into his.

"The Baxters?"

She nodded. "I keep thinking about that woman, and how I'd feel if my little girl was... lost or taken."

Their faces were close; their voices were low, intimate, interspersed with little pauses.

"Do you want to go see her?" He put his hand into her hair, feeling the soft, silky tresses, thinking they were like a shimmering waterfall.

"I don't... know. I don't want to see her, and yet, I

do. I want to think that I belong here with Mamma and Papa and you." She moved and made a soft little whimpering sound.

"You'll always belong here . . . with me."

"No. It wouldn't be the same. If I came back, it would be like I was coming for a . . . visit." Her voice broke, and she turned her face to his shoulder. Daniel's hand burrowed beneath the pillow and he cuddled her close in his arms. His lips found the dampness of her temple, and his nose the softness of her hair. "What am I going to do?" She sobbed the words against his neck.

"I can't tell you that, love. But I can tell you this: Whatever you decide to do, I'll be with you. If you want to go see the Baxter woman, *we'll* go, and then we'll come back home. If you don't want to go, I'll see to it that Lenny and Bernie leave here, and you won't have to see them again."

"How can you do that?"

"I have ways. You'll just have to leave it to me."

Mercy's hand wriggled out of his, and she cupped his cheek with her palm, then moved the tip of her forefinger to the dent in his chin and held it there. "Ah, Danny . . . you've done so much for me already."

He swallowed before he could answer, and his arms tightened around her. "I've never done anything for you that I didn't want to do. Since the first, I've felt that you belonged to me, and I to you."

"I never knew that, Daniel." Her fingers moved up over his face to brush back the unruly hair on his brow. "I can't remember how things were at the very first, but it must have been awful for you."

"Having you helped."

"I'm sorry I didn't cook your supper. Jeems left the chicken all ready to put in the pot. I think I had an attack of self-pity."

"You can cook the chicken tomorrow."

Daniel looked down at Mercy's quiet, beautiful face. She was calm now. Her breath was sweet on his mouth, her hair tumbled down in beguiling disarray, as he had not seen it in years. He wanted to stay there forever holding her in his arms, warm and soft and dear, and to tell her how much she meant to him. A smile softened the line of his mouth.

"What are you smiling about?"

"I'm thinking I'm going to pull you out of this bed if you don't get up and get dressed. I'll fix us some supper. You'll feel better when you've eaten."

While he spoke, his arm slid from beneath the pillow. He stood and moved away from her, wanting to stay but knowing it best to put distance between them.

"Daniel." He turned at the door when she said his name. "The woman who gets you will be so lucky."

She was leaning up on her elbow, her hair curled down about her shoulders, a perfect frame for the peach-gold skin of her face. Her eyes watched him through the heavy frame of lashes. He could see the shape of her high, uptilted breasts beneath the thin coverlet, and suddenly he was holding his breath. He stood staring, remembering the feel of her in his arms, the scent of her skin, the warmth of her breath on his face.

Beyond the smile he gave her, his mind raced furiously. It was unthinkable that he would ever love another woman, and the thought of her with another man was as painful as a knife stab. He wanted to say something because she was waiting, but what he said was totally unrelated to his thoughts.

"Get your lazy bones up out of that bed, Miss Quill, and come on downstairs. I'm hungry."

CHAPTER SIX

Mercy walked along the bank of the shallow stream that ran from the spring house to the larger creek. The sun felt warm on her back. It was warmer outside the house than inside, once she left the warmth of the cook stove. Green grass edged the banks, and here and there a patch of gold dandelion blossoms poked through the grass. They reminded her of when she and Amy had picked green in the spring. She stopped at the place where Daniel had placed rocks in the creek years ago so she could cross, and she watched the water travel over the stones.

Pleasant childhood memories leaked into her mind, all connected with Daniel, her protector, friend, and counselor. He had always been there to take her side in a dispute or to see that an older student didn't force her to give up a swing or her place in line at the outhouse. No one hit her or pushed her when Daniel was around. She thought now of the time, during her early adolescent years, when she had refused to wear her knit cap to school because it would muss her hair. In the afternoon a blizzard had come up, and Daniel had put his cap on her head when they left the school. On the way home his ears were frostbitten.

This morning he had told her that she must make a decision today about the Baxters. Tomorrow at dawn the brothers were leaving Quill's Station. If she wished to see the woman who had birthed her, Daniel would go with her, stay with her, and bring her back. One way or the other, the Baxters were leaving, he had said. There was something about the intensity of the words when he said them that bothered her.

In the distance Mercy could see the cabin where Jeems and Gerrit lived. The old man was plowing in the field just beyond the cabin. She would tell him to take the excess milk and eggs and the slab of bacon from the smokehouse. Her mother had taught her never to let food go to waste. Her *mother*. Mercy's feet stumbled on the ground, even as her mind stumbled over the word. Mother was Liberty Quill. How could she call another woman Mother?

Before she reached the cabin, she veered off across the field toward Jeems. She was walking over corn stubble, holding her skirt just above her shoe tops so that it would not catch and tear, when a growl, like that of an angry animal, came from behind her. Startled, she jerked around. Her breath tore into her lungs and caught at the sight of a huge Negro man, held fast by a chain on his leg, the other end secured to a heavy post. He stood on spread legs, his arms reaching out toward her. A good fifty feet separated them, but she could see the rage in his eyes as he strained to free himself from the shackles that held him. His breath rasped in and out through a cavernous red mouth. Long black wiry hair stood straight out from his head. The hands at the end of his arms were huge; the growls coming from his throat were like the sounds of an angry dog.

"Missy! Missy!" Mercy heard old Jeems calling and was aware that he was running across the field to her, but she was mesmerized by the sight of his son and could not turn away. "Missy! Come back." Jeems reached her and gently pulled on her arm. "Please, Missy, please—"

"Oh, Jeems. I didn't realize . . ."

She retraced her steps, walking so fast that the old man had to hurry to keep up with her. Gerrit continued to yell something over and over, something she did not understand.

"What's he saying?" she asked after a fearful look over her shoulder.

"He sayin' . . . yo is purty, purty, Missy. He don't mean no harm. He donno no better."

"I know that. He's so big! I guess I was still thinking of him as a little boy. The last time I saw him he was not as tall as you, Jeems."

"Yass'm. He growed some."

"I'm sorry if I got him stirred up."

"He don't see nobody much a-tall. When he do, he get all stirred 'n' he talk, talk, talk."

"I don't know how you handle him."

"It do be gettin' hard, Missy. Mistah Dan, he say he help make a pen ta hold him."

"Oh, Jeems. I'm sorry it's come to that."

"But he alive, Missy. 'N' he my boy." Jeems' seamed face broke into a smile.

"I came to tell you to take the milk in the springhouse and a slab of bacon. When you gather the eggs, take them too. There's more than we can use."

"Gerrit like dat clabber milk mighty fine. Thanky, Missy."

"I'll be all right now," Mercy said when they reached the shallow creek. "Be careful, Jeems."

"I do dat, Missy." Jeems bobbed his head before he turned back.

Blackbird came from the barn and sat waiting for Mercy. The cat meowed and walked over to rub against her legs. He looked up at her with his slanting eyes and meowed again. She reached down and stroked his humped back.

"You look as if you're getting enough to eat."

"Meow!"

"Someone has been giving you milk too," she said, glancing at the pan beside the barn door. "You've got it pretty good here, Blackbird."

On her way to the kitchen door the words were repeated in her mind. *You've got it pretty good here, too, Mercy.* She took off her shawl and hung it on the peg beside the door. The kitchen was warm and pleasant. The aroma of cooked chicken mingled with the smell of the cinnamon she had put in the dried apple pie she had baked that morning.

Did Mrs. Baxter—she couldn't call her Mother, even in her thoughts—have someone to make chicken and dumplings for her? Did the wife of one of her sons take care of her? The questions tormented Mercy. Had the woman loved her as Jeems loved his demented child? Or as Dovie loved her baby? Everything she said, everything she did, seemed to Mercy to take on a new meaning. She clamped her hands over her ears and stood in the middle of the floor shaking her head.

Daniel said to decide by suppertime if she was going to Kentucky. Either way, he said, he had arrangements to make. Daniel, dear Daniel, was willing to leave his farm, his mill, leave his commitment to Levi Coffin to others to carry on while he was away. He would do all of this in order to go with her to Kentucky to visit the family of her birth.

She sank down into the rocking chair beside the kitchen stove. It was so odd to be sitting there, thinking about whether or not to go to see her *real* mother. It occurred to her that Mrs. Baxter would tell her her *real* birthdate. She had always celebrated the day Farrway Quill had found her as her birthday. Mercy rocked gently, her hands palms up, lying in her lap. She was remembering how welcome the Quills had made her feel, and how lovely her childhood had been with them and Daniel.

She leaned forward and looked through the window. There were shadows now where a short time before there had been sunlight. The sun had gone down, and soon she would see Daniel's tall, familiar form coming up the path to the house.

Mercy sat rocking, her hands holding on to each other. She had been fortunate to have been found by Farrway Quill. It was a wonderful thing to have been brought up in a family where goodness, honesty, and respect were important. The feelings inside Mercy stirred, unfolded, and were clear.

She knew what she was going to do.

There was a light in the window to greet Daniel when he came up the path. He called a greeting as soon as he opened the door, then came to stand in the kitchen doorway, his dark head almost reaching the top, his eyes on her face. There was a half smile on her lips when she turned to look at him. Her brow was smooth, her eyes no longer worried. Daniel knew immediately that she had made a decision and would tell him when she was ready. He shed his short leather coat and hung it on a peg beside the back door.

"Something smells good."

"Something? You know what it is. There's a lot of it, too, so you'd better be hungry."

"I am. I'll wash up."

Mercy carried the teakettle to the washstand beside the door and poured hot water into the basin. Daniel followed and ladled in a few dipperfuls of cold water from the water bucket.

"Thanks," he said as he took the soap from the china soap dish. "Hot water and apple pie, what more could a man ask for?"

"How do you know it's apple?" she quirked an eyebrow with her question.

"I can smell the cinnamon."

"It's pumpkin."

"It's apple. The pumpkins are all gone." A grin danced about his mouth.

They both knew they were making idle conversation to prolong the time when they must discuss what was really on both their minds.

Mercy dished up the meal while he washed. He watched her in the small mirror above the washstand. Neat and slender, her golden hair piled on top of her head, she seemed to float rather than walk. She moved from stove to table and back again to pour water over the tea in the pitcher, placing a plate on top of it so the tea would steep. This was what he wanted to come home to every night for the rest of his life—a warm kitchen and this sweet woman waiting for him.

Daniel took the comb from the comb case that hung beside the mirror, dipped it into the water in the washdish, and ran it through his hair. A stubborn lock refused to obey the comb and fell forward on his brow. He gave it several licks with the comb, then gave up and dropped the comb back into the case.

"You need a haircut," Mercy said when he came to the table.

"It's too damn short as it is. I took my knife to it, and now it won't stay back."

"I'll cut it for you after supper, or you'll have to braid it in the back."

Mercy took her place at the table, and Daniel sat

down opposite her. He reached for the lamp on the table between them, moving it to one side so that he could see her. Tenderness was in the eyes that looked at her, but she didn't notice. Her eyes were on her plate.

"Do you mind if I say the blessing?" she asked quietly, and lifted her eyes to his. Her look of deep anxiety erased all other matters from his mind as he resolutely kept his eyes on her face.

He nodded.

Mercy clasped her hands together on the edge of the table and bowed her head.

"Lord, I want to thank thee for bringing me to this place. I want to thank thee for letting me be a part of this family, who clothed and fed me, who cared for me when I was sick, who saw to my education, and who taught me love and respect. Thank thee for Farrway Quill, who in every way has been like a father to me. Thank thee for Liberty Quill; no young girl ever had a more loving and understanding mother. And thank thee, especially, for Daniel. He is so much a part of my life, I cannot imagine life without him. Bless him and keep him safe as we journey to Kentucky. Amen."

Her voice shook at the last, and tears were in her eyes when she raised her lashes to look at him. Yet, now her eyes still did not look unhappy. She seemed quite peaceful and resigned, but there was a certain tenseness in her manner as she watched him to see how he reacted to her decision to go visit the family that claimed she was one of them.

"May I eat now?" he asked, reaching for the bowl of tender chicken and big fluffy dumplings. His face gave away nothing at all, but he was feeling elation, not only because she had mentioned him in her prayer but because he had been right about what she would do.

"I put a speck of sage in the dumplings, the way you like them."

"I see you did. I'm surprised you remembered." He forked a piece of chicken out of the broth and put it on his plate. "You've had a busy day."

"I walked down to the where Jeems lives . . ."

Daniel's hand, reaching for the bread plate, paused in midair. "And?"

"I shouldn't have gone. I didn't realize Gerrit was so big, and so violent."

"You didn't get close to him?"

"No, but he saw me and got excited."

"I'm worried he'll hurt Jeems." Daniel dipped into the butter bowl with his knife while still looking at her. "As soon as we get back from Kentucky, George and I will go down there to build something for him to keep Gerrit in. He's big and he's as strong as a bull. I hate to think of what will happen if he outlives Jeems."

"Jeems is such a kind man. He lives to take care of Gerrit. It would break his heart if anything happened to his son."

Mercy worried the dumpling around on her plate with her fork and took a small bite now and then. Daniel emptied his plate and helped himself to more. They didn't speak again until after Mercy poured the tea.

"What did George have to say about Hammond Perry?" she asked. "I hope he doesn't do anything foolish and let himself get caught down by the state line. Papa has warned him about that."

"I've warned him too. He followed Perry across the river and trailed him until he was well on his way to Newport. Levi Coffin hoped to throw Perry off Turley's trail, and he did. He's a sly fox."

"He must be a awfully good man to take the chances he does. Does Papa know what you and Turley do?"

"We've talked about it."

"I thought of Mamma when I was with Dovie and her

baby. She would approve, although she would be worried if she knew Hammond Perry had been here."

"We won't worry her with it now. We'll tell her about it when they come home at Christmas."

"I wish she knew I was going to Kentucky, and why."

Mercy's large blue eyes were more beautiful than ever—more brilliant with the moistness of tears she refused to acknowledge. Daniel's eyes moved to her mouth, sweet and young and vulnerable. Absently a part of his mind noted that during the last few days she had changed. Her face now had the look of a serious young woman rather than that of a carefree girl. She seemed paler, her eyes a deeper blue. He enjoyed the sight of her lovely face in the glow of the lamp.

"I've made the arrangements necessary to be away for a while. We can leave at dawn."

"Were you so sure I would go?"

He looked at her across the table, his dark eyes earnest, warm, and caressing on her face.

"You forget, Mercy, that I've known you for a long time. I may know you even better than you know yourself. I was almost a hundred percent sure that I knew what you would do."

"I wouldn't even have considered going if you had not offered to go with me."

"I know that too."

"Daniel, I feel so guilty taking you away from the mill and the farm. Spring is a busy time. Are you sure you can spare the time?"

Can I spare the time? Good Lord, he thought, she had no idea what she meant to him. The farm, the mill, even his desire to help Levi Coffin, were all as nothing compared to his desire to be with her, keep her safe, bring her back here, where she belonged—with him. These thoughts went through his mind, but when he spoke, it was casually.

"Oh, yes. I can spare the time. Jasper and Gus know

what to do at the farm. They'll get advice from Mike if something comes up. Turley and George can run the mill as well as I can, and Gavin will be back in a day or two."

"I wonder what Eleanor and Tennessee will think. I wish I could see them before I go."

"They'll be here when we get back."

Mercy stared wide-eyed into the corner of the room. Things will never be the same again, she thought. She would never sit at this table as Mercy Quill. How did she know this? Her hand crawled across the table toward Daniel's as if to hold on to the past. He placed his knife across the edge of his plate, met her hand in the middle of the table, and covered it with his. He looked at her searchingly; she met his eyes earnestly, with a kind of pleading for understanding.

"Do you think I'm doing the right thing? A part of me doesn't want to know any more about the Baxters than I know already. The other part wants to see *her* and let her know I've had a happy life."

"If you don't go see her, you may regret it later. And you'd wonder about the rest of them, thinking that someday they might show up here again."

"I know you're right. I've got to face up to what I am, don't I?"

"Dammit, Mercy! You're what you are, regardless of what *they* are. They could be the scum of the earth, and it wouldn't make you any different!"

"How long will it take us to get there?" she asked with torturous slowness.

"Three, maybe four days. We'll take the road wagon Farr bought when you were going to the Jefferson Academy in Vincennes. It will take a little longer, but it will be more comfortable."

"I could ride. A couple of dresses and heavy shoes are about all I'll need."

"Pack what you want. We'll take the wagon. Farr

would insist on it. I'm sure we'll be able to find places to stay along the way."

"What if they won't let me . . . come back?" She turned her palm up and laced her fingers between his.

"They'll not have anything to say about it!" He gripped her hand tightly. "You're going for a visit and that's all." Then, in a voice that was more commanding than appealing, "You're not to worry about that."

"I can't help thinking about them. I wonder if all the Baxters are as strange as Bernie and Lenny. They acted as if they owned me."

"They're strange compared to the way we were brought up. I've heard that the hill families down there have peculiar ways. They are close-knit, clannish as hell, and keep to themselves. But they don't *own* you or have any claim to you other than what you want to give them."

"Daniel, you're so levelheaded," she said with a wistful smile. "You make things sound so reasonable. Sometimes I wonder why you put up with me."

God in heaven, he thought. *It's because I love you, have always loved you*. He couldn't say the words; this was not the time; so he slipped his hand from hers and said, "Eat your supper. It's getting cold."

Mercy heard Daniel shake the ashes from the cook stove and knew that dawn was near. She threw back the covers, got out of the bed, and lit a candle. She gasped as she splashed the cold water on her face, then dried it on the towel that lay on her washstand. She dressed quickly in the gray dress she had decided to wear for the trip. The dress would be warm enough for this time of year. She would take a heavy shawl and a light one. Mercy folded her nightdress and the three dresses she had chosen to take; a blue one of soft material, a light gray with a white collar, and a dark brown work dress. She placed them with the stockings, underthings, several fine handkerchiefs, and toilet articles, including two bars of scented soap, in the open carpetbag on Mary Elizabeth's bed where the night before she had packed the supply of soft cloths she used for her monthly flow. Mercy added a soft white shawl, knitted in an open, lacy pattern and a packet of her sewing equipment, with knitting needles and several balls of wool yarn for stockings, in case she would need something to keep her hands busy.

She straightened her bed and tidied the room before she took down her hair and brushed it, braided it, and wound the thick braids around her head, securing them with the silver hairpins her parents had given her on her eighteenth birthday. Before closing the bag, she put in her comb, brush, and an extra towel. As an afterthought she packed a pair of soft slippers.

When she was ready to leave, Mercy picked up her carpetbag and looked about the room. It seemed lonely, somehow. She couldn't believe that she was leaving it. When she looked at the candle flame, it was blurred. She blinked her eyes until they cleared, picked up the candle, and left the room.

Daniel was in the kitchen. Mercy left her bag beside his pack, just inside the kitchen door. In the lamplight he looked rested, although she knew he had made a trip out to his farm after she had gone to bed. He had shaved, and his hair was damp and had been briskly combed.

"I forgot about your haircut, but I'm taking my sewing things. I'll cut it sometime soon."

"I've made tea. How about cold dumplings and pie for breakfast?"

"We have to eat it or give it to Blackbird. I must wash the pans before we go."

"Blackbird is *not* getting the pie," Daniel said with a grin. He poured tea in a cup and set it on the table beside the place he had set for her. "Is that all you're taking?" he jerked his head toward the small bag beside the door.

"It's all I'll need."

"You're a rare woman. Gavin says Eleanor takes everything she owns, even when they go to Vincennes for a few days."

"How long do you think we'll be gone?"

"It depends on how long you want to stay. A few weeks, maybe." He sat down at the table, put a large piece of pie in a bowl, and poured milk on it. "I told Jeems to come in the house once a day and make sure it was all right. Mike and Gavin will keep an eye on the place too."

Mercy took a few bites of the cold dumplings, ate a small sliver of pie, and drank the tea. When Daniel finished, he carried the dumpling pan out to the barn and scraped out what was left in a trough for Blackbird. They were both quiet as they went about the task of getting ready to leave. Mercy cleaned up the breakfast things while Daniel carried the water bucket to the fireplace and then to the kitchen stove to wet down the ashes as a precaution against fire. When he went to the barn to get his horse and one to hitch to the light wagon, he took his pack and Mercy's bag with him.

Alone in the house, Mercy went upstairs to get the chamber pot. She carried it out the front door and emptied it away from the house. Her mother wouldn't mind if she didn't carry it to the outhouse just this one time, she told herself. She took it back upstairs and slid it under her bed. Mercy felt as if her past were ending, and from this day on it would exist only in her memory. This had been her home. There was a dear memory tucked into each corner of the house, into each piece of furniture, each windowpane. The people who lived here and who had made this house into a home were her family.

Determinedly she dismissed that thought from her mind and concentrated on another. Daniel had said that she was what she was, regardless of the Baxters who had passed their blood down through the generations to her.

"Oh, Daniel, my dear, dear one," she whispered. "How unbearable this would all be without you."

When Mercy heard the horses stamping at the back gate, she flung her shawl about her shoulders, blew out the candle, and went out into the brisk, dark morning, closing the kitchen door firmly behind her. The night wind had cleaned and freshened the air. It was sharp and cold against her cheeks. In the eastern sky a faint hint of light was coming into the blackness. She walked rapidly to where Daniel was working with the harness and hitching the mare to a short, light, high-wheeled spring wagon.

"Zelda is anxious to go," he said, patting the neck of the sorrel mare. "She's gentle, she's got an easy gait, and she likes pulling the wagon."

"We drew straws to see who got to name her. Remember? Mary Elizabeth got the shortest straw."

Daniel finished hitching the mare and tied the reins to the brake handle. He fastened a lead rope to the halter of his mount, a big buckskin gelding that stood a good two hands taller than the mare, and tied it to the tailgate. He stood for a moment looking at Mercy over the back of the horse. Her face and hair were a faint light spot in the darkness.

"Don't be sad. We'll be back," he said, his whisper sounding thick, almost desperate.

"I'm trying not to be sad." Then she said the next thing that came into her mind. "Do you want to stop by and tell Belinda Martin you're going?"

He said nothing for a long while, as if her words had rendered him speechless. His face was a blur in the darkness, but she could see the outline of his hat brim, and the breadth of his shoulders. He was standing very still. She could feel his eyes on her face. A sudden warmth suffused her cheeks and neck. She had no right to pry into his private affairs, and wondered what had possessed her to say such a thing.

"Why in hell would I want to do that?" he asked with quiet sincerity.

"Oh, I don't know. I just . . . thought you m-might want to," she stammered.

"We'd better get started if we're going to get past Granny Halpen's before she's out on the porch," he said abruptly as he went to the hitching post to unsnap the holding rope. Mercy was on the seat when he climbed up beside her. "Do you have something for your head? It's cold down on the river road."

Mercy folded a square she'd pulled from her pocket, placed the triangle on her head, and tied the ends beneath her chin. Daniel picked up the reins and urged the mare out onto the road. They drove away in the still of the morning with only the song of the mourning doves in the trees above the house to bid them good-bye.

Not a single light glowed in any of the houses in Quill's Station when they passed through it. But now there was definite early-morning light along the tops of the trees that edged the river road. It was still very dark, but Mercy could make out the line of Daniel's profile. His face was still, his brows drawn together as if he were in deep thought. Was he angry because she had mentioned Belinda Martin?

The thought of the small, plump widow and Daniel set a nagging thought worrying her mind. Was that the kind of woman who appealed to Daniel? Did he like a woman who would keep her mouth shut and obey him without question? Daniel deserved more, much, much more, than what Belinda Martin could offer.

Daniel turned the horse down a little used road that

led to the river, and Mercy brought her thoughts back to the present. It was darker here and so quiet that the horses' hooves and the wagon wheels made scarcely a sound on the thick mat of damp leaves. They came into a small clearing. Mercy opened her mouth to question but closed it when she sensed movement ahead. There was a stirring in the darkness, then a form stood beside the mare. She could make out the shape of a pointed leather hat and the barrel of a musket.

"She goin'?" Lenny's voice.

"Yes."

"She got her plunder?"

"Yes."

"Then we ain't got no more use fer ya, mister. Ya can head on back."

"No."

"Ya ain't goin'!"

"Try and stop me."

"Bernie's got a bead on ya."

"And I've got one on you." The unmistakable sound of a pistol being cocked was loud in the quiet that followed Daniel's words.

Mercy suddenly realized the undertone of the conversation. *They didn't want Daniel to go with her!*

"What are you talking about?" she said, her voice shrill. "Are you saying you don't want Daniel to go with me?" Mercy turned in the seat and leaned across Daniel's lap so she could peer into the darkness. "He goes or I don't! Is that understood? I wouldn't even consider going all the way to Kentucky with you if he didn't go!"

"He ain't yore kin! Ya ain't needin' him, 'n' he ain't got no business trailin' along where he ain't wanted," Lenny said with a snort of disgust. "Now, I'm tellin' ya, yore goin' ta get yoreself in a peck a trouble diddling' 'round with a feller what ain't yore man!"

"You . . . hare-brained, shiedpoke! You're not telling

me anything about Daniel or anyone else!" Mercy shouted, her temper flaring.

"Dang bust it! Ya'd better pay a mind ta what I'm telling ya!" Lenny's shout matched hers.

"Don't you yell at me, Lenny Baxter!" Mercy scanned the darkness behind him. "Bernie, put that gun down and get out here or . . . or I'll take this horsewhip to you," she yelled, then she turned the full force of her wrath back on Lenny. "You pig-ugly, mindless . . . worm! Don't you even attempt to tell me what to do. You've already caused me to lose my teaching job," she charged bitterly. "I'm going to your . . . Mud Creek only because Daniel is going with me. He's in charge here! Complete charge. Do you understand that? If you or Bernie give him any trouble, you'll be sorry you ever came to Quill's Station. What's more, if you touch a hair on his head, I'll . . . I'll shoot you! So help me God, I will!"

Daniel watched and listened with a half smile on his face. This was his Mercy, the real Mercy. She was leaning firmly against him, her shoulder against his chest, her hand on his knee. Once again she had been jarred out of her depression, as she had been when she raked Glenn Knibee over the coals. He sat quietly, enjoying her closeness and her handling of the situation.

Bernie came out of the shadows, an old musket in the crook of his arm.

"Put that gun down, you fool," she snapped.

"It ain't right. I ain't likin' it."

"It doesn't matter a whit to me if you like it or not. But it *does* matter to me how you treat Daniel. If you don't back off and behave yourselves, he and I will turn back, and if you ever come near me again, I'll fill your tail so full of buckshot, you'll not sit on it again."

"Well, it 'pears like ya got me o'er a barrel . . . this time. He can come," Lenny said begrudgingly, "but Hod 'n' Wyatt ain't goin' to like it none a-tall."

"To hell with Hod and Wyatt." Mercy slid her hand inside the crook of Daniel's arm.

"Ya better not let Maw hear ya swearin'," Lenny cautioned. "She'd be plumb misput."

"Are we going, or do you intend to stand there all day jawing about it?" she asked crossly.

"We're goin'. Bernie, get the mules."

"Ya're lettin' him off the hook?"

"Ya heared me, didn't ya? Get the mules!"

"Well, it plumb flummoxes me why ya're lettin' a *woman* call the shots, 'n' say what's what. If 'n word get out 'bout this, we couldn't look folks in the eye down on Mud Creek. This feller's goin' ta be nothin' but a peck a trouble. I swan, Lenny, ya beat all I've seen in all my born days. Ya've done let Hester muddy yore mind."

"Shut up! Get the mules. I've had a bellyfull a yore back talk. Sister," he said to Mercy, "I've got my craw full of yore sass too."

"That's too bad, *brother*!" Mercy said the word scathingly. "Because you're going to hear a lot more. And I don't give a doodle-d-squat if you like it or not."

"Ya just better have a mind ta who ya're talkin' to, Missy. I ain't never heared of no woman what so lippy as you is," Bernie muttered. "A taste of a willow switch is what ya be needin'. Book learnin's done ruint ye fer mindin' what ya're menfolk say."

"Book learning never ruined anyone. The lack of it sure ruined you," Mercy retorted.

"We'll jist see what Wyatt 'n' Hod got to say 'bout ya runnin' off at the mouth. They ain't goin' ta like a know-it-all sister none a-tall. It'll be plain as a nose on yore face that they ain't goin' ta."

"It may surprise you to know that I'm not concerned with their opinion of me any more than I am with yours. I want to know what you meant about letting Daniel off the hook," Mercy demanded. "I demand to know just what you two were planning to do to Daniel."

"It was nothing," Daniel said quickly, causing her to turn to look into his face. "We had an agreement. I told them the decision was yours, that if you decided to go to Kentucky, I would bring you here."

"And if I decided not to go?"

"Then I'd meet them here and tell them you were not going. Let's move on out. We've wasted enough time here," he added impatiently, and slapped the reins against Zelda's back. The wagon moved suddenly. Mercy leaned heavily against Daniel until she could straighten herself on the seat.

There was definite light now. Daniel turned the wagon around in the clearing and headed back toward the river road. Mercy moved to withdraw her hand from the crook of his arm. He pressed it tightly to his side and tilted his face down toward her.

Smiling, he looked at her. Smiling, she looked at him and snuggled her shoulder behind his.

CHAPTER SEVEN

D aniel turned south at the river road, let Zelda have her head, and urged her into an even trot. The light vehicle moved smoothly over the hard-packed road that ran parallel with the river. At New Harmony they would take the ferry across the Wabash into Indiana and travel south into Kentucky. It was always cool and quiet along this part of the road except for the birds and squirrels.

The sun came up, sending streaks of brightness through the budding trees. The birches that mingled with the oak along the riverbank stood white and clean. The squirrels scampered among their branches. A mockingbird, swaying on a slender branch at the very top, trilled, and was scolded by a sassy bluejay from the sumac bush below.

Mercy didn't look behind them, but she knew that Bernie and Lenny were following. Now and then she could hear Bernie's voice raised in heated argument. Finally she heard Lenny telling him to hush his mouth, and he did.

The second seat in the light spring wagon had been removed to make room for Daniel's saddle, his pack, Mercy's carpetbag, a bag of grain, a covered basket, and a wooden box that held extra powder and shot, as well as tools. Daniel's rifle, powder, and shot bags were within easy reach beneath the seat. The pistol was beside him.

Mercy leaned against the comfortable padded seat and was glad Daniel had insisted on bringing the wagon. She glanced at him. No words had passed between them for some time. He sat with one booted foot on the dash, his forearm on his thigh, the reins in his hands. He appeared to be deep in thought. She wondered if it was because they were nearing the Crawford homestead where Belinda Martin and her son lived with her parents.

An uneasiness crept into her mind that had nothing to do with the Baxters or the trip to Kentucky. It lingered there like a nagging toothache. Was Belinda Martin the type of woman Daniel would pick for a wife? Was he attracted to her plump, soft body, her cow eyes? A vision of Daniel with the widow in his arms suddenly appeared before Mercy's eyes. Belinda's arms were about his neck, and he was holding her, kissing her. Mercy's heart began to pound with a frightening force, her face tingling with the heat of her jealousy. The hands in her lap gripped each other, as a bewildering complex of thoughts, each fleeting, merging into one another, filled her mind until one managed to stick, demanding an answer. Was she, Mercy Quill, in love with Daniel?

Her eyes were drawn to him. He was looking straight ahead. She glanced away quickly lest he look at her and read in her hot face what she was thinking. Mercy could feel the pulse in her throat, throbbing with each beat of her heart. She shifted in the seat so that her shoulder was no longer touching his as thoughts tumbled in and out of her mind. It was Mercy and Daniel, Daniel and Mercy, together . . . forever. That thought had begun to formulate in her mind, she realized now, when she saw him with Belinda Martin at the Humphrey barn-raising and had gathered strength when she saw him with Belinda's son perched on his shoulder. That was long before the Baxters had accused them of having more than a brother-sister relationship.

Of course, she was in love with him!

At first she loved Daniel as a younger sister loves an older brother. Now, she realized, a corner of her heart that had never been filled was suddenly overflowing with a different kind of love. She loved him as a woman loves the man with whom she wants to mate, have children, share life. Dear God, how did this happen? She must be careful, very careful. Daniel must not know how she felt about him until she was sure he felt more than brotherly love for her. Her heart shook with apprehension. Years of habit were hard to break. He had always been so protective of her. She was certain that he would sacrifice his own happiness before he would hurt her. But she didn't want him that way! She wanted him to love her as Papa had loved Mamma all these years, as if his life would not be complete without her.

She dared another look at him. He was so dear to her! She knew every line in his face, the dent in his chin, the way his hair grew back from his forehead. She knew what he liked to eat, the clothes he liked to wear, his feelings about politics, justice, slavery. He was a man of integrity and occasional violence. He was not a bully, but when he was pushed, he enjoyed the fight. He seemed to get some kind of satisfaction out of the combat.

Her thoughts shifted to how absolutely handsome he was. A shiver of pure physical awareness ran down her spine. Unconscious of time or place, she stared at his profile as if she had not seen it before.

He turned his head slowly; their eyes caught and held. She saw the question in those deep, beautiful brown eyes. Her blue ones lost themselves in their dark, velvety depths, and she seemed to be filled with a warmth and completeness that was new to her.

"What are you thinking when you look at me like that?" he said softly, breaking into her thoughts.

Ten seconds passed while Mercy drew a shallow breath, followed by a deeper one. She had a mad impulse to move close to him, grab his arm, and hug it to her.

"I was thinking that you have beautiful eyes. It's no wonder Belinda is in love with you."

'Who says she is?"

"She would be crazy not to be."

"That so?"

He turned his eyes away. Mercy wished fervently she had not mentioned Belinda and vowed not to do so again. The thought of him and the widow ravaged her, sending a shiver of dread down her spine.

"Speaking of Belinda," Daniel was saying, "there she is. We'll have to stop now that she's seen us."

"Yes, of course." A feeling of misery and loneliness washed over Mercy like a rolling tide.

Belinda Martin stepped off the porch and walked out to the road when Daniel stopped the wagon. Her young son raced ahead of her, his small, freckled face wreathed in smiles.

"Mr. Phelps!" the boy squealed. "Are you comin' to see Ma?" he asked hopefully. "Is them men with ya? Ma cooked a pie."

"Hello, Homer." Daniel handed the reins to Mercy and got down off the wagon.

"He knew it was you," Belinda said, tucking stray wisps of hair into the loose knot at the nape of her neck. "And he hasn't seen you in this wagon before." Her eyes remained on Daniel's face for a long while, then she glanced up at Mercy. "Hello, Mercy."

"Hello, Belinda."

"I heard that school has been dismissed for the year," she said, her eyes leaving Mercy to glance behind the wagon at the two men on the mules. Lenny and Bernie had stopped a short distance behind them. They sat watching while their mules cropped the grass alongside the road.

"Yes," Mercy answered. There seemed to be nothing else to say. She had no doubt Belinda had heard the whole story from the Knibees. Now she would have something to add to the gossip, she thought, looking down into the pretty, face of the widow. Belinda turned from Mercy, dismissing her. She was looking up at Daniel as if he were the sun and the moon, Mercy thought, feeling irritation and trying to ignore the fluttering sensation dancing in her stomach.

"Homer was talking about you only this morning, Daniel. He was wondering when you would be coming out again."

Daniel ruffled the hair on the top of the boy's head. "He was thinking about that sweet tooth of his." He reached into his shirt pocket and brought out a small, paper-wrapped package. "Here you are, squirt. Here's the sugarhards you're so fond of."

"Oh, Daniel! You shouldn't have," Belinda gushed. "You're spoiling him!"

"It'll take more than a few sugarhards to spoil him." He smiled down at the boy and chuckled when the child unrolled the paper and a piece of the confection fell into the dirt. Homer picked it up quickly, wiped each side on his shirt sleeve, and put it into his mouth, looking up at Daniel with a snaggle toothed smile.

"Are you taking your sister to Vandalia?" Belinda asked.

"Vandalia is to the west of here. No. Mercy and I are going to Kentucky." Daniel started to the back of the wagon, then paused and looked up at Mercy. "I'll ride Buck if you'll drive for a while. It'll lighten up the load for Zelda."

Mercy nodded and moved to the middle of the seat.

"Will you be gone long?" Belinda moved along the wagon box to where Daniel was lifting his saddle from the back.

"We're not sure. I left a penny with Mike, Homer.

The next time you're in the store, he'll give you a penny's worth of licorice."

"What do you say, Homer?" Belinda prompted.

"Gee! Thanks, Mr. Phelps!"

Mercy could almost, but not quite, feel sorry for Belinda. She was so anxious to make conversation with Daniel, and he was making it difficult for her. Mercy wondered if he was uncomfortable because she was along. Belinda's next low-voiced question wiped all pity from Mercy's heart.

"Is it true that Mercy's . . . kinfolk have come to claim her? Are you taking her to them?"

"Why don't you ask Mercy?"

"Well . . . I don't want to . . . embarrass her."

"Why would it embarrass her?"

"Oh, you know. I'd be embarrassed enough to die to have people know *they* were related to *me*."

"I don't see why. They haven't stolen anything or harmed anyone. If they had a bath, clean clothes, and were riding good horses, you'd think differently about them." Daniel detached Buck's lead rope from the wagon and threw the saddle over the back of the buckskin while he was talking.

"No, I wouldn't. I'd still be able to tell what they were," Belinda murmured, loud enough that the words carried to Mercy.

"And what is that?"

Irrationally Mercy felt angry at Daniel, as well as at Belinda, for talking about her and the Baxters as if they weren't there. Her anger ignited into full-fledged rage after she heard Belinda's next comment.

"Trash. Breeding tells, Daniel. Everyone knows that. Oh, I feel so sorry for poor Mercy."

How dare that . . . dumpling of a woman pity her! Mercy was painfully aware that her temper was about to explode all over Belinda Martin. The man-hungry bitch had no right to say that about Lenny and Bernie. They had done nothing to her. They had not even come close to her. Completely unaware that a part of her anger was due to a remote sense of loyalty to the two brothers, Mercy breathed deeply and gave herself a full moment to pull herself together.

"Daniel," she called in a carefully controlled voice. "I'll go on and give Belinda a chance to visit with you . . . alone. I'm sure that's what she's hoping for. She wants to know about my trashy kinfolk. You can tell her all about them and why we're making this trip." Her voice rose at the last in spite of her determination to stay calm. " 'Bye, Belinda," she called with drippy sweetness and slapped the reins against Zelda's back with such force that the mare was startled. The wagon lurched forward, creaked, moved quickly, and Mercy fervently hoped the wheel would run over Belinda's foot.

" 'Bye." Belinda's voice barely reached her. "Have a good trip."

"You're darn right I'll have a good trip, you . . . soft, sweet-smelling, little butterball," Mercy muttered. "I just bet my last button you'd give your front teeth to be going on a trip with Daniel. It will never happen, Mrs. Uppity Martin. You'll not use his love for children to get your claws in Daniel. It's taken me a long time to realize it, but he's mine, and I'll fight tooth and nail to keep him."

Not five minutes later, although it seemed an hour to Mercy, Daniel rode past the wagon and took the lead to set the pace. He didn't look at her or speak. He was angry.

Yesterday she would have merely regretted angering him. Today it devastated her.

On another road in southern Indiana, another wagon was headed east, pulled by a team of tired horses. Levi Coffin, the Quaker, sat on the wagon seat, the noonday sun beating down on his dusty black coat and his high-topped hat. He pulled out his pocket watch, opened it and checked the time, replaced it, and calmly stared off down the road. He figured that he should be hearing hoofbeats behind him at almost any time—that is, if Daniel Phelps had been able to draw Hammond Perry off the trail of the woman and babe.

Good man, Phelps, Levi mused. Farr Quill had done a good job raising him. There was not a more respected man in the state than Quill. He was badly needed in the legislature if they were going to keep Illinois a slave-free state. Concessions had already been made to allow a slave owner to come into the state to look for fugitives. If found, the owner was allowed to take them back over the state line.

Phelps was following along in his stepfather's footsteps. He was building a reputation that someday would equal that of Farrway Quill. He was becoming known as a man of high principles, totally trustworthy, and dedicated to a cause if he considered it right. Levi and Daniel had met only one other time in Evansville, but Levi knew about the place called Sugar Tree and that at least a dozen people had passed through it on their way to the North and freedom.

Levi wiped the sweat from his brow with a handkerchief that once had been white. The road was passing through the rocky bed of a creek. Levi pulled up on the reins and stopped the horses so they could drink. He had business south. Soon he would be forced to turn north to make it appear that he was headed for Newport. John Ingle, a settler a few miles back with whom he had spent the night, had said that this was a dangerous road. Travelers were often waylaid and robbed. He wished Perry would catch up if he were going to.

The thought was no more than completed in his mind when he heard the sound of hoofbeats on the road behind him. Levi turned to see a group of horseman galloping toward him. He urged the horses up out of the stream and on down the dusty road. Levi thought of what John Ingle had told him and prayed a silent prayer. The last house he had passed was several miles back, and according to Ingle, it was a good ten miles to the next one. Of course, there was a chance this was not a band of robbers or Hammond Perry. A glance behind him told him it was Perry.

"Hold up!" Hammond Perry came alongside the wagon. He spoke in a commanding tone as if he were leading a military patrol.

Levi had met Hammond once before in Louisville and knew he was a thoroughly unpleasant man. He pulled up on the reins, took off his hat, and wiped his forehead.

"Good day to thee."

"Goddamn you, Quaker! I've chased you for three days. You've got my nigger and her whelp, and, by God, I mean to have her back!" He wheeled his horse so that he could reach the ropes holding the cover over the wagon bed. He began to cut the ropes with a long knife. "Get that cover off! Empty the wagon and get that wench out of there!" he yelled to the men, who jumped off their horses to obey.

"What are thee doing, friend? I pray thee stop this destruction of my property. Who are thee searching for?" Levi wrapped the reins around the brake handle and climbed down over the wheel. The canvas had been ripped off the wagon bed, exposing the rug samples, boxes of buttons, an assortment of thread, and carefully wrapped bolts of cloth and lace. The men were tossing them out of the wagon. "Stop! Stop! Thee are ruining my trade goods."

"Trade goods, hell!" Hammond snarled. "I'll break every bone in your mangy body if I don't find my nigger. I know you took her from Evansville. By God, I'll make you sorry, you . . . Bible-thumping son-of-a-bitch!"

"There's nothin' here," one of the men said when he could see the bare floor of the wagon bed.

"Get everything out, you fool!" Hammond shouted. "There's got to be a false bottom in that wagon!"

Levi stood by, wringing his bony hands. He ran to

pick up a bolt of fine lace that had been tossed into the dirt and clutched it to his chest.

"Thee are ruining me, thee are ruining me," he chanted sorrowfully.

"Turn the goddamn wagon over," Hammond roared.

"No!" Levi pleaded. "Thee will hurt the beast."

One of the men, a man with a stubble of red beard on his face, quickly unhitched the team and stung each of the animals on the rump with his whip. They took off down the road and were quickly out of sight. The wagon was tipped on its side and examined.

"There ain't no double floor in this wagon." The man who spoke went to his horse and mounted when he saw the rage on Hammond Perry's face.

Four of the men began rummaging in the goods they had tossed out of the wagon. One of them picked up a bolt of material and took it to his horse.

"The nigger ain't here, but I'll have me some of this dress goods fer my trouble. By jinks' damn! I know me a woman who'd shine up ta me for a hunk of this."

The red-bearded man who had freed the horses stood watching Hammond whose eyes were on Levi Coffin. Hate and rage contorted his face.

"You thieving son-of-a-bitch! You left her at Quill's." Hammond spoke calmly, but his hands were trembling violently. He suddenly pulled his gun from the boot on his saddle and pointed it at Levi. "That's the last nigger you'll steal."

The red-bearded man sprang forward and grabbed Hammond's arm.

"You're not killing him. He doesn't have your nigger."

"Get your hands off me, you scum!"

"You're not killing him," the man repeated as he held Hammond's arm in an iron grip. "You don't know for certain that he hides your runaways."

"Damn you! A man who works for me stays in his place and does as he's told." Hammond's face was livid with anger.

"You said nothing of murder."

"I aim to put a ball in his knee, damn you! I'll cripple the thieving Bible spouter."

"It's the same thing. He'd die out here."

"You ... you lily-livered bastard," Hammond shouted. "You're done!"

"Then give me my pay." The steely eyes of the red-bearded man bored into Hammond's.

Growling with frustration, Hammond shoved his gun back into the boot, took some coins from his pocket, and threw them into the dirt at the man's feet.

"Goddamn your creeping, crawling soul! Grovel for them!" He yanked on the reins, causing his horse to spin around. "Take what you want and let's go," he yelled to the men still rummaging among Levi's trade goods.

Several of the men grabbed up bolts of cloth or lace before they mounted and rode after Perry.

"Thank thee, Edward." Levi wiped the sweat dripping from his face.

"He's a mean one, Levi. I'll not be any more use in keeping an eye on him for you now." Edward Ashton stooped and picked up the coins Hammond had thrown on the ground at his feet. "It's just as well. Another day and I'd have split the bastard's gullet."

"What happened at Quill's Station?"

"Nothing much. First Phelps made Perry madder than a stepped-on snake so that he wasn't thinking straight. Then he let it slip that you were headed for Springfield. Perry took it that Phelps was trying to throw him off the track. We headed south for the ferry like a prairie fire was behind us. It wasn't hard to pick up your trail."

"Good man, Phelps."

"I'd hate to go up against him myself. He's got a look about him that says he'll not back down, and he's got the size to back it up. Say, Levi, I'm almost sure a feller trailed us across the river. Does Phelps have a young, light-colored nigger with hair braided like an Indian's working for him?"

"Yes. I met him at the mill. He's the son of a Negro and a Shawnee woman."

"I saw the same feller a couple of times. He was sly about his trailing, but he's a man who stands out. He had on Indian dress, but there was no mistaking his color."

"Did Perry see him?"

"Perry was like a hound dog on a scent. He had his nose to the ground and was too hot on your trail to notice anything. But he knows about the boy. He's heard that he's a pet of Mrs. Quill. He said that if he had him, he'd put him to a high-colored wench and get whelps that would bring top price."

"Such inhumanity intensifies my hatred of slavery and inspires me to devote myself to the cause of the helpless and oppressed," Levi said fervently.

"Yeah? You're not going to help anybody if you're left beside the road with your throat cut. I'm almost sure Hammond Perry is a member of the Mystic Clan, James Murrell's outlaws, who rob, steal slaves, and pass counterfeit. He'll put the word out on you. You'd better not be roaming around alone."

"Is he also a partner to John Crenshaw at the salt works known as Half Moon?"

"I don't think he's a full partner. Crenshaw is too smart for that. Perry is more than likely associated with Crenshaw in the Negro-napping operation. He furnishes slaves for the salt works at a good price. It saves Crenshaw from renting them from planters across the line."

"'Tis said Crenshaw not only profits from human bondage and enforced servitude, but he also is cruel man. Slaves are under the whip and treated like animals."

"I know one slave who doesn't think Crenshaw is a cruel man. He's the one that Crenshaw keeps to service the young, healthy females. He's got a smile on his face a yard wide." Edward's blue eyes slitted with amusement at the horrified look on Levi's face.

"Edward! That's against God's teachings and not to be made light of."

"Yeah, so it is." The grin disappeared from Edward's mouth, but the twinkle remained in his eyes. "We'd better get the wagon turned upright. You can put your goods back in while I get the horses." Edward shook his head. "Beats me all hollow how you've kept from being killed roaming around on these roads all by yourself. You've got to start using some horse sense, Levi. You're getting pretty well known to the slave hunters. If Perry don't get you, some of the others will."

"The Lord is with me, friend."

"Yeah? Let's hope the Lord gets you to Newport. If he does, stay there and take care of your store. You're better suited to setting up a network of places along the way where a runaway would be safe. Leave the transporting across country to others. Help me turn the wagon over." Edward brought a stout branch from a deadfall beside the road. "When I lift, shove this under the wagon bed."

Edward went after the horses while Levi reloaded the wagon. When the team was hitched in place, Levi climbed up on the wagon seat.

"I thank thee. I will take thy advice and return to Newport. Get word to Phelps that Hammond Perry has his eye on George and will seek revenge."

"I'm on my way." Edward mounted his horse. "A few miles from here there's a family by the name of Rankin. He's a son of John Rankin of Ripley who has helped so many runaways. Stop and make yourself known to him. He may be able to send one of his sons with you."

"I will be all right, Edward."

"Dammit, Levi—"

"Thee must not swear."

"All right, but seek help from the Rankins. I'd ride with you, but I want to see what Perry will do next."

"He could kill thee."

"He couldn't, but he might hire someone else to do the job. I've got to be going. Take care, Levi."

"God go with thee, Edward."

"Shut up!" Hammond Perry turned in the saddle and shouted to his men. The fact that he had been outwitted by Daniel Phelps was a cancer gnawing at his insides. He was nursing a resentment that flared into rage given the slightest provocation.

The men riding behind him had been laughing and talking. They were excited over the goods they had taken from Levi Coffin's wagon and were boasting about the favors it would buy from the trollops along the river. A quiet settled among them. Each man secretly despised the small, cocky man who sat his saddle with his back straight as a board and his head tilted back. They put up with his overbearing ways because the pay was good.

Retaliation was on Hammond's mind. He had suffered another indignity at the hands of his old enemies, the Quills. He knew just how to make them pay. He would capture the nigger known as George Washington and take him to Crenshaw. If he didn't want to use him as a stud, he would be put to work in the salt mine. Before he was finished, Hammond vowed, he would have every Negro who worked on Daniel Phelps's land.

Hammond's mind drifted back to the time before the War of 1812. He had been a lieutenant in the militia serving under Major Zachary Taylor and stationed at Ford Knox, a few miles from Vincennes. Liberty Quill had married Hammond's brother Jubal, in upstate New York and, with her father and sister, had set out to homestead along the Wabash. Jubal had died on the journey to the Illinois Territory, and later Liberty had married Farrway Quill. She had conspired against Hammond Perry when he had Quill arrested for treason and tried at Fort Knox. Major Zachary Taylor had sided with the Quills, and Perry had been banished to Fort Dearborn to serve for two years, a duty dreaded by all militiamen.

Perry's hatred for the Quills even surpassed his hatred of Major William Bradford, who had been given the assignment of establishing Fort Smith, an assignment Perry had coveted with every fiber of his being. He would have been chosen if not for the lies told by Bradford. Shortly after that he had left the service. For a time Hammond's hatred had been directed toward Bradford, and he had schemed to kidnap Bradford's prospective bride, Eleanor Woodbury. In that effort he had been thwarted by Rain Tallman, another one of Farrway Quill's strays.

A growl came from Hammond's throat at the thought of all the frustrations that had been dealt to him by the Quills. This time he would win. His first move would be to take George, the son of that uppity nigger who ran the ferry back in the days before the war. If Crenshaw didn't want him, he'd transport the damn nigger so far south that Quill would never find him, or else he would kill him. Then he would concentrate on the niggers on Phelps's farm. After that there was Eleanor McCourtney and that big Scot she had married.

Hammond rode with his head down. If Quill had not crossed him, none of this would be necessary. Revenge would be sweet.

"We'll just see who has the last word, you bastard," he whispered. "We'll just see."

CHAPTER EIGHT

When the sun was directly overhead, Daniel signaled for Mercy to pull off the road and stop beneath the branches of a spreading maple tree. He helped her alight from the wagon, then lifted the covered basket out of the back and set it on the ground. Mercy spread a cloth from the basket and laid out buttered bread and cooked chicken while Daniel unhitched Zelda and led her and his mount to the river to drink.

Lenny and Bernie stopped a good fifty feet behind them, talked in low tones, then rode toward the river. Daniel returned and picketed the horses. He lifted a jug of water from the wagon and brought it to where Mercy sat on her shawl beneath the tree.

"Where's Lenny and Bernie?" She took the tin drinking cup from the basket and set it on the ground beside him, then handed him a chicken leg and two slices of buttered bread, laid face-to-face.

"Watering their mules. I don't think they'll wander off," he said dryly, and filled the cup from the jug.

"Minnie must have worked all night cooking this

food. She packed food for several days. We'd better eat the meat. It'll not keep like the eggs and the huckleberry pies." She lifted the cup of water to her lips and drank deeply.

"I sent word to her in the afternoon. She had the basket ready when I went out to the farm last night."

Mercy ate the buttered bread before she spoke again. "It's hot for this time of year."

"It'll cool off toward evening." Daniel took off his hat, placed it on the ground beside him, and wiped his forehead with the sleeve of his shirt. He sat with his elbow on his bent knee and ate slowly while staring off down the road.

"Daniel?" Mercy waited until his eyes turned to meet hers. "I didn't like it one bit, what Belinda said about me." She tilted her head and raised her chin a fraction. "It was rude of you and Belinda to talk about me as if I weren't there. She was mighty quick to name Lenny and Bernie trash because of . . . how they look."

"Didn't you do the same?"

For a moment she was incapable of replying. There was a tightness across her chest and a fullness in her throat, and she couldn't utter a word. He was looking directly into her eyes as if he were seeing straight into her inner self. She lowered her lashes and bit her bottom lip, knowing that what he said was true.

"Yes," she said, her voice shaky. "But I was wrong to judge them so hastily. I realize that now. Not because they are my brothers but because Mamma taught me to give respect and consideration to others, even if they are different. I didn't appreciate hearing Belinda's remarks." Mercy's voice firmed. "And I don't want *pity* from anyone."

"You were there. Why didn't you speak up and say so?"

"Speak up?" She met his gaze and blinked. "The two of you were having a private conversation."

"Not as far as I was concerned. You ran off in a snit when you heard something you didn't like. Next time stay and take up for yourself."

"Well, for goodness sake! What did you expect me to do? Pull her hair out? I wanted to!"

He lifted his shoulders, and his face broke into a grin. He looked at her for so long, her face began to redden. She was grateful when Lenny and Bernie came back up onto the road and drew his attention from her.

"Lenny," Mercy called when the brothers settled down on their haunches beneath a persimmon tree. "There's plenty of food here. Come have something to eat."

"We ain't hungry."

"You must be. There's enough meat and bread for all of us."

"We don't want none. We ain't beggars." Bernie had taken off his hat and was poking a bluejay feather in the band around the crown. More than ever, his thick, straw-colored hair looked like a sloppy haystack.

"For crying out loud! I'm *offering* the food to you. That's not begging!"

"It's his grub, ain't it?"

"Well, yes, but what difference does that make?"

"Hit makes a heap ta us. We'll shoot us a bird along come suppertime."

A look of exasperation came over Mercy's face. She grabbed several slices of bread and a couple pieces of chicken and started to get up. Daniel's hand on her arm stopped her.

"If they're too stubborn to come be sociable, let them go without."

"But . . . we've got plenty."

"You heard what I said, Mercy. Sit down."

"I don't like for food to go to waste."

"It won't go to waste. Eat up so we can go. It's only a few miles to the ferry. I'll ride ahead and make sure it's there when you get there. There's an inn about twenty miles south of New Harmony where we can stay. We'll have to hustle to get there before dark."

Mercy sat down and nibbled at her food. Daniel watched he as he drank from the cup they shared. She was hurting. Belinda had been cruel, and he told her so in no uncertain words after Mercy had left them. But he would not always be with Mercy, and she was going to have to get used to holding up her head and fighting back. It had angered him that she had broken and run. He had fully expected her to turn on Belinda like a spitting cat and tell her to shut her gossipy mouth.

"Are you sorry that you came with me?" Mercy asked, and quickly turned away from him so that he wouldn't see the anxiety in her face. She wrapped the bread in the cloth and put it back in the basket.

"No."

"I don't seem to be doing anything that pleases you."

"Leave the Baxters their pride, Mercy. They've had to swallow having me along. Let them get used to it. You invited them to eat and they refused. Either they are going to accept us or continue being hostile. It's up to them."

"And Belinda?"

Daniel stood abruptly. "We'd better get to moving. Do you want another drink before I take the jug and basket to the wagon?"

"No thank you."

Mercy shook the leaves and dried grass from her shawl and folded it over her arm. She moved behind the screen of hazel bushes and grapevines so that she could relieve her full bladder. She was puzzled by Daniel's manner. If she had stayed to defend herself against Belinda's catty remarks, she would have made a fool of herself and embarrassed him. It was plain enough that he had a fondness for Belinda's little boy. Had he brought the sugarhards thinking he would stop at the homestead? He had already made arrangements with Mike to give Homer licorice when he came to the store. Did Daniel remember his longing for male companionship when he was a little boy? So many questions floated around in Mercy's mind that she drew in a deep, pained breath and moved out from behind the bushes.

Zelda was hitched, and Daniel was waiting to help Mercy up onto the wagon seat. She placed her hand in his without looking at him. The hand that had clasped hers many times before felt warmer and stronger to her now that she was aware of him in a completely different way. Her thoughts in disorder, she set her foot on the spoke of the wheel, and as she reached to grasp the rail to pull herself up, her foot slipped. With a cry she fell backward.

"Oh! Oh!" She gasped, flinging her arms in an attempt to catch herself.

Daniel caught her in a tight embrace when she tumbled against him. The force of her unexpected body caused him to backtrack a few steps. When he had regained his balance and stood holding her, sudden laughter burst from her lips. He watched in fascination as the sky-blue eyes sent shards of sparkling sunshine that penetrated his very soul. He heard himself laughing too. A deep, rumbling, uncontrollable sound. Her face was close to his. He could smell the warmth of her womanly body. Christ! She was his love, his own sweet woman. He wanted to hold her forever, kiss her, make love to her.

"You wouldn't have thought it so funny if I had dropped you on your behind," he heard himself saying while his eyes devoured her face, and he wondered if ever a man in love had had the problem he now faced.

"You haven't held me like this since I lost my shoe in the river and you had to carry me home because my foot was bleeding. I was ten or eleven and thinking I was a young lady. You complained all the way." Her lashes fanned down, then lifted over mischievous, laughing eyes.

"You said I was a stupid child and that I was muddle-headed."

"I remember," he said softly, his eyes holding hers.

The pulse in Mercy's throat throbbed, and suddenly it was hard to breathe. She had a fierce desire to encircle his neck with her arms, but one of them was pinned between them, and the other clutched her shawl.

"I'm still muddleheaded, Daniel," she whispered.

"Yes, you are," he said with a grin that deepened the creases on each side of his mouth. He took the two steps necessary to reach the wagon and lifted her so that her feet were in the space in front of the seat. "I think I'll add 'clumsy' to that."

"What an unflattering thing to say," she snapped, but she was smiling because his twinkling brown eyes were teasing her all the way down to her toes.

"I've never been accused of having a way with words." He put the reins in her hands. "I'm going on ahead to the ferry, like I said. I've all ready told Lenny. They'll be with you."

"No doubt about that," Mercy said dryly. "I don't think I could shake them if I had the plague."

Half an hour later, Mercy came to the place where the riverbank had been cut away and a long log ramp had been laid. The ferry was tied to the dock, and Daniel was waiting to lead Zelda onto the gently rocking raft that would take them across the Wabash. After the horse and wagon were secured, Mercy got down off the seat to stand at the rail.

Lenny and Bernie had stopped on the riverbank. Daniel walked up the log ramp and called to them.

"Come on aboard. We're not waiting for you."

"We ain't crossin' here," Bernie said.

"Why not?"

"We can cross on down a ways," Bernie said to

Lenny, ignoring Daniel. "We ain't takin' no handouts from the likes a him."

"Hush up. I'm thinkin'." Lenny spit a stream of tobacco juice into the dirt, churned into powder by the traffic coming to the ferry landing.

"Suit yourself. Your fare is paid." Daniel shrugged and walked back onto the ferry.

"Ain't no use getting wet if'n we ain't got to," Lenny said.

"I swear! Ain't ya got no pride a-tall?"

"Yeah, but I ain't wantin' ter drown, neither. The waters is up since we crossed afore." Lenny followed Daniel onto the ferry.

"I ain't a-likin' it," Bernie protested, even as he slid from his mule to lead it onto the rocking craft.

Lenny tied his mule to the side post where Daniel indicated, but Bernie defiantly moved past him to the front of the boat.

"Tie that mule to the side post or get off," the ferry operator yelled as the raft tilted and rocked.

Bernie snorted, cast Daniel an angry look, and reluctantly tied his mule to the side post.

When all was secure, Daniel took a stout pole and helped the ferryman push the raft out into deeper water. A thick rope running through a pulley lashed to an oak tree ran to the other side of the river. The ferryman began to turn the windlass. He had wide shoulders and thick arms. He strained against the crank and finally the rope began to move through the pulleys and the wide log raft was pulled out into the river toward the eastern bank.

Mercy had crossed on the ferry many times. It always reminded her of Mr. Washington's ferry, which had been farther upriver, closer to Quill's Station. Mr. Washington, George's father, had been a huge freedman who wore his hair cut in the fashion of the Mohawks. He had large silver rings swinging from his earlobes and a small one from his nostrils. He would set Mercy a-straddle his neck and gallop like a horse. She would scream with laughter and hold on to his topknot. Sugar Tree, his Shawnee wife, would scold and caution him to be careful. Mercy thought now that she couldn't have had a happier childhood. What kind of childhood memories would she have, she asked herself, if Farrway Quill had not found her?

"I always think of Mr. Washington when I cross the river," Mercy said to Daniel when he came to stand beside her.

"So do I. Life was a lot less complicated then. We only had the Indians to worry about." He smiled down at her, and she returned his smile.

They stood silently. Mercy was aware of Daniel in a way she never had been before. His arm touched hers and she wanted to lean into it. *How can I be so happy*? she thought. *My life has been turned upside down since the Baxters found me*. It did one thing for her, she decided. It made her realize how much she loved Daniel. Her thoughts shifted to how capable he was, how dependable, how wonderful, how . . . handsome. No other woman will have him, she vowed. She had been a fool to run away and leave him with Belinda. That was a mistake she would not make a second time.

Together they watched the waterfowl swarm up as they approached the other side. Mercy could feel the warmth of Daniel's arm against hers, and the warmth of the telltale blood that covered her neck and face. She bent her head and occupied herself with watching the water that lapped at the side of the craft.

"Stay here." Daniel's hand was on her arm for just an instant. "Hold on. I'll help ease the raft up to the ramp."

As soon as the raft bumped the log landing, Daniel tossed a thick rope around the stout post set on the shore. The ferryman left the windlass and secured the other side. When they were ready to disembark, Mercy climbed upon the wagon seat, and Daniel led Zelda up the ramp and onto the hard-packed landing.

They headed south at the fork in the road. Daniel led the way, urging them to move along briskly. Toward late afternoon, after only one stop to water and rest the horses, Mercy's arms felt as if each were trying to lift a hundred-pound weight, and the seat that had felt so soft that morning was now hard and uncomfortable.

They passed a number of homesteads. The women came outside, each usually with a child in her arms, and waved as they passed. Most of the homesteads were neat and well planned, with a goodly number of acres cleared and planted. A few were ramshackle affairs with crops planted amid tree stumps and a woodpile that consisted of a deadfall pulled into the yard, and chopped as the woman of the house needed it. Several log houses or barns had been burned out. Fire was the dread of all. It was usually caused by a hastily, carelessly built fireplace, or an overturned candle.

The sun sank behind the thick grove of trees to the west. As the air became cooler, Mercy wrapped her shawl around her. The silence of the deep forest seemed strangely oppressive. Birds fluttered in the newly leafed trees. Otherwise the stillness was unbroken. It was almost dusk when Daniel reined in so that the wagon could come alongside.

"The inn is up ahead."

"Thank goodness."

"It isn't much, but it's lodging."

Peering through the gloom, Mercy saw a good-sized barn with a rail fence attached. Beyond that, sitting close to the road, was a long, narrow log building. Mercy sighed, thinking of a comfortable resting place for her aching limbs. They passed the barn and stopped in front of the inn. A chill of disappointment came over her. It was as uninviting a place as she had ever seen. Signs of neglect were everywhere. A heavy cloth was nailed over a broken window, the cross pole was missing from the hitching rail, an empty watering trough lay on its side. Through the open door they could hear loud and boisterous voices. On a shingle above the door a crudely printed sign hung by one leather strap: BED AND EATS.

"It's hardly the place I remembered," Daniel said, frowning.

"Welcome, folks!"

The man who appeared in the doorway was wiping his hands on the once white cloth tied about his waist. He was an odd-looking person, rather slight and short in stature. His large, prominent features were overshadowed by a shock of coarse yellow hair that gave him a wild and savage look, especially as his hair and his complexion seemed almost one color.

"Are you the landlord?" Daniel asked. He stepped down from his horse with his rifle in his hand. The pistol was tucked in his belt.

"Lyman Sickles, sir."

"What happened to James Looney?"

"Dead. God rest his soul. Died of snakebite a year ago. Bought the place from his poor grievin' widow. Are you wantin' lodgin'?"

"Yes. For me and the lady."

"Come in. Come right in. The woman is 'bout to dish out supper. Pearl," he shouted back over his shoulder. "We got two more. One's a woman."

Lenny and Bernie had stopped their mules behind the wagon. They sat watching, making no move to get down.

"Are they with you?" the landlord asked.

"Are you?" Daniel directed his question to Lenny.

"We ain't goin' in thar."

"Supper and lodging for two," Daniel said to the innkeeper. "They'll fend for themselves." He helped Mercy down, then lifted her carpetbag out of the wagon. "Come morning, there had better not be anything missing out of that wagon or there'll be a hell of a ruckus."

"My man is honest as the day is long, sir." Sickles said with a wounded look on his face. "But"—he glanced at Lenny and Bernie—"I don't know 'bout them."

"Don't worry about them. They're as honest as the day is long," Daniel echoed.

With his rifle in one hand, he took Mercy's elbow with the other and ushered her into the inn. The inn seemed to consist of three distinct buildings, probably put up at different times. The room they entered was used as a barroom according to the counter that was made of the roughest construction—two tree stumps with boards laid across them. Planks nailed to the wall served as benches.

The landlord led them through a wide doorway and into the kitchen. Talk ceased among the four men seated at a trestle table. They stared curiously at Daniel and with open admiration at Mercy. Three of the men were dressed in the rough clothes of rivermen; the fourth man, who had on a well-worn, dusty black coat, sat a little apart from the others. The man looked Daniel over briefly before his dark eyes honed in on Mercy and stayed there.

A woman of perhaps thirty years was waiting on the table. She held the bail of an iron kettle in one hand and a ladle in the other. In the light from the two candles on the table, Mercy could see that the woman was plain and old-fashioned, almost beyond her memory. Her dress was a thick-striped material, woven to defy time and wear. It was unlike any fabric Mercy had ever seen. The dress fitted the woman closely, was low in the neck, with sleeves coming to below the elbow. She was tall, and the dress was extremely short-waisted, without a particle of fullness in the skirt. She had on no shoes or stockings, and a faded piece of cloth was tied in a loose knot around her neck. Her dark hair was bound straight around her head and fastened with a metal comb on top.

"Stop your lollygaggin', Pearl." The landlord's voice was loud and harsh. He nudged the woman in the back with his elbow. "Make room for the gent and his missus."

"We want to wash before we eat."

Daniel released Mercy's arm, but she stayed close to him, wondering if she would be able to eat in this place. She gave a glance of scrutiny to the dishes on the table and the eating spoons. They were clean, as was the scrubbed tabletop. The woman appeared to be clean, for all her odd appearance.

Sickles waved them toward the other end of the room where a window of four small panes let in a meager light. A wash bench was attached to the wall. Mercy set her bag down against the wall, took the shawl from around her shoulders, and looked for a peg to hang it on. When she found none, she folded it and laid it on the bag.

"I don't like this place," she whispered while Daniel dipped water into a washdish from a wooden bucket. The basin was surprisingly clean, as was the towel that hung on the bar beside it.

"I don't like it either, but it'll have to do."

"Where will we sleep?"

"There's a room up above for the men. There's another room off the kitchen. I'll ask about it for you."

"I'm not staying in there by myself!"

"Don't panic. I'll not be far away."

Mercy washed her hands and splashed the cold water on her face, wishing for the luxury of warm water from the teakettle back home. She tidied her hair while Daniel washed.

The boards, or rather planks, of the floor were hand-hewn and laid down so unequally as to make walking on them perilous. Daniel kept a firm hold on Mercy's elbow and led her back to the table. The innkeeper was not in sight, but the silent woman placed plates of food at the end of the table and indicated that they were to sit down. Daniel leaned his rifle against the wall within easy reach and sat down beside Mercy.

The meal was meat, cabbage, and turnips. Bread that appeared to have been baked in an open kettle was placed beside each plate. Neither milk nor butter were offered. Mercy's eyes swept the table, and she saw that the men were breaking up the bread, putting it on their plates, and shoveling such great quantities of food into their mouths that grease was running down their chins.

The meat was in large chunks. It was difficult to eat it with a spoon. While wondering how she was going to manage without a knife, Mercy raised her eyes and met the gleaming black eyes of the man across from her. He had a narrow hawklike face that was in variance with his thick shoulders and the hamlike fist that gripped a long hunting knife. The end of the hilt rested on the table, a piece of speared meat was on the point, the juice running down the blade and onto his clenched fist. He sat as still as a stone with his unblinking eyes on her face.

Daniel's elbow nudged hers. Then he pulled her plate toward him and cut the meat with his hunting knife. "Eat," he said.

She ate quickly, wishing to hurry and get out from under the intense gaze of the man across from her before Daniel took offense at his staring. Daniel cleaned his plate and shook his head when the woman offered to refill it. Mercy laid down her spoon although her plate was still half full.

"I'm ready," she whispered.

Daniel picked up his rifle, Mercy the carpetbag, and they went into the barroom. The flame from a single candle was the only light. The air in the barroom was fouled with the odor of stale ale. It tickled Mercy's nostrils. Daniel's hand on her elbow urged her over near the door where he stopped, glanced outside, then down at her anxious face.

"I wish we hadn't stopped here. We could have camped out in the open," she whispered.

"It's too late now."

"Why can't we just leave? I don't like the looks of those men in there . . . or the landlord."

"The one across from you is the one we have to worry about. I wouldn't be surprised if he didn't have a little robbery on his mind. The other three are river drifters."

"How do you know?"

"I just know. If we leave now, he'll follow if he has mischief in mind. You'll be safer here."

"Don't leave me alone."

"I won't."

"Can we go outside while they're eating?"

"Sure. We'll go out and check on the wagon. Leave your bag here." Daniel picked up her shawl and put it around her shoulders.

As soon as they stepped out the door, they saw the innkeeper coming from the barn. They moved out away from the house before Daniel called to him.

"What accommodations do you have for us, Sickles?"

"We got a room for you and your lady. The woman'll get it ready soon as supper is over."

"We'll walk down to the barn and see about the horses while we wait."

"They've been taken care of. They got a good measure of grain."

"Much obliged."

"What did you say your name was?"

"I didn't say, but it's Phelps."

"Headed for Evansville, are you?"

"We haven't decided."

"I don't see them fellows that rode in with you. They must have gone on."

"Must have." Daniel and Mercy moved on down the path toward the barn.

"There's a lantern inside the door," the landlord called.

After Daniel looked in on the horses they walked around to where the wagon was parked in an open shed. Daniel checked the lock on the wooden box that held his extra powder and shot. Then he lifted several heavy blankets from the basket containing the food and set the basket out on the ground.

"The rats will be in this by morning. We'd better take it in with us."

"Where did Lenny and Bernie go? They could have eaten the chicken if they hadn't been so stubborn."

"I'm thinking the meat will be spoiled by morning. Why don't you lay it out there on the end of the wagon and let the rats or the coons have it."

"I'll not do—" The pressure of Daniel's hand on her arm shut off her protest. She looked up and saw that laugh lines crinkled the corners of his eyes. He put his face close to hers and winked. Mercy suddenly felt extremely happy. "That's a good idea," she said, trying to keep the laughter out of her voice. "I'm glad you thought of it. We don't want spoiled meat stinking up the basket."

Mercy spread a cloth on the folded-down tailgate and placed the chicken, several pieces of buttered bread, and two boiled eggs on it. When she finished, Daniel took the lantern back to the barn, and they went back toward the inn.

"How did you know they were there?" Mercy whispered.

"I smelled them," Daniel said bluntly. "After I smelled them, I started looking, and one of them was hunkered down in the tall weeds beside the shed. The peaked hat gave him away."

"They've got more pride than brains," Mercy said fretfully.

"Maybe. But with them out there our horses and the

wagon will be all right. The next time we'll not wait so late to find a place for the night."

The woman was waiting when they returned to the inn. Without speaking, she picked up a candle and indicated to them to follow her into a room that had been added to the original building. She set the candle on a table and quickly departed.

"She's strange," Mercy said. "I wonder if she talks. Oh, well, she brought in my carpetbag."

Daniel was examining the door. After he closed it, he tried to fit the bar into a slot on the either side, but it was broken. He murmured a few curses, then stood the bar in he corner.

"That's useless," he grumbled. "There's no way in hell to bar this door!"

"You aren't going to leave me in here by myself?"

"You'll be all right if we can figure out a way to bar the door. I'll be right outside."

"Even if I can bar the door, I don't want to stay in here by myself. There's the window. And besides that . . . they could gang up on you. I don't trust that landlord."

"I don't either. I'm trying to think of where I've seen that fellow in the black coat." Daniel took off his hat and placed it on the floor beside his rifle. "I'll leave you for a while, but I'll be watching the door." He took the pistol from his belt, checked the load, and put it back.

"Are you expecting trouble?"

"I'm always expecting trouble, and when it doesn't happen, I'm pleasantly surprised." He smiled down at her. "Don't worry. You'll be all right."

"I'm worried about you. You can't sleep outside that door. I'll take one of the feather ticks off the bed and make a pallet here on the floor. Stay in here with me. The landlord will think it funny if you don't. He thinks we're . . . married." Mercy's fingers gripped his wrist. Very softly she said, "Please, Daniel."

"You're in enough trouble with Lenny and Bernie." She caught the devilish glint in the depths of his eyes.

"They already think you've ravished me." She almost choked on the giggle that bubbled up inside her. Her eyes danced and played with his, glowing happily.

"Ravished you? That's a good idea. I'm glad you thought of it."

"Daniel! You idiot!"

"I'll leave you alone for a while. Don't worry. I'll watch the door."

"I wish Lenny and Bernie had come in. They would be some help."

"Help for what?" Daniel chuckled. "They'd more than likely start something, and I'd have to help them. I'll be back in a little while."

The first thing Mercy did when she was alone was to look for the chamber pot. She found it beneath the bed, pulled it out, and removed the lid. She sighed with relief. She had been afraid there wouldn't be one, and she would have to go outside.

As she was arranging her clothes so she could use the chamber, she glanced at the high, small window above the bed. The shape of a man's face was there, his nose pressed to the windowpane. For several seconds she was paralyzed with fear. Then she turned and quickly blew out the candle, plunging the room into total darkness. Mercy fought against momentary giddiness and the desire to rush out of the room and find Daniel. She pressed her fingertips to her temples and waited for her galloping heart to slow and her eyes to become accustomed to the darkness.

Her fright at seeing the man's face in the window eased. The pain of her swollen bladder did not. She had to use the chamber before Daniel returned. Fumbling in the darkness, she managed to perform the chore, cover the chamber, and slide it back under the bed. Moving carefully, trying to remember where the table was located in the room, she found her carpetbag and carried it back to the bed. Then she removed the top feather tick, folded it, and made a pallet on the floor.

A wave of fatigue washed over her. Her shoulders slumped, and a longing for her comfortable room at home brought a mistiness to her eyes. She sat on the edge of the bed, took the pins from her hair, and put them in her pocket. With the tips of her fingers she massaged her scalp and combed through the heavy hair that hung to her hips.

The low murmur of voices coming from the barroom reached her, as well as the sounds made by the woman cleaning up after the evening meal. Mercy loosened the buttons at the neck of her dress and lay back on the bed. Her spine straightened painfully. She flexed her shoulders and rolled her head from side to side to ease her tense muscles. Her body was tired to the point of collapse.

"What will happen next?" she whispered into a silence that gave no answer. She was sure that she and Daniel were in a nest of cutthroats and robbers. But even when they left this place and reached Mud Creek, he would be among people who were hostile to him. The Baxters would not harm her, but what about Daniel? She knew nothing of the people who were her kin. "My God! I couldn't bear it if anything happened to him!" Her faced twisted in agony.

Some time later Mercy heard the creak of the door and sat up quickly.

"It's me."

Daniel's voice came out of the darkness. Mercy was almost giddy with relief and lay back down on the bed as if she didn't have the strength to sit up.

"Don't light the candle."

"It's so dark in here that I couldn't even find the candle if I wanted to." She heard him stumble. "Christ! What's this on the floor?"

"It's the feather tick. I made a pallet for you. I knew you wouldn't take the bed and let me have the pallet."

"You're right, I wouldn't."

"Daniel, someone was looking in the window." She strained to keep the fear out of her voice.

"The hell there was! I thought it was too high." His whispered voice was near. She held out her hand. When her fingers touched his trousers, she tugged on them and he sat down beside her. "Could you tell who it was?"

"No."

"He had to be eight feet tall, or else he pulled up a barrel to stand on." His hand found her arm, his fingers moving down to her wrist. "Are you still dressed?"

"Yes. I didn't even take off my shoes. I'm scared in this place."

Suddenly Daniel was kneeling down beside the bed. His fingers went into the thick, loose hair that lay on her shoulders, then moved up to her cheek and looped the heavy masses behind her ear.

"You don't need to be scared." His voice was the merest of whispers. "Go to sleep. I'm going to be right here with you. They've all gone to bed and I'll be there by the door."

"Will you hold me . . . for just a minute?" She couldn't have kept the sob out of her voice if her life depended on it.

CHAPTER NINE

Daniel's arms went around her. His hand slid across her back beneath her hair, and he wrapped her in his arms. He gathered her to him gently, carefully, as if she were the most fragile thing in the world. He burrowed his face deep into the fragrance of her hair and abandoned himself to the heavenly feeling of having her in his arms. His heart was drumming so hard that he could scarcely breathe; his love was choking him. He breathed in the scent of lavender as his whole self hardened and trembled.

His desire for her was so great that for an instant he feared he would be unable to keep his arms from crushing her to him and his lips from saying the words that leaped to his mind. *I love you, love you! Ah, sweet woman, I love you!* Hair, soft as silk caught on his whiskered cheeks, and round, firm breasts pressed against his chest. His pretty childhood companion had grown into a beautiful woman and was bound to every sweet memory he could recall. Daniel felt his body reverberate with unspoken love.

In a daze of joy Mercy clung to him. She wondered if he loved her as a woman, or if he was fond of her because she was his foster sister. Did she only imagine she felt his lips nuzzling her ear? In the warmth of his embrace, she longed to whisper that the love she felt for him was the all-consuming love of a woman for her man. She wanted to tell him to please take her as his mate, to join his body with hers, to plant the seeds of his children in her womb. What would he say? Would he be shocked? Disgusted by her boldness?

"Danny..." Mercy murmured, cuddling into him, pressing her face to his throat and moving her arm up to encircle his neck.

"Are you all right now?" he whispered. He settled himself more firmly on his haunches and moved a hand to cup the back of her head. His eyes closed, he felt the softness of her woman's body, he breathed her woman's scent, heard the little murmur of contentment that came from her lips. Several minutes passed before he heard her whisper.

"I'm all right...now."

"I'll be between you and anyone who tries to come in."

"It's always been that way." Her voice grew throaty as she pulled her face away from his neck and her hand stroked his cheek. She was awash with a warm wave of tenderness and maternal protectiveness toward him. "Are you tired? You didn't get much sleep last night."

"I got enough. I'll sleep with my back against the door. You're not to worry."

"I can't imagine life without you, Danny." The words came in a quivering voice.

"I can't imagine life without you, either," he said hoarsely.

"We were two little orphans. I...thought you the most wonderful boy in the world. You were my protector, friend, playmate. We played together, ate together, slept together. You were always calm, sensible, and made things right. I was your shadow, Mamma said." Mercy lay very still after her whispered words, barely breathing.

"Yes . . ." Daniel clutched her to him in an almost crushing embrace and nestled his mouth below her ear. "It . . . was like that."

"And here we are, grown up. I should be taking care of my own problems, and you're still taking care of me."

"Yes," he said again, and sighed deeply.

"Do you resent me taking up so much of your time?" she asked against his neck.

In response, he held her even more tightly. "God! No! Whatever gave you that idea?"

"You're a man with a lot of responsibilities."

"I'm a man and I can do as I please. It pleases me to take care of you. Now, you've got to get some sleep and I've got to get over to the door. We don't want any surprises."

As Daniel gently eased her away from him, her arm fell from around his neck. It was one of the hardest things he'd ever had to do. His arms felt empty. He had no recollection of ever feeling quite so bereft. This yearning for her went beyond what he had known—that his feelings for her were fierce, consuming. Gnawing at the edge of his consciousness was the fear that she would be repulsed should she learn the depth of his love for her.

Mercy lay with her head pillowed on her arm. The room was pitch-dark, and she wondered how Daniel could see. She heard him move the feather tick over in front of the door, and that was the last sound she heard. She closed her eyes tightly, still feeling the warmth of his arms, the smell of his skin, and wished fervently that she had moved her lips along the column of his strong throat. She gritted her teeth, trying to fight down a wave of agonizing jealousy at the thought of Daniel holding Belinda in his arms.

With her eyes tightly closed, she rejected the image. He was her love! Why had she not realized that before now?

When a hand touched her shoulder, she awakened immediately and blinked against the light of the candle.

"It's almost dawn," Daniel whispered.

"Already? It seems like only a few minutes have passed."

Mercy sat up on the edge of the bed and looked around. The feather tick lay in a heap in the corner, and Daniel's rifle was wedged against the door. She took her hairbrush from her carpetbag, smoothed the tangles from her hair, and quickly braided it into one long strand.

"I want to wait until there's enough light to see before we leave. I'll step outside the door while you . . . do whatever you need to do." He saw her glance quickly toward the window, then back to meet his eyes. "I covered it before I lit the candle. You needn't worry about someone spying on you."

Daniel went to the door, removed the rifle, and, taking it with him, stepped out and closed the door. Mercy pulled the chamber pot from beneath the bed. She despised the tinkling sound she made when she relieved herself and prayed the noise could not be heard outside the room. When she finished, she covered the pot, shoved it out of sight, and went to tap gently on the door.

Daniel came in and went to the window. Pulling back a corner of the cloth he had used to cover the pane, he looked out. Dawn was streaking an overcast sky. There was a bank of rain clouds in the south. His eyes searched for a sign of Lenny or Bernie, but it was still too dark to see anything but the shape of the barn.

"We'll wait a little while," he whispered. "Get ready

to leave and we'll put out the candle so that our eyes will get used to the dark."

Mercy put her shawl around her shoulders, closed her carpetbag, and set it on the floor beside her. Daniel hung his powder and shot bags around his neck, checked the load in the pistol, and thrust it into his belt. With rifle in hand he nodded for her to blow out the candle; the room was plunged into darkness.

Daniel removed the covering and stood beside the window. It was too high for Mercy to see out, but after her eyes became accustomed to the darkness, she could see the faint light of morning coming through the dirty glass windowpane. She stood silently waiting for Daniel to tell her when it was time to go. After what seemed to her an eternity of waiting, he left the window and came to her.

"Let's go. Stay close to me."

The door opened silently on its leather hinges. Daniel stepped out into the kitchen, looked around, and then, with Mercy close behind him, they went to the door and stepped out into the crisp morning. Mercy felt the throbbing beat of her pulse high in her throat, fluttering to her very ears. She sensed danger to her beloved. Her heart thumped as her eyes strained to penetrate the morning gloom. She was startled when a rooster crowed, proclaiming his dominance over the hens that came from their roosting places in the low brush near the barn to start their daily search for food.

Daniel headed for the barn, then stopped. To the south, beside the fenced enclosure, he saw the wagon. Zelda was hitched, and his buckskin was tied behind. There was no sign of Lenny or Bernie. With his hand holding Mercy's elbow, he urged her toward the wagon, silently thanking the Baxter brothers because he would not have to take Mercy into the dark barn.

As the rounded the end of the log building, Daniel heard a whirling sound, followed by a dull thud, and then a grunt. He spun around, rifle up. On the ground not six feet behind him was a black-clad man sinking to his knees, then collapsing in a heap. Daniel moved the end of the barrel in an arc as he surveyed the area. Two familiar figures came silently out of the brush at the side of the barn and walked leisurely toward them.

Lenny pushed the man on the ground over with his foot. Blood oozed from his temple. It was the dark man who had sat across the table and stared at Mercy during the evening meal. He had a knife in his hand.

"I didn't hear him," Daniel said simply.

"Ya would've," Bernie said. "He warn't no good a-tall at sneakin'."

Lenny squatted down beside the man on the ground. "It was a fair shot, Bernie, but a mite high."

"'Twarn't high a-tall. Three fingers above the ear be the best ta lay a man low."

"What did you hit him with?" Daniel asked.

"With a rock." Bernie held up a leather sling.

"Goddam you! You could have hit Mercy with that stone!"

"He was fixin' to put a knife in yore back."

Daniel glanced toward the brush, then back at the man on the ground. "That stone passed within a foot of her."

"What're ya so riled up fer? Bernie's been knockin' down squirrels with that sling since he was ass-high to a piss-ant. He warn't goin' to hit sister."

"Did he kill him?" Mercy asked.

"I'm not caring if he did or not." Daniel urged her toward the wagon, took her bag from her hand, and flung it into the back. After he helped Mercy up onto the seat, he turned to the brothers. "I'm obliged to you . . . and for hitching up too. We'd better make tracks. He may not be the only cutthroat in this bunch."

Daniel slapped the reins against Zelda's back and they drove out of the yard. Out on the road they were soon rolling along at a steady pace. Mercy looked back to see the Baxters riding close behind the wagon, and she felt a surge of relief. She was reasonably sure now that they would back Daniel . . . at least until they got to Mud Creek.

During the early-morning hours they passed several travelers going north toward New Harmony. Daniel pulled the wagon to the side so they could pass. By mid-morning the slight breeze had blown the rain clouds away, and the sun came out. Mercy glanced from time to time at Daniel's profile. Few words had passed between them since leaving the inn. They enjoyed a comfortable silence. He seemed to be wrapped in his own thoughts, and she in hers.

When they came to a small pond made from water that seeped out of a bluff, Daniel pulled Zelda to a stop.

"There's good water here." He watered the horses and held their water jug beneath the trickle that came from the rocks. The Baxters disappeared into the woods east of the road. After Mercy drank from the jug Daniel offered, she started to ease behind the screen of pines to the west to relieve herself. Daniel's voice stopped her.

"Hold on, Mercy," he said softly.

She turned questioning eyes to him when he came up close behind her, his rifle cradled in his arms, and placed a hand on his shoulder.

"I thought I heard something when we first pulled up. Let me go first," Daniel added.

Mercy followed Daniel into the cool, dark shadows of the pine trees. She stayed close behind, trembling, scarcely daring to breathe, expecting any moment to hear some suspicious sound. She kept turning her head slowly, listening first in one direction and then another. About twenty paces from the road Daniel stopped so suddenly that she ran into him. She moved up beside him and saw a black face with huge eyes staring at them from behind a screen of cut cedar boughs.

"Come out of there," Daniel commanded.

A Negro parted the boughs and stepped out. He was young and gaunt, and the clothes that hung on his thin frame were not much more than rags, yet he stood with dignity, his head up, looking Daniel in the eye.

"What are you doing here?" Daniel asked. When he received no answer, he said, "Are you a runaway?" The Negro shook his head vigorously. "I'm not a hunter, man. If you need help, say so." The man continued to shake his head. Daniel saw his eyes dart to his right. "Is anyone with you?"

"No, sah!"

The words had no more than left the Negro's mouth when a whimpering sound came from behind him. His nostrils flared, but he faced Daniel without the slightest change in his expression.

"Drop the gun!" The command came suddenly from behind them, and Mercy gasped in surprise and fear.

Daniel muttered a curse word, blaming himself for being a careless fool. He lowered the barrel of the gun and turned slowly. A red-bearded man came out of the underbrush, a pistol in his hand. Daniel recognized him at once. It was one of Hammond Perry's men who had been at the mill a few days ago. For an instant Daniel toyed with the idea of thrusting Mercy behind him and raising the rifle. He was about ready to spring when the man lowered his gun.

"Phelps? By God, it's Phelps!" The red-bearded man shoved his pistol into his belt, came forward, and held out his hand. "Edward Ashton. I'm a friend of Levi Coffin."

Daniel hesitated before he extended his hand. "Then what the hell were you doing with Hammond Perry?"

"Do you know a better way to find out what the bastard's up to than to ride with him? I had to show my hand yesterday when Perry was going to shoot Levi. I was on my way back to Quill's Station when I ran into these people."

"People?" Daniel inquired while shaking the man's hand.

"Four of them. They're damn near starved. I was about to leave to find something for them to eat."

"Why didn't you?"

"When I saw you stop here, I had to come back." Edward Ashton's eyes darted from Daniel to Mercy, who stood close beside him.

"This is Miss Quill."

"How-do, ma'am."

"We have food, Daniel." Mercy's hand slipped from Daniel's arm. "Shall I get it?"

"What about the Baxters? We don't want them to know about this."

"We done know it." Lenny spoke and moved out where they could see him. "We ain't helpin' no hunters, 'n' we ain't helpin' no niggers neither."

"You'll keep your mouth shut?" Daniel asked.

"Baxters ain't got no niggers."

"That isn't what I asked, dammit!"

"I said we ain't takin' sides."

"What about Bernie?"

"He be a Baxter, ain't he?"

Daniel turned back to Edward. "His word is good. I'll get what food we have, then we'd better talk."

The four runaways—a man, his wife and child, and his mother—had traveled from lower Tennessee, trying to reach relatives in the North. They had been told to watch for a white man with a blue feather in his hatband. The day before they had seen Hammond Perry pass by, and early this morning Edward Ashton, with a blue feather in his hatband, had found them after being alerted by a sympathetic homesteader from whom they had begged food.

They ate the food from the basket sparingly, although Mercy could tell they were ravenous. The young woman slipped a small fried pie beneath her shawl when she thought Mercy wasn't looking. *Poor soul,* Mercy thought. *She's not sure we mean for them to have it all.* The little girl who clung to her mother was so pitifully thin that Mercy wanted to cry. She wished she had more to give, then thought of the coins in her purse. She turned her back, reached into her pocket, selected one, and when she thought she was unobserved, pressed it into the woman's hand. Tears flooded the woman's large, pensive eyes when she realized the coin was for her.

Daniel and Edward Ashton walked away a few paces, and Edward told him about his concern that Hammond Perry would find a way to take George.

"George has been warned," Daniel said. "He'll not do anything foolish. I hope to get back to Quill's Station before Perry knows I'm gone. Meanwhile Gavin McCourtney will be there. George can tell you where to find him. He's a good man and has no use for Hammond Perry. As a matter of fact, he'll kill him if given the chance."

"I'd not mind that a-tall," Edward said with a grin.

"How do you plan to get these people across the river?"

"We'll not cross. I'll take them to the next stop where they'll be sent on to Newport. Levi will take care of them from there on."

"Look out for Perry. I don't believe the man is more than a little crazy."

"He's tied in with a fellow named Crenshaw," Edward said. "They're two of a kind in my way a thinkin'. Crenshaw has built himself a three-story mansion down in southern Illinois. The top floor is where he keeps his stud to service the young females. It's said he's as cruel a master as ever there was, using the whip and shackles even on the children. The people are treated like animals and work long hours in the salt mine. Most don't last over a year. He and Perry have got it in their minds to breed a strong strain of Negroes. Crenshaw has political influence. So far no one has been able to prove anything. If Perry gets his hands on George, that's where he'll go."

"And that's where I'll go looking for him," Daniel said firmly.

Edward shrugged. "You'd better take the militia with you."

"I'm obliged to you for the warning." Daniel held out his hand.

Mercy left the basket with the pitiful group and walked beside Daniel back to the wagon.

"We don't realize how fortunate we are to have been born white, do we Daniel?"

"No," he said thoughtfully. Then, "We've got to make up this lost time. I want to be across the Ohio and down into Kentucky before nightfall."

They stopped at a store in Evansville where Daniel bought some supplies; cornmeal, jerky, raisins, salt, tea, a jug of sorghum syrup, and a bag of sweet potatoes. Mercy went into the store with him and looked at the yard goods while he was making his purchases.

The storekeeper was a scholarly-looking man with a flowing white beard and scarcely any hair on his head. The well-dressed strangers aroused his curiosity, and after trying to draw Daniel into conversation several times with no results, he tried another tactic.

"Your missus would sure look pretty in a dress made out of that blue goods," he said to Daniel.

Daniel's eye sought Mercy's. She saw the mischievous twinkle there as he waited several minutes before answering the storekeeper.

"She looks pretty in most anything. The blue is her color, matches her eyes. Do you want some of that goods for a dress, sweetheart?"

"Can we afford it?" Mercy turned her face away to keep him from seeing the flush of pleasure that covered it.

"I think I can spare a few coins for my *wife* to have a new dress," Daniel said smoothly.

Mercy's eyes flew to his face. His wife! If only it were true! His eyes held hers teasingly, and she wondered if he were aware of her inner trembling.

"Thank you, dear," she managed to say calmly. "You've given me six new dresses this year, but if you're sure you don't mind, I'd like enough of this for a dress and a bonnet too." Mercy picked up the bolt and carried it to the counter. She looked directly into Daniel's brown eyes. Hers had a look of complete innocence.

"Women are never satisfied," Daniel said seriously to the storekeeper. "Give them a dress and they want a bonnet. Give them stockings and they want shoes."

The clerk cut a generous length of the material, folded it, and tied it with a string. After Daniel paid for the purchases, they left the store, laughing like children.

"I'll pay you for the goods, Daniel," Mercy said when they reached the wagon.

"My treat. See that you behave yourself or I'll take it back and have Rose make me a shirt." He smiled at her fondly, and her heart pounded with pleasure.

The sun poured its heat directly down upon them as they crossed the Ohio on the ferry and headed southeast with Lenny and Bernie pointing the way. The brothers were in a noticeably better mood now that they were on Kentucky soil. It seemed they no longer feared that Daniel would turn back. While in the open, they rode a quarter of a mile ahead.

"We ort ta be pert nigh home this time tomorry," Bernie said.

"If'n it was just us, we'd be home tomorry night. I figger it'll be mid-mornin' the next day 'fore we get ta Mud Creek."

"I sure do hope Maw's not . . . gone."

"I hope it too."

"What're we goin' to do 'bout Hester 'n' that feller, Lenny? It pure rattles my mind to think of what Maw 'n' Hod 'n' Wyatt'll say. They'll be plumb 'shamed over the way she carries on."

"She be ruint fer another man, it's sure."

"It's sure!" Bernie shifted his weight on the mule so he could look at his brother. "There warn't but one bed in that room, Lenny. I seen there warn't when I looked in the winder, 'n' I ain't likin' what went on none a-tall."

"It warn't a made no difference if'n there'd been a dozen beds. Ain't no blood-'n'-guts man goin' to stay cooped up with a sightly woman 'n' not diddle with her some. This feller ain't no different than a Mud Creek feller when it comes to that. Hod would've diddled, Wyatt would've diddled plenty. I shore would'nta let the chance get by. Gid woulda been on 'er like a fly on fresh shit. Hester's sightly. Ya got to own up to that. She ain't got no worts on her face, 'n' she's got her teeth yet."

"We could let it slide 'n' not tell it."

"I ain't never lied to Maw. She'd see it soon enuff. He ain't a-lettin' her outta his sight. 'N' what'd we do if Hester come up with a belly big as a whuskey barrel? Could ya say we didn't know? Hod 'n' Wyatt'd say we was slack-handed on lookin' out fer our sister, is what they'd say. They'd be plumb flummoxed that we let it go on."

"We can't kill him. Sister'd be plumb put out," Bernie said.

"I'm thinkin' ya're right. But somethin's got ta be done afore we get home."

"But what?"

"I know the *what*. I jist ain't figgered out the *how*. They ain't goin' to like nothin' we do none a-tall."

"But, Len, what if'n that feller bows his neck?"

"We jist got to figger a way to unbow it, is all."

At dusk they made camp. Lenny found a suitable place in a clearing off the road, near a fast-moving stream. By the time Daniel and Lenny had watered and staked out the horses in the knee-high grass, Mercy had unloaded their food supplies and gathered dry wood for a fire. Bernie had crept upstream to the edge of a clear, cold pool, and ten minutes later a dozen trout lay flopping on the bank.

Fascinated, Mercy watched him. He scooped a small hole in the bank and filled it with pieces of dry oak bark. He covered this with green branches so that when he lit the fire, there was only one small air hole. The bark produced a single wisp of smoke. After he cleaned the fish, he removed the green branches and placed the fish on the white-hot coals. Soon the sizzling smell of fish drifted up to her.

Daniel quickly built a small, hot fire and raked aside some of the coals to cover several large sweet potatoes. It all went so quickly that before it was completely dark, the meal was ready. Bernie and Lenny brought tin cups from their packs and accepted tea, sweet potatoes and hoecake. Bernie brought his fish to their fire on a slab of white poplar bark.

Hungrily, the four of them devoured the dozen trout, the sweet potatoes, and the hoecake.

"I coulda caught more," Bernie said.

"How did you catch them so fast?" Mercy asked.

"It warn't nothin'." Bernie drew a line from his pocket. Attached to the end was a hook fashioned out of the thighbone of a rabbit. The bone of a chicken leg came out with the string. Bernie quickly kicked it away with his foot. Mercy suppressed a smile. They had eaten the chicken the night before, and Bernie had saved some to use for fish bait.

"I'd like to learn how to do that," Mercy said. Bernie didn't answer. He shuffled his feet as if he were going to get up and leave, but he didn't. They all sat quietly, drinking their tea. This was the first time the Baxters had been the least bit friendly. They were rested and fed and presented with an hour's leisure, Mercy decided to try and draw them out.

"Lenny, tell me what to expect when we get to Mud Creek."

"We dunno if Maw's there," he said crossly. "We been gone nigh on two weeks."

"Oh, I hope she is!" Mercy said in a small voice as her eyes sought Daniel's.

After a silence Lenny said in a resigned voice, "We done as good as we could."

"Who's taking care of her?"

"Hod's woman does most of it."

"Do they have children?"

"Hod claims four."

"And Wyatt?"

"Claims one, 'n' one comin'."

"You've not said much about the younger boy. What's his name?" It seemed to Mercy that the only way she would find out anything about the Baxters was to ask.

"Gideon."

"How old is he?"

"Fourteen, fifteen, somewhere in there."

"Does he go to school?"

"School? Hell, no! Gid's wild as a deer 'n' horny as a

billy goat. Gid's done already poked half the women in the county. Young, old, wedded or not. It makes no never mind to Gid," Bernie added proudly.

"I don't think that's anything to brag about," Mercy said in her schoolteacher voice and raised the cup to her lips. She took several gulps of the hot tea to hide her embarrassment.

"Ain't nothin' to be 'shamed for," Bernie said stubbornly.

"Did any of you go to school?"

"What fer? Maw learnt us how to make our name on paper."

"Do you farm?"

"Some. Baxters is best at makin' whuskey." Lenny threw the dregs from the tea in his cup over his shoulder.

"Whiskey?"

"Yup. We make nigh on to ten barrel a year. Sell it fer a dollar a gallon. Makes all the cash money we need." He grinned proudly. "I'd sure like to have me a jug a Baxter whuskey right now."

Daniel was sitting with his back to a small sapling, listening and watching her. Mercy looked at him, thinking of how comfortable she was with him and how she would hate to have anyone other than Daniel hear those things about her real family. She decided that she could almost like Bernie and Lenny. They were open and honest, and their love for their mother was the reason they had come looking for her. It was also evident to Mercy that the Baxter clan was close-knit and that she would *never* fit into the family. But then she wouldn't have to. Daniel was with her, and after the visit he would take her back home to Quill's Station.

"It's about time to turn in." Daniel's voice broke into the quiet. "Do you want to sleep in the wagon?"

Mercy laughed. "It's too short. My legs would hang off."

"All right. I'll fix you a place under the wagon."

"Where will you be?" Mercy asked anxiously.

"Here, with you. You know this country, Lenny. Do we need to set up a watch?"

"We be nearby," Lenny said stiffly, and Daniel saw the look that passed between him and Bernie. "Ain't nobody goin' to sneak up on ya."

"I'll sleep with one eye open to make sure. Mercy, I'll hang a blanket over the side of the wagon if you want to get behind it and undress. We'll let the fire burn down." He kicked at the fire with his booted foot to scatter the embers.

"I'd like that. I've had these clothes on for two days."

Lenny and Bernie wandered off toward the pool where Bernie had caught the fish. Daniel hung up the blanket. Mercy took off her clothes, slipped into a nightgown, and wrapped the blanket around her. Daniel spread a blanket on the grass, and Mercy sat down to take down her hair and watch him make up the bed beneath the wagon.

"Lenny and Bernie can be quite agreeable . . . sometimes. But I hope the others are not as contrary as they are. I never know what to say to them." Mercy had loosened her hair from the braid and was brushing it.

"They've lived their lives one way and you another. I'm sure our ways are strange to them." When Daniel finished making the bed, he lifted his own bedroll from the wagon bed.

"Oh, Daniel, I hope *she's* not . . . gone! I want to see her and let her know I'm all right and that I have people who want me. If she's gone, Lenny and Bernie will have come all the way to Quill's Station for nothing."

"No. Not for nothing," he said quietly as he spread his bedroll on the grass.

* * *

The clouds scudded low over a rising full moon, letting patches of moonlight shine through. Mercy, lying on the pallet beneath the wagon, thought of Daniel's words, "Not for nothing," and her mind hung on them. He was right. Lenny and Bernie's arrival at Quill's Station had opened her eyes to a lot of things. It made her aware of how fortunate she was to have been found by Farrway Quill and raised in his home. Most of all, she was now aware of her love for Daniel.

Mercy was dozing when she was jerked alert by a distant sound—a howling that swelled and grew. *Wolves*. The word never failed to strike terror in her heart, since as a child she had heard tales of the gray killers. She leaned up on her elbow, her eyes probing the shadows where Daniel lay.

"Daniel . . ." Her voice was thick and strangled, and her heart raced wildly.

He rolled from his blanket and came quickly to kneel beside the wagon. "What is it?"

"Was that . . . wolves?"

The howl came again before he could answer. "Yes, it's a wolf, but it's not near."

"But they hunt in packs."

"It sounds like a single wolf calling its mate. You needn't be afraid. He sounds much closer than he is."

"I can't help it. I've heard . . . stories."

"All exaggerated, I'm sure. I'll move my blanket closer if it'll ease your mind."

"Please . . ."

Daniel threw his bedroll on the ground beside the wagon, placed his rifle and pistol within reach, and laid down with his back to her. His head was even with her knees, and she could look down on his dark head, lying on his bent arm. She wished with all her heart that she had the right to reach out and touch him, ask him to move up beside her and let her hold him, pillow his head on her breast and share her warmth with him. *It's all so one-sided, my love,* she told him silently. She didn't have anything to offer him but herself, not even a good family background. All she had was a heart full of love for him.

The wolf continued to send its lonely message to the female, who never answered his call. The moon rose reluctantly in the sky, dimming the stars. The wind came up. The air cooled, and Mercy pulled the blanket up around her neck. She was no longer uneasy about the wolf. Daniel was with her. She dozed and drifted off to sleep.

As Mercy came slowly out of a dream, she became aware of the warm hand caressing her ankle. She was not the least bit frightened by the touch. She lay with her eyes closed, her chin buried in the blanket, savoring the wonderful touch that could only be Daniel's hand. She lifted her lashes a mere fraction to look down. They were lying on their sides facing each other, his face tilted upward toward her face. She could see the gleam of his eyes, watching her in the moonlight, and they felt like a warm hand caressing her cheeks.

She tried to keep her breathing even, lest he know the turmoil of her emotions, but it was difficult. All her senses were focused on that warm hand on her foot. Gradually the warming sensation crept upward to her thigh, and upward still to settle with a powerful throb in the area below her stomach.

The almost overwhelming desire to rub her thighs together caused her mouth to go dry. She closed her eyes tightly. Despite the drowning feeling his touch evoked, Mercy lay as still as a stone lest he take his hand away. Slowly, hesitantly, his fingers moved upward to the calf of her leg and stroked lightly all the way down to her heel. There his hand stayed curled about her ankle.

As she watched, he lowered his face and settled his head more firmly on his arm. Was that a deep sigh she heard? Mercy wondered if she had stirred in her sleep and if his hand on her foot was to reassure her that he was near. Regardless of the reason for his hand being there, this moment was to be remembered as one of the most precious moments in her life.

At the edge of the clearing the two Baxter brothers squatted in the shadows, their backs to a tree, their rifles on the ground beside them. They had been sitting there since shortly after they left the campfire. With infinite patience they watched the wagon. They heard the wolf howl and knew it for what it was, a loner calling its mate. When they saw Daniel move his bedroll, Bernie threw down the twig he had been chewing on and snorted with disgust.

"See thar! I tol' ya he'd be under that wagon by mornin'!"

"By granny! Ya was right!"

"We ort to do . . . somethin'. It pure gets my dander up. That thar is our sister he's diddlin' with."

"Don't make such a racket," Lenny cautioned. "He's as flap-eared as a deer, 'n' got eyes like a hawk, 'n' a plumb whirlwind when he's riled. Ya've had a couple settos with him already. Didn't ya learn nothin'?"

"It's a plumb disgrace how they carry on. Ya reckon she be one a them loose women what carries on with any man a-tall?"

"I don't reckon that. Not with Baxter blood! But I'm right bambozzled over it. It's got ta be put right. There ain't no two ways about it. I ain't takin' no whore home to Maw."

"If'n Maw's there." Bernie's words came after a long sigh.

"She said she'd hold on," Lenny said carefully.

There was a silence as both the brothers pondered the sorrow that might await them when they reached home.

"Hit's just come to me!" Lenny stood and picked up his rifle. "I done got me a idea what we got to do, Bernie, 'n' we can do it tomorry. By jigger! It'll take some doin', but a Baxter don't back down from a hard chore."

"I'll be hornswoggled if'n I know what ya're talkin' about. I done thought on it till I'm tired."

"I'm talkin' about puttin' it right, ya dunderhead! If'n ya'd use yore head for somethin' besides scratchin', you'd know there ain't but one thin' to do."

"We ain't got no time to do nothin' but to kill him."

"We ain't killin' him! We ain't never done a man in if'n he warn't tryin' to do us in. The fellers been kinda . . . decent, considerin'.'"

"Guess we ain't ort to kill him. Sister'd be sure to tell Maw, 'n' she don't sit still for killin', exceptin' if they're shootin' at us."

The brothers went back to where they had unpacked their mules. Bernie sank down on his blanket and stretched out.

"I'm just plumb petered out, Lenny. When we get home, I'm goin' ta sleep a week."

"Get up! Ya ain't home yet," Lenny said sharply. "We got plannin' to do."

CHAPTER TEN

Morning came, and Mercy tried to meet Daniel's look with smiling calm while an almost frantic thrill leapt within her at the thought of his warm fingers on her foot. Nothing in his manner indicated that for him that morning was different from any other. He made tea and they used it to wash down the hoecake left over from the night before. When they finished, they went about breaking camp and packing the wagon as the sun was sending streaks of light up over the eastern hills.

The Baxters didn't come to their breakfast fire, but they were waiting on the trail when Daniel guided Zelda out onto the road. They rode ahead without as much as a greeting.

"I wonder what's got into them," Mercy said when the brothers moved their mules on ahead at a brisk trot.

Daniel chuckled. "Who knows. I thought you softened them up last night."

"They're hard to talk to. They don't tell me a thing unless I ask."

"You'll know about them soon enough. Lenny said we should be there by mid-morning tomorrow."

"Will we camp out again tonight?"

"If we don't come to a place where I can get a bed for you, we'll have to."

"I'd rather camp than stay in a place like we stayed the first night."

Mercy watched a large snake slither across the trail ahead. Zelda broke stride and whinnied.

Daniel slapped the reins gently. "Go on girl. That's just a harmless old grass snake. It's scared of you too."

"Ugh!" Mercy shivered. "I don't blame Zelda. Snakes give me the chills. I even hate a big worm."

"Then there'd be no point in taking you fishing." Daniel looked down at her. His deep, dark eyes were dancing with devilment, and the slight, upturning smile of his lips was boyish.

Mercy swallowed the large lump blocking her throat. Today everything seemed to take on a new, different, and wonderful meaning. He was an extraordinarily handsome man: broad shoulders, trim waist, long legs, and the most beautiful eyes in the world. She wanted to ask, "When did you shave?" Instead she said, "Bernie caught the fish last night with chicken meat. Did you see the chicken bone fall out of his pocket?"

"I saw it." Daniel chuckled again. "They're quite a pair. I could almost like them if they weren't so bull-headed."

"I suspect it's a Baxter trait."

He smiled down at her again. "I suspect you're right."

"I wonder what the rest of the Baxters are like. I hope they're not all like that young Gideon. It sounds like he's had no upbringing at all."

"What's wrong with wild and horny?" Daniel asked with an innocent look on his face.

"What's wrong? Why . . . why, Daniel Phelps, you know what's wrong!"

"There you go . . . sputtering. You don't even know what it means." Laughter rippled in his voice.

"I do too know what it means. It means that at age fifteen he's got bastards spread all over the county!" Her voice was curt, her chin up, and her face as red as the morning sunrise. "They were so quick to condemn me because you spent the night in the house with me, but they think it's funny that Gideon . . . does what he does."

"It seems that they have a different set of rules for the women of the family," Daniel said patiently, trying not to laugh at the indignant look on her face.

"Well! They're not telling *me* what to do. I'll set them straight about that."

"You do that and I'll back you up."

"You're laughing at me!"

"Yeah, I am." He smiled into her eyes, reached across her lap, and patted her bent knee. "It's fun to get you riled up. It used to be my favorite thing to do. You'd shout, 'You don't know everything, Daniel Phelps.' Remember saying that?"

"And you'd say, 'You silly girl. I know more than you do, I'm older.' You would make me so mad that I'd cry."

"I remember."

"We've been together a long time, Daniel."

"Yes, a long time," he said quietly.

They passed through the rich bottomland stretching black and loamy on either side of the Green River, which cut a deep gash through central Kentucky, and entered low, clustering green hills. They followed a pike that wound around jutting slopes and across small rocky streams that divided the hills that rammed each other. At times the pike clung to the rocky ledges; at other times it passed through woods so dense and dark that no brush grew beneath the trees.

Although Mercy and Daniel had not seen Bernie and Lenny since they'd entered the hills, there was only one track, and they kept a steady pace. Daniel led the way on his buckskin, and Zelda followed him across rocky streams and through thick, sweet-smelling pines.

Stopping at noon beside a clear, gurgling creek, they ate jerky and raisins and drank water from the fast-moving stream. When they started up again, Daniel was on the seat beside Mercy, and his buckskin was tied behind the wagon. Mercy had never felt so good, so free, so happy. Being alone with Daniel in the deep woods was like a dream. A sudden worry caused her to frown. *Dreams seldom came true.* She looked at Daniel's profile; concentration furrowed his brow. *I love you,* she told him silently. She didn't want this to be a dream. She wanted to be with him forever, but not as a sister. She wanted to be his lover, his friend, his mate.

"Why are you frowning?" Daniel's voice broke into her thoughts. "Are you worried about meeting the rest of the Baxters?"

His serious eyes looked into hers. He was so very dear to her that she couldn't lie to him. Yet she couldn't tell him her thoughts.

"What if Mrs. . . . Baxter has already passed on?"

"Then we'll go home." He passed the reins to his left hand and reached for her with his right. "Come closer."

She went willingly, her shoulder tucked behind his, her hip and thigh in contact with his.

"You're not to worry." He said the words simply. "We'll see her, then we'll go home."

Mercy placed her hand on his thigh, and his hand dropped immediately to cover it. She turned her face away, but he saw a glimmer of tears.

"You trust me, don't you, Mercy?" he asked in a voice so low and concerned that she looked at him quickly. "I said I'd take you home, and I will."

"I know you will, Danny," she said softly, turning her palm up to lace her fingers between his. Theirs was a companionship that needed no words. Being with Daniel was all the security she needed.

In the middle of the afternoon they came out of the low hills and into a wide valley. In the distance, a small settlement squatted on the flatland. As they drew nearer, the buildings took the shape of a gristmill, a blacksmith shop, a store, and perhaps half a dozen houses. A church spire loomed up between the store and the blacksmith shop, and as they came closer they could see a small stained-glass window in the church. Smoke curled up from the smithy's forge and from the chimneys of several houses. The clang of the blacksmith's hammer rang out with regularity. It was not an unpleasant sound.

Their arrival was announced by several dogs that came bounding out from beneath the store's porch, yelping and scattering squawking chickens. The wiry birds ran a few yards, then flew a few yards, in their rush to get out of the way of the dogs and the approaching wagon. Zelda kicked halfheartedly at the curs that nipped at her heels. The buckskin snorted, and the dogs kept their distance from his sharp hooves.

"This must be Coon Hollow." Daniel pulled Zelda to a stop in front of the blacksmith shop.

"Is this the nearest town to the Baxters?" Mercy asked.

"No. Lenny said the closest settlement didn't have a blacksmith. So there must be one more."

A man came from beneath the shed. He was bare to the waist, and his body glistened with sweat. His shoulders seemed to be a yard wide, and his arms were knotted with muscles. He held a hammer in a hand that looked as if it could knock a mule to its knees.

"How do. If ye be Phelps, Lenny Baxter said tell ya to keep goin'. He be waitin' up ahead."

"I'm obliged to you."

Mercy wanted to ask him if there was any news about Mrs. Baxter, but the man turned and went back to his anvil, took up a shoe with his tongs, and shoved it into the fire. They drove out of the settlement with the same racket as when they entered: yelping dogs and squawking chickens.

The valley was longer than it appeared to be. It was late afternoon when they left it, crossed through a pass between two sets of hills, and entered another valley. The sun was sinking behind the hills to the west when they smelled wood smoke and saw the black curl that came from a chimney in the distance.

On this, the third and last night before reaching the Baxters, Mercy hoped they could stay at a place that would provide her enough privacy for a bath. She was disappointed to discover that the house they approached was not much larger than a good-sized wagon. However, there was a shed attached, and out back she could see the Baxters' mules and a horse tethered.

Lenny stood in the doorway. As they neared, he came out and signaled for Daniel to bring the wagon to the side of the house. Daniel complied, pulling Zelda to a stop. He jumped down and lifted Mercy from a high seat.

"This ain't much of a place," Lenny said. "But it's better'n in the open."

"Who lives here?" Mercy reached into the wagon for her bag as Daniel began unhitching Zelda.

"Nobody. It was Old Man Mertser's, but he passed on." Lenny untied Daniel's buckskin and led him away without another word.

Mercy stood beside the wagon holding her carpetbag

and wondered how it could be that she could be a sister to Lenny and Bernie Baxter. Their ways, their dress, their speech—all were so foreign to her. She had to admit to a family resemblance—the blond hair and blue eyes. But there was not the slightest bit of warmth in the brothers' eyes when they looked at her.

She heard a scraping sound inside the cabin, as if someone had moved a chair over a rough floor. It came to Mercy that if no one lived here, who did the horse belong to? Daniel came back to the wagon, followed by Lenny.

"Lenny, who's in there with Bernie?" she asked.

"Some of the kin. He'll be ridin' out."

"Did he bring news of... your mother?" In her thoughts the woman was Mrs. Baxter, and she could not bring herself to say *my* mother. Somehow it would seem disloyal to Liberty Quill, who had been the only mother she could remember.

"Nope. He ain't heard."

Mercy stepped into the cabin. There was a front door and a back door but no windows. Both doors stood open, and a fire blazed in a cobbledstone hearth. Bernie stood back in a corner, his wiry blond hair looking as if it had never known the feel of a brush. He evaded her eyes when she looked at him. Of the two brothers, she decided, Lenny was the more reasonable.

A thin man with a head of white hair and a beard that came down to the middle of his chest pushed a chair back from a table and stood up when they entered. He wore a black coat that was much too large for his thin frame. It sagged on his shoulders, and the sleeves hung down over his hands.

"What the hell!"

Startled, Mercy turned quickly to Daniel. He had let her bag fall to the floor and tried to grab the pistol from his belt. The barrel of Lenny's rifle was in the middle of his back, and he was forced to toss the pistol aside.

"Lenny!" Mercy's heart dropped to her toes when she saw the snarl on brother's face. "What are you doing? Are you out of your mind?"

"Ain't nothin' like that. Stand still," he snapped at Daniel. "I'd jist as soon shoot ya 'n' be done with it." He emphasized each of his words with a vicious poke of the rifle barrel.

"Stop that!"

"Hush up, Hester! This here's men's business. I've had me enough o' yore woman's sass. Cousin Farley, here, is goin' to wed ya up to this son of a bitch what ruint ya from ever gettin' a decent man. We is seein' that ya is done right by afore we take ya home to Maw."

Mercy could scarcely believe what she heard. It took a minute before she could gather her wits to reply. When she did, angry words poured out of her mouth.

"You blundering, empty-headed, stupid idiot!" she yelled. "What the hell do you mean, *ruined*? Daniel is the most honorable man I know. He's done nothing! Nothing!"

"Hester, I done tole ya, ya ain't better let Maw hear ya talk like no fallen woman. She'd have me or Hod ta upend ya 'n' whip your butt if she heared ya swear."

"I'll swear if I want to! What do you mean about Daniel? He's looked after me all my life. Where in the hell were you when I needed you?"

"Right here on Mud Creek with my folks where I belonged," Lenny said with a superior look on his face.

"We done seen what the feller done, Hester. Ain't no use a-lyin'," Bernie said.

"Shut up, you . . . horse's ass. You've *seen* nothing!" Mercy threw the wild words over her shoulder at Bernie, then turned the full force of her anger on the other brother. "You've got a dirty mind, Lenny. You'd better not hurt Daniel! I'm telling you now, I'll shoot you! I swear it! I'll shoot you down like a mad dog if I have to wait ten years to do it!"

"He ain't goin' ta get no hurt if'n he behaves," Lenny said impatiently.

"Cousin Farley can wed ya up proper. Give ya a paper 'n' all."

Bernie's voice came to Mercy as if from a deep well as her stricken eyes sought Daniel's. She felt her breath catch in her throat, felt her insides turn cold as she looked into his anxious eyes. They relayed a message for her to stay calm. Daniel was everything in the world that was dear to her, and she would not allow her brothers to force him to marry her against his will.

"I won't do it! I'll not be forced upon Daniel! I'm telling you that we have done nothing wrong. I'm as virginal as the day I was born," she gasped through wobbly lips.

"Hush, Mercy. You don't have to explain anything to them. Lenny isn't going to shoot me because he'd have to shoot you, too, or you'd tell about it. They can't force us to marry if we don't wish to. You don't have to do anything that you don't want to do. Remember that and stay calm."

"Mister . . ." The bearded man spoke for the first time. His voice was unusually loud for such a thin man. "The Lord brings down his wrath upon the sinner! If ya've fornicated 'n' sinned, it's best ya put it right. Our God is a just and forgivin' God. When you meet your maker—"

"Fornicated!" Mercy said in a voice that screeched in spite of her attempt at control.

"More'n once," Bernie said. "And we ain't takin' no whore home to Maw."

Mercy took two steps toward Bernie and raised her hand as if to slap him. "Don't you dare say those things about Daniel, and don't you dare call me a whore!"

Daniel lurched forward when Bernie grabbed her arm. A loop suddenly flew over his head, settled about his neck, and he was jerked back. Lenny wound the end of the rope around a log that protruded out from high on the wall. Daniel clawed at the rope around his neck, and Mercy screamed and fought against the hands holding her. Bernie's hand dug cruelly into her arm and kept her from going to him.

"We're going to have us a weddin' here 'n' now, and there ain't no two ways 'bout it." Lenny picked up the rifle he'd let slip from his hand when he dropped the loop. Once again the barrel was pressed into Daniel's back. He had to stand on his toes to keep the loop loose enough so he could breathe. Mercy's eyes were huge, fastened on him in horror, and changed to blue, cold fury when she turned them on Lenny.

"I'm so ashamed," she said slowly, and shook her head. "I'm so ashamed that the same blood that runs in your veins runs in mine."

"Mercy. . ." Daniel spoke her name and her eyes went back to his. "I'll not be forced. They can't make us say the words that will wed us. Stand your ground, honey. They're a couple of misguided, ignorant fools if they think they can make us wed against our wills."

"Well, I guess thar ain't nothin' else to do but some persuadin', is thar, Lenny? It ain't pleasin' me to do it, but if I got to, I will. Stubborn 'n' bullheaded as they be, I feared it'd come to this."

Bernie kept a tight hold on Mercy's arm, and with the other hand he reached behind him for a long, slender stick that stood in the corner. He carefully lifted the stick out of a sack lying on the floor. Because of the intense look on his face, Mercy looked down and froze with fear. Tied to the end of the stick was a small, writhing snake, its body curled around the stick, its small mouth open, its forked tongue flicking in and out. The rattles on the end of its tail shook angrily.

Daniel tried to claw the noose from his neck. "My God!" he croaked. "Get that away from her!"

"Ya best be still or Bernie'll lose his hold on that stick." Lenny poked Daniel viciously with the gun barrel. "It's just a little bitty old rattler. It ain't got up a full head a pison yet. It won't make sister dead if'n it bites her down on the leg, but it'll make her powerful sick."

"Daniel!" Mercy's eyes pleaded.

"Stand still! Do what they want."

"Daniel!" she screeched again, and moved away as far as the hand on her arm would allow. Bernie moved the stick along the floor until the snake was within a foot of Mercy.

"God damn you!" Daniel shouted. "I'll break every bone in your damn body for this. Can't you see she's scared half to death?"

"Shore we can see it. If she don't behave, Bernie'll just move his little purty overhere 'n' let it get a taste a yore hide. Start the words, Cousin Farley," Lenny said calmly.

"I'm sorry, Daniel. I'm sorry I've got you into this." Mercy's voice, weakened by her fear, came out in a hoarse whisper.

"I'm going to beat you half to death when this is over." Daniel glared at Bernie. His voice was soft, but the measured words left no doubt as to his rock-hard determination.

Bernie grinned cockily, but his eyes darted nervously to Lenny. Daniel's face had a harshness that made him uneasy.

"Ya goin' ta fight family 'cause we bested ya?" Bernie's grin faded. "Start the words, Cousin Farley. This here rattler's gettin' riled aplenty. He jist might come loose from that there stick."

"If'n ya don't answer right, mister, by night Sister'll be sicker than a dog what's eat the ass outa a skunk. Start the weddin', Cousin Farley."

"Huh?"

"Start the weddin'."

"Huh?"

"Start the weddin'!" Lenny shouted.

"Why didn't ya say so in the first place?"

The book the preacher held had a wooden cover. He opened it, being careful of the dried flowers pressed between the pages. He moistened his finger with his tongue and turned the pages. Finally he rocked back on his heels and looked first at Mercy, then at Daniel.

"Dearly beloved..." Cousin Farley's voice boomed in the closed room as if they were all as deaf as he was.

"Danny, I'm sorry they're making you do this." Mercy blurted the words.

"Hush, honey. It's all right."

"We are gathered here today to unite this man—what's yore name, mister?"

"Daniel Phelps."

"Huh?"

"Daniel Phelps!"

"To unite this man, Randall Phelps, to this woman, Hester Baxter, in holy wedlock."

"Daniel, Cousin Farley," Bernie yelled.

"Daniel, ya say? To unite this man, Daniel Phelps, to this woman, Hester Baxter, in holy wedlock."

Mercy's eyes locked with Daniel's. Tears rolled unchecked down her cheeks. Her heart felt as if it were being squeezed by a cold hand. What should be the happiest day of her life had become a nightmare. Daniel was being forced to take her as his wife. She never would have the chance to win his love now. He would resent her for the rest of his life.

"Daniel Phelps, do you take this woman to be your lawfully wedded wife, to have and to hold, in sickness and in health, until death do you part?"

Daniel saw the look of despair on Mercy's face. For a moment he thought of refusing to answer. He glanced at

Bernie, saw him move the stick a fraction closer to Mercy's leg. *Sweetheart! Oh, my love.* His heart felt like a great, hard lump in his chest. He loved her so much, and he had failed her. He had waited, wanting her to be free to make a choice after they returned to Quill's Station. He didn't want her to love him out of obligation. He wanted her whole heart. In the space of a few minutes a decision that would affect them for the rest of their lives had been made for them.

"Air ya goin' to answer or not?" Lenny said from behind him and pulled up on the noose.

"I will . . . do." Daniel's voice was a strangled sound.

"Speak up!" What'd ya say?" the preacher asked.

"I said, I will."

"Huh?"

"He said yes," Bernie shouted.

"I thought that's what he said." Cousin Farley snorted, then turned his sharp eyes on Mercy. "Do you, Hester Baxter, take this here man, Daniel Phelps, to be your lawfully wedded husband? Do you promise to love him, obey him, in sickness and in health, until death do you part?"

Mercy saw that Daniel's eyes were filled with loving concern for her. Her mouth moved a fraction, and the words came from the center of her being.

"I do promise."

"What'd ya say? Stop mumblin'. Do ya take him or not?"

"I said I'll take him," Mercy shouted angrily.

"You are man and wife." Cousin Farley closed the book, picked up his hat, and shoved it down on his head. "The weddin' paper's made out. I'll leave it on the wagon. Put your mark on it, mister, and don't be thinkin' you can crawl out of it. I got the preachin' papers that says it's lawful for me to wed ya. It'll be marked down in the church at Coon Hollow."

"Much obliged, Cousin. We knowed we could count on you," Bernie said.

"What'd ya say?"

"Nothin'."

"There ain't no point in tellin' the folks 'bout this," Lenny said loudly.

"It'd grieve 'em to know it, is what it'd do," the preacher agreed. He looked at Bernie. "Now get that goddamn snake out of here, Bernie. You never did have the brains of a flea. If you'da let that viper bite that gal, I'd have stomped your ass into the ground." The shocking words coming from the preacher would have amused Mercy at any other time. But her mind was too numb with misery to grasp them.

"Yes, sir!" Bernie said meekly.

Cousin Farley left by the back door. Bernie inched the snake across the floor toward the open doorway. He put it out the door, stepped out, and slammed the door shut behind him. At the same time Lenny backed out the front and closed the door.

They were alone.

Mercy stood for only a second in the firelit room, then went quickly to where Lenny had tied the rope. She jerked on the end, pulling the slipknot free, and the noose loosened. Daniel lifted the loop over his head and threw it to the floor.

Suddenly it was too much to hold inside her. She went into Daniel's arms, huge racking sobs coming from deep within her and disrupting the silence of the nearly dark room. Something deep and primitive screamed from the very center of her being that it wasn't fair that this should happen to her. The tears came in a torrent from the depths of her misery. Her arms closed frantically around Daniel's neck, and she clung to him as harsh sobs came from her throat. She could no more stop them than she could a runaway horse. She cried for herself, and she cried for Daniel.

For the first time in her life she was totally beaten, totally humiliated.

"Ah, honey, don't cry! Shh . . . hush, dear heart." His voice against her ear was pleading, but she wouldn't be comforted. The shame and humiliation she felt at having Daniel forced to wed her was like a knife in her breast. Soon the sobs ceased and were replaced with faint grieving moans.

He tried to pull away from her so he could see her face.

"Oh, please! Don't . . . look at me. I'm so ashamed! I'm so sorry! I've ruined your life. You can't . . . can't—"

"Can't what? I'm sorry I didn't keep you safe like I promised. But . . . is it so bad being wed to me?" His voice quavered, and even more tears squeezed out from under her closed lids.

"You . . . don't love me." The agonized voice came from against his chest.

"Of course I love you. I've always loved you."

His casual words were not comforting. Mercy wished with all her heart that he hadn't said them. She knew he was fond of her, even loved her with that special, protective kind of love a man had for the women of his family. To hear him say it made her misery all the more acute.

"I'm going to break that bastard's neck for scaring you with that snake." Daniel's voice lowered to a husky whisper.

"I hate them! I wish they hadn't found me!"

"Things could be a lot worse."

"I don't see how!"

"Now that we're wed, your duty is to me, not to them. After you see your mother, I'll take you home and they can all go straight to hell as far as I'm concerned. Dry your eyes, honey. You've shed enough tears over them."

"Danny! How can you be so calm? So reasonable?

You may . . . want to marry someone else someday! Now you won't be able to. I've ruined your life."

"What about *your* life? Is there someone else you want to marry? Is it Mike? Are you in love with him?" he lifted her chin with his fingers and nudged it until she lifted her lashes to meet his eyes. This was something he had to know. While he waited for her answer he felt as if he were standing on the edge of a deep, dark pit and the next few seconds meant life or death for him.

"In love with Mike? Heavens, no! I love him, but like a sister loves a brother. He's in love with Tennessee and has been ever since Eleanor and Gavin brought her home with them from the Arkansas. Didn't you know?"

"No, I didn't know." There was a long, breathless silence while they looked at each other.

"She loves him desperately but made me swear not to tell him. She thinks he won't want to marry her because her mother is Shawnee."

"How do you know that Mike's in love with her, Miss Smarty?"

"Because of the way he looks at her. Oh, men! They are so dumb sometimes."

Daniel suddenly began to smile, first at the corners of his eyes; then the slashes in his cheeks deepened as his lips spread. She leaned away from him, but her arms were still around his neck.

"How can you smile after what's happened?"

"Because I just remembered something. You just promised to obey me."

Confusion darkened her eyes for a moment, then her mind cleared. "Oh, that." Her arms slid from around his neck, and her palms lay flat against his chest.

"The preacher forgot to tell me to kiss my bride." His voice was thick. "Do you think I should?"

His words sent a thrill of excitement through her, but she made an attempt to assert control over her mind. She failed miserably, because she said the first thing that came into it.

"Kiss me? You don't . . . have to."

"What if I want to?" It was scarcely more than a whisper.

"Well . . ."

"Put your arms around my neck again." He covered her hands with his and moved them upward.

Mercy drew the tip of her tongue across dry lips while her eyes focused on the sensual fullness of his mouth. Her brain commanded her to back away, but her legs refused to move.

"I . . . you don't have to—"

"Shh. You promised to obey. Remember?"

Mercy closed her eyes at the first gentle touch of his lips against her cheek. They traveled upward to sip at the tears that hung on her lashes, then across the bridge of her nose and back down her cheek to her mouth. They pressed softly, nibbled, caressed and possessed. His lips were soft, his cheeks rough. She had been close to Daniel before, but not like this. His arms held her so tightly against him that she could feel the wild beating of his heart against her breasts. She was aware of the tangy smell of his skin; and his mouth, as it meshed with hers, tasted of the sweet they had shared that afternoon. Then the kiss changed and became more demanding. Her lips parted, but she wasn't quite sure why. She was completely unaware that her arms had tightened about his neck, and she was pressing her lips tightly to his.

It was a strange, yet exciting, feeling. Her brain refused to acknowledge the fact that Daniel was trembling, or that his hand had moved down to her hips and was pressing her to him, or that his hold across her back had flattened her breast against his chest. His lips gentled as he tasted the sweetness of her mouth. The tip of his tongue was sending hot little sparks throughout her body. She sagged in his arms.

When he finally lifted his lips from hers, Mercy opened her eyes, now shining, but not from tears. Her lips were moist and parted, the pulse in her throat making her breathless. She didn't know what to say or do. Her heart thudded under her ribs in a strange and urgent way. She stood locked in his embrace breathing deeply and erratically. Slowly he let his arms slide from around her, and she saw a look of deep frustration on his face. Daniel reached for her hands and drew her arms down from about his neck.

"I'm sorry. I didn't intend to do that." His voice was uneven. A movement in his throat betrayed the fact that he was swallowing hard. "But . . . ah, hell!" He turned, angrily shoved a chair out of his way, and went to the door.

Mercy had been kissed a few times before, but she had been totally unprepared for the storm of emotions that swamped her when her lips and Daniel's met, and she felt the hardness of his body pressing against her. Now he was angry. Why? Had he not wanted to kiss her? A feeling of mortification caused her cheeks to flame. *He had kissed her because he thought she had expected it!*

It was almost dark in the room, and hot.

"What the hell!" Daniel kicked the door savagely when it failed to open. He went to the back door. When it resisted the first attempt to open, he put his shoulder against it. The top leather hinge tore away, leaving an open wedge. He picked up the pistol he had been forced to toss aside and squeezed through the opening. A few minutes later he had kicked away the post wedged against the front door and opened it.

The cool night air fanned Mercy's hot face. "Are they gone?" she asked as soon as she stepped outside.

"The mules are gone, but they're somewhere close. You can bet on that," he growled.

Daniel built up the fire in the hearth so they could see, then brought in the food box and her bedroll and placed it on the platform in the corner of the cabin. He went back to the wagon for their water jug and set it inside the door.

Mercy dampened a cloth by pouring water over it and washed her face and hands. She was drained and empty, choked with misery, and glad to be alone. Knowing that they had to eat, she put a couple of sweet potatoes in the coals to bake, filled the kettle from the water jug, and set it to heat for tea. When this was done, she went outside and leaned against the rough logs of the house.

The night seemed to be unusually quiet, the stars bright against the black void above. The moon had not yet appeared, and the cabin was surrounded by a velvety darkness. It seemed to Mercy that she could very well be alone in the world. Then a squeal came from Zelda behind the cabin. Daniel's buckskin had come too close, and she was protesting.

Where was Daniel? When Mercy's eyes became accustomed to the darkness, she saw him. He had put distance and darkness between them. He stood on a small rise, looking down the slope toward a creek they had crossed to get to this place. His arms were folded across his chest, his feet spread, his head tilted slightly to the side. He stood so still, looking so alone.

Wells of grief for what had happened to him because of her strained for release inside the tight walls of her chest. Unless they could get the governor of Kentucky to annul the marriage, Daniel would be tied to her until one of them died. She could see the years stretching ahead of them. Daniel, forced by circumstances to live with her, would come to resent her, maybe even to despise her. The thought was almost more than she could endure.

CHAPTER ELEVEN

Mercy was standing beside the fire when Daniel came in. The firelight played over her. She stood still and small, as if she were depleted of all strength, and looked down at her hands, clasped in front of her.

The muscles clamped above the jawline of Daniel's face as he bent to throw another log on the fire.

"There's a trickle of a creek out back. I can bring in enough water for you to wash decently if you want me to." His voice was not quite even. "This is a hell of a place," he went on gruffly. "Damn creek's not even deep enough to wet your ankles."

Mercy's face in the firelight was without expression. Her eyes were like empty stars. She said nothing and her hands pressed down the sides of her dress nervously. Daniel turned and walked away, out the door, as if he had to be alone. Mercy went to the door and watched his tall figure merge with the darkness. Then he was gone, as if forever.

Her frozen voice suddenly thawed.

"Daniel . . . you don't need . . . to bring in more water.

I can manage with what's here." She wanted to cry again. She had not realized he was so miserable in her presence.

"I've already got it." His voice, coming from the side of the cabin, held a note of irritation. "I'll leave it here because the goddamn bucket leaks."

"Thank you. Come eat something." Mercy lifted a tired hand and brushed wisps of hair from her face. Misery swelled her throat.

There was a long pause.

"I'll be there in a minute."

Mercy had poured the tea and laid out the sweet potatoes and a handful of raisins by the time Daniel came in. The firelight illuminated her face. The eyes that sought his were wide and uncertain. Her braid had come loose, and hair hung down over her shoulders and back. In the firelight she looked young and slim; she was like a wraith out of a man's dream.

"I'm sorry if I seemed out of sorts. My anger was not directed at you. Never at you, Mercy. I want you to believe that."

There was a silence while Mercy waited until she could trust herself to speak evenly.

"I understand."

"No, you don't understand," Daniel said with unexpected fervor. "But let's drop it for now." His features took on a look of carved stone, and his dark eyes grew cold and unseeing before he turned away from her.

She opened her mouth to reply, but no words came out. Whatever she had been going to say was frozen in the silence of bewilderment.

Daniel ate in silence. Mercy made a halfhearted attempt to eat the sweet potato and to nibble on the raisins. She felt sick, and it was an effort to swallow. While they were drinking their tea Daniel drew a paper from inside his shirt and handed it to her.

"Here's the marriage paper. You should keep it in your carpetbag."

Mercy took it from his hand. Without looking at it, she slipped it down inside her open bag. After several minutes of silence she cleared her throat.

"I've been thinking of what we can do, Daniel. Papa knows people in Kentucky. We can ask him to write to the governor. And, due to the circumstances, he may . . . ah . . . undo this and divorce us."

"Is that what you want?" Daniel's face was inscrutable as he looked into Mercy's eyes. "Do you want to carry the stigma of a divorced woman around with you for the rest of your life? It would certainly limit your chances of marrying again."

"I know you have your own life to live, and I'd rather do that than see you . . . unhappy." Tears flooded her eyes, and she blinked rapidly.

"Dammit! Don't cry again," he said angrily, and got to his feet. He busied himself repacking the food box and shoved it into the corner. "I'll bring in the water and refill the kettle. After you've had a good wash and a night's sleep, you'll feel better."

Mercy wasn't sure if it was anger or hurt she saw in his eyes before he turned from her. She wanted desperately to ask him if he was going to sleep inside the cabin, but his abrupt manner was a barrier between them.

Later, after she had washed and put on her nightdress, she laid out the clothes she would wear the following day. Mercy lay in the bedroll on the platform in the corner of the crude cabin. She wished that she felt free to call out to Daniel, to ask him to bring his bedroll inside. But his last words to her had been said so abruptly that they had thickened the barrier between them. A sense of hopelessness consumed her.

Her mind went back to the night before when she and Daniel had been linked by his hand on her ankle. Had she dreamed it? She must have been dreadfully tired to have supposed, even dreamed, that Daniel's touch was a loving one.

Mercy slept the sleep of exhaustion. When she awakened, daylight was streaming through the open door. Her head was throbbing. She put her hand over her eyes for a moment, to block out the light. When she could see clearly, she looked around the box of a cabin where the most important event in her life had taken place. The little cabin was well built. It had been a home spot for people. It had sheltered them from the weather, given them a place to come back to. But it was not her home, and she couldn't wait to get away from it.

Mercy swung her feet off the bed. The feel of the rough planks against her bare feet brought to her mind the writhing rattlesnake. Her skin prickled; she held her feet up off the floor and reached for her shoes and stockings. She dressed quickly and went to the door.

Daniel squatted beside a small fire he had built in the yard. The carcasses of two rabbits hung on a spit over it, and a delicious aroma tantalized her nostrils. He looked up, saw her, and grinned.

"Hungry?"

"Starved."

"I set a couple of snares last night. If you're a good girl, you can have one of my rabbits."

He was in a better mood this morning. That was the thought that pierced Mercy's mind as she washed her face and hands in the cold water. She took extra time with her hair, letting the short hair dip on her forehead. She brushed the rest of it up and twisted it into an attractive knot that she fastened to the back of her head, allowing one loop to hang on the nape of her neck. She had put on the light blue dress with the white collar. After a hasty trip to the woods behind the house to take care of her bodily needs, she came back through the cabin to wash her hands. Then, wondering what her reception would be, she stepped out into the yard.

"Sleep good?" Daniel asked without looking up. "You look better this morning. You should tie your old dirty dress around your neck or you'll get that one all splattered with meat juice."

"I don't want to meet the Baxters all meat-splattered. Maybe I'll change back into the other dress. I can wear it until we're ready to leave."

"There's no hurry this morning. We can take our time. I saw smoke coming up over that ridge. I suspect we're closer to our destination than I thought."

While she changed back into her soiled dress Mercy thought about the day ahead. Before the sun set again, she would see the place where she was born, and perhaps the woman who was her mother. Strangely she was unconcerned about the meeting. Daniel filled her thoughts. She wanted so badly to have their relationship be as it had been before. Later, much later, when he became used to the idea that he was married to her, he might even learn to love her a little.

She sat on a stump and ate the leg of rabbit. Daniel had cut up her portion and put it on one of the plates from their food box. He was ravenous and ate one whole rabbit by himself, tossing the bones back into the fire.

"Two snares, two rabbits," Mercy said teasingly. "You must be pretty proud of yourself."

"It's no more than I expected." His eyes lit up with mischievous delight.

"You had a good teacher. Admit it."

"I admit it. I had the best. Uncle Juicy taught Farr; Farr taught me."

"I wonder what Papa and Mamma will think of . . . all that's happened."

Daniel made no reply, and Mercy looked off toward the line of timber climbing the hills. They seemed so serene and blue in the quiet morning sun. Somehow she wished they didn't have to go over the hill to that unknown place. Her thoughts raced around and around, in and out, and finally she turned worried eyes to Daniel. He had been watching her but turned his eyes away and picked up his mug of tea when she looked at him.

Before she said anything, Mercy pondered for quite a while about what she would say, and when she did speak, it was not what she wanted to say at all.

"I'm sorry. . ." Mercy was astonished to feel the crimson flush that crept up, up, up, and over her throat and face. She could have cried with mortification, but she remembered his words of last night. "I'm . . . sorry."

Daniel stood and looked down at her. "I don't want you to apologize to me again. What is done is done, and there's nothing we can do about it now. We'll go on just as we have before this . . . thing happened. After we get back home, we'll decide what to do."

Mercy nodded, relief flooding her heart. He was willing to go on as before. It was enough for now.

They traveled across the valley and up the hill between the trees. The grass on either side of the tract seemed alive with small birds whirring up as they passed. Robins flitted from bush to bush, bluejays scolded, and a sparrow diving after a blackbird swooped down in front of them. Piny squirrels chased each other around and around the trunk of a large oak. A red-tailed hawk screeched high over the treetops, protesting their invasion of his territory.

It was a beautiful spring day in the heart of the Kentucky hills.

"Don't be nervous." Daniel's eyes were dark, concerned pools that looked into her bright ones.

"How did you know?" Her eyes did not leave his face.

"By the way your fingers tremble and because you haven't taken a deep breath since I lifted you up on the wagon seat." He reached for her hand, placed it on his thigh, and covered it with his.

"I'm glad you're not mad anymore," she said urgently.

"I was never angry at you. I was angry at them, and disgusted with myself for letting us get into such a fix." His voice held a baffled regret.

"What will you do?"

"To Lenny and Bernie? Nothing now, but before we leave here, I'm going to do my level best to see that they gum their food for the rest of their lives."

Mercy smiled. "I want to see it. I might want to get in a few licks myself."

"You'll have to be faster than you were with Glenn Knibee."

"I learned my lesson. I'll get my licks in first." Mercy laughed, yet there were tears in her laughter: tears of happiness because there was a new understanding between her and her love, even if he was unaware of it. As long as he didn't hate and resent her, there was hope that someday he would love her.

They came up over a ridge to see a house and several outbuildings nestled among the trees not a quarter of a mile ahead. Two gray mules were tied beneath a spreading oak.

"Could this be it?" Mercy asked. "I thought we'd pass through Mud Creek, the settlement they were always talking about."

"Mud Creek could be beyond." Daniel pulled his hat down to shade his eyes when the trail turned slightly east.

"This is the Baxter place. I've been looking at the back end of those mules for a hundred miles. I'd know them anywhere."

Smoke curled up from a rock chimney that soared up above the steep, slanting roof of the house, which was built of rough, heavy timber. The chinking between the logs, which had once been white, had long since weathered to a soft, mellow gray. The house sat high off the ground on blocks, and covered by the slanting roof was a porch stretching along the front. Two front doors stood open to the morning sun. Mercy would see the figure of a woman standing in one of them.

The ground surrounding the house was bare, except for a few clumps of bushes. Chickens, two dozen or more, picked and scratched in the dirt. Blue-blossomed vines climbed thickly over a stump beside the huge woodpile. A rosebush clambered valiantly up the cobblestones of the chimney. Mercy could see a shed attached to the back of the house. In the area between the house and the creek were a smokehouse, several three-sided sheds, a garden, and a pole enclosure for hogs.

"It looks like it's been here for a long, long time," Mercy murmured. She turned her palm up and gripped Daniel's hand tightly.

Bernie led the mules to the back of the house as they approached. Dogs darted out from under the porch and barked furiously, then slunk back under the porch when Lenny came out and shouted at them.

Several people followed Lenny to the porch: a woman with a babe in her arms; a man who was larger, older version of Lenny, and several children. Two small children ran screeching to the vine-covered stump, climbed on top, and stood staring at them. One, a girl with two fingers in her mouth, pushed the smaller child, a boy, off the stump. He fell but climbed back on.

Daniel stopped the wagon beneath the tree. While he

tied Zelda to a hitching rail Mercy took off her white shawl, folded it, and placed it on the seat. She didn't want to appear to be too well dressed.

"Are you all right?" Daniel murmured when he lifted her down.

"I'm fine." She felt strangely detached, and it showed in the lift of her chin and eyes. She looked calmly at the group on the porch. She smiled faintly at Daniel and took his hand.

Daniel thought she had never looked lovelier. She was regally beautiful, calm and serene. At this moment he was enormously proud that she was his wife, even if the ceremony had been forced upon them.

They passed the children on the stump, and Mercy smiled at them. "Hello," she said softly.

"Are ya Hester?" the girl shouted after they passed.

Lenny stayed on the porch beside the woman holding the baby, and the other man came to meet them. He was almost as tall as Daniel, and heavier. His face was clean-shaven, but his straw-colored hair was long and unkempt. He wore a shirt made from homespun, and his britches were held up by leather straps that crossed in front, as well as in the back. His piercing blue eyes honed in on Mercy's face.

"Lenny says you're Hester."

"It appears that I am."

"You've got the mole on yer eye. Lenny says ya've got the Baxter brown spot too."

"Yes."

"I'm Hod Baxter."

"I'm called Mercy, and this is Daniel Phelps."

Daniel held out his hand.

While Hod shook hands with Daniel he looked him over closely, sizing him up. Not many men topped Hod in height or had shoulders as wide. Daniel gave him back look for look, and Hod finally turned back to Mercy.

"Maw's holdin' on. We mostly give up that the boys'd find ya 'n' fetch ya home in time."

"Does she know I'm . . . here?"

"We ain't tol' her. C'mon in."

When they stepped up onto the porch, Lenny moved quickly to the other end. Both Mercy and Daniel ignored him.

"Hello," Mercy said quietly to the woman holding the baby.

The woman acknowledged her greeting with a slight bob of her head. She was large and robust and looked as if she could do a man's work. There was no softness about her. Her hair was slicked back in a knot so tight, it seemed to pull at the corners of her eyes. Her dress was a faded brown linsey that had seen much wear, the bodice soiled by milk that had leaked from her heavy breasts. In spite of all this, Mercy could see compassion in her soft brown eyes.

Hod went through the door and beckoned to Mercy.

She tugged on Daniel's hand. "Come with me, Daniel."

The room was large with an open door as well as an open window on the back. Deer antlers were attached to the wall beside the back door, and a familiar, peaked leather hat swung from one of the horns. A massive stone fireplace was set into the wall at the end of the room, and a log crackled and popped on the grate in spite of the open door and the open window. A frame bedstead sat in the middle of the room across from the back window, its head against the front wall. A handmade hickory rocker sat beside it, and farther along the wall was a four-drawer chest with two smaller drawers at the top. On the mantel, strangely out of place in its crude surroundings, a massive, elaborately carved wooden clock with a glass door, its pendulum swaying gently back and forth.

Mercy was only vaguely aware of all these things. It was as if she were off someplace looking down on things that were not quite real. Her eyes were on the face of the woman on the bed, and the woman's eyes were on her. Her slight body made only a small hump beneath the patchwork quilt that covered her. The skin on her face was soft and white, with scarcely any wrinkles. Her snow-white hair lay in soft curls around her small-boned face. Her eyes were large and as blue as the sky.

Hod went to the bed and knelt down beside it. "Maw," he said low-voiced and gently. "Looky here who's come home."

The woman's gaze remained on Mercy's face. "I know. It's Hester." Her voice was barely above a whisper. Tears filled her eyes, overflowed, and ran from the corners into the hair at her temple.

Hod got to his feet, and Daniel urged Mercy forward. She dropped to her knees beside the bed and took her mother's frail hand in both of hers. Blue eyes looked into blue eyes for a long moment.

"Hello . . . Mamma." Tears filled Mercy's eyes and rolled down her cheeks. All the resentment she had felt toward the Baxters for disrupting her life faded into nothing in the instant she saw the look of joy come over her mother's face.

"I've been waitin' fer ya to come home."

"I'd have come sooner if I'd known about you."

"Yore as purty as ya ever was. I'da knowed ya in a crowd."

"And you're just like I hoped my real mother would be."

"That mole on yore eye got a mite bigger."

"I expect it has."

"And ya got the brown spot on yer hinder?"

"Yes, ma'am."

"I pined fer ya, Hester." The soft lips trembled but held firm.

"I've had a good life. I've been with good people. I'll tell you all about them."

"I never gave up on ya. I knowed someday you'd come." Her mouth turned down like a child's, as if she no longer had the strength to hold it straight. She closed her eyes and cried silently.

"I'm here now, Mamma. Don't cry." Mercy held her mother's hand to her cheek and fought her own tears. She was conscious that Daniel stood close behind her, and that Hod stood at the head of the bed, as if to protect his mother from the strangers.

The storm of tears passed, and Mercy wiped her mother's soft cheeks with a hankerchief she drew from her pocket.

"I'm . . . a-thinkin' ya got ya a good strong man, Hester."

"Yes, ma'am." Mercy tugged on Daniel's pant leg, and he knelt down beside her. "This is Daniel."

"Hello, Mrs. Baxter."

"Yer big, like my William was. He was strong as a bull, gentle as a lamb, but meaner'n sin when riled. Air ya takin' good care a Hester?"

"Yes, ma'am. I'm doin' my best."

"That's all a body can ask," she said tiredly. "I like the looks of ya."

"Thank you, ma'am."

"You got any younguns, Hester?"

"No, Mamma."

"I take it he knows what to do to get 'em. Ain't never seen no man what didn't. He looks to have good sproutin' seed in 'em. He'll give ya younguns."

"That's what I've been telling her, Mrs. Baxter," Daniel said smoothly, and nudged Mercy's knee with his.

"His eyes ain't too close together, neither. It's the sign of a providin' man."

Mercy turned to look at Daniel. "I hadn't noticed."

He slipped his arm across her shoulders, gave her a smile and a brief hug. He picked his hat up off the floor and got to his feet. "I'll tend to the horses if you'll tell me where to put them," he said to Hod.

"Hod, where's yer manners?" Mrs. Baxter said, as if speaking to a small child. "Show Daniel where to put the horses."

"I just now been asked, Maw."

"Don't ya be givin' no sass, Hod. Where's Lenny? Tell 'em to go kill some chickens. Tell Marthy to . . . slice up a ham and cook a cobbler. We got a . . . homecomin' to plan." She became breathless and had to stop talking.

"You needn't put on anything special for us," Mercy said quickly, getting to her feet slowly because her legs were numb from kneeling so long.

"Maw still rules this roost," Hod said firmly. "If she says have special fixin's, we have special fixin's."

"Of course, I only meant . . ."

Hod went out and Daniel followed.

"Hester?" The weak voice came from the bed. "Pull up the rocker and set a spell."

"I don't want to tire you."

"Sit," she commanded, and Mercy sank down in the rocker. "I just ain't believin' yore here. There's so much to tell ya, so much to hear."

"We can talk later if you want to rest for a while."

Her mother rolled her head back and forth on the pillow. "Soon I'll be . . . restin' for . . ." Her words trailed away and her lids drooped.

Alarmed, Mercy jumped to her feet and bent over her. The skin on her face had taken on a bluish tinge.

"She drops off like that."

Mercy looked up to see Hod's wife standing in the doorway. She came to the end of the bed.

"She's asleep? Oh, thank goodness! It scared me."

"She ain't got no strength a-tall." Martha went to the

side of the bed and gently lifted Mrs. Baxter's hand and covered it with the quilt. "She be a-sinkin' fast," she said sadly.

"What's the matter with her?"

"When her man was took, she jist give up. When she come down with a fever, she hardly had no flesh on her bones a-tall. It jist cooked up what was left, 'spite of all the doctorin' we could do. Maw says she ain't goin' ta get up." Martha put her hand to her chest. "I reckon her heart's plumb wore out." She tiptoed to the door.

"Martha"—Mercy followed her out onto the porch—"I want to be a help to you."

The big, plain woman looked at Mercy, and her eyes settled on the lace collar of her dress.

"Why, I don't know nary a thing ya can do," she said slowly. "I done sent Lenny out to kill the chickens, 'n' Dora's comin' with a mess of greens."

"Dora?"

"Wyatt's woman. She's havin' another youngun 'n' she ain't up to snuff, but she's willin'."

Daniel came to the porch with Mercy's carpetbag. "Where do you want this?"

Mercy looked at Martha. "I'd like to change out of my good dress." It suddenly occurred to her that Martha thought she was dressed too fine to help.

"Maw. . ." The small girl came around the side of the house with the baby astraddle her hip. "He's messed! It's a-runnin' down."

"Hold him jist a minute more. We'll take 'em down to the creek and wash him up," Martha said patiently, and turned back to Mercy. "Ya can go up to the loft. It's where the boys sleep, but they ain't there. I thought ta bed ya 'n' yer man in the eatin' room. It's the best bed."

"No," Mercy said quickly, hoping the color that rose to her cheeks went unnoticed. "You needn't do that. Daniel and I can spread our bedrolls outside."

Martha looked shocked. "Company sleep out? Maw'd be plumb 'shamed," she said, and her mouth snapped shut like a clam.

"But where do you sleep?"

"I been stayin' here nights. Hod takes the younguns on to our place."

"You don't live here?"

"We got a cabin out yonder a ways. Go on up to the loft if ya want to. Maw'll think she dreamed ya if she wakes up 'n' ya ain't there."

"I'll take the bag up for you," Daniel said when Martha walked away with the little girl and the baby.

"I can take it."

"You'd better look at the ladder first," he said with raised brows.

They went into the eating room. It was larger that the other room and had an even larger fireplace at the end. A large assortment of cook pots, ladles, trivets, and scoops hung close to the fireplace. A long plank was fastened waist-high to the wall, and on it were wooden bowls and kitchen equipment. Beneath the work shelf were several baskets and some tall covered tins. The table with benches on each side sat in the middle of the room. Two three-legged stools, a cupboard build against the wall, and a platform bed in the corner made up the furnishings.

At the far end of the room, in the corner opposite the bed, a ladder stretched up into a hole in the ceiling floor. Built about a foot from the wall, the ladder went straight up. When she saw it, Mercy understood why Daniel had offered to take the bag up for her.

"Can you make it up there?" he murmured close to her ear.

"I'll have to."

"Let me go first. I'll reach down and give you a hand."

Daniel went up easily, as Mercy knew he would. She

climbed the first few rungs of the ladder, trying to keep from stepping on her skirt. She hung there until Daniel reached down and grasped her hand. After that it was easy, and soon she was hauled up into the nearly dark loft.

"Heavens! I hope I don't have to do that often."

Mercy looked around at the pallets scattered on the floor, the clothes, the personal belongings of the Baxter brothers. She wrinkled her nose at the odor of unwashed bedclothes and dirty feet. Daniel had turned to back down the ladder. Mercy put her hand on his arm.

"Daniel, I'm so glad I came to see her."

"I thought you would be."

"Have you seen Lenny or Bernie?"

"They're keeping their distance. Hod seems to be more reasonable. Don't worry about me. Enjoy your visit with your mother."

Mercy wanted desperately to ask him what they were going to do about the sleeping arrangements, but she couldn't find the words. He had heard what Martha had said. Maybe by night he would think of something.

"I don't want to leave my bag up here. I'm afraid mice will get in it."

"Change your dress and hand it down to me. I'll be waiting below."

As soon as Daniel's head disappeared, Mercy quickly changed into her brown work dress, carefully folded the blue one and put it back in the bag. She didn't want to stay in the loft any longer than she had to. When she was ready to leave, she leaned over the hole in the floor and looked down. Daniel was there looking up.

Mercy dropped the bag and Daniel caught it. "Back down," he said. "I'll guide your feet."

It was far easier going down than it was going up. When her feet touched solid floor, Mercy turned and leaned for a delicious moment against the only familiar thing in this whole, new, strange world.

"It ain't so bad, is it?" Daniel murmured, and cuddled her against him.

"No. But I'd not be able to bear it without you. It's all so strange. Yet I came from this place. I was born here. She's my mother, and I've got a father buried somewhere nearby."

"It will all get straight in your mind. Just take things a little at a time."

They heard something drop and roll across the sagging, uneven floor, and Mercy moved reluctantly from Daniel's arms.

A woman stood beside the table staring at them. Her eyes flicked to the wooden bowl on the floor, then back. She was young and pregnant. Her dress was hitched up in front, leaving her bare legs exposed halfway to her knees. The corners of her wide mouth tilted, as if it were used to smiling. The skin was taut over her cheekbones. Dark, rough, springy hair was clubbed at the back of her neck. Her expressive eyes were as dark as soot but held a bright flame as they looked straight into Mercy's. Then she smiled, and her face lit up like sunlight. It was the first smile Mercy had seen from any of the Baxters since she and Daniel had arrived.

"Hello. I'm called Mercy. I was once called... Hester."

"I figgered ya was. Ya jist had to be Hester. I'm Dora. Wyatt's my man. My, yore purty. Yer jist the purtiest thin' I ever did see! Lordy! The horny men in these hill'll go plumb loony when they set their sights on ya."

"Well... thank you." *I guess*, Mercy added to herself.

"This yore man?" Dora asked, then answered herself before Mercy could speak. "'Course he is. Wouldn'ta come if he warn't. I just can't get over how purty ya are, 'n' how fine yore dress is. Ya got on store-bought shoes! Now ain't that something? Bernie said ya was sightly, but Bernie's as muddleheaded as a horny goose most a the time. Ever'body 'round here knows that 'n' pays him no mind."

If Dora thought this dress fine, Mercy wondered what she would think of the blue one. At least she'll talk, she thought, and cast her twinkling eyes in Daniel's direction. He was smiling too.

"I'll get on outside." Daniel's hand lingered on her arm.

Dora's eyes followed Daniel out the door. "Lordy, Hester. Ya got yourself a real eye-buster. He's about the most man I've clapped my eyes on fer a spell. Ha! Wyatt thinks he's the best-lookin' thin' in these parts. He'll be mad enough to kick a stump when he sees yore man."

"Daniel is handsome and . . . kind, and very dear to me."

"Love 'em, do ya?"

Mercy looked into the girl's open, smiling face, and decided she liked her very much. "Yes," she said simply.

"Now, ain't that nice? Maw loved Paw Baxter somethin' fierce. It tore her up when he was took." Dora looked over her shoulder when Martha came in with the baby on her hip. "I got the greens, Marthy. I washed 'em down at the creek."

"Wyatt 'n' the boys workin' on the barrels?"

"No. Hod put 'em ta pullin' stumps. How'd Maw take ta seein' Hester?"

"Took it good. Go in 'n' set with her, Hester. I'll put this youngun down and clean them chickens Lenny killed."

The floorboards under Mercy's feet suddenly shook, a dog growled menacingly, followed by more heavy thuds beneath the floor. Martha picked up a piece of firewood and thumped the floor. The growling stopped.

"Hogs root under the house," Dora explained. "Sometimes they get to fightin' with the dogs 'n' make a racket enough to wake the dead."

"Best way ta keep snakes outa the house, to my way of thinkin'," Marthy said.

"Do you have a lot of . . . snakes?"

"I ain't seen many lately. Hogs keep 'em cleaned out."

"I'd better see if Maw's woke up." Dora went into the other room.

Mercy followed Dora and stood at the end of the bed while the small, dark-haired woman went to the side and leaned over.

"Ye've waked up," she crooned as if to a baby. "Now, ain't ya glad ya let me brush yore hair this mornin'? If I'da minded ya, ya woulda looked like a burr head 'n' scared Hester silly."

Mercy watched Dora smile fondly at her mother-in-law and thought that she must be a special woman to command so much love from her sons and their wives.

"Yer jist talkin' to hear yore head rattle, gal."

"'Course. Didn't Wyatt say he brung me home 'cause ya needed sunshine 'n' foolishness?"

The sky-blue eyes looked pointedly at Dora's bulging belly, then to Mercy.

"That ain't why he brung her."

"There ya go, tellin' tales on Wyatt," Dora said, teasing. "Is there something ya want, Maw? If there ain't, Hester'll sit with ya 'n' I'll give Marthy a hand after I go see about my youngun."

"Is your sister here?"

"Wyatt fetched her to stay a spell. Ya want the shutters pushed back so ya can see the trees?"

Dora adjusted the shutters and left the room. Mercy drew the hickory rocker up close to the bed and sat down. Now that she was alone with her mother, she didn't know what to say.

"Ya feelin' kinda at odds, Hester?"

Mercy smiled. "How did you know?"

"Ya got a pucker to yore brow like Will had."

"Tell me about him."

"He fetched me here when I warn't more'n fourteen. This here was the purtiest, wildest place ya ever saw. Turkeys come right up to the door, deer, elk, and possum aplenty. Big, Will was. Me 'n' him . . . built this . . . place." Her breath left her, and she had to rest.

"The land is flat back in Illinois where I've been living," Mercy said to fill the void.

"It pert nigh kilt Will when he went to fetch ya home, 'n' the folks was all dead 'n' no sign of ya." Mrs. Baxter rolled her head on the pillow and looked out the window. He was powerful cut up over it 'n' grieved 'n' grieved. It was a bad time."

Mercy leaned over and took her hand. "I was found in the cellar by a man named Farrway Quill. They had put me there to keep me safe. He said they were killed by river pirates for the oxen and the horses. He didn't know what to do with me. He thought my folks had been killed, so he took me home with him."

"They was good to ya?"

"Very good. They raised me as if I were their own."

"I'm glad to hear it." Her lids drooped, and Mercy thought she had fallen asleep. Soon she opened her eyes and said, "I've got yore Paw's death crown. I knowed he'd have one. He was a strong-willed man. It was in the pillow he died on. I want ya to have it."

Mercy looked puzzled. "What is it? You found something in his pillow?"

"Ain't ya never heard of a death crown?"

"No, ma'am."

"Landsakes! Get in the bottom drawer in the chest 'n' get out that wood box on this end."

Mercy found the small, square box and took it to the bed. It was made from thin sheets of wood smoothed to a satiny finish. A rose was carved on the top. A faded ribbon was wrapped around it and tied with a bow.

Mrs. Baxter ran her fingers over the top of the box. "Hod made this here box. He done good. Open it up, Hester."

Mercy untied the ribbon and lifted up the lid. Inside was a group of feathers formed in a knot about the size and the shape of a clenched fist set on end. The white-and-gray feathers were swirled in the same direction, even on the top.

"Any loose ones in the bottom?"

Mercy tilted the box and looked closely. "No. They're all stuck in this . . . knot."

"There is feathers in the bottom of the box sometimes. Other times they're all put back where they ort ta be 'n' not a loose one a-tall. Pick it up. Ya can hold it."

Mercy's fingers closed around it. She lifted it out of the box and placed it on the palm of her hand. It was a *solid* ball of feathers. Each of the gray-and-white goose feathers was firmly in place. She stroked the smooth top of the knot with her fingertip. Never had she seen anything or heard of anything like it.

"There's times when I hold it, I can feel Will's heart a beatin', beatin', beatin'." The eyes that looked into Mercy's were clear, or she would have thought her mother's mind was wandering. "Will fought the black hand a-pullin' him. He warn't wantin' to leave me behind. He knowed how I'd take on."

"What do you think it means?" Mercy asked.

"Why . . . it means dyin' ain't the end. What was put in graveyard warn't nothin' but Will's shell. He's here." She lifted her hand and moved her fingers as if she were caressing something. "Times is . . . I can see him sittin' in . . . his chair, or feel him on the bed a-huggin' me. He's in the . . . boys. In you, Hester. Ya was his seed, 'n' I growed ya for him. Ah . . . Will, Will . . ." Her voice trailed away, but her mouth made movements as if she were still speaking.

When her mother's mouth stilled, Mercy placed the ball of feathers back in the box and tied the lid in place. She returned it to the drawer and sat back down in the chair. Her mother's eyes were closed. She was sleeping.

CHAPTER TWELVE

Daniel wiped the sweat from his forehead with the sleeve of his shirt, placed his foot up on the stump, and leaned on the ax handle. He had split wood for the past hour. He welcomed the labor. It was not in him to sit idle. Hod had been polite but had not invited him to go along when he left the homestead and disappeared in the timber along the creek. Daniel suspected that was where the still was located.

The homestead was well laid out. Daniel slowly and methodically surveyed the area. North of the house, a good piece of flat land was planted in corn. Hod had told him that there was another patch of corn beyond the screen of cedars to the west, and that his cabin was there. Wyatt had a cabin in the hills across the creek. A well-tended garden spot, over which hung strings of cloth fluttering in the breeze to scare away the birds, was between the house and the fast-moving creek that flowed from north to south between the homestead and the hills. Old Man Baxter had placed his home so that it was shielded from the north wind by the hills, had plenty of water, and judging from the looks of the thickly timbered hills, game.

Daniel watched the two Baxter women working at the outdoor cook fire. Martha had set a flat iron pan in the oven. The oven was like the ones he had seen used in the Arkansas Territory.

A stump had been hewn perfectly flat on the top with a slab hewn out and laid upon it. On this was spread a thick layer of clay. A wooden frame of hickory was made in the shape of an oven and filled with wood. It was placed on the clay slab. The frame, except for a small opening at one end, was covered with a thick layer of clay and set out to dry. After it had stood several days, the wood inside was set on fire and burned out. The clay oven was then used over a slow fire or placed among hot coals.

Daniel carried several armloads of split wood to the well-used, three-sided stone-and-mortar fireplace and stacked it nearby.

"Thanky." Martha looked up and then away.

"There's sweet potatoes, raisins, sorghum syrup, and a few other things in the box on the porch," Daniel said. "They should be used, or they'll spoil if left in that hot box."

Martha nodded but didn't say anything. Daniel went back to work on the woodpile. An hour passed, and she hadn't gone near the box on the porch.

"Poor and proud," Daniel murmured to himself. He chose a piece of pine and swung the ax down. He let the feel of the pine splitting run up his arm. It was a good feeling: something done, something completed. He selected another chunk of wood and set it upright on the wood block. Work was what he needed right now, work to keep his thoughts at bay.

Later, when Mercy came out onto the porch, he stopped and leaned on the ax handle again. He could not describe how he felt when they were apart and he could stand back and look at her. He had not wanted this to happen to him. The gut-wrenching feeling that came over him now was pure misery. Her brothers had forced him upon her. At the moment when they were united in marriage, he had lost the thing he wanted most, her love. He remembered his heart-stopping fear when Bernie pulled the snake out of the bag, and the look of terror in Mercy's eyes. Just thinking about it made him cold with fear. His fear now summoned up his anger, and he vowed to beat Bernie and Lenny to within an inch of their lives before he left this place.

Daniel watched Mercy move across the yard to where Martha stood at the cook fire. He felt that he knew Mercy as well as he knew himself, yet he had never felt the weight of her breasts in his hands, or stroked the satiny skin of her thighs. Hunger for her had gnawed at him for weeks. The desire to touch her had been overwhelming the night they'd camped out under the stars. His hand, as if acting independently of his brain, had burrowed beneath the blanket to hold her warm, slim ankle. His touch had not awakened her, and he had lain awake thinking of what it would be like to have her move down into his arms: naked; sweet-smelling; her soft arms around him; his aching flesh buried in the sweet, dark cavern of her body.

Mercy looked his way and waved.

It had not occurred to him that she would suggest that they be divorced. His mind skittered away from the thought as if it would bite him. They were wed, and it was now up to him to see that she wanted to stay wed to him. At times he thought he glimpsed something in her eyes that made him think she returned his love. At other times he was sure that what she felt for him was the fondness a sister had for an older brother because she was not nearly as shy with him as he was with her.

The kiss they had shared after the wedding had jarred him to the center of his being. Every inch of his skin had come alive, and wild tremors of passion surged through him, sending a primitive need to feel himself enclosed within her warmth. His muscles had knotted with strain as reasoning took control. He had forced himself away from her before she felt the insistence of that part of him that had leapt to life and begged for release. Thinking about it, Daniel felt his body tighten, his breath quicken, and his male member come alive. He was hopelessly, desperately in love with her, and wondered if he had the strength to endure the time it would take for her to become used to the fact that they were husband and wife before he declared his love.

Two hours after the sun had reached its zenith, the Baxter brothers came back to the homestead. They lined up at the wash trough. The trough, hollowed out of a poplar log, sat on a shelf attached to the back of the house. They washed, smoothed down their wiry straw-colored hair, and tiptoed into the room where their mother lay.

The women had carried the kitchen table to the yard. It was set and ready for the meal. Martha brought to the table the iron pot of cooked chicken with fat bread dumplings floating in the broth. Dora followed with a platter heaped with slabs of fried ham. There was red-eye gravy, hominy, boiled beans, greens, and corn bread with plenty of butter, and honey in the comb. Martha had made a juicy cobbler from dried apples and a sauce flavored with whiskey to go over it. She explained to Mercy that the reason for the late meal was that the men were taking the rest of the day off from their work to celebrate her homecoming.

Mercy was surprised to see Hob carry his mother, snugly wrapped in the quilt, out of the house and into the yard. He walked slowly along the table so she could view the repast. She looked like a small child, except for her thick gray hair. Martha and Dora stood by, as if awaiting her approval. She was quick to give praise.

"Ya done real good, Marthy, for havin' no more time than ya had. Land, but yore good at fixin' up greens. Ya make that old hominy look good too."

"Yore the one what made that old hominy, Maw."

"I see yore hand in . . . the fixin's, Dory. Ain't that some a the honey ya . . . made Wyatt get the time he got . . . stung."

"Yes, ma'am. That little old sting didn't hurt him none. Ya want I bring ya some on some corn bread?"

Mercy and Daniel stood apart from the family and watched them gather around her mother. Wyatt and Gideon, the two brothers she hadn't met, had given them only a curious glance. All their attention was on the woman Hod held in his arms. Even the children who had raced and played in the yard stood quietly and watched.

Hod carried his mother back inside, and the brothers followed. Soon Mercy understood why. The men had picked up their mother's bed and moved it so she could look out the door. Martha hurried in to put more covers over her.

When the men came out again, Wyatt came directly to Mercy. He had smooth, suntanned skin; a wide, generous mouth; and good teeth. His hair was thick and bushy but not as wiry as that of his brothers. He had a blond mustache, merry blue eyes, and an infectious grin.

"Now ain't ya jist as purty as a June bug? I was thinkin' I was the only Baxter what was good ta look at."

"Don't pay him no mind, Hester," Dora said in passing. "He ain't near as handsome as yore man."

Wyatt turned his grin on his wife and playfully nipped her bottom with his fingers. "Yore lible to get a switchin' fer that, Dorybelle."

"Hello." Mercy held out her hand. "Have you met Daniel?"

"No, I ain't. But I heared plenty." He extended his hand to Daniel. "I hear ya hunt bear with a willow switch."

Daniel laughed. "Not quite."

"I'm Gid."

The boy who spoke was as tall as Wyatt but whiplash thin. He was the handsome one in the family. Mercy saw that at once. She realized that Gideon was well aware of that fact also, and was plenty proud of himself. His hair was very blond, as fine as silk and carefully brushed back from his forehead. His features were not as rugged as his brothers', and when he smiled, his face lit up.

"Hello, Gideon." Mercy held out her hand. The boy took it in both of his and smiled into her eyes.

"Hello, Hester." He spoke as if she were the only person in the world. Mercy knew immediately that this was part of his charm, the charm that allowed him to do what Lenny and Bernie had bragged about. She felt a strong desire to let him know she thought him an irresponsible child.

"Practicin', Gid?" Wyatt hit his brother so hard on the back, the boy took a step toward Mercy. "Charmin' womenfolk is his way a-passin' the time. He do love womenfolk. Ain't that right, Gid, boy?"

"Y'all quit yore jawin'. It's eatin' time." Dora came up beside her husband, and he threw an arm across her shoulders. "Stay way from Emmajean, Gid." Dora said bluntly. "My sister ain't but twelve. I ain't havin' ya diddlin' with her 'n' ruinin', like ya done the Morgan girl."

Gideon laughed. "Then ya better tell her to stay way from me, Dorybelle."

"Take yore places," Hod roared.

After the men were seated, there was one place left. Martha and Dora stood ready to serve, and the children lined up behind Hod with a plate in their hands.

"I'll wait and eat with Martha and Dora," Mercy said when Hod waved her toward the vacant place beside Daniel. Bernie and Lenny had moved as far away from him as was possible.

"Sit down, Hester. This here's yore homecomin'."

While Mercy was taking her place the dogs slunk out from under the porch. Hod's roar sent them scampering back. Then he stood and held his palms together in front of him.

"God, it was good a ya to send our sister, Hester, home. We thank ya fer it. We ain't never been askin' ya fer much, but food fer our belly 'n' wood fer our fire. Now we be askin' ya fer somethin' that means a heap to us. We be wantin' ya to make our Maw's passin' easy. And when she gets over thar, we want ya to let 'er meet up first off with our Paw, 'cause it's with him she's wantin' ta be. Thanky fer the food, 'n' fer keepin' us all fit. Amen."

Mercy's throat was so full of sobs, she thought she would choke. She raised her eyes and looked at her brothers. Their eyes were closed. Hod finished the prayer, sat down, and began to fill the children's plates.

As the late afternoon turned into evening, Mercy was as tired as she had ever been in her entire life. She wondered how Martha stood up to the work. The only time she had sat down was when she nursed her baby. Dora worked alongside Martha, doing the lighter chores. Both women insisted that Mercy sit with her mother, whose bed had been moved back from the door.

Daniel visited with Hod and Wyatt. The older Baxters seemed interested in what he had to say about farming, and asked him questions about his mill. Bernie and Lenny sat at the other end of the porch, played with the children, and every once in a while sent one of them for the whiskey jug being passed between Hod and Wyatt. They had offered the jug to Daniel and laughed when the fiery drink took his breath away. The strong drink didn't seem to affect the Baxters. But after the first few swigs Daniel's speech began to slur, and he realized he'd had enough.

Mercy came out of the house at dusk. The hills

seemed to close in when the sun went down. Both Wyatt and Hod held sleeping children in their arms.

"How's Maw?" Hod asked.

"Sleeping again. She's eaten very little today."

"She ain't et enough to keep a bird alive fer a week now."

"It seems she's having a harder time getting her breath than when we first arrived," Mercy said worriedly.

"I noticed it," Hod said.

Dora came hurrying around the end of the house and made straight for Wyatt. "I can't find Emmajean, 'n' I can't find Gid. If he's taken her off 'n' crawled on her, I'm goin' to fix him so's he won't be ruttin' fer a while. What he needs is a horsewhippin'."

"I thought Emmajean went off to put Hod's younguns to bed."

"She didn't. Hod's younguns is in there sleepin' on a pallet. Where's Bernie? Where's Lenny?"

"Gone to bed, I reckon."

"Damn that Gid! I told Emmajean what he was like. She ain't used to havin' a feller courtin' her. He's a horny little toad, is what he is! He's going to get somebody killed sure as shootin' if'n he don't quit droppin' his britches ever' time he sees a woman."

"Calm down, Dorybelle." Wyatt shifted the sleeping child over onto Daniel's lap and got to his feet.

"Calm down! If it was yore sister Gid was fornicatin' with, ya'd bash his head in. Then you 'n' Hod'd wear yore tails off runnin' fer the preacher!"

"Yore makin' a lot outa nothin'," Wyatt said patiently. "Gid ain't never took no woman what wasn't willin'. Me 'n' Hod'd bash his head, 'n' he knows it. But if'n yore so all-fired worried, c'mon, we'll go find Emmajean."

Mercy's face burned with embarrassment. The Baxters were the plainest-talking people she'd ever been around. There was just nothing they didn't talk about. She looked down at Daniel. He didn't seem to be uncomfortable at all holding the sleeping child. She thanked God for his quiet presence. She moved up close behind him and placed her hand on his shoulder, as if he were the only steady thing in a tilting world. He looked up. Their eyes met. There was no need for words between them.

Hod's sudden laughter drew Mercy's attention.

"If thar's a skirt in a mile, ya can bet that Gid'll be under it if he gets half a chance. He's the horniest little sucker I ever knowed!"

"And you think that's funny?" Mercy asked coldly. She looked down her nose at her brother. Disapproval was evident in the way she held her head and in the clipped way she spoke. Daniel knew the signs. Mercy was getting her back up.

"Well . . . it ain't nothin' to be 'shamed for."

"And you think it's an admirable trait?"

"What're ya talkin' about?"

"How would you like to have a 'horny little sucker' like Gid violate your daughters?" Mercy's anger was making her speak her mind, regardless of the consequences.

"Violate?"

"Do wrong to . . . misuse."

Hod was taken back by her frankness and didn't answer for a minute. "I reckon it'd depend on if'n she wanted it. If'n she did, it'd be all right. But he'd make it right."

"By making it right, you mean you'd force her to marry him, and she'd have to live with the 'horny little sucker' for the rest of her life while he continued to beget bastards?"

"We have our ways here," Hod said, his voice rising with anger.

"I see that you do." Mercy's voice matched his in tone.

"What're ya gettin' so het up fer? It be a natural thin' a man be doin'." There was a puzzled look on Hod's face.

He really doesn't know! The thought crossed Mercy's mind. It was beyond her understanding how a father could talk so about his daughter. It puzzled her that they could love their mother so much, yet put such a small value on the virtue of a young girl. Her lips formed the question, but it was not voiced.

Dora came around the end of the house with her hand firmly attached to the arm of a young girl who was crying. Wyatt followed, pushing his brother in front of him. Gideon showed none of the shamefacedness that would be expected under these circumstances. He walked like a proud little rooster, and he was grinning broadly.

Dora reached up and yanked straw out of the girl's hair. "I warned ya, Emmajean. Yore goin' home come sunup. I ain't got no time to be ridin' yore tail to keep Gid off'n it."

"I don't know why yore in a lather, Dorybelle. I didn't do nothin' but kiss her a little."

"Jist shut yore mouth, Gid Baxter! I know what ya done, 'n' I know what ya was tryin' to do. Wyatt snatched ya off afore ya had time to do it." Dora put her hand on her hip and shook her finger in Gid's face. "All the brains ya got is in that thin' hangin' 'tween yore legs, Gid! Beats me why yore so all-fired proud of it. It ain't like yore the only man in the world what's got one. I'm hopin' ya get it caught in somethin' 'n' it get tore right off ya, afore ya ruin ever girl in these hills!"

"Ohhh! Ohhh!" Gid grabbed his privates and staggered back in a dramatic show of misery. "Don't even think such a thing, Dorybelle." He glanced at Mercy to see if she was enjoying his performance.

Mercy decided then and there that she didn't like this younger brother who had nothing but fornication on his mind. Her mouth tightened, and she looked away from him. Hod's sharp eyes read the message of disgust on her face.

"Stop actin' the fool, Gid," he said sharply. "Let Emmajean be. If'n yore itch is such ya can't abide it, find one what's willin' to oblige ya."

"She was willin' enough. It ain't like she ain't been used." Gid grinned openly at the still sobbing girl who hid her face behind Dora.

"That's a lie," Dora shouted.

"Why's it a lie about her? It warn't no lie 'bout you, Dorybelle! Yore belly was all puffed out when Wyatt brung ya home," Gid said nastily.

"Shut your mouth, boy!" Wyatt said quietly. "Ya talk respectful to my wife. Hear?"

"Emmajean's goin' home at sunup," Dora said staunchly. "Pa'll handle Gid if he goes smellin' 'round over there." Dora took her sleeping child from Daniel's arms. "We'll be goin' on home now. You comin', Wyatt?"

"Soon's I look in on Maw."

Hod, carrying one sleeping child and leading two more, went home to the cabin behind the pines. Martha had prepared a pallet for herself and her baby on the floor beside Mrs. Baxter's bed, leaving the bed in the kitchen for Mercy and Daniel. Mercy had tried to convince her that she could look after her mother through the night, but Martha had insisted in her quiet way that it was more "fit" that she get a good night's sleep after such a long journey. Mercy had watched her bring a pan of warm water and a clean rag and bathe her mother's face. For such a big woman, Martha had a gentle touch, and it was obvious that she loved the frail little woman. Mrs. Baxter had been still and trusting under Martha's hands.

"Yore jist to rest yerself now," Martha had said. "I be here on the floor by ya if 'n ya want nary a thin'."

"I'm a thankin' ya, Marthy."

"I know ya are. Ya go back ta sleep."

Mercy went out to the porch and sat down beside Daniel. The moon was up and flooded the homestead with light. The silence was absolute, except for the occasional grunts of the hogs under the house. Without these sounds, Mercy thought, one might think the world had gone away, leaving only her and Daniel here on the end of the porch.

It was cool, and she had not brought out her shawl. Daniel saw her shiver and put his arm around her. She turned to him, tucked her shoulder beneath his armpit, leaned her head against him, and cuddled against his warmth. She was weary and closed her eyes for a moment.

"It's been a long day, hasn't it?" he murmured against her forehead.

"Yes, and one I'll never forget. What do you think about my family now?"

"They're a typical hill family: proud, hardworking. This is home to them, just like Quill's Station is home to us."

"They have strange ways—and stranger values," Mercy said slowly.

"Probably forced upon them by circumstances."

"That's no excuse for the way Gideon behaves."

"There are many Gideons in the world, honey. You just haven't run into one before."

"I keep thinking about how it would be to live here, have hogs under the house, chickens coming up onto the porch and wandering in, not being able to read or write, not knowing what went on in the world outside these hills."

"You would have been happy. Dora seems to be, and Martha appears to be content. There's no need for you to think about that now. You don't live here, will never live here."

"It makes me look at myself differently," she whispered against his neck. "I feel sorry that my mother grieved for me, and I hate myself for being glad that I was raised by the Quills, but—"

"Shhh. You're not to feel guilty. None of it was your doing."

"I couldn't live here now. Poor Martha works like a horse. Hod seems to have absolute control. He assigns the work, tells everyone what to do. I suppose he took over after . . . after my father died."

"He's a fair man. He's doing the best he can to keep the farm going."

"The main thing they do is make . . . whiskey."

"There's no law against it."

"He'd make me stay here, if he could."

"He knows better than that. He has nothing to say about you. Lenny and Bernie may have done us a favor. You're my wife now, my responsibility. When the time comes, you'll go home with me."

Mercy encircled his waist with her arms and tilted her face so she could look up at him. "I wonder what's happening at home. Do you think Gavin and Eleanor got back from Vincennes?"

"I'm sure they're back by now. Gavin has several big orders for lumber to fill."

"Was Mike going to send Papa a letter telling him about us coming to Kentucky?"

"No, I asked him not to. Without knowing the whole story, Mamma would worry."

"Don't you know that the whole town is talking about us leaving together? Granny Halpen's mouth has been worked so hard, it's probably sore by now," Mercy said with a giggle in her voice.

"She's having the time of her life," Daniel replied with a chuckle.

"Daniel, what if Papa Farr hadn't found me? I'd not have known you!" Mercy's arms tightened around him.

"Somebody up there must have made plans for us, honey."

"I like it when you call me that. You didn't used to."

"I know. I called you brat, or silly girl. You're grown-up now, but your mouth is still getting you into trouble. Tonight when you got your back up over Gid, I thought I might have to fight Hod over you."

"I was right, you know. His attitude made me mad! I couldn't keep quiet."

Daniel laughed a deep, chuckling laugh that vibrated against Mercy's cheek. "You just thought you'd burst if you couldn't say what was on your mind, didn't you?"

"Right's right!"

"You're not going to change their way of thinking. Their way of life is as deeply ingrained in them as yours is in you."

"I had to try."

"Why don't you go in and go to bed? You'll feel better in the morning."

"That's what you said last night. You were so angry at Lenny and Bernie—"

"We agreed not to talk about that. We're going to let it rest for now and take one day at a time. We'll have plenty of time to talk about it on the way home."

"But . . . what about tonight?"

"What about it? We'll go in and go to bed. It would be hard to explain if you slept in there and I slept out here."

"But . . ."

"But what? We were together in the same room at the inn that first night. We slept side by side the next night. Tonight will be no different. Are you afraid that I'll . . . take advantage of you?"

"No!" She drew back and looked into his face. "You know better than that! You're just so calm, so reasonable. Sometimes I don't know how you put up with me."

"It's easy. I'm used to it."

"Did you like kissing me last night?"

"Couldn't you tell?"

"You left so quickly. I thought you didn't like it." Tired but feeling happy and safe in his arms, Mercy loved the feeling of his fingers moving up and down her spine.

"Of course I liked it," he said matter-of-factly. He wanted to tell her that he loved it, that the most gut-wrenching thing he had ever had to do was to walk away and leave her. Instead he said lightly, "It was the first time I kissed my wife."

"I liked kissing you too. It wasn't a brotherly kiss, was it?"

"No. It wasn't meant to be."

"Daniel—"

Mercy didn't know what she had intended to say, because Daniel silenced her. She was looking up at him. His chin scraped her forehead as he lowered his head and brushed his mouth against hers. It was the softest of touches. He looked into her eyes, then his fingers slowly spread against the side of her face, and he held her head to his shoulder. Almost mindless with wanting, he kissed her again. The soft, hesitant caress changed to one of intense longing, and he delved into the sweetness of her mouth as if he could never get enough of her. Her mouth quivered weakly under the persuasion of his kiss. The searching movement parted her lips, and the tip of his tongue slipped inside her mouth. Spasms of unfamiliar joy obliterated all from Mercy's mind. She wanted him closer, closer. Her insides strained, reaching out for fulfillment of the strange, delicious hunger he aroused in her.

Daniel knew he should stop and was about to pull away when her hand moved up and her palm cupped his face. His fingers traced her spine to her hips, caressing, while his mouth pressed against hers with a hungry urgency. His rapidly disintegrating common sense told him he was treading on dangerous ground, that this was not the time or the place to consummate their marriage. It could leave her dissatisfied and humiliated. He caressed her upper lip with the tip of his tongue before he raised his head to look at her.

Her eyes were misty, and her parted lips beckoned him to taste them again. He wanted to say something that made his action sensible. But the truth was that he had done it simply because he could not help himself.

"Honey," he whispered thickly, "I think you'd better go on in and go to bed".

"Are you coming in?" Her soft whisper came from beneath his chin.

"In a while." His mouth traced a pattern along her jawline. His body throbbed with want, and it took a supreme act of will to let his arms drop away from her. Only God knew how much he wanted her, but he could wait.

Why does he have to be so dammed noble? Mercy thought. Her insides warmed with pleasure when she looked into his quiet face and dark eyes. She didn't want to leave the warmth of his arms. She could hear the scrape of his whiskers on her cheek as she laid hers against it for a brief moment, could feel the pounding of his heart against her breasts. Then there was nothing to do but get to her feet and into the house.

Mercy groped her way to the bed and found her carpetbag at the end of it. She pawed in her bag for her nightdress, undressed, and slipped the gown over her head. She took the pins out of her hair and, not knowing a safe place to put them, dropped them in her shoe. Just as she placed her folded dress on the floor beside her shoes, one of the hogs under the house bumped the floor beneath her feet. Shaking her head at the absurdity of it, she got into the bed, moved over next to the wall, and pulled the quilt up around her neck.

Mercy's eyes probed the darkness toward the door. Didn't these people ever close doors in this house? It seemed to Mercy that the family lived outside as much as they lived inside. Her mind roamed over the events of the day. Her mother was a gentle woman yet had an iron will. She'd done something right because her family loved her fiercely. Mercy thought about the death crown her mother had said was to be hers. What did it mean? Was something of her father holding together the feathers that had been in his pillow when he died?

Mercy's thoughts turned to home—Quill's Station. How surprised they would be to discover that she and Daniel were wed. She dozed as visions of her and Daniel at home floated through her mind.

Sometime later, when the quilt lifted, letting the cold air hit her warm body, it brought Mercy groggily out of a sound sleep. Daniel had slipped into the bed. He lay on the edge, his back to her. Only half awake, she pulled the quilt up over his shoulders, and sighing contentedly, she snuggled against his bare back. Her arm worked its way around him. He took her hand in his and held her palm flat against his chest. Warm, content, and happy, her cheek resting on his back between his shoulder blades, she went back to sleep.

Sleep for Daniel did not come easy. The feel of her firm breasts against his back, her knees behind his, her breath on his shoulders, sent a fiery message to his loins. All those nights of aching loneliness were nothing compared to the misery of having her cuddle against him and not be free to turn to her for the comfort only she could give.

When he was sure he wouldn't awaken her, he turned over, slid his arm beneath her shoulders, and held her to him. She lay quietly in his arms, soft, fragrant, trusting. Love and tenderness welled within him. This woman, this sweet woman, was his whole world. He had been bound to her since the moment they met in the wilderness along the Wabash. Feeling like a thief, he settled his mouth gently on hers and kissed her moist, parted lips.

He could feel the steady beat of her heart against his hand, could feel each of her ribs through the thin night-dress. His fingers inched upward until his thumb nudge the fullness of her breast.

Mercy stirred and snuggled closer, pressing her miraculous softness against him. Her thigh came in contact with his hard, throbbing sex, which strained against his britches. A small grunt came from his lips before he could hold it back. He quickly moved his hips away from the sweet contact and gently turned her so he could fold his long frame snugly around her. Mercy cushioned the side of her cheek on his arm and wiggled her backside against him to get more comfortable. Kissing her shoulder, her hair, hungry for the taste of any part of her, he silently told her of his love for her. She was his, all his, for the rest of their lives.

Coming out of a deep sleep, Mercy was aware that she was wrapped in Daniel's arms, her back pressed against his chest, his knees behind hers. A wonderfully safe and happy feeling unfolded within her. She almost feared that this was a dream from which she was bound to awaken alone in her bed.

Daniel, darling, I love you. She wanted to sleep in his arms every night for the rest of her life. Reaching for his hand, she pulled his arm up until it rested between her breasts, placed her cheek on the palm of his hand, and went back to sleep.

CHAPTER THIRTEEN

When Mercy awakened, she could see the shape of the cupboard because of a faint light coming in the open doorway. She knew it was dawn because of the racket made by the birds in the trees above the house, and because the hogs beneath it were moving again. She felt in the place where Daniel had lain beside her. It was cold, which meant he had left their bed a while ago. She lay for a moment and thought about how wonderful it had been to sleep in his arms, how warm and protected she'd felt. What would it be like to lie beside him naked, become one with him? A thrill tingled down her spine. Only her thin nightdress had been between her breast and his bare chest. He had worn his britches, but his feet had been bare, and in the night she had rested the bottoms of her feet on the tops of his. Had he kissed her during the night, or had she only dreamed it?

Now she could hear the steady thuds of an ax hitting wood and smell fresh wood smoke. The younger Baxters would be coming down from the loft. She got up and dressed quickly, listening for sounds from overhead. After running the brush through her hair she twisted it and pinned it to the top of her head, repacked her carpetbag, and set it on the bed.

The morning was cool, but no fire had been built in the kitchen. Mercy wrapped her shawl about her shoulders and went out onto the porch. A fire blazed in the fireplace in the yard, and Daniel was in front of it adding more wood. Martha stood at the table slicing meat and placing long, thick strips in a skillet. Mercy was surprised to see her baby sleeping snugly in a sling on her back.

"Morning. I'll help you, Martha, as soon as I wash."

Daniel turned on hearing her voice. It was still too dark to see his eyes, but Mercy could feel them on her as she went around to the washbench at the back of the house. Hod was there, splashing water on his face.

"Morning, Hod."

"Mornin'." He didn't say anything more, and after he dried his face he went into his mother's room. The doors were closed, and smoke came from the chimney. Streaks of light, from a candle or a lamp, came through the cracks in the door.

Mercy wondered if she should look in on her mother or go help Martha with the morning meal. She decided to wait until Hod came out of her mother's room before she went in.

"Martha, how is Mamma this morning?"

"She jist layin' there. Don't seem to be hurtin' none."

"Did you get up with her in the night?"

"Only fer a sip a water. She's sinkin'," Martha said, and looked down at her feet.

"Isn't there anything we can do?"

"She ain't wantin' us to do nothin'."

"Oh, but—"

"It's what Maw wants," Martha said firmly. "Ain't nothin' can mend a wore-out heart, nohow." She went to the big skillet on the grate and forked the meat over.

Mercy followed her. "What can I do?"

"Ya can add that meal ta the pot when it boils." She nodded to the iron kettle hanging on a spit over the flames.

Mercy added the cornmeal to the water a little at a time, stirring it with a big wooden paddle so it would be smooth. The rest of the family came out onto the porch, stretched, yawned, and went around to the washing trough. When Hod came from his mother's room, he spoke quietly to Martha for several minutes, then took his place at the table.

While the men were eating, Mercy went to sit with her mother. It was warm, even hot, in the closed room. She put her shawl on the back of the chair and sat down. A small, weak voice came from the bed.

"I cain't abide bein' shut in, Hester. Open the door."

Mercy jumped up to obey, then went back to the chair, sat down, and leaned toward the bed. "Do you feel like eating something this morning?"

"No. Hod done give me a swig a whuskey." She closed her eyes.

Mercy leaned back and looked at her. Her eyes seemed to have sunk in since yesterday, and the bones in her face were more prominent. Her skin, which was white yesterday, had a bluish tinge. Mercy rationalized that it could be from the glow of the lamp, but she knew better. Martha was right; she was sinking. She leaned closer when her mother's lips moved.

"Hester . . . come home, Will. Ya . . . promised me I'd see her . . . someday. She growed to be a . . . sightly woman . . ."

Tears filled Mercy's eyes, and she tried to not think about how she had dreaded coming to Kentucky, and wouldn't have if not for Daniel. She thought of William Baxter, the man who sired her. Because her mother had loved him, he must have been a good man. She sat beside her mother, who appeared to be sleeping, until it was fully daylight. When she went out onto the porch, the men had finished eating and had left the table. The younger brothers were gathered around Hod, who was talking and gesturing with his hands. Martha sat at the table, her baby on her lap. There was no sign of Daniel.

Mercy spooned mush into a bowl, poured herself some tea, and sat down at the table across from Martha.

"Ya want meat?" Martha asked.

"No. But I'll have some sorghum to go on my mush." Martha pushed the pitcher toward her. While she ladled out a spoonful of the thick, dark syrup, Mercy said, "She's worse, isn't she?"

"I'm thinkin' she is. Hod 'n' the boys'll stay by today."

"She was talking to Will."

"It's somethin' she does more 'n' more."

Mercy ate a few bites. "Where's Daniel?"

"Hod ask him ta go up 'n' tell Wyatt ta come. He's thinkin' they ort ta be here."

Lenny went past without looking at them and entered his mother's room. He was still there when Mercy finished her mush and brought a big dishpan to the table and filled it with the soiled dishes. Bernie brought a bucket of water and sat it on the end of the table. His face was so drawn with worry lines that Mercy could almost forgive him for threatening her with the snake.

One by one the men in the family went to sit with their mother. Daniel, and Wyatt, carrying a small child, came through the woods with Dora and her sister following. Dora had not made good her threat to send her sister home at sunup. It might be, Mercy decided, that Hod's summons had come in time to prevent Wyatt from taking her.

Mercy and Martha cleaned up after the morning meal. Lenny and Bernie moved the hogs out from under the house and drove them into a pen attached to a shed. Mercy wondered why they were not kept there in the first place. Dora sat on the end of the porch, worked the dasher up and down in the tall wooden churn, and watched the children playing quietly under the elm tree. Mercy suspected she was keeping her eye on Emmajean, who sat on a quilt with Dora's child and Martha's baby. No one talked much. The whiskey jug sat undisturbed, but the big teakettle was filled and refilled as mugs of tea were consumed.

It wasn't easy for the men to sit idle. Wyatt sought the shade at the side of the house and squatted on his heels to whittle on a stick with a long knife. The others worked on harnesses they brought from the shed. Daniel continued to work at the woodpile. He had cut several cords of wood during the last two days and shaved a good supply of kindling. Now he sat on a stump, sharpening the ax with a whetstone.

Shortly before noon, Hod came out onto the porch. His shoulders were slumped dejectedly, and his craggy face was drawn with lines of worry. The family knew that what he had to say was not something they wanted to hear. He stood for a moment before he spoke.

"C'mon in. Maw wants ta see us—all a ya."

Each and every one of them knew in their hearts that this was the moment they dreaded. No one spoke. They got slowly to their feet and filed into the room behind Hod.

Mercy was the last to enter her mother's room. She had waved to Daniel to come to her, waited for him, grasped his hand, and pulled him along with her. Standing with her brothers in a circle around the bed, she felt for the first time the bond of common kinship. Blood tied them all together and bound them to the small, white-haired woman who lay on the bed gasping for breath. A harsh hand began to squeeze Mercy's throat dry.

What followed was the stillest stillness Mercy had ever known. There was no sound from the children playing beneath the oak tree, or from the dogs under the porch. Not even a squawk came from the chickens in the yard. For a long while there was no sound except for the ticking of the mantel clock, and the song of a mockingbird in the tree outside the window.

When their mother opened her eyes, she looked long at each of them. A peaceful look settled on her face, and her eyes were clear. When she began to talk, her voice was barely above a whisper, and every ear strained to catch every word.

"Yore . . . Baxters. Yore what . . . me 'n' Will made. Ya ain't ne'er ta shame your paw's name."

It was difficult for her to talk, and she paused after each word. Her eyes drifted shut, as if it were too much of an effort to hold them open. Hod knelt down beside the bed and placed his big rough hand over hers.

"Hod," she said with her eyes still closed. "Ya 'n' Marthy move in here. Lenny can go over ta yore place." There was a long pause. "Wyatt's got his land. There's aplenty left fer Bernie 'n' Gideon . . . when they're ready to settle. Ya . . . hear me, Hod?"

"Yes, ma'am. I hear ya. Thin's will be done jist as ya want."

They all waited in an agony of suspense. Their mother's fingers were plucking at the bed covers. Finally she opened her eyes and looked at Martha.

"Ya been as good a daughter as ever a woman had, Marthy. I want ya ta have my clock . . ."

"I love ya, Maw. Ya don't need to be givin' me nothin'."

"I want to." Her eyes met Hod's steadily. "It ain't my business ta be sayin' this, but ya be good ta Marthy."

"Yes, ma'am. I will."

"Dory, ya brought me sunshine 'n' foolishness, jist as Wyatt said ya would. I got cash money laid back ta buy ya a store-bought dress 'n' shoes. Ya'll be purty in 'em. I wish I could see ya . . ."

"Ah . . . Maw." Dora turned her face to her husband's shoulder and sobbed.

"Hush yore caterwaulin', Dorybelle." The whispered words were a command. "I got thin's ta say."

"Yes, ma'am," Dora said, and sniffed back the tears.

"Will said Lenny was . . . the best shot of any of ya." There was a long pause while she regained her breath. "He wanted him to have . . . his rifle. Ya take care of it. Hear?"

"I will, Maw."

"Bernie, ya ain't the . . . muddlehead they be sayin' ya are. Ya got a hand with hogs. I done told Hod ta give ya a good start of them hogs, 'n' help ya fix up a . . . place fer 'em. Will said any fool could make whuskey, but it took . . . special sense to raise hogs." She closed her eyes wearily.

It seemed to the waiting group that it was a long time before the frail-looking little woman spoke again. All eyes were on her face. Tears rolled from Wyatt's eyes. He held his wife to him and cried silently. Hod's face looked as if it were etched in stone, as did Lenny's. Bernie bit his lips and gripped his hands together as tears ran down his cheeks. For once Gideon was not preening and smiling. He stood with his arms folded across his chest, his head down. He lifted his head when his mother spoke his name.

"Gideon?"

"Yes, ma'am."

"I fear I spoilt ya rotten, son. Ya . . . was purty as any girl baby I ever saw, 'n' my last youngun. I want . . . ya to be payin' heed to Wyatt 'n' Hod. If'n ya ain't careful, ya'll fiddle yore life away on fast women 'n' tomfoolery."

"I . . . won't, Maw."

"Don't ya be promisin' what . . . ya can't keep, son. If'n ya got to see what's beyond . . . the hills, go." She drew rasping breaths in through her open mouth. "Come back. These hills be yore home. Ya liked yore paw's squeeze box when ya was a tad. Ya danced 'n' sung like a bird when he played. Take it, keep it fer yore younguns."

"I'll take care of it." Tears streamed down Gideon's cheeks, but he spoke without a trace of them in his voice.

Mercy held tightly to Daniel's hand when her mother turned her eyes on her. And then Mrs. Baxter's breath choked her. She gasped, then lay quietly for a long space of time before she spoke.

"I had my heart set on seein' ya . . . afore I passed on. I owe it ta Lenny 'n' Bernie fer fetchin' ya." She paused and took several shallow breaths. "I ain't a bit put out with what ya are, Hester. Yore a fine woman 'n' ya . . . make me plumb proud."

"I'm not . . . disappointed in you, either, Mamma."

"Ya ain't needin' nothin' here. Ya got a good man who's got love for ya like my Will had for me. That's worth a heap more'n gold. Carry her back ta Illinois, Dan'l. Take care of her 'n' give her a parcel a younguns ta do fer. A . . . woman ain't much without . . . younguns."

"I'll do that, ma'am."

"Hod? Where's Hod?"

"I'm here, Maw."

"I want Hester ta . . . have yore paw's death crown, Hod."

"All right, Maw."

"Ya carry it home with ya, Hester. It's somethin' yore paw left behind when he was took." Her eyes had closed, her voice fading until the last word came out on a breath.

The family stood around the bed, their eyes on their mother's face. She rolled her head on the pillow ever so slightly, and her mouth worked. She seemed to be talking, but no words came out. After what seemed an awfully long time she opened her eyes again. They went to the door, as if she could see beyond and, seeing, nodded her head slowly. Her lips curved in a slight smile. She looked back at her children

"I ain't wantin' ya ta be cryin' 'n' carryin' on. Hear me now?"

Even lying on her deathbed, she was still in charge. Mercy wondered if in facing death she could be so strong.

Her mother was worn and weary, but she was not defeated. She had married her man and borne him as many children as God had seen fit to give them. She had buried some of them and commanded obedience from those who lived. Her life must have been hard, but she had had the love of her husband and the love and respect of her children to sustain her through years of toil and grief.

"Give yore maw a last kiss," she commanded in a voice that was somewhat stronger.

No protest and no sounds of weeping came from the big men. With tears streaming down their weathered cheeks they filed past the bed, bent, and placed a kiss on their mother's brow. After the men, Mercy went to the head of the bed and kissed her mother, then back to take Daniel's hand and follow the Baxter brothers to the porch.

The day wore on. It seemed to Mercy an awfully long time since morning. She helped Martha put food on the table. The family, worn out with grief and worry, didn't eat much, but everyone made a show of swallowing a few bites. They conversed in low voices when it was necessary to speak. First one, and then another, sat in the hickory rocker beside the bed and watched as their mother's head moved restlessly on the pillow and the slow, gasping breaths went in and out of her open mouth.

The sun was almost at the crest of the hills to the west. The day's last ray of sunshine came through the doorway and made a path across the floor. Mercy, alone with her mother, suddenly realized that her eyes had opened and she was looking at her. She leaned close to the bed.

"Mamma? Do you want something?"

"Take my hand, Will."

The words were clearly spoken, and then her lids fluttered closed. Mercy watched and waited anxiously. After a moment one side of her mother's face pulled down, as if drawn by an invisible hand. The thin hand on the bed at her side twitched, then stopped. Panic, sudden and acute, knifed through Mercy. She hurried to the door.

"Martha! Hod! Everyone!"

The family filed in quickly and stood around the bed. Hod knelt on the floor beside his mother and held her hand. Her labored breathing sounded like sobbing grief. The rest of the family stood helplessly, quietly, and waited for it to stop. Gideon started for the door, as if the waiting were more than he could bear. Wyatt's hand, on his arm, stopped him and held him at his side. The sun passed beyond the hills, and the streak of sunlight vanished from the floor.

And then it stopped. The sobbing, gasping, dragging sound stopped. No one moved. The tall, rough men and the three white-faced women stood as still as stones, waiting for the hand on the bed to move, or an eyelid to flicker. Time went by. Slowly they accepted the fact that what had happened would not be altered or undone. The hand that had wiped their noses and soothed their fevered brows had moved for the last time. The eyelids over the blue, laughing, all-knowing eyes were closed forever. Their hurt was real, their grief deep, and it pressed down upon them.

It occurred to Mercy that this was the way death comes. You are breathing air into your body, pushing it out again. You are real, warm, and living. You eat, sleep, laugh, love, and feel pain. Then, when the breathing stops, you are nothing. The world still turns. The sun comes up in the morning, the moon at night. The stars are still bright, the rain falls, the flowers grow, and the seasons change. But you, who have been living, producing the next generation, are nothing.

Daniel's hands slipped from her shoulders and went around her, pulling her back against him. Gratefully she leaned on his strength. This was the closest she had been to death, and the awful finality of it was like a tight hand at her throat.

Quietly the family went about doing what had to be done as if it had all been rehearsed. Hod took charge as was expected. Lenny would go to the still to tend to the mash they had neglected for several days. Hod sent Gideon in one direction and Bernie in another, to notify the neighbors. Wyatt would go to Coon Hollow to fetch the minister. Daniel saddled his big buckskin and brought it to the front of the house when Wyatt was ready to leave. Wyatt pressed his shoulder gratefully and rode away from the homestead.

The grimmest task of all was left to Hod and Daniel. They went to the shed behind the house. Hod pulled wide, sawed boards from the rafters where they had been stored for just this purpose and wiped the dust and chicken droppings off them. From the box in the wagon Daniel brought a handful of square, iron nails, a saw, and a hammer. Nails were a scarce commodity in the hills, and Hod at first refused them, saying he would use pegs. Later he accepted them after Daniel remarked that the coffin they were building was for his wife's mother.

After her mother was washed, dressed, and laid out on the bed to wait for Hod and Daniel to finish the box, Mercy brought her soft white shawl, folded it, and placed it beneath her mother's head. Candles were lit when darkness fell. The older children were put to bed in the loft, the younger ones in the bed in the kitchen.

The family sat with their mother's body all through the night. Bernie and Gideon returned. Wyatt wasn't expected back until morning. Hod and Daniel had spent most of the night making the coffin by the light of a fire in the yard. After it was finished, the women lined it with their best quilts and gently placed their mother's body inside, her head resting on Mercy's white shawl.

At dawn Daniel went with Hod and Lenny to the burial ground to dig the grave. When they returned, the Baxter brothers began to dress for the funeral. One after the other, they sat on the stump by the woodpile and Dora cut their hair. Then, wordless, they went to the creek to bathe and to the loft to dress. Hod was the only one who wore a coat, which was much too small for his broad shoulders. The faces of the brothers were nicked where they had scraped off their whiskers, and their wild blond hair was slicked down with grease.

Dora and Martha wore loose, dark dresses that looked to Mercy like granny gowns worn by the older women at Vincennes and Louisville. The dresses were not trimmed with collar, cuffs, or pockets and hung from the shoulders with nothing to indicate a waistline. Dora's hair was puffed and coiled and held in place with a wooden comb. Martha's dark hair was as slick and tight as the day Mercy first met her.

Wagonload after wagonload of neighbors began to arrive an hour after sunup. They brought food hastily gathered from their storehouses: hams, venison, hominy, dried beans, and freshly baked bread. The women took over the cooking and the feeding of the more than seventy people that gathered at the homestead. Quilts were spread beneath the trees for the little ones, and the older children were cautioned to be quiet out of respect for the dead. The children, all dressed in their best, obeyed and tried to conceal their excitement.

A wedding, a burial, or a house-raising was almost the only occasion to bring neighbors together. It was a chance to visit and to exchange news. All were curious about Mercy and Daniel. All had heard the story about little Hester, who had been lost so many years ago. Mercy left it to the Baxters to tell the story of how she had been found at Quill's Station.

Wyatt returned with Cousin Farley, the deaf old man

who had married Daniel and Mercy. He wore the same oversize black coat and carried his Bible clutched to this thin chest. He looked over the crowd and then headed straight for Daniel.

"Do I know you?"

"I don't know," Daniel growled impatiently. "Do you?"

"Huh? What'd ya say."

"I said, you don't *know* me!" Daniel raised his voice.

"Caroliny! I thought that's where I met ya. Long time ago, warn't it? Air ya from there?"

Daniel shook his head. Hod came to take the old man's arm and lead him to a seat at the table. The noon meal was served, after which Cousin Farley stood on the porch and preached a sermon.

"They ain't one among us what someday won't meet our maker and atone fer our sins," he shouted. "Repent, all ye sinners! God begins life; he ends life. Ye must repent yore sins or be cast into everlasting hell . . ."

In her good dark dress, now devoid of collar and braid, Mercy stood beside Daniel while the preacher's voice droned on. She looked at the lines of the homely, weathered faces around her. They were arranged somberly to fit the occasion. A few tears squeezed from the eyes of some of the woman, but they blinked them away.

After the sermon they all filed past the box for one last look at their mother. When the last neighbor had walked past the coffin, Hod nodded to Daniel. He stepped forward, placed the lid on the box, took nails from his pocket, and nailed it firmly in place.

The five Baxter brothers then lifted their mother's coffin to their shoulders and carried it out the door. The mourners followed them up the hill to the final resting place of the Baxters who had gone before. There were the graves of two children, both girls, who had been stillborn, and the graves of two more, a boy and a girl, who had not yet reached the age of three years when they died. William Baxter, who had sired them all, rested there. His name was carved on the wooden slab that marked his grave. It was a sweet plot of ground with honeysuckle and wild roses running over it, and tall trees shading it.

After the coffin was lowered into the ground, Mercy stood beside her brothers with her eyes lifted to the hills while Cousin Farley consigned her mother's body to the earth.

"Dear God, here's yore servant, Mary Len Baxter. Take her to yore kingdom so that she may walk the streets o' gold and know no pain or sorrow." The old man's voice boomed in the quiet of the hillside. "Ashes to ashes, dust to dust . . ."

The ceremony was brief. As soon as the first clods of dirt tapped a knocking on the wooden box, Dora cried out and leaned heavily on Wyatt's arm. Martha stood beside Hod, dry-eyed, her baby nestled in her arms. Mercy knew Martha felt the loss even more than she did, for she had been with her, tending her. It was strange to think of it now, but she had known her own mother for only two short days. Tears filled Mercy's eyes as the mourners raised their voices in song.

> Rock of Ages, cleft for me,
>   Let me hide myself in Thee:
> Let the water and the blood,
>   From Thy wounded side which flow'd,
> Be of sin and double cure,
>   Save from wrath and make me pure.

Mercy lifted her eyes beyond the open hole in the earth and closed her ears against the sound of the earth spilling onto the wooden box. As the mourners continued to sing, occasionally a sob from one of the women could be heard. When it was over and the fresh earth was rounded over the new grave, Mercy stepped forward and scattered a handful of roses she had picked from the bush that clambered up the stone chimney of the cabin where Mary Len Baxter had spent most of her life.

Mercy and Daniel lingered at the burial site until everyone had gone back down the hill to the homestead. Then they went to stand at each of the graves in the small plot and read the inscriptions on the boards. At her father's grave she read the crudely printed words.

WILLIAM LUTHER BAXTER
1780–1828
Beloved husband and father

Each of the children had a marker. Some of the boards were so weathered that Mercy had to kneel down and trace the letters with her fingers. Gladys, 1809. Maude, 1811. Myrtle, 1812–1815, Robert, 1814–1816. Mercy realized that it was when Maude was born that her father had taken her to relatives on the Green River to stay until her mother recovered from the birth.

Daniel stood quietly by until Mercy was ready to leave the burial plot, then he took her hand and they walked back down the hill to the homestead.

Mercy came out of the house and sat down on the edge of the porch beside Daniel. The night was clear and cool, the stars bright. She could see the Big Dipper tipping its empty cup over the trees. She was homesick, terribly homesick, for Quill's Station, for Mamma and Papa, for Mary Elizabeth and Zack.

Not long after the last wagonload of neighbors departed, Hod had taken his family and gone to the cabin beyond the pines. Wyatt and Dora also had gone home.

Cousin Farley, tired from the long ride, had gone to bed. The younger brothers had not shown themselves since their mother's funeral.

As soon as Mercy sat down, Daniel put his arm around her and pulled her close to his side.

"When can we go home, Daniel?"

"As soon as you want to."

"Let's go tomorrow. There's nothing to keep us here now." She leaned her head against his shoulder.

"We'll leave in the morning. Don't you want to go to bed? You're worn-out," he whispered, his lips against her forehead.

"I am tired," she said wearily. Then, "We got here just in time, didn't we?"

"Yes, we did. I understand now why Lennie and Bernie were in such a hurry to get back. It was quite an undertaking for them to go all the way to Quill's Station just on the rumor that they might find their long-lost sister there."

"Daniel, I don't want to be mad at them anymore for forcing me to come here."

"Think about it, honey. They didn't force you."

"They made me feel guilty. That's why I came. It wasn't out of love for my mother. I couldn't even think of anyone except Liberty as Mother. I'm glad I came. I'm no longer ashamed of being a Baxter. They're good, honest, hardworking people."

"Yes they are that. Their ways are not our ways, but that doesn't necessarily make them wrong."

"Now we've got to think about our other problem," Mercy murmured.

"Is it really a problem?" he asked softly.

She raised her head so that she could look at him, and his heartbeat picked up speed. Looking into her face, he marveled that she was so beautiful. His eyes feasted on her face, surrounded by its golden aureole of hair. Her eyes were like stars, the curve of her lips perfect.

"I think it is, don't you?"

"Why is it such a problem? No, don't answer," he said quickly, not wanting to hear what she would say. "We promised we wouldn't talk about it until we were on the way home." With his hands at her waist he put her from him and they got to their feet. "Go on, honey. Get ready for bed."

"You . . . kissed me last night."

He looked down at her for a long moment. "Then maybe you'd better kiss me tonight," he whispered.

Mercy's hands moved up his chest to his face. She held her palms against his cheeks, stood on tiptoes, and gently placed her mouth against his. He increased the pressure, and his hungry mouth drank in the sweetness of hers. She made no effort to move away from him. His hands tightened around her waist; his breathing and heartbeat were all mixed up. With utmost tenderness she moved her lips against his. He thought surely she would feel the evidence of his desire that throbbed so hurtfully between them, and be frightened of it.

Her arms slid down to wrap tightly around his waist. She pressed the full length of her body against him and was made instantly aware of the elongated hardness pressing against her stomach. She felt him tremble when she moved against it, and wild, sweet enchantment rippled through her. His lips had moved against hers urgently when she kissed him. His pulse was racing as wildly as hers, his virile body reacting to hers. Daniel was no longer thinking of her as his sister but as a lover!

Stirred by the incredible discovery of his hard male sex pressing against her, she kissed him again with intimate sensuousness and parted her lips to run the tip of her tongue across his mouth.

Finally, reluctantly, he put her from him. "Go to bed, sweet one." The words seemed to be wrenched from him.

Disappointment knocked at her heart. She raised her

eyes to look into his, but he bent his head and placed a gentle kiss on her forehead.

"You'll come in . . . soon?"

"In a while."

Daniel did not come to their bed. It seemed to Mercy that hours passed while she lay waiting hopefully for him. Finally she got out of bed and went to look out the door. He was clearly visible in the moonlight, sitting on the stump beside the woodpile. He was not coming to bed until he was sure that she was asleep. The thought ran wildly through her mind as she watched him. On the heels of that disappointing thought there was another brighter one—the next night they would be alone.

Daniel saw the blur of white in the doorway. Mercy was waiting for him to come in. She had clung to him the last few days as she had when she was a child—moving close to him, taking his hand when she was confused or unsure. He understood that. They had grown up together—he was familiar, safe. She had been thrust among strangers who expected her to feel as if she belonged here. They and their ways were as foreign to her as hers had been to Lenny and Bernie when they came to Quill's Station.

Dear Lord! How he wanted to go to her! But he could not endure the torture of another night like the one before. It had taken all of his willpower to keep from blurting out his love for her, and taking all her sweet woman's body had to give. There wasn't the slightest doubt in his mind that she would have surrendered to him. But he was certain that all it would have been for her would have been a painful taking of her maidenhead; and for him, a quick, temporary relief.

If it should happen, a small voice whispered in a corner of his mind, there would be no possibility of a divorce. If he got her with child, she would be his forever. Daniel firmly shoved the thought aside. He wanted her desperately, but not that way! He thought of her trusting acceptance of him the previous night. She had curled in his arms with only her thin nightdress and his britches between them. In the night she had taken his hand and placed it on her breast, totally unaware that the feeling of her soft breast in his palm sent shock waves to his already painful loins. Early that morning she had turned to him and slept with her face against his neck, her thigh over his, her arm across his chest.

Daniel looked at the moon riding high in the sky and wished for its swift passage. He looked forward to the dawn of a new day. It couldn't come quickly enough to suit him. He and Mercy would leave this place, and he would have her all to himself. He would tell her of his love for her and that he wanted nothing more than for her to spend the rest of her life as his wife. If she wanted a wedding to remember, they could be married again by a minister in Evansville. He was determined that they would spend their first night as husband and wife with a complete understanding between them.

Daniel picked up a limb from the woodpile and began to shave it into kindling. Mercy hadn't thought of what they faced when they got back to Quill's Station. As for himself, he didn't care what people thought, but he knew it was different for a woman. By now Belinda Martin would have spread the news that the two backwoods men who had come riding into town on mules were Mercy's brothers. That, coupled with the fact that Glenn Knibee would see to it that the whole town knew Daniel had spent the night alone in the house with her was enough to ostracize her. Outside of Eleanor McCourtney and Tennessee, he doubted if there was another woman in town who would dare speak to her. This would hurt her unbearably, and there was no way he could shield her from that hurt.

An hour later there was enough kindling in the pile at Daniel's feet to start a dozen fires. His thoughts had turned to George, to Turley Blaine, and to the people on his farm. They would be tilling the soil and putting in the crops. Gavin would be on the lookout for Hammond Perry after George told him what happened at the mill. But Gavin would be busy with his lumber business, and he was sure Perry would give Gavin a wide berth, knowing the big man would kill him if given half a chance.

The news Edward Ashton had given Daniel about Perry wanting George worried him some. There was only one way to stop a bastard like Hammond Perry, and that was to kill him.

Some of Daniel's most frightening memories as a child were of Hammond Perry. He remembered when Perry came to Quill's Station to take Farr to Vincennes to stand trial for treason. He remembered standing beside Mercy while she cried when the soldiers took Farr away. Then, later, he had heard the story of how Perry had sent men to kill Rain Tallman and to take Eleanor, who at the time was engaged to marry Will Bradford, another man Perry hated. There was nothing the man wouldn't do for revenge.

Daniel thought of the Negroes on his farm—Jasper, Gus, and their families, and poor old Jeems and his demented son, Gerrit. They were gentle, good people, and the thought of any of them in the hands of Hammond Perry set his blood to boiling.

Suddenly tired in mind and body, Daniel sank the ax in the stump and went to the porch. He spread out his blanket and stretched out.

Thank God, with any luck at all, he and Mercy would be home in three days.

CHAPTER FOURTEEN

Moonlight shimmered on the waters of the Wabash. The beauty of the night was not only unappreciated but also cursed by the three men in the flat-bottom boat that slid silently beneath the screen of willows lining the pond above the falls that turned the mill wheel.

"By God! I ain't likin' gettin' in that cold water."

"We ain't gettin' that nigger no other way, so get in thar."

"We'll drown 'em gettin' him back in the boat."

"God damn you, Knibee. This was yore idea. You told Perry you could get in the mill. Now get yore ass in the water."

"What'll we do if the nigger drowns?"

"We'll let him float on downriver 'n' head fer Saint Louie. Perry ain't one ta overlook bunglin'. Get on out."

"Hang right in close, hear?" Glenn Knibee said to the man at the oars.

"I hear you. I ain't deaf."

Two of the men slipped silently out of the boat and into the water. After a swim of no more than half a dozen feet, they reached the overhang of the flume that led into the wheel housing. The structure hung over the water, projecting from the side of the mill. The first man took a deep breath, sank beneath the surface of the water, and came up under the housing sill. He waited for the second man to join him, and then they climbed up into the mill. They waited a few minutes to get their breath, then, with Glenn Knibee leading the way, they silently moved up the ladder, into the storage room, and on to the living quarters.

Hammond Perry paced the length of the barroom and back. He paused, glazed at Lyman Sickles, the landlord, and continued his pacing.

"Are ya wantin' anythin', Mr. Perry?"

"You don't have anything here I'd spit on, Sickles."

The landlord turned his face to hide his resentment and moved behind the bar before he spoke.

"Ya was glad enough to get the word about Phelps and the woman."

"I paid you for it. You didn't tell me how you knew it was him."

"One of my other lodgers recognized him 'n' the woman. They're the brats Farrway Quill raised. Then Knibee come in, said Phelps and the woman were goin' down to Kentucky. The woman's a looker, a real looker."

Sickles stopped talking when Hammond stood in front of him and looked him in the eyes. It was not often that Hammond was able to look down at a man shorter than he was, and he enjoyed doing it.

"So she's a looker. You've said that a dozen times. If you're going to talk, tell me something new."

Resentment tightened the lines of Sickles's face again. "Phelps stays as close to her as skin on a sausage. They slept together."

"Wouldn't you, if you got the chance? Hell, that woman of yours looks like she's been dragged behind a wagon for half a day. Don't she talk?"

"Not that I ever heared," the landlord said dryly.

"Who was the damn fool who tried to stab Phelps? Stupid son of a bitch got what was coming to him for pulling such a stunt. Why didn't he shoot him?"

"I didn't ask him. He was dead. Looked like he was hit with a rock."

"A rock? Shit!" Hammond paced to the end of the room and back. "Went down to Kentucky," he said, as if to himself. "He'll be coming back this way."

The years had not been kind to Hammond Perry. He had the stamp of greed and malevolence on his face. Puffy red pouches hung beneath his watery eyes. His hair lay against his scalp in strings. To make up for the loss of hair on his head, he had allowed his sideburns and his whiskers to grow long, which gave him a top-heavy look. He held his thin body ramrod-straight, which made his protruding abdomen all the more pronounced.

Hammond took a watch from his pocket, flipped open the case, and looked at it. "Midnight," he murmured.

"They ort ta be gettin' back."

"How long have you known this fellow, Knibee?"

"Year or two. He ain't got no use for Quill or Phelps. I heared Phelps knocked him on his arse a while back."

"Good. Good. He'll be wanting to get even."

Another hour passed before a heavy hand pounded on the back door of the inn. The landlord lifted the bar and swung the door back. Two men staggered in, holding George between them. His hands were bound behind his back. A loop around his ankles allowed him to take only short hopping steps.

"Get that nigger outa here!" Sickles snarled.

The men ignored Sickles and looked beyond him to Hammond. "We got him, Mr. Perry."

"I can see that. Take him to the barn and tie him up."

"He's wet as a drowned rat."

"Bein' wet ain't goin' to hurt a nigger none," Knibee said, and yanked George back toward the door.

"Wait!" Hammond strode past Sickles. "Slit his drawers. I want to see his dong."

George began to struggle when one of the men pulled out a long, thin-bladed knife.

"Ya best stand still, nigger, or this blade might make a geldin' of ya."

George froze, then flinched when the tip of the knife nicked the skin beneath his pubic hair as it slit open his britches. Humiliated, he had to stand and suffer the indignity of having his private parts examined. He looked at the ceiling and vowed to kill each and every one of these men who prodded and snickered at his manly endowment.

"Christ!" Knibee explained. "He's hung like a horse."

"All niggers have big peckers. Didn't ya know that?"

"When it swells, it'll reach to his belly hole and pump seed," Perry said, and flipped it with the back of his hand. "It's what Crenshaw wants. Take him to the barn, tie him good, and throw a horse blanket over him. We don't want him sick."

Two of the men dragged George out. The third man, James Howell, walked over to a jug, and helped himself to a drink.

"How'd it go?" Hammond asked.

"All right. Knibee's a bitcher. Bitched all the way down, and bitched all the way back."

"Anyone see you?"

"I stayed in the boat. They said the old man who works at the mill came storming in while they wrestled the nigger. He'll not tell anybody. Knibee bashed his head."

"Kill him?"

"Probably. Tell that woman of yours to get me something to eat, Sickles. I must of rowed that damn boat twenty miles, and my stomach's rubbing my backbone."

James Howell was a noted slave stealer and was connected with John Crenshaw in his slave operation at the salt mine. He masterminded the plans but seldom did the actual kidnapping.

"I've got another job for you," Perry said impatiently.

The man's tone rankled Howell, and he turned his back on him and sat down at the table.

"I'm not beggin' for *jobs*, Perry."

"It'll pay a hell of a lot more than stealing a nigger."

"What've you got in mind? I suppose you want me to go to Vandalia and kill Farrway Quill for you."

Hammond ignored the jibe. His hatred of Quill was a well-known fact, and he never made an attempt to conceal it.

"Daniel Phelps runs the mill at Quill's Station, and—"

"I know that. I just come from there."

"He's a nigger lover. And—"

"I know that too." Howell enjoyed seeing the corners of Perry's eyes twitch when he was angry. The man hated to be interrupted. He talked as if he were giving orders to a troop under his command.

"Phelps will be coming this way in a few days, maybe a week. He'll not stay away from the mill very long this time of year. He'll be with a blond woman. Sickles can give you his description, and those of the horses and the wagon. I want him stopped. Understand?"

"Killed?"

"It will be the only way to stop him."

"The woman too?"

"Do what you want with her, as long as she never gets back to Quill's Station."

"What's in it for me?"

"Five hundred in gold and about a dozen niggers up on Phelps's farm. Without him there to tell them what to do, it'll be like picking apples off a tree."

"I'll think about it."

"Think about it? Hell! I want to know *now,* Howell. If you're not interested, I'll get someone else."

"All right." Howell pursed his lips and looked from Sickle to Perry. "I'll take care of it. I know just the man for the job."

"No! I want you to do it yourself."

"Don't be telling me how to run my business, Perry." James Howell looked Hammond straight in the eye. He didn't like the cocky little son of a bitch, but John Crenshaw did, so he had to put up with him. That didn't mean he had to knuckle down or do any of his dirty work regardless of the pay. "If I take on this job, I do it my way or not at all." He helped himself to a hunk of bread and plunged his knife into the crock of butter Sickles set on the table.

"Five hundred is a lot of money," Hammond said. "A man can do a lot with that much money."

"Yeah? I could poke that much up my arse and not even know it." Howell began to eat.

Hammond paced back and forth, the heels of his boots making the only sound other than the slurping Howell made when he drank from his mug. Hammond didn't like having a third party involved, but if that was the only way he could get the job done, he would go along with it this one time.

"All right," Hammond agreed reluctantly. "All right. But, by God, the job had better be done."

"Half now, the rest when the job's done," Howell said, knowing Perry would not agree.

"I'll not pay for a pig in a poke," Hammond shouted. "I'll leave the money with Crenshaw. When Phelps is dead, you'll be paid."

James Howell shrugged his shoulders. "Then I'll be at Crenshaw's house in a couple of weeks to collect."

Moonlight came in through the window at the McCourtney house, set back from the Wabash along the road to Vincennes. It was a neat, well-built house with four rooms below, two above, and a porch that fronted the width of the house. In the bedroom at the back of the house, Gavin lay in the oversize bed that was needed for his large frame. Eleanor cuddled close to his side.

"I'm glad to be home and in our own bed, Gavin. I love this place."

"Aye, lass. Me feets been hangin' over the end of the bed for the past two weeks."

Eleanor laughed softly and swirled the hair on his chest with her fingertips.

"I wish we had come home sooner. We'd have been here when the two men came from Kentucky to see Mercy. Oh, that poor girl. She must have been shocked. Imagine, Gavin. She hasn't known who she was for all these years. If not for Daniel—"

A loud pounding on the door cut off Eleanor's words. Gavin sat up in bed. The pounding came again.

"Someone be at the door." Gavin was swinging his huge body out of the bed when the sharp raps sounded again.

"Hurry, Gavin," Eleanor said. "No one would come knocking this time of night if there wasn't something wrong.

"He be in a snit, whoever he be." Gavin pulled on his britches. "I be comin'," he yelled.

A blanket wrapped around her, Eleanor followed her husband out of the bedroom and through the kitchen. She hung back when he went to the door leading to the porch.

Gavin lifted the latch and opened the door. A man with a head of white hair, blood streaming down his face, sagged against the doorjamb.

"Turley! Godamighty, mon!" Gavin exclaimed. He grabbed the old man and half dragged, half carried him into the house, then eased him down into a chair. "Eleanor!" Gavin roared, only to find his wife beside him. "Turley's hurt," he said in a softer voice.

"Oh, Turley! Oh, your poor head! We must stop the blood. Tennessee!" Eleanor called as she ran to get a cloth.

A dark-haired girl came down out of the room above.

"What happened to Turley?"

"Get whiskey," Gavin commanded, and Tennessee hurried to obey. "What happened to ye, mon?"

"Took . . . George . . ."

"Took George?" Eleanor gasped. "Who took George?"

"Hush, love. Let the mon speak."

"One was . . . Knibee . . ." Turley's voice faded to nothing, his head fell to the side, and he would have slid from the chair except for Gavin's strong arms."

"Oh, Gavin! Is he dead?"

"I be thinkin' he almost is. Run fix the bed, love. I be takin' him to it. He be an ol' mon to be struck such a blow."

Gavin placed Turley on the bed and moved away so that Eleanor could wash the gash on his head with the whiskey Tennessee had brought too late for Turley to drink. She snipped the hair away with her scissors so that Tennessee could see to close the wound with a few stitches. He was still unconscious when they finished.

"Is there anything else we can do?" Eleanor asked the girl who was like a daughter to her and Gavin.

Kneeling beside the old man, Tennessee looked more Indian than white with her dark hair parted in the middle and two thick braids hanging over her breasts.

"I don't know if his skull is cracked. I do know it is good to put ice on a head wound. That was told to me by a doctor in Vincennes."

"Do we have ice left in the sawdust pit, Gavin?"

Gavin scratched his shaggy head. "I'm believin' we do, love. I'll be fetchin' it."

Later they tried to spoon whiskey into Turley's mouth, but it ran out the side. He lay as still as death.

Eleanor, curled up in her husband's lap, watched Tennessee change the ice packs and put the hot bricks at the old man's feet.

"Gavin, Turley said 'Knibee.' Do you suppose Glenn Knibee had anything to do with someone taking George?"

"Knibee has not the brains to act on his own. I be seein' Perry's hand in this."

"What can we do to get George back? Oh, poor George. He's so proud. It'll kill him to be treated like a slave."

"There's nothin' we can be doin' tonight. Ye ain't to be frettin' 'bout it nohow. It'll be back to bed for ye, Mrs. McCourtney. Tennessee, with me help, will be lookin' after Turley." Gavin stood with his wife in his arms.

"Gavin McCourtney! You're impossible! Since I told you we were having a baby, you've been like a mother hen. You've hardly let me wipe my nose."

"If ye'er nose needs wipin', I'll be wipin' it," he said with a grin. "We be waitin' ten years fer this bairn, Nora, me girl. He'll be rested when he gets here."

"You stop treating me like an invalid, or . . . or I'll have a girl just for spite."

"Ye'll have what I planted, is what ye'll have."

"Tennessee, tell him women have been having babies since the beginning of time. Tell him—"

"Hush yer yappin', wench." Gavin shut her mouth with a quick kiss.

Gavin loved his wife with every fiber of his being. Even after ten years of marriage his greatest pleasure was to look at her. It still astounded him that a beautiful living doll, such as she was, could love a big, ignorant riverman. She was his world; his life revolved around his beloved Eleanor.

Tennessee, kneeling on the floor beside Turley Blaine, saw the love on Gavin's face when he looked at his wife. She hoped, she prayed, that someday the man she loved would love her half as much.

"Put the kettle on, lass," Gavin said to Tennessee. "I'll take this sassy wench to bed and make her a toddy. Her hands are like ice."

"She'll not stay in there, Gavin." Tennessee got to her feet. "Sit down with her and let me make the toddy. That way you'll be sure that she drinks it."

The three of them stayed by Turley's bedside throughout the long night. Eleanor went to sleep in her husband's arms. He continued to hold her. Tennessee added more fuel to the fire, changed the ice pack, wrapped blankets around Turley Blaine's thin body, and kept the warm bricks at his feet.

"It's unthinkable that anyone would do this to Turley. He's such a good and gentle man," Tennessee said after a long silence, and tucked covers closely around his thin shoulders.

"Aye, lass. It's greed what makes a mon strike down what stands in his way."

"Turley wouldn't hurt anyone. He's old and not very strong. A man would have to be awfully mean to hit him."

Gavin gazed fondly at the French and Indian girl who sat so patiently beside the old man. She had formed an attachment for his Eleanor many years ago, and when Eleanor and Amy Devereau were taken from the village of Davidsonville while Gavin and Rain Tallman were away, the girl had run five miles alongside a rocky creek to see where Hammond Perry's henchmen were taking them. Without the help of this lass he might never have known the bliss of having Eleanor as his wife. Aye, he loved the girl as if she were his own.

"Ye've seen the ways of a mon, lass. They be good ones and they be the bad ones. 'Tis Perry's hand in this. God! But if I could get me hands on the mon, I would be throttlin' him."

"Will you go looking for George, Gavin?"

"I be thinkin' on it, Tenny. I be wishin' Daniel was back. With Turley laid low, I cannot be leavin' the mill. I'd not be knowin' where to look for George if I did."

"Mike doesn't expect Daniel and Mercy back for several weeks. Mike is worried about the talk. He said the whole town knows about the men coming to get Mercy, about Daniel staying at the house with her, and about them leaving together. He said Mr. Knibee is behind most of it."

"A fiddle on the talk," Gavin said with a snort. "Busy bodies is what they be. Daniel be an honorable mon."

"What can we do?" Tennessee asked.

"I'll be callin' on Knibee come mornin'. If 'n the mon had a hand in the takin' of George, 'n' strikin' down Turley, I'll know."

Tennessee lifted the cloth from Turley's head to turn it over. She paused, looked into his face, then sat back on her heels.

"Oh, Gavin! Turley's not breathing!"

"Air ya sure, lass?"

Tennessee nodded tearfully.

Gavin got to his feet and carried his wife into the other room, put her into the bed, then hurried back. He knelt down beside the bed and placed his fingers on the old man's neck.

"He be gone, Tenny," Gavin said sorrowfully. He lifted Turley's sagging lower jaw to close his mouth.

Tennessee bowed her head and made the sign of the cross on her breast.

"God rest his soul," Gavin murmured, and pulled the blanket up over Turley Blaine's face.

CHAPTER FIFTEEN

There had been a flurry of activity at the Baxter homestead since the first light of dawn, and now the sun was slanting through the tall cottonwood trees. Mercy stood in the yard with the other family members, saying good-bye to Cousin Farley, who was going on south to visit relatives at Mud Creek.

"Yore maw was second cousin to Aunt Fanny, Hod. Or maybe it were Cousin Bessie Mae. If I recollect, a Varney married up with a Cartwright gal and they had Fanny, Oscar, Maynard, Eldon, Percy, Fletta Mae..." Cousin Farley counted on his fingers, repeating the same names. Finally he said, "Yup, I was right. Yore maw, Mary Len, was second cousin to Aunt Fanny."

"I never knowed how it was ya was kin. Maw always called ya Cousin Farley. We're obliged to ya fer comin' so quick," Hod yelled with his hand cupped around his mouth.

"Huh? Oh, yes, they be glad to see me at Mud Crick. They be graves to preach over, and a weddin' or two. I reckon that horny bunch's got a heap a younguns on the way. I ain't done a weddin' in a while"—he paused and scratched his head thoughtfully—"or have I? Seems like I done one some time back, 'n' it were a hurry-up too."

"Here's yore horse, Cousin Farley," Lenny shouted. "He's all saddled 'n' ready ta go."

"What ya say, Lenny? Of course that's my horse. I rid him here, didn't I? Where's Bernie? That damn muddle-head ort to stop foolin' with them snakes."

"Here's a packet a grub Marthy fixed up fer ya, Cousin Farley," Hod said. "Stop 'n' stay with us when ya come back this way."

"Yep, it sure is. It's goin' to be a dandy day. May the good Lord look kindly on ya 'n' keep your feet on the straight and narrow," the old man shouted above the clatter of hoofbeats as the horse took off on the run.

Lenny breathed a sigh of relief as he watched him leave. With Farley's black coat flying out behind him, he reminded Lenny of a black crow. If the old fool didn't break his neck before he got to Mud Creek, he'd be surprised. Lenny glanced at Mercy, then away. He had been sure Cousin Farley was going to tell Hod and Wyatt that he and Bernie had forced their sister to wed. He was not sure how his brothers would have reacted to the news. They had taken to Daniel like a duck to water, but then they didn't know the man as he and Bernie did.

Mercy tied the strings of her bonnet beneath her chin and waited on the porch for Daniel to bring the wagon up to the front of the house. Gideon, following Daniel, led his buckskin. He looked the animal over appreciatively, stroked his neck, and tied him to the end of the wagon. Martha had filled their food box with slices of leftover ham, bread, and gooseberry jam. Gideon moved Daniel's saddle and made room for the box.

Hod came out of the house with the small, square box containing the death crown. He held it reverently in his big hands before he handed it over to Mercy.

"I don't feel like this belongs to me, Hod. I wish

Mamma hadn't said for me to take it. It should stay here with you and the others."

"Maw was right in sayin' fer ya to take it. She wanted ya ta be feelin' ya was a Baxter. Hand it down to yore younguns, Hester. Mayhap some will come settle in the hills. Hills is in Baxter blood."

"I'll take care of it always," Mercy whispered. When Daniel brought her carpetbag, she opened it, put the box inside, and packed her clothes carefully around it.

"When ya get a hankerin' fer real whuskey, Dan'l, try some of this." Wyatt set two jugs in the back of the wagon. "That be pure Baxter whuskey. The best in these hills."

"Thank you, Wyatt. A man never knows when he's going to get snakebit." Daniel cast a glance in Bernie's direction as he set the carpetbag back in the wagon.

Daniel shook hands with Wyatt and Hod, then stood back while Mercy said good-bye to her family.

"'Bye, Martha. Thank you for making me welcome." She hugged the big, plain woman.

"We was glad to have ya. Ya was a comfort to Maw in her last days." Martha patted her shoulder.

"'Bye, Dora. Take care of yourself and that baby you're carrying."

"'Bye. I wish ya wasn't going, Hester."

"Maybe you and Wyatt can come see us sometime." She held out her hand to her brother.

"Ya come back, hear?" Wyatt said gruffly, and squeezed her hand.

"'Bye, Hod. I was scared of you at first, but not now."

"This be yore home, Hester," the big gruff man said sincerely, and held her hand in both of his. "If'n ever yore in need or want to come back, yore welcome."

"Thank you, Hod." Mercy sniffed back a tear. "'Bye, Gideon." She held out her hand to her younger brother. He clasped it, shuffled his feet, and grinned nervously.

Lenny and Bernie were standing off to one side.

Mercy wanted to make peace with them before she left. As she started toward them Daniel stepped out quickly and firmly took her arm.

"Stay here," he said softly.

Daniel's lengthy strides took him to the two brothers. They scarcely realized his intentions before he lashed out with first one fist, then the other. Lenny took three steps backward before he hit the ground. Daniel's fist had split his lips when it collided with his mouth. Bernie went sprawling, blood spurting from his nose. Both men lay on the ground where they had fallen. Neither made an attempt to get up.

"You know what that's for," Daniel said.

"Whoa, now!" Hod shouted. He and Wyatt stepped out and grasped Daniel's arms. "What's this about?"

Daniel shook loose from the hands holding him and spoke to the two men on the ground.

"I promised myself I'd beat you to a pulp. The reason I don't is out of respect for your brothers. I've taken a liking to *them*. What I just did will have to do, unless you want to take it farther. In that case I'll take on both of you, as I figure two of you don't make one of me." He rubbed the knuckles of one hand with the palm of the other.

"What's this about?" Hod asked again, gruffly.

"Ask them." Daniel looked Hod in the eye, then back down at Lenny and Bernie. "As far as I'm concerned, it's settled." He turned to Mercy. "Ready to go, honey?"

"I thank you for coming to get me, Lenny. You, too, Bernie," Mercy said. "I want you to know that I'm glad I came, and I'm sorry I gave you so much trouble at first. It was such a shock to me to know I had a family, and I didn't understand your need to hurry back here." She turned and went to the wagon when they didn't speak.

"Me 'n' Wyatt had no idee there was hard feelin's twixt you and the boys," Hod said.

Daniel took out his handkerchief and wiped the blood from his knuckles. "It's settled."

"We been figgerin' on them seein' ya back home. We ain't likin' ya bein' on the road by yoreself in these troubled times of robbers 'n' runaway niggers."

"I'll keep an eye out," Daniel said, and helped Mercy up onto the wagon seat.

"They be robbers aplenty travelin' the roads. These be hard times, Dan'l. They'll slit yore throat fer a fancy wagon 'n' a good horse." Wyatt spoke as Daniel came around to check Zelda's harness and adjust the cheek straps.

"I'll not be caught unaware, Wyatt," Daniel said, and held out his hand. "No hard feelings about that?" He jerked his head toward Bernie and Lenny.

Wyatt grinned. "Glad it warn't me. Ya pack a wallop."

"You, Hod?" Daniel asked.

"Not if'n they had it comin', 'n' I reckon they did. I'm thinkin' yore a fair man."

"Thank you for that. I'll take care of your sister, just as I promised your mother."

"I figger ya can do it."

"Come back," Dora yelled when Daniel was settled in the seat.

"'Bye," Mercy called.

Daniel flicked the reins, and Zelda moved briskly out onto the track leading away from the homestead. Mercy looked back and waved to the group in the yard. She looked back once again before they reached the timber. Hod and Wyatt stood with their wives and Gideon. There was no sign of Lenny or Bernie.

"It's going to be a dandy day, just like Cousin Farley said." Mercy smiled at Daniel, removed her bonnet, and loosened the shawl from around her shoulders.

Daniel grinned back. "He's a wiry old coot, even if he can't hear himself think. He rode that horse out of the yard as if the devil were after him."

"Maybe he was." Mercy's laughter was a tinkling, musical sound that drew his eyes to her face again.

"Are you glad to be going home?" Daniel knew she was but wanted to hear her say it.

"Oh, yes. Aren't you?"

"You bet!" After a while he said, "I liked them. I didn't think I would, but I did."

"So did I."

Along the trail, the brush was beginning to flower. Mercy breathed deeply of the sweet, warm air and felt her spirits soar. They splashed across the shallow rock-bottomed creek that curled behind the Baxter homestead, and Zelda, happy to be on the trail, moved briskly on up the track.

Mercy's gaze strayed over to Daniel. She loved the rugged planes of his face and the hole in the middle of his chin. He had the most beautiful eyes beneath the straight black brows, and when he smiled, as he had just done, they wrinkled at the corners. Her eyes went to his hands— they were long, slender, and strong. Her body quivered at the thought of them on her naked flesh. He was her husband, and he had every right to touch her breasts, to touch any of her secret places if he wanted to. Oh, she hoped that he wanted to make her his mate in every way. Her heart began to race at the thought of what could happen during the night to come.

Daniel glanced at Mercy for what seemed to him the hundredth time since they'd left the Baxter homestead. This was what he had been waiting for. He had her all to himself, but how was he going to bring up the subject of their marriage? He couldn't just ask her if she loved him and wanted to stay married to him. She would say that she did out of gratitude, if it was what she thought he wanted to hear. He had to know if she *loved* him as a wife loved her husband, as Liberty Quill loved Farrway Quill, as Eleanor loved Gavin, as Amy loved Rain Tallman.

Rain and Amy lived in the Arkansas Territory, twenty miles from their nearest neighbors. Months went by when

Amy didn't see another human being but Rain and their two boys. It was enough for Amy; she loved Rain that much.

Daniel had to force himself to look away from the woman beside him. Once he had taken her sweet body, there would be no turning back. He had to be sure that she wanted him and no other for the rest of her life before he dared to claim her as his own. Daniel began to wonder how she would feel warm and naked in his arms, her mouth and her body open to him. Would she be repulsed by the act of mating with him? From what he had heard, most women didn't like it. The few men who had women who enjoyed that part of their married life didn't talk about it. Good Lord! He had to stop thinking about her.

With doglike determination Daniel began to concentrate on the terrain, the curve in the trail ahead, the bushes along the track that could conceal a man. He didn't think there was much of a chance they would be jumped this close to the Baxter homestead, but he must be vigilant. A frown settled on his face, and his hands tightened on the reins as the thought of some unknown danger threatening Mercy flashed through his mind. He glanced at her. Her head was tilted, and she was smiling as she watched a hawk soar in the sky. His whole body yearned to hold her and tell her of his dreams.

Mercy didn't think she had ever been happier than she was at this moment. It was a beautiful, cloudless day; she was alone with Daniel, her love, and they were going home. Up ahead, through the trees, was the cabin where they had been married. Looking back on that day, she decided that it was not so terrible an experience as she thought it was at the time. Even the snake Bernie used to frighten her didn't seem to be as deadly as it had then. As they passed the cabin Daniel looked over at her and smiled as if he knew what she was thinking.

Later, when he took the reins in his left hand, flexed the fingers of his right, and flattened his palm on his thigh, she took his hand in hers and gently ran her fingertips over his cut knuckles.

"You had to hit them, didn't you? I had almost forgotten that you said you were going to."

"I hadn't forgotten. If the damn fools had let that snake bite you, I would have killed someone."

"Did you see the surprised look on Bernie's face after you hit him?" Mercy's musical laugh floated away on the breeze.

"I was too busy aiming my other fist at Lenny's mouth."

"It happened so fast that Hod and Wyatt were stunned."

"Lenny and Bernie didn't want Hod and Wyatt to know what they had done." Daniel chuckled. "Lenny fairly sagged with relief when Cousin Farley rode out."

"Why do you suppose they did it? Right from the start they were angry because you stayed the night in the house with me. They couldn't have thought that I was a . . . a loose woman."

"After seeing the way they regarded Gideon's adventures, I think what they couldn't believe was that I hadn't taken advantage of you." Daniel looked into her eyes and just barely stopped himself from saying, "Not that I didn't want to."

"Adventures! I think Gideon's *adventures* are disgraceful."

"They don't think so."

"I realize that it would have been difficult to explain our . . . relationship to Hod and Wyatt. They took it for granted right from the start that you and I were—that you were my husband. So did my mother."

"They would have been as put out as Lenny and Bernie if we had told them differently," Daniel said thoughtfully.

"Daniel," Mercy said, and giggled, "let me see your

eyes. I didn't know that you could tell if a man was a providing man by how close his eyes were set together."

Watching as laughter burst from her lips, Daniel laughed, too—a deep, rumbling, uncontrollable sound that he hadn't heard for so long, it almost startled him.

"Your mother was a smart woman," he said, focusing his gaze on the trail ahead. The urge was on him to hold her against him, nuzzle her ear with his nose, taste the sweetness of her full, smiling lips.

At mid-morning Daniel stopped in an open place near a clump of bushes where he could see for a good distance in all directions.

"We'll rest the horses for a half hour, and you can walk a bit and stretch your legs."

He had been thinking about the warning Hod had given about robbers along the trail. He knew that from now until they reached home, he would have to be on his guard. He was reluctant to worry Mercy about it, but sooner or later he would have to tell her about the possible dangers.

She jumped down from the wagon, stretched wearily, and headed for the bushes, welcoming the privacy they afforded. When she returned to the wagon, Daniel was waiting with a cup of water in his hand. She drank it gratefully and smiled her thanks.

"We're making good time, aren't we?" She handed him the cup. He refilled it and offered it to her. When she shook her head, he lifted it to his lips and emptied it.

"Yes. Coon Hollow isn't far from here. We'll stop there and eat." He looked at the sun. "We'll not make it by noon. Think you can hold out for another three hours?"

"Sure, but can Zelda?"

"I'm sure she can. It's downhill going." After they had started up again, Daniel said, "I'll ride Buck this afternoon. It'll lighten up the load for Zelda." He didn't add that he would be in a better position to watch ahead and behind if he was on horseback.

They heard the clang of the blacksmith hammer as they came into Coon Hollow. The dogs raced out to yip and snarl, and chickens ran squawking because their hunt for food had been interrupted. The blacksmith paused and nodded as they passed. A woman with a basket on her arm stopped and stared. Daniel tipped his hat politely, then looked over at Mercy.

"Is there anything you want at the store?"

"I can't think of anything."

"We need to stop at the livery and buy grain for the horses. Then we'll go on out of town and eat down by the creek."

While Mercy waited on the wagon seat for Daniel to come out of the livery, her eyes wandered over the town. She was glad they would not be spending the night here. The building with the sign that said BED AND EATS looked to be one of those small inns that had only one dormitory-type sleeping room. She would much rather she and Daniel camp out in the open.

The thump of the grain sack in the back of the wagon told her that Daniel had returned. The liveryman stood in the door and watched as Daniel climbed up on the seat and slapped Zelda into motion.

"The man was a damned robber," Daniel said disgustedly. "I could have bought three bags of grain in Evansville for what that one cost."

"He probably thought you'd never be by this way again."

"If I am, I'll know where *not* to stop," Daniel growled.

Half a mile out of town, he pulled off the trail and stopped beneath an oak. He immediately unhooked Zelda from the wagon and began to rub her down. After that he led her to water, filled a feed bag, and slipped it over her head. Mercy walked down to the creek, relieved her aching bladder, then washed her face and hands. Daniel passed her, leading his buckskin, as she returned to the wagon.

She had the food box open, and meat and bread laid out when he returned. He took off his hat, finger-combed his hair, and took from her hand the bread and meat. They stood at the end of the wagon and ate in silence. He poured water from the jug and they drank from the same cup.

Mercy was surprised to discover that she was shy with Daniel, the man she had been with almost every day of her life until a few years ago. She found herself perspiring with nervousness. Why didn't he say something? She had turned to see him darting glances at her, but he hadn't said half a dozen words since they stopped to eat. Mercy wondered if he was getting tired of her company. She knew that he was eager to get home. Turning away to hide her face, she forced from her mind the thought that his feelings for her were the same as they had been when she was a child —that he was still taking care of her as he had then. She remembered hearing Liberty Quill say that there was nothing more agonizing or embarrassing than unrequited love. She was going to have to be careful not to let her feelings for Daniel be an embarrassment to him.

A sigh escaped Daniel's lips. Being constantly on guard with Mercy took more energy than lifting heavy sacks of grain all day. Now, as he watched her, he instinctively sensed a fawnlike unease she had not shown before. Was it because they were alone? She began to repack the food box. When she flicked a glance at him, there was none of the warmth in her eyes he had seen that morning. He wanted that warmth, needed it desperately.

"We'll have enough meat and bread for supper," Mercy said as she repacked the food box.

Daniel saddled the buckskin before he hitched Zelda to the wagon. He checked the load in his rifle and in the pistol. He put the rifle in the scabbard attached to the saddle and placed the pistol under the wagon seat. Mercy glanced at him. His brows were drawn together as if in deep concentration. She climbed up onto the wagon seat and waited for him to mount and come up alongside.

"I'll be right ahead of you. If there are times you don't see me, don't worry, because I'll be able to see you."

Mercy nodded. She looked into his eyes and was startled by the tenderness she saw there. Her tongue was stuck to the roof of her mouth, but she didn't know what she wanted to say, anyway.

Zelda followed the buckskin. The track crossed the creek and cut through a thick stand of spruce and pine. They came out into an open meadow. The sky overhead was clear blue, with a few puffy white clouds rolling lazily along on a slight breeze. The long, magnificent sweep of landscape was green, glistening in the afternoon sun, providing a vivid contrast to the blue sky above.

A two-wheeled cart came toward them from the other end of the meadow. Daniel slowed the buckskin until he was riding alongside Zelda. Mercy watched the cart approach, saw a man, a woman in a stiff-brimmed sunbonnet, and a child in the cart. She pulled Zelda to the side so the cart could pass.

"Howdy." The man who spoke had long, unkempt whiskers, and the woman's face was brown and wrinkled from long hours in the sun.

Mercy nodded and smiled but received no answering smile from the woman or the child.

Shortly after that they entered the pines again, and Daniel rode ahead. At one time Mercy was alone for a long stretch of time, yet she wasn't frightened. Daniel had taken his rifle, but the pistol was on the floor of the wagon at her feet. It seemed hours before they came out of the dark woods and into the sunshine, and shortly after that the sun was a red ball in the west.

Daniel motioned for her to stop. He tied the buckskin on behind and climbed up into the seat to take the reins.

"We should reach the place where we camped before in

about an hour. I think that's a good place to stop for the night."

"I could use a cup of tea." In the setting sun the air was cooler. Mercy hugged her shawl around her.

"I'd rather not have a fire, honey. You can smell wood smoke for miles."

He had said it again. *Honey*. Mercy's need for tea suddenly vanished.

"You did take stock in what Hod said about robbers, didn't you?"

"I knew the risk even before he voiced it. Don't worry, we'll not take any chances."

Mercy moved over until her shoulder was tucked behind his. His body was so solid, so warm. She felt her insides warm with pleasure when his hand found hers and tucked it in the crook of his arm.

"I'm not the least bit worried. Between us we should be able to handle a couple of robbers," she said lightly.

He turned his head toward her, and his eyes held hers like magnets. The touch of his body, the warm caress of his smiling eyes, called out to something deep inside her. Ten seconds passed while they looked at each other. Mercy drew a shallow breath, followed by a deeper one.

It was dusk when they reached the curve in the creek where they had camped with Bernie and Lenny. Daniel stopped the wagon in the same place where he had stopped it before.

"I'll take care of the horses," Daniel said, jumping down from the wagon. "You go on down to the creek. Get behind that bank out of sight and wash, or do what you want to do. No one can come up on you unless I see them from here."

Mercy took soap and towel from her carpetbag. "Don't you want to water the horses first?"

"There's a backwater along here that will do for them."

The creek water was icy cold. Mercy washed her face

and hands and ran the cloth over her neck to wipe away the film of dust. She longed for a tub of warm water. She was hungry and her stomach growled. She hurried back to the campsite. It was going to be cool tonight without a fire.

When Daniel returned from washing at the creek, they sat on the tailgate of the wagon, ate bread and ham, and washed it down with creek water. Mercy smeared the gooseberry jam on bread and held it to Daniel's mouth. He took a bite and almost nipped her fingers.

"Ouch!" Her eyes smiled into his, and she lifted a finger and wiped jam from the corner of his mouth. "Ungrateful is what you are," she said, teasing. "From now on you can put jam on your own bread."

"You've got some on your upper lip. I think I'll take that."

He leaned toward her, and his tongue swiped the jam from her mouth. She didn't move. She looked into his quiet, smiling face and the soft brown eyes that now anxiously waited to see if she would throw back a sassy retort. Love and tenderness welled up within her. She lifted her free hand and held it to his cheek. Still holding her eyes with his, he turned his lips into her palm. She felt them move, felt the warmth of his breath, and her heart tried to leap from her breast.

"It'll be dark soon." He said the first words that came to his mind and slid off the end of the wagon. "There'll not be moonlight tonight if that cloud bank coming up out of the south keeps coming."

Mercy was only half aware of what he was saying. His hands at her waist lifted her off the end of the wagon.

"Do you think it will rain?"

"It could." Daniel climbed up into the wagon bed and threw out the bedrolls, then arranged his saddle and Mercy's carpetbag, the grain sack and the food box, and covered them with a canvas. "If we should have visitors in the night, I want them to think we're sleeping in the wagon."

"Where will we sleep?"

"I've got it figured out. I've staked Buck here close to the wagon. He'll let us know if anyone comes nosing around. Bring the blankets, I'll carry the rest."

Mercy followed him toward the willows that lined the creek bank. When he reached them, he stopped and looked back toward the wagon. Its shape was clearly visible. At the base of a large oak he stopped again and looked back.

"This will do. If it rains, we'll get under the willows."

Mercy looked at him blankly when he took the blanket from her hand and spread it on the soft grass beneath the tree. She remembered Hod's warning, and for a moment she was alarmed.

"You think someone will try to sneak up on us?"

"I'm not planning on it, but if they do, I want to be ready. Come on. Sit down." She sat down with her back to the tree, and Daniel sat down beside her, his rifle, pistol, powder, and shot within reach. "Are you cold?" He flung out another blanket, pulled it up around her, and felt her tremble. "Don't be afraid. Between me and old Buck out there, there's not a chance of anyone sneaking up on you."

"Do you think I'm afraid just for myself?" she said, flaring. "Oh, Daniel—sometimes you make me so mad!" She clutched his arm and shook it.

"Now, don't get all riled up." His arm went around her and pulled her close to him. "Tomorrow night we'll stay in Evansville. I know of an inn where you can get a good warm bath, and we'll eat in style in a private dining room. Will that make up for having to sleep in your clothes on this hard ground?"

"I don't mind the hard ground or sleeping in my clothes. I just want you . . . safe." She wiggled out of the confining blanket, and throwing it over the both of them, she turned and snuggled against his side. He was solid flesh and bone, and his heart beat steadily against her breast. She could smell the masculine smell of his body and . . . gooseberry jam too.

"Danny . . ." Her hand moved up his chest to his throat. "If anything happened to you, I'd just . . . die."

Daniel's chest was so tight, he could scarcely breathe. He was aware of every soft curve of the body pressed to his. Every time he touched her, it was harder to keep from crushing her to him and blurting out his love for her. Slowly he sucked in a fortifying breath. This was the time to get things settled between them. He couldn't put it off any longer, nor could he bear for another hour to go by, not knowing if she was going to be truly his. While he thought of what he was going to say, his hand stroked the arm that lay across his chest.

"We need to have a talk, Mercy."

Mercy, he'd said. Not *honey!* A cold chill traveled down Mercy's spine. He wanted the marriage put aside! Her arm slid around him and tightened unknowingly. She closed her eyes. Please, God, don't let him say that! She strived for calmness by telling herself that she would accept it, if it was what he wanted. She would not hang on him, cry, or make him feel guilty. She loved him enough to turn him loose, didn't she?

"Did you hear me?"

"I heard you, Danny. What . . . is it you want to talk about?"

"Don't make it difficult for me. You know we have to decide how we're going to deal with this . . . this situation we're in."

"Have you thought about what we should do?"

"I didn't have to think about it. I want to know how you feel."

"You know how I feel about you." *Oh, Danny,* her heart cried. *Don't make me say it.*

"I know that you're fond of me. We've known each other for almost as long as I can remember. We're comfortable together, and we share many memories. The fact that we were both orphans drew us together when we were children."

"I had a wonderful childhood—"

"We're no longer children." He took a deep, trembly breath. "We're a man and a woman. Being fond of a man is not the same as . . . loving the man who is your husband, or the woman who is your wife."

Mercy was still for a long while, trying to analyze what he had said. Then it dawned on her. He wanted to be free, and he was trying to make it easy for her. Swallowing the lump that rose to her throat, she tried to make her voice natural when she spoke but failed miserably. The words came out gravelly, as if she had rocks in her throat.

"What you're trying to say is that you're fond of me as a sister, but you do not . . . love me as a man loves his wife." She heard Daniel's indrawn breath and felt him stiffen.

"Goddammit! I didn't say that at all!"

"Well . . . I thought you did—"

"I've got to know how you feel about *me!*" he demanded in a voice as angry as any he had ever used with her. "Are you merely fond of me? I want to know, right now!" He threw the blanket aside and gripped her arms. His face was close, and his lips were curled in a snarl. "Can't you understand? I don't want to be your brother!" He spaced the words for emphasis.

"You're not—"

"I want you in my bed as my wife . . . my lover! I want to hold you in my arms every night for the rest of my life! Are you horrified, embarrassed, to know your *brother* wants to love you?"

"Love me?" she echoed. New life surged through her. It shut off her ability to think. She gazed at him in stunned silence.

"Dammit! Say something!"

"Give me time. You . . . love me? Really love me?"

"Don't you know?" he answered gruffly. "How could you not know? I can hardly keep my hands off you."

"You don't want the marriage put aside!" Tears filled

her eyes. With a sob she launched herself at him and threw her arms tightly about his neck. With her mouth pressed against the indentation in his chin, she whispered, "Oh, Danny. I was so afraid you'd not want me . . . for your wife. I love you. I want to be your wife, your lover. I want us to make babies together!"

"You do?" he croaked, and crushed her to him, rocking back and forth. "Ah, sweet woman!" His lips found her eyes and tasted her tears. "I love you. I don't have the words to tell how much."

"Why didn't you tell me?"

"I was afraid to."

"Afraid? Oh, darling, I can't imagine you being afraid of anything."

"I was. You purely scared the hell out of me!"

"I thought I'd lost you. You were so angry . . . the night we were wed."

"I didn't want to be forced on you. I wanted you to *choose* me over all other men." He moved her onto his lap and wrapped his arms more tightly about her. "Darlin', darlin'," he crooned. "Didn't my kisses tell you how much I wanted you?"

"I just knew that I liked them and didn't want you to stop. I waited for you to come to bed last night. I wanted you to hold me again."

"I didn't dare lie down beside you again. I . . . wanted you so much." His hungry lips sought hers, but his kiss was gentle, reverent, loving.

"I wanted to sleep in your arms again," she whispered against his mouth.

He moved form her mouth and worshiped each feature of her face with his lips, pressing soft kisses and murmuring words of love. "Sweetheart . . . you're so sweet, smell so good. Ah, my love, my love, you're as soft as a cotton ball. Don't you have bones in this sweet body?" His lips moved back to hers, and fitting her head in the crook of his arm, he deepened his kiss, sending her blood thundering through her ears.

Caught in a spinning whirlwind of desire, Mercy was aware that his heart was racing as fast as hers. She met his passion with intimate sensuousness and parted her lips to run the tip of her tongue across his mouth. She moved her lips against his in an instinctive invitation as old as time. When she felt his mouth leaving hers, she held the back of his head with one hand more tightly.

The weight on his lap felt so good. He moved one hand down to cup her buttocks and press her to his swelling desire. Stirred by his incredible arousal, he jerked his lips from hers and pressed them to the side of her face.

"Sweetheart! We've got to stop this while we can."

"I don't want . . . to stop." Her arms strained him to her.

He moaned and buried his face against the side of her neck. "We'll not spend our wedding night here on a blanket. Tomorrow night, in a soft bed, I'm going to love you all night long."

"And I'll love you," she whispered. Her hands framed his face, and she looked deeply, lovingly, into his eyes.

"Mercy, honey . . ." He drew her hands down from his face and held them to his lips. "You know what . . . happens, when I . . . when we come together in our marriage bed?"

She laughed, placed a tender kiss on his lips, and nestled down in his arms.

"Oh, Daniel! You still think of me as a child. I've known *that* since I was ten years old—even if you wouldn't let me in the barn when the bull was in with the cow."

"I suppose you asked someone. You were always full of questions," he said with a happy chuckle.

"I asked Mamma and Amy."

"When was this?"

"It was while you were gone to Louisville with Rain. I told Mamma I knew she didn't get Mary Elizabeth by sitting on Papa's lap, because her dress wasn't up." Mercy giggled happily. "Then I said that if they didn't tell me how they got babies, I would ask Mike. That got them riled up."

"I bet. What did Mamma say?"

"She said, 'Young lady, it's time you and I had a walk down by the creek'. She told me everything I wanted to know. At the time I was pretty shocked by some of it. Later, when I was older, we had another talk, and she told me that for a woman to be intimately entwined with the man she loved was one of God's greatest gifts."

"Farr said something like that to me one time," Daniel said slowly. "He said it was a lucky man whose wife enjoyed the marriage bed. He also said it was the man's duty to see that she did. I'll be gentle, sweetheart. . . ." His breath almost left him.

She sat up and looked into his face. His eyes were so close to hers that she could see the glints in them, and his breath was warm on her wet lips. She placed her nose alongside his and spoke against his lips. "I'll not be one of those women who cringe from the marriage bed, love. I want to be yours, you to be mine, have you go inside my body and give me your child." The last words were whispered with trembling desire.

Daniel's throat was so tight, he couldn't speak. He swallowed with difficulty, closed his eyes, and leaned his open mouth against her cheek.

"Mercy, little Mercy," he murmured, "you fill my life completely." He kissed her, his lips demanding yet tender. His tongue deeply invaded the mouth that parted so eagerly, and grazed over pearl-white teeth. Her lips clung moistly to his. The kiss was long and deep and full of promised passion. She took his kiss thirstily. She wanted to stay there in his arms forever. His lips pulled away, but he drew her closer to him and chuckled softly.

"What are you laughing about?" she asked.

"I feel like I'm floating above the ground."

"I feel like I'm hanging from a cloud."

"I love you," he said quietly.

"I love you too."

A great wave of love and pride swept him; his heart beat with pure joy as his hands moved over her breasts lovingly, stroking, caressing. It was like a dream having her here in his arms, knowing she was his, from the top of her shining head to the soles of her feet—his to love and to care for. He adjusted her on his lap, pressed her head to his shoulder, and wrapped the blanket snuggly around her.

They sat quietly, listening to the music of the night and talking softly of the past, the future, the discovery of their love. After a while Mercy's quiet, even breathing told him she was drifting off to sleep. Content to hold her, Daniel closed his eyes, and his mind filled with an indelible picture of golden hair and sky-blue eyes.

The voice of a wolf shattered the stillness and startled Mercy from sleep.

Daniel smiled against her forehead and whispered, "Go back to sleep. It's just that old wolf calling his mate."

"If she has any brains at all, she'll go looking for him," she said sleepily, and curled her arm about his neck. "Crazy old she-wolf doesn't know what she's missing."

CHAPTER SIXTEEN

"Are you going to sleep all day?"

The husky velvet tone reached into Mercy's sleep-drugged mind. She moved against the warm body holding her and slowly opened her eyes.

"Is it morning?"

"Almost."

"I don't want to move." There was a seductive huskiness in her voice. She moved her hand across his chest and into the neck of his shirt. Her fingers stroked the skin over his collarbone. "Have you been holding me all night?"

"No. I left you lying here all by yourself," he said, teasing.

"You didn't." She sat up so she could see his face. "Did you sleep at all?"

"A little." He didn't tell her that it was damned little, and that a few times he had laid her down, covered her, and circled their campsite. Neither did he tell her that once in the night he had heard hoofbeats, and at another time the peeper frogs along the creek bank had stopped their cadence, disturbed by something they didn't understand, and he had knelt over her, his rifle ready, until the frogs started up again.

"Did I dream that you said you loved me and wanted us to stay married?" she whispered drowsily.

"No, love. You didn't dream it." His hands moved up to frame her face, and he pulled it to his and placed a tender kiss on her lips. His fingers then moved into the hair next to her scalp. "I like to see you with your hair all messed up."

Her hands moved up to his. "Did I lose my hairpins?"

"If you did, I'll buy you some more when we get to Evansville. As soon as it's daylight, I'll build a fire. You can have that cup of tea this morning."

"Let's stay here a few more minutes." She burrowed her face in the warm flesh of his neck. "I love this place, I love this tree, I love you. Oh, Daniel, I'm as happy as a dog with two tails!"

"And too lazy to wag either of them," he said with a chuckle, and blew the strands of her hair from his lips.

She licked his neck with her tongue, then fastened her lips to the spot and began to suck vigorously. His fingers found her ribs, and their laughter mingled. They were like excited children. Everything was new and wonderful.

"Don't! Don't! I'm too full. I've got to— Oh, Daniel, don't. You know I can't stand to be tickled." Her eyes sparkled at him through thick lashes.

"Kiss me and I'll stop."

It was fully daylight before they picked up the blankets and went back to the wagon. Daniel put the pistol on the wagon seat, within reach of her hand.

"Stay here and let me look around, and then you can go down to the creek and wash up."

Mercy's eyes followed his tall, lean-limbed figure as he walked away from her. When he walked, his feet hit the ground lightly. He didn't lumber along as her brothers did. He carried the rifle with the stock under his armpit, his hand on the trigger, as he had been taught by Uncle Juicy a long time ago. The old mountain man who had raised Farrway Quill would be proud of Daniel, she thought suddenly, and smiled.

It was so wonderful to be with him, to know that he was hers. No other woman would ever know the feel of his arms or the gentle touch of his lips. Mercy was adrift in a sea of happiness.

When Daniel returned, he told her that there was no great hurry for them to leave. They would be at the river in the middle of the afternoon, and in Evansville a short time later. They sat by the small fire, drank tea, and ate bread and ham again.

"I'll not want ham for supper tonight," Mercy said firmly. Her eyes traveled lovingly over Daniel's face, and her smile was one of girlish sweetness.

"I'll not want it for a week, if ever." Daniel was hardly aware of what he was saying. He found such joy and exquisite pleasure in being with her, watching her radiant face, he could have been eating a leather boot.

"I'd like a nice crusty meat pie, fresh bread and butter, peach cobbler with cream—"

"Is that all, Mrs. Phelps?" The very realness of her happiness was a miracle of every-expanding proportions.

"No, husband, I want a bath!" The laughing words gushed out of her mouth.

Daniel got up to put the campfire out with the water left in the teakettle. "I thought of something last night while you were asleep. We can be married again by another preacher, or we can go to the courthouse in Evansville and be married by a magistrate if you want."

"Would you feel more married if we did?"

"No, but I thought you might want a nice wedding to remember."

Mercy laughed in joyful abandonment. The sound soared, pure and sweet, right up to the tops of the giant tree.

"I've got a wedding to remember. I may be the only

bride in the world that shouted, 'Yes, I'll take him,' to the preacher who was so deaf, he couldn't hear. Let's keep our wedding, Daniel. It's a wedding to tell our children about."

When they left the clearing in the bend of the creek, the sky above was overcast, but they could see the sun shining on the hills ahead. Sitting close beside Daniel, her shoulder behind his, her hip and thigh snugly against his, Mercy had no thoughts except of him. She was happy, so happy! There would be no lonely future for her; she and Daniel would be together forever.

Daniel, however, was thinking about the fresh tracks on the trail. Two riders were up ahead. Between them and the river, where they would take the ferry, was a twisting, winding trail through dense woods. The perfect place for robbers lay along that stretch. Daniel reasoned that as long as he could see the tracks of the two horsemen, they were in no danger from them. But if they cut off into the woods, it would mean trouble.

Beside him, totally unaware of any danger, Mercy chatted happily. "Mamma is going to be pleased. Now that I think about it, I think she wished for us to fall in love. She said that cowlick, that thing that causes your hair to grow in the wrong direction, and the dimple in your chin were signs of admirable qualities. Did you know that?"

"I didn't know that. I hope that you're suitably impressed with your husband's admirable qualities."

"Oh, you!" Her laughter rang in the quiet stillness. It had a joyous, earthy quality, like the wind.

Daniel's eyes, dark and intense, clung to her like a caressing hand for long seconds. They traveled lovingly over her face, her passionate red mouth, laughing eyes, windtousled hair, and down the tight, slim body and firm, round breasts. This was his bride, the love of his life. Now a silent prayer was in his heart: *Dear God, let me keep her safe.*

They entered the woods, and Mercy lapsed into silence, sensing Daniel's preoccupation. He watched the trail ahead, his face still, his eyes moving from side to side. She felt his arm tense, and her eyes were drawn to the pistol on the floor. If it became necessary, if someone threatened Daniel, she could grab it and shoot.

The thought had just crossed her mind when Daniel spoke softly. "Pick up the pistol, honey. Hold it in your lap."

Mercy obeyed. She held the barrel in her hand, the butt toward Daniel. In the stillness of the woods there was only the muffled sounds of the wagon wheels and the horses' hooves. It was dark and cool. There was an eerie stillness. Mercy set her eyes on the farthest point of the trail and kept them there, watching for any movement. The trees had closed in on them, the branches meshing into a canopy overhead. There was no undergrowth of brush beneath the thick foliage, but the ground was padded with years of dried leaves. The tree trunks were so close together, you could see no more than ten feet into the forest on either side of the trail, which was so narrow that two wagons could scarcely pass each other.

The sound of a running horse coming toward them was sudden. Daniel hauled up on the reins, bringing Zelda to a halt so quickly that her front feet left the ground and she edged toward the trees. Daniel wrapped the reins about the brake and quickly pushed a protesting Mercy down on the floor between the seat and the footboard.

"Get under the seat," he hissed when she attempted to raise her head. He leapt over the seat and into the wagon bed. From behind the seat he watched the trail, his rifle, and the pistol he had jerked from Mercy's lap beside him, in his hands.

"What is it?" she whispered.

"I don't know. Stay there. No matter what I do, stay there!" he ordered sharply.

The sound of the pounding hoofbeats became louder. The horse was traveling fast. Daniel watched the bend in the trail ahead. The horse, when it burst into view, was riderless. The stirrups of the saddle on its back flopped against its heaving sides as it ran at full speed. With head up, eyes rolling, and wet with sweat, the horse thundered toward them. Frightened, Zelda whinnied and danced sideways. The buckskin tied behind the wagon jerked on the lead rope, rocking the wagon, and kicked out behind him. The big gray came on at breakneck speed, then swerved around the wagon and raced on down the trail.

Daniel waited for a full five minutes, watching ahead and behind. It was quiet after the sound of pounding hooves were swallowed by their distance. He stood up, and Mercy crawled out from under the seat.

"Who was it? I couldn't see."

"A riderless horse. Someone must have scared hell out of it." He handed her the pistol. "A snake or a bear could have caused it to bolt and throw the rider."

"A bear?"

Daniel grinned and said lightly, to ease her fear, "Don't worry, I'm a good shot." He placed the rifle across his lap and shook the reins to get Zelda moving.

"My goodness, but that was exciting." Mercy adjusted her shawl and looked at Daniel. The intense look on his face caused her heart to make a frantic leap. She bit her lips and said nothing. It would be time enough to know what he was thinking when they were out in the open again.

They passed through the dense, dark forest and into one that was lush and green and allowed scattered patches of sunlight through. Alongside the trail was a thick grove of stately pines, and beneath the branches was an abundance of ferns and wildflowers. Mercy heard the plaintive call of the mourning dove and the happier sound of a bobolink. Another time she would have enjoyed this beautiful place, but now, knowing that Daniel was tense and alert, she wanted only to hurry through it to the open stretches beyond.

When they finally came out into the full sunlight, she let out a long sigh. A warm breeze drifted over them, bringing a scent of the river ahead. They turned at the same time to look at each other.

"I'm glad to be out of there," Mercy admitted. "Where do you suppose the horse came from?"

"I don't know, but I don't think it's anything for us to worry about."

The tracks of the two horses were still on the trail ahead of them. Daniel had seen where the running horse had come out of the woods. He doubted, now, that the two riding ahead of them had any interest in what was coming along behind. They were probably just two travelers going to Evansville, as they were.

Daniel, however, was relieved when they rounded a bend and went down the trail toward the Ohio River and the ferry that would take them across the river. Somewhere along the way amid a growing number of tracks, he lost the prints of the horses and forgot about them.

While they waited for the ferry at the landing Mercy got down and walked back and forth to ease her aching muscles. Daniel watered the horses and hung the feed bags over their heads. It had been a long morning for the horses and for them.

Evansville, when they reached it, was a bustling river town of several thousand inhabitants. Twelve years ago, in 1818, it was made the county seat of Vanderburg County. The first session of circuit court was held in the home of one of the town founders. At that time the town was only a cluster of log cabins. Now the seat of government was housed in a two-storied brick courthouse, set in the middle of the town square.

Daniel drove down a street lined with shops fronted by a boardwalk. Freight wagons, buggies, carts and horsemen clogged the street, but Daniel skillfully guided Zelda through the traffic to a framed and painted building at the end of the street. He stopped in front. A small Negro boy jumped off the porch with a huge smile on his face.

"I watch yo' wagon, sah."

"All right." Daniel smiled and rubbed his knuckles over the woolly head. "I'll take the lady inside and I'll be back." With his hands at her waist, he swung Mercy down to the boardwalk.

"Is this where we'll stay?" Mercy glanced at the open door and beyond to a carpeted floor. "It looks nice."

"It's the best the town has to offer." Daniel took her elbow and escorted her inside. He set the carpetbag down, left her, and went to the counter.

"Welcome, sir. Are you needing lodging?"

"The best room you have."

"Yes, sir. Sign here please." Long, slender hands that looked as if they had never done a day's work turned the open register toward Daniel. The young man's dark eyes went from Mercy to Daniel and back. Ooo, la, la, to have such a wife, he thought, or a mistress. He revised his thoughts to *wife* when he looked at the neat script on the register—Daniel Phelps and wife. He adjusted the lace at his cuffs. Oh, well, some men were born lucky, even this rough, crudely dressed one.

"My wife will want a bath."

"It will be extra."

"No matter."

"Yes, sir. I'll see to it at once. You will be in Room Two, directly above." He took a key from a board on the wall behind him and placed it on the counter.

"Meals?" Daniel asked, picking up the key.

"We start serving at six o'clock—in the dining room."

Daniel turned away. He didn't like the way the man eyed Mercy, but as long as the young popinjay kept his thoughts to himself, he'd tolerate him. He picked up Mercy's bag, cupped her elbow with his hand, and led her up the stairs.

The first thing Mercy saw when Daniel opened the door and she entered the room was a big, high, four-poster bed with two plump pillows. A washstand with china pitcher and bowl stood against one wall. Beside it on the floor was a blue-flowered chamber pot. A bureau, with a straight-backed chair beside it, stood against the other wall. A square of carpet lay on the floor beside the bed. The room was small, and when she turned, she came up against Daniel's tall, hard body. Her skin began to tingle. This was their wedding night. They would be together in that soft bed!

"They'll bring up a bath." Daniel's voice was raspy. He set her carpetbag down, and they came together, wrapping their arms about each other. "I'll go find a livery while you take your bath." His lips moved against her ear.

"Kiss me before you go."

"I've been wanting to for hours."

His brown fingers lifted her chin and his eyes searched hers. He lowered his head and kissed her softly, reverently. There was no haste in it. She kissed him back hungrily, her lips moving beneath his. A slow fire began to seep upward from his toes, and he turned his lips toward her cheek. His arms loosened and his hands came up to cup her head. A rap on the door caused him to step away from her.

Daniel opened the door to a maid with a tin hip bath and a burly man with huge buckets of water hanging from each arm. The maid placed the tub in the corner of the room, and the man emptied the water into it and went out.

"I vill bring the kettle ta hot the vater." The maid, a plump German girl, placed towels on the chair, curtsied in an old-world manner, and left the room.

Mercy opened her carpetbag and searched for her soap.

"I didn't think they'd bring it so soon."

"I'll wait until she comes with the hot water. After I go, I want you to bar the door."

The maid returned with the kettle of boiling hot water and poured it in the tub, trailed her fingers through the water, then nodded approvingly to Mercy and went out.

"Enjoy your bath, honey. I'll be back in about an hour, and we'll go down to the dining room."

"I'll be ready." She looked into his quiet face, and her eyes mirrored the love in her heart.

"If you look at me like that, sweetheart, I'll not go."

She moved close to him, snuggling in his arms, and held her lips up for his kiss.

He kissed her quickly. "If I don't leave now, I'll not go, and your bath will get cold."

"Then I'll bathe in cold water," she said against his lips before she pulled away from him. "You're the dearest man in the world," she declared.

"Of course." His eyes teased her. "I'm dear, I'm handsome, I'm kind, and . . . I'm leaving." He laughed and his dark eyes glowed warmly, the creases in his cheeks making arcs around his smiling lips. "Drop the bar," he said before he closed the door.

Mercy felt a sudden, delicious rush of joy. This was her wedding night, and she was totally, completely, utterly in love with her husband.

It was purely wonderful to sink into the bath of warm water, but Mercy didn't linger. There was too much to do before Daniel came back. After her bath she laid the blue dress out on the bed and ran a damp cloth down the skirt to help rid it of wrinkles. While it was drying, she put on her last set of clean underclothes and brushed her hair vigorously. After she was dressed, she made a coiled rope of her hair, wound it, fastened it to the top of her head, and then carefully pulled a few curls loose above her ears and at her temples.

It was slightly more than an hour before Daniel returned to the inn. He had managed to accomplish a lot in that short time. After he had found a livery and arranged for the animals to be cared for, he had sought out a barber. Bathed, shaved, and in clean clothes, he'd had a short conversation with the barber, then headed for a merchant a few blocks down the street.

Now, with his purchase tucked safely in his pocket, he rapped on the door of Room 2.

"It's me, Mercy."

Mercy opened the door and stepped back so he could come in. He closed the door behind him, leaned against it, and looked at her. They stood quietly, as if to absorb the presence of each other.

"You had a bath too." Her voice was weakened by the depth of her emotion.

"Uh-huh. You're so pretty! I want to kiss you, but I'm afraid I'll mess your hair." He tossed his hat on the bed.

Laughter bubbled up. "We're acting so shy, you'd think we didn't know each other. Do you think we'll ever get used to this new feeling? Oh, Daniel, I hope not!" She went to him, and her arms went around his neck. "It's just so wonderful to be free to put my arms around you," she whispered, pressing the full length of her body against his.

He took her mouth in a hard, swift kiss. "I have something for my wife."

She leaned back and looked into his eyes. "For me?"

"You're the only wife I have, love." His smile covered his face, making his eyes shine. The fingers of one hand closed over hers while with the other he delved into his pocket. She was still looking into his eyes when he slipped the ring on her finger. They both looked down at his big hand holding hers; the wide gold band had slipped easily over her knuckle and glinted there on her third finger.

"Oh, Daniel! I had forgotten about a wedding ring!"

"I hadn't. I want the world to know you're mine."

"It's beautiful."

"I told the merchant to stay open. If it didn't fit, we'd be back."

"We don't have to. It's perfect!" She held her hand up and twisted the ring around on her finger. "See. I'll not lose it."

He brought her hand to his lips and kissed it. "Let's

go eat, honey," he said, and draped her shawl about her shoulders.

The maid was lingering outside the door when they opened it. "I come vor the tub," she said, not looking at them.

Daniel nodded, and he and Mercy went down the stairs and into the dining room. At the entrance he paused and looked the place over. There was a long communal table where several men sat eating, and two small tables. He led Mercy to the small table covered with a white cloth and seated her.

The slick-haired young man who had been behind the counter when they arrived nodded to one of the serving women. She left the long table and hurried to the kitchen. The clerk wondered about the big, broad-shouldered man named Daniel Phelps. Since leaving Boston to come to this uncivilized place, he had seen few men who moved with such ease and spoke with such quiet authority. Phelps had stopped on his way out that afternoon and demanded, not asked, that they be served crusted meat pie, fresh bread and butter, and peach cobbler. The clerk had opened his mouth to say the evening menu was planned but closed it and went to the kitchen immediately to order the cook to make the cobbler, the rest being already on the evening menu.

Mercy's shining eyes went from Daniel's face to the ring on her finger. She looked around the dining room and wondered if everyone knew that this was their wedding night. She caught the dark-haired man looking at her and quickly turned away. He knew, or else he was curious about them.

Mercy's smile widened when the woman brought the hot, crusty meat pie and the fresh bread and butter.

"Just this morning I was wishing for this."

"I remember."

"Peach cobbler too?" she exclaimed when the woman

brought the dish, set it on the table, and moved away swiftly. "You asked for it!" she accused happily.

"Yes." He smiled into her eyes.

They were not as hungry as they thought they would be, but they spent three quarters of an hour at the table.

"I can hardly wait to get home, Daniel. Will we go right out to your farm? I'll not spend another night away from you," she warned.

"It'll depend on what time it is when we get to Quill's Station. I suppose we'll stay at the house. If we leave early and make good connections at the ferry, we could be home by dusk. If I think we can't make it home, we'll stop in the afternoon at New Harmony."

"I won't mind the long day. I'll be with you."

People passed and the lovers didn't even look up. They had eyes only for each other. Light faded and lamps were lit. They finished eating and drank the hot, sweet tea.

"Would you like to walk a bit?" Daniel asked when they'd left the dining room.

"Would you?" She looked shyly up at him.

"No."

"Neither would I."

He took her arm and they went up the stairs. Mercy paused in the doorway of their room and waited while Daniel lit the lamp, then moved inside, closed the door, and dropped the bar across it. She stood quietly and watched him go to the window and pull the curtains together, enclosing them in their own little heaven. He turned and opened his arms, and she ran to him.

His embrace enfolded her. Mercy loved the lean hardness of his body and closed her eyes as she lifted her face to meet his. Trembling lips softened and parted as his mouth possessed hers. A warm tide of tingling excitement flooded her when his kisses turned fierce and devouring as tongues met and mouths slanted across each other with hungry impatience.

"Sweet, sweet . . . wife."

"We can be together . . . all night long." Mercy pulled back, and her eyes searched his quiet, dark face.

"All night long," he echoed softly, and smiled. "Do you want me to leave while you get ready?"

"No," she said quickly. "Don't leave." She reached into her hair for her hairpins. His fingers covered hers and sought out the pins. He placed them on the bureau and finger-combed her hair. It hung down to her waist. She brought it over her shoulder, and with her eyes holding his, she loosely braided it in one long plait, deftly twisting a length of loose hair at the end to hold it.

Sitting on the edge of the bed, she removed her shoes and stockings, then stood and unbuttoned her dress. She pulled her nightdress from her carpetbag. Daniel stood at the end of the bed, suddenly shy. How could he undress and expose his arousal to her innocent eyes? Her effect on him was devastating to his self-control. He wanted to see her, yet he could tell by the way her eyes flicked toward him and then away that she was shy about taking off her clothes in front of him. He turned to the bureau, stood there for a moment, then lifted the chimney and blew out the lamp.

Mercy was relieved. She was not as uninhibited as she thought she would be. Being with him was too new. She quickly removed the rest of her clothing and slipped the gown over her naked body. The bed felt wonderfully soft when she got into it and moved over to the far side. She closed her eyes tightly, almost dizzy from the blood pounding in her ears. Anticipation sent her heart galloping madly. She heard him moving in the room, then felt the covers lift and the bed tilt as he slid in beside her.

With a low, wordless moan he reached for her, enclosed her in his arms, and brought her against his hard-muscled chest. His mouth found hers and, gently, softly, reverently, he kissed her. Her smooth, womanly arms crept about his neck. The fragrance of her filled his brain, and her lovely, curving form nestled against him. The sweetness of her filled his senses.

Mercy's hand moved over his back and down to his bare buttocks, rested there hesitantly. He moved his head slightly and took his lips from hers.

"I don't even own a nightshirt."

The absurdity of it made her giggle. Her hand stroked his buttocks and moved to the small of his back, over his ribs, his hipbones, learning the feel of him. Every few breaths, she turned her lips to his, caressing his mouth with haunting gentleness.

His hands were rough and callused but amazingly gentle as they stroked the length of her body from her shoulders to her waist, to her thighs and buttocks. He wanted her out of her nightdress, wanted her naked breasts against his chest, wanted the soft down where her legs joined to be pressed against his rigid flesh. It seemed to him that he had waited forever for this moment. His kisses grew deeper. His tongue invaded her mouth and she welcomed it.

Mercy felt her body catching fire from his. She felt an unbearable tension growing deep in her belly, then spreading to a throbbing ache between her legs. She moved her mouth from his.

"Daniel, do we . . . ?" she breathed.

He waited, but no more words came from the soft lips pressed to his.

"Do we what, love?"

"Do we . . . do I take off my nightdress?"

"Would you mind?" His whisper was ragged against her ear.

"Not if you want me to. Tell me what to do."

"Just love me . . . and let me love you."

"Darling . . ."

"It was torture to lie beside you and not do this!"

"It's over, darling. Hold me. Love me."

Her heart soared with love and pride. She moved

away from him and slipped the nightdress over her head. In an instant they were back together, naked and straining, feeling every inch of each other.

"There's nothing between us. You feel so good!" His voice was choked with the harsh sound of desire.

Her breasts pressed into the silky hair on his chest, his hand cupped her buttocks and pressed her soft down to his rigid arousal. He claimed her mouth once more, filling it with the sensual caress of his tongue. She gave herself up to his kiss with an abandon that made the clawing hunger in his loins an agony.

He bent over her breasts, kissing first one and then the other, until she arched in a silent plea. He took her breast in his mouth, drawing, sucking, tugging on her with a slow rhythm. The rough drag of his tongue was so painfully exquisite, she drew in a gasping breath. When his fingers moved into the mound of tangled hair that hid the hot core of her and slid, caressingly, inside, pleasure speared through her body, bringing soft cries. She moaned and arched against his probing fingers. Her world began to careen crazily beneath the savage urgency of the wild emotions that claimed her.

Trembling from the force of his need, Daniel pulled her thigh up over his. He clutched her buttocks with strong fingers and held her while his aching flesh slid across her soft thigh, then pressed hungrily at the entrance of even greater softness. When the tip of him entered her body, his open mouth sought her lips, parting them. Their breathing became one, and Mercy lost her last touch with reality. Swimming in a black void, she was totally unaware that as soon as his blunt hardness touched her intimately, intruding into her soft, womanly flesh, his life-giving seed pumped into her.

Mercy awakened to soft words and gentle kisses.

"Sweetheart . . . love . . ."

The sweet, familiar smell of his breath and the light

touch of his lips at the corner of her mouth brought a small, inarticulate sound from her.

"Darling?" Daniel whispered anxiously. She lay on her back as he bent over her.

"Did we . . . do it?" Her hands moved up into his tumbled hair, fondled his neck and the strong line of his shoulders, then came up to stroke his cheeks and caress his ears. His lips, sweet and firm, moved over hers. She felt the rough drag of his cheeks, the caressing touch of his hair against her forehead. Her legs were entwined with his.

"Not all. I couldn't . . . help myself," he muttered against her cheek. "There's more, love. Much more. I've spent so many nights wanting you, I couldn't hold back."

"What do you mean, more? What could be better than this?"

"I'll have to show you."

"You were . . . hard and trembly."

"I barely got inside you," he whispered apologetically against her shoulder.

"I remember only . . . that. It was so wonderful, I must have swooned."

"Swooned! Oh, love . . ." His voice was a moan of agony.

"It's all right. I was just . . . so excited."

A groan started deep in his throat as he felt desire that had been only momentarily appeased stir in his loins. His mouth closed hungrily over hers in a moist, deep, endless kiss. She gave herself up to his kiss with an abandon that made hunger leap even deeper inside of him. The palms of his hands moved over her breasts, rousing her nipples to hard buds. A powerful, sweeping tide of love flowed over her, making her feel stronger than the hard-muscled body entwined with hers.

"I like for you to do that." She pushed her breast harder against his palm and raked her fingers through the soft fur on his chest.

"I like doing it. I like touching all of you. Ah, love, the nights will never be long enough for me to love you like I want to," he whispered urgently, kissing her, stroking her lips with his tongue, kissing again. "I want to lose myself . . . inside of you." His breathing was shallow and rapid, while her heart thudded a wild, frantic rhythm.

"You can . . . you can," she crooned. Hesitantly she brushed her fingers along the tense muscles of his stomach. "Can I touch you?"

He drew in a long, torturous breath as he guided her hand to his hard, heated, elongated flesh where throbbed the pulsing hot blood of his desire. His whole being turned to liquid as her slender fingers gently explored the length of his rigid flesh, then circled him with her hand. Her touch sent an agony of sensation through him. He was glad now that the edge had been taken off his passion and he was able to control his desire.

"You were like this that night down in Kentucky when you kissed me. I felt it against me."

"Yes . . . I was afraid it would frighten you."

"You could never frighten me!"

"When I go inside you, it may hurt you." He pressed the throbbing flesh against her hand. "Tell me if I do and I'll stop."

Daniel moved to bring her beneath him and lowered his hips between her thighs. It was her hand that guided him into the warm cavern of her body. She swallowed a strangled moan as he probed with gentle, but unrelenting, pressure at her tight, resisting flesh. She felt herself stretching to accommodate him, aching for fulfillment. When she arched against him, a small, sharp pain exploded in her innermost recesses, and there was a sense of delicious fullness as he plunged deep within.

"Oh . . . oh . . ." she whispered when it finally seemed that she could breathe. Feeling that her heart would stop, she pressed her face against the base of his neck. His hungering mouth would not allow hers to hide. He searched out her lips, and he kissed her slowly, deliberately. The touch of his tongue was persuasive rather than demanding. She gave herself up to the waves of emotion crashing over her, and the ache of his intrusion subsided.

Mercy was not aware of the precise moment he began to move within her. Her hands roamed his back, feeling hard ridges of his muscles body, enjoying the feel of his strength under her hands.

She responded to his wild, ardent kisses, her tongue playing with his. Suddenly she was quite incapable of reason. She arched against him and met his thrust instinctively. Each movement now was forceful and hard, as if he were trying to reach her very soul. It brought her to a new plateau of pleasure, and each level seemed to her to be as high as she could go, yet she was filled so completely with bliss that she continued to soar up and up. Somewhere along the way she had lost her fumbling innocence and was driven by a fierce desire to keep him there, inside her, the tip of his heated shaft moved inside her in an ever-increasing rhythm, knocking with sweet symphony against her womb. She buried her face in the hollow of his throat, whimpering at the glorious agony of sensations he was creating in her. His hands, on her hips, pressed her to him. She was consumed by rippling waves of exquisite sensation as the warm, healing fluid from his body passed into hers.

Shaken and exhausted, he rolled so that they lay locked together on their sides, and their minds drifted back from the nether ends of the universe where they had fled during their joining.

"Sweetheart . . . did I hurt you too much?" he whispered between kisses on her damp forehead.

"You didn't hurt me at all." Her hand moved down to where they were joined. "I never realized that . . . all of you would go inside me." She could feel his smile against her face. "Do married people do this every night?"

"Some do . . . at first."

"It's all right with me if you want to." She giggled happily and laid her head back against his arm to observe his face, but all she could see was the white flash of his teeth when he smiled. "I lost my virginity!" she said, as if she had just thought of it."

"Yes. You're no longer a maiden."

"If you hadn't married me, I would've stayed a maiden forever," she said staunchly, then moved her head and kissed his lips lingeringly. "I love you," she whispered, sighing. "We were playmates, then friends. Now we're lovers!"

"I love you," he murmured huskily. His hand slid down the warm, smooth curve of her back, pulling her so tightly to him that her breasts were flattened against his chest.

Her body trembled against his; his lips found hers gently, sweetly. They were lost in a mindless vortex of pleasure created by caressing fingers, biting teeth, warm lips, and closely entwined limbs. They made love deep into the night, until sheer exhaustion sent them to sleep, her cheek nestled in the warm hollow of his shoulder, her naked body molded to his.

CHAPTER SEVENTEEN

"**A**re you going home with me today?"

"Is it morning already?" She opened one eye, then closed it against the light from the lamp on the table beside the bed. She ran her fingertips lightly over the face bending over hers. He was real. "Danny, when did you light the lamp?" Her words melted on her lips and were swept away by his kisses.

"About an hour ago. I wanted to see my wife."

"Have you forgotten what I looked like already?" she said teasingly.

"I wanted to see you after I made love to you, your lips puffed from my kisses, your hair in a mess. And I wanted to see these." He moved the covers down to bare her breasts. His eyes held hers, then he looked down and back into her eyes before he bent his head to kiss them reverently. When he lifted his eyes to hers again, he held them tenderly. On his face was the look of unfettered love.

"It was a wonderful . . . night." She let her fingers wander across his chest to a nipple, and gently stroked it.

"Are you very sore?" His face was buried between her

breasts. Her thighs were tightly locked between his, the hardness of his aroused flesh pressed against her leg.

"Danny..." A sudden flood of tenderness overwhelmed her, and she lifted his face to hers, longing to kiss his lips with sweet, lingering softness.

His lips covered hers, murmuring between kisses. "I'm so hungry for you. I want to...love my wife... again."

"Then why don't you?"

"I won't...if you're too sore."

"I have an ache there that only you can take away." Her hands glided over the firm muscles of his shoulders and into the silky down on his chest, wanting to touch him, satisfy the longing in him. Her hands instinctively knew what he wanted. His bare skin surprised her with its smoothness, and her hand fluttered down his side over his hipbone to his groin. His body answered the movement of her hands with a violent trembling.

He covered her, murmuring between kisses. "I love you...love you."

When his entire length was buried inside her, Mercy was lost to her own throbbing need. His arms were the only arms in the world, his lips the only lips. Words were not needed now. Their bodies conveyed the message of love.

Mercy washed and dressed while Daniel went to the kitchen to order their breakfast, and food packed for a noon meal.

She had an uncomfortable moment when she saw the small spot of blood on the bedclothes and knew the maid would see it and recognize it for what it was. But her joy in her husband was real, blotting out all else. They had spent the night in each other's arms. She knew that even if she looked the same that morning, she would be forever different. Her body had known the sharp thrusts of her lover's body. He had caressed and possessed every inch of her. She was a woman, a wife. Nothing in her life up to now had prepared her for the emotions that churned inside her when she was fully joined with her husband.

It was daylight when Daniel drew up in front of the inn. Mercy picked up her carpetbag and went out onto the boardwalk. Their eyes caught and held, and Mercy thought she would stop breathing. Daniel jumped down and made a courtly bow.

"Good morning, Mrs. Phelps. Are you going somewhere?" He took the carpetbag out of her hand.

"I'm thinking about going home. That is, if my husband can stir his lazyself to help me up onto the seat," she replied haughtily.

"Poor Mr. Phelps sure has a bossy wife," he announced to the sky above. He set the bag in the back of the wagon and lifted her up onto the seat. He sprang up beside her.

Zelda moved out into the street at a flick of the reins.

Mercy glanced at his profile. He was so handsome. His hat was pushed back, and dark hair hung down on his forehead and over his ears. She could see the deep creases in his cheeks.

"Why are you smiling?"

He turned his head to look at her. His eyes were twinkling. "Because I can't help it. I have the prettiest wife in Indiana, Illinois, *and* Kentucky. I'm taking her home to my house and to my bed. Get along, Zelda. Let's get home."

"You didn't seem to mind the bed last night," she said teasing.

"My feet hung over the end. Didn't you notice?"

"No! And I don't think you did, either."

Their eyes caught and held, and they smiled. He

grasped her hand, placed it on his thigh, and covered it with his.

As they passed through town the streets were empty except for an occasional dray wagon or a traveler headed for the ferry. They passed the store where Daniel had bought her the dress goods. The white-aproned proprietor was sweeping the porch. He raised his hand in recognition as they passed. In the open, Zelda picked up speed as if she knew she would be in her own stall come nightfall.

Mercy could hardly contain her bubbling spirit. She and Daniel would be making their home together, and she couldn't help speaking of it.

"Someday we'll tell our children about our wedding. Oh, Daniel, we'll have a home that is ours, children that are ours. We'll grow old together!"

He smiled at her with amused tenderness, and the smile reached all the way into her heart. She smiled back. He looked as happy as a small boy at Christmas. He filled every corner of her heart now. The world was suddenly bright and shining. Laughter bubbled up inside her, and a smile of pure delight curved her mouth. She even pushed to the back of her mind the gossip that caused the parents to stop sending their children to her school. There was no room for anything now but the thought of making a home for Daniel.

The morning sped by on wings of pure happiness. They talked and they talked. Would their children have his dark hair and eyes, or her blue eyes and blond hair? He wanted the girls to be blond, she wanted the boys to be dark and have their father's dimple in their chins. The boys would be tall like their father, the girls small-boned like their mother. She would teach the girls to sew; he would teach the boys to hunt and to run the mill. She would teach them all to read and to write and to enjoy the classics.

Her eyes sought his, and her heart pounded furiously. She placed her hand on her stomach. Was his seed there?

Had they already begun a child that she would someday teach all those things?

The sun had been warm on her face, but when they reached the cottonwood trees that grew along the river, the trail narrowed and the air cooled. Mercy had taken her hand from beneath Daniel's to pull her shawl up around her shoulders when she heard the first loud crack of a rifle and then felt the whoosh of air as the bullet passed between her and Daniel.

"Down, Mercy!" Daniel yelled. He let up on the reins, to urge Zelda into a run, and Mercy grabbed the seat.

Someone was shooting at them! The thought had no more than passed through Mercy's mind than a gun roared again. Daniel lurched against her. He dropped the reins; Zelda stumbled and went to her knees. The wagon jolted to a halt, and Mercy went sailing out of the seat. She hit the ground on her back. The breath had been knocked out of her, and she lay gasping, her head reeling. More shots were fired.

"Daniel!" she screamed.

Mercy felt something heavy fall across her as the boom from a gun nearby echoed in her head. The sounds of more shots reached her. She tried to get up. She had to get to Daniel, but something was holding her down. Frantically, she shoved, then realized it was Daniel's body that lay atop hers. He didn't move when she pushed at him.

"Daniel! Oh, God! Daniel!" Through the blackness that clouded her mind she knew he was covering her body with his. Their bodies were glued together with something . . . wet! "Oh, my God! Help me!"

Panic blotted her vision. She batted her eyes so she could see who was bending over them. She wrapped her arms around Daniel, holding him, protecting him.

"Get away! Don't hurt him!" Someone was trying to take him from her, trying to lift his precious weight from her body. She struggled to hold him and felt him slipping away from her. She closed her eyes and screamed, opened them, and saw someone in a peaked hat bending over them.

"Sister? Air ya all right?" It was Lenny or Bernie, she couldn't tell which.

"Oh, my God! Oh, damn, damn you! I'll kill you!"

"Help me get him turned over," Lenny said to someone she couldn't see.

Bernie knelt on the other side of them, and they lifted Daniel up and laid him on his back. Mercy reared up and leaned over him.

"What have you done? Oh, dear God! Danny! Danny!" His chest, his face, and his neck were covered with blood. He lay like a limp doll. She lifted his hand, released it, and it fell back to the ground. Black spots appeared before her eyes and she felt herself sinking away from reality and into a black void.

When Mercy came to, she was lying on her back, her face in the sun. It was wet! She lifted a hand to wipe the water from her eyes.

"Ya swooned, Sister. Wake up." It was Lenny talking.

"Daniel," she whimpered, then rolled over and crawled to him. "Oh, dear God!" Reason suddenly left her. She sprang at Lenny, hitting, clawing, scratching. "Damn you to hell! You've killed him!"

"Hold on, Sister!" Lenny tried to ward off her blows. "Get 'er, Bernie. She's gone plumb crazy."

"Stop it! He ain't dead!" Bernie grabbed her from the back and held her. "We ain't the ones what done it, nohow. We done kilt them two fellows what was doin' the shootin'."

The words began to sink into her mind slowly. It wasn't her brothers who had shot Daniel! They had come to help him. It didn't occur to her to ask what they were doing there, two days from the Baxter homestead. They were there. They would help them.

"Get your mind together, Hester, if'n yore goin' ta help him," Lenny said sharply.

Mercy's face crumbled when Bernie released her arms, and she sank to her knees beside Daniel's still form.

"How bad is he?"

"I dunno. If'n yore thinkin' straight, get somethin' to stop the bleedin'." Bernie's hand on her shoulder shook her.

"In my carpetbag." Mercy looked wildly around when Bernie left her. The wagon lay on its side, with Zelda still in the traces. The buckskin had broken loose from the wagon and stood a few yards away. She saw all this in a glance while she lifted Daniel's hand and held it to her cheek. This was not the time for her to panic, she told herself. Daniel needed her. She looked at Lenny. "Where . . . was he hit?"

"Here's one." He moved aside the sleeveless vest, split the laces on Daniel's shirt, and pulled it back to reveal a gaping hole. There was some blood, but not as much as streamed down his face from the wound on his head. "Fellers waited till ya went by. Hit him in the back 'n' it come out here. Then he got a slice 'cross his head. It's bleedin' a heap but ain't too deep, far as I can tell. He was crawlin' onto ya when he got a good'n in his leg."

"He was shot three times? We've got to do something or he'll die!"

"We best tie up his leg first off. It's bleedin' most."

Bernie tore strips from something he took from her carpetbag while Lenny slit Daniel's pant leg with his knife. Before they bound the leg, Lenny soaked a rag in whiskey from the jug Wyatt had put in the wagon and pressed it to the gaping wound in his thigh. He did the same with the shoulder wound, both front and back.

"How come you're here?" Mercy asked after Bernie

had gently lifted Daniel so Lenny could reach the wound in his back.

"Hod said to come. Said we owed it ta ya ta see ya got back. We warn't goin' ta show ourselves knowin' how ya was feelin' 'bout what we done."

"You've been with us all the way?"

"Ahead or behind. We passed by them fellers a while ago. Bernie looked back 'n' seen 'em scutterin' off the road, quick like. We figgered they was goin' ta waylay ya. We come a-hightailin' it."

"Did you kill them? Oh, I hope you did!"

"Deader 'n' hell. It's certain they was set fer killin' Dan'l. Shootin' at 'em, they was, while he was crawlin' ta ya."

"He covered me," she whispered. "He was trying to protect me."

Mercy carefully washed the blood from the crease on the top of Daniel's head. There was a groove, but it appeared to be the least serious of his wounds.

"He goin' ta have a hell of a headache. I got one like that once. I figger that's the one that killed the horse," Bernie said. "Hit's a good thin' Dan'l ducked his head." Mercy looked up at her brother and saw compassion in his eyes. "Them fellers warn't good shots a-tall. Any kid down on Mud Creek could've done a heap better."

"What do we do now, Bernie?" Mercy asked softly.

"We get the wagon turned up, 'n' my mule hitched ta it. Ya ain't ta worry, Hester. Me 'n' Lenny'll see ya on home."

Tears sprang to her eyes. "Thank you."

Mercy was surprised by her brother's cleverness in devising a place for Daniel. They knocked out the wagon seat and used the padded seat and back for a bed. Daniel's legs were too long for the short wagon bed. Lenny tied the saddle on the very end of the wagon where it would be beneath Daniel's knees. They had to keep his knee raised because of the wound in the back of his thigh.

Bernie rode one mule and led the one hitched to the wagon. Lenny rode behind on the buckskin, his rifle in his hands. Mercy sat beside her husband, her hair hanging down her back, the front of her dress bloodstained. They passed the inn where they had stayed the first night. The landlord, Sickles, stood in the doorway. He raised a hand in greeting. Mercy and her brothers ignored him.

For long, agonizing hours they pressed on. Mercy drank water from the water jug and dampened a cloth to wipe he blood from Daniel's face. From time to time he stirred restlessly but didn't regain consciousness. Lenny, Bernie, and their mules seemed tireless. Mercy told them there was food in the food box if they wanted to eat. They said they weren't hungry, but they'd take cup of water and a drink from the whiskey jug. The wagon didn't stop. Lenny took the water and the jug to Bernie, then brought it back to the wagon.

They came into New Harmony in the late afternoon. Mercy wondered if they should stop there and try to find a doctor. She thought of putting Daniel's life in the hands of strangers, and a shiver went down her spine. If he was going to get well, it would be at home with her. Tennessee was as good a doctor as there was in these parts. Many people went to Tennessee for doctoring in spite of the fact that she was part Indian.

The ferry was at the landing when they reached it. The ferryman stood with hands on his hips and looked over the strange procession. Mercy waved to him. While he walked up the ramp to the wagon she took several coins from the bag Daniel had concealed inside his shirt.

"Ma'am? Ain't this Daniel Phelp's outfit?"

"Yes." She moved the blanket aside so the man could see Daniel's face. "He's been shot. We need to get him home. Can we cross now?" She held out the coins. "Is this enough?"

"We shore can cross now, and I ain't takin' no coin from Dan Phelps when he's layin' flat on his back." He rolled his eyes toward Bernie on the mule, remembering a few days back when he had been so contrary.

"We got waylaid by robbers. My brothers were riding ahead of us and came back, or we'd have been killed." Mercy looked the man in the eyes. "They'll see that we get home to Quill's Station."

"Well, ma'am, come on aboard. Hey, there," He called to Bernie. "Will that stubborn jackass let me lead him on?"

"Nope. Jobe ain't likin' strangers. Lenny'll put the horse on, then come back fer Jobe."

Bernie stood beside the mule, hitched to the wagon, while they crossed. Lenny helped Mercy out of the wagon. She was so stiff, she could hardly stand. Her back and shoulders ached as if she had been beaten with a stick. She stood for a while, then climbed back into the wagon. She couldn't bear to be away from Daniel. Her heart felt like a lump of lead in her chest. If only he would wake up and look at her.

Daniel awakened at dusk. Slowly, hazily, he became aware of movement. He was riding, riding, riding. Suddenly he became conscious of pain. Pain that raked him like a giant claw. Darkness was hemming him in, heat was melting his bones, and he ached in every fiber of his being. His eyes grated open and he stared at the sky; then they drifted closed and opened wide again. Sweet Jesus! Mercy. Where was she? He must have said her name, because she was there, bending over him.

"I'm here, sweetheart. Are you awake?"

"Mercy. . ." A terrified look came over his face at his instant recall. "Are you . . . are you all right?"

"I'm just fine. Lenny and Bernie came in time. They

were seeing us home, like Hod said. They were riding ahead and came back."

"So it *was* their tracks I saw ahead of us. They must have spooked the horse too. I remember the shot in the back. Where else was I hit?"

"The bullet went in your back and came out the front. You have a crease on your head from another bullet. Bernie said that was the one that hit Zelda. And you were hit in the back of the thigh."

"They wanted to make sure they got me. Who were they?"

"I don't know. They were killed by Lenny and Bernie. They're taking us home."

"Tell them . . . I'm obliged."

"They know that." She smoothed the hair back from his face with gentle fingers.

"Where are we?"

"We've already crossed the Wabash. We're going up the river road."

"I'm awfully thirsty."

Mercy poured a cup of water from the jug and attempted to raise his head so he could drink. He closed his eyes and groaned.

"Oh, God! Honey, I can't. My head feels like it's been split with an ax. I can't move it."

"Lie still." Mercy reached into her carpetbag, brought out a clean handkerchief, and dipped it in the water. "Open your mouth." She squeezed the cloth, and the water dripped into his mouth.

"He come to yet?" Lenny asked as he came up beside the wagon.

"He's thirsty. If you got a dry reed, he could use it to suck the water out of the cup."

"No chore to get it." Lenny wheeled the horse around.

"Lenny will get a reed and you can drink all the water you want." She wiped his forehead with the wet handkerchief and followed it with her lips. "Oh, darling, I've been so scared. I love you."

He opened his eyes and looked at her through a cloud of pain. "I love you, honey. My wanting you all to myself almost got you . . . killed."

"Don't think about it." She put another blanket over him when he started to shake. "We've got to keep you warm."

Lenny brought the reed. "Whuskey'll keep him warm, Hester. Water it down if'n it's too strong fer him."

Mercy poured whiskey in the cup and added water. Daniel sucked it up through the reed and made a face.

"I know you don't like it, love, but it'll help."

He drank the whiskey. After a while he slipped into insensibility and dreamed he was being poked viciously with a pitchfork, and then being chased down a dim, narrow road. There was a light at the end, if only he could reach it in time. That dream faded into one where Mercy was standing against the trunk of a tree and a snake was dangling from the limb over her head. She was unaware of it, and he didn't have a voice to call out to her.

When he roused, it was dark. Mercy held the reed to his lips, and he drank cool water and sank into a dreamless sleep.

The moon was up and shining through drifting clouds when they passed the dark homestead where Belinda Martin lived. Farther down the road, old Mr. Blalock's dog came out and barked as they passed. The old man yelled, and the dog slunk back under the porch.

It was the middle of the night when they came to Quill's Station. Not a light flickered anywhere. Mercy told her brother to stop at the store and bang on the door to wake Mike. He came hurrying through the store carrying a lantern. Cautiously he held it up to see who was at the door. The light fell on Mercy, standing in the wagon so he could see her. Her hair hung down her back, her dress was stained. Mike hurried out the door. Now he could see that her skin seemed to have shrunk and that her eyes were circled with dark lines of fatigue.

"My God! What's happened?"

"Daniel's been shot. He's hurt bad, Mike. It happened about the middle of the morning, down below New Harmony. I didn't know what else to do but to come on home."

"You did right, honey. Sweet Jesus! Take him on up to the house, and I'll go get Eleanor and Tennessee."

"We had a hard time getting him in the wagon. We hurt him. I don't think we can get him out."

"You're home now, honey. Gavin and I will take him in." Mike turned away from her, but not before she saw the contemptuous look he shot at Lenny. Mercy caught the look, and her anger flared.

"Mike! Lenny and Bernie are my brothers. Don't you *dare* look down your nose at them! If not for them, we'd be . . . dead!" She began to cry. Loud sobs that came roaring up out of the depth of her misery.

"Why, honey, I didn't mean anything. Don't cry! You've been through a lot and you're worn out."

"I don't care! We've got to get help for Daniel."

Mike looked at Lenny. "Could you ride on the wagon? If I took Daniel's horse, I could get there faster." Lenny slid down. Mike started to mount. "You been riding this sucker bareback?"

"'Pears that I have," Lenny said dryly.

"Jesus! Give me a boost up." Mike set the lantern on the end of the wagon. "Take this with you. I'll be there as soon as I can."

Bernie pulled the wagon up close to the front door. Mercy and Lenny went into the house. It was cold and damp from being shut up for more than a week. Lenny built up a fire in the hearth. She lit the lamps and kindled a fire in the kitchen stove, knowing they would need hot water. After she prepared a bed in the room off the kitchen, she went back to the wagon to wait with Daniel. It seemed to her an awfully long time before she heard hoofbeats coming up the drive.

Pain awakened Daniel when they moved him from the wagon to the house, and again when Mercy and Tennessee had stripped him to wash away the blood so they could see the wounds. It had been so painful to watch as Tennessee probed into gaping holes for foreign matter and then stitched his flesh that Mercy had run out of the room in tears. Gavin had come to help the calm Tennessee, who went about doing what had to be done.

Now Mercy stood beside the bed and watched the flicker of lamplight play over Daniel's still features. Her own eyes were glazed with fatigue. She bent and placed small, feathery kisses on his mouth, his cheeks, and his eyes. When she straightened, she saw Mike, Eleanor, and Gavin watching her.

"He is my husband!" she lashed out with unreasonable anger. "I have every right to kiss him if I want to." She burst into tears.

"Ah . . ." Eleanor came to her and put her arms around her. "Of course you do. I was wondering when you two would wake up and realize you were meant for each other."

"I'm afraid! Oh, Eleanor! I'm so afraid."

Gavin put his hand on her shoulder. "Buck up, lassie. Dan'l be a strong mon. He'll come through, ye'll see."

"Tennessee gave him something to make him sleep," Eleanor said. "Come sit down. Oh, my, so much has happened. I can hardly take it all in."

Mercy's mind ran rampant over the events of the last two days, especially about the runaway horse that charged down the trail toward them and the two men who were waiting to kill Daniel. She looked around for her brothers.

"Where's Lenny and Bernie?"

"On the porch, I think," Mike said.

Mercy went quickly to the porch. "Lenny," she called, "are you and Bernie out here?"

Lenny got up from where he sat on the porch, leaning against the house. "We're here."

"Why don't you come in?" She went to them. "Please, come in. Let me fix you something to eat."

"We ain't hungry."

"Damn you! You've got to be. You haven't eaten all day."

"We had somethin' this mornin'."

"Don't you dare leave without talking to Daniel."

"He might not be talkin' fer a while. We got ta be gettin' on back."

"Not for a day or two. Please, Lenny. Daniel will want to know as much as you can tell him about the men who were trying to kill him. He'll want to know if you had anything to do with a big gray horse that came running toward us yesterday."

"Oh, that." Lenny grinned and glanced at his brother. "Bernie stung him a bit with his slingshot. The feller ridin' 'em flew off'n him like he was a bird."

"Was he waiting . . . for us?"

"I dunno. He was in the bushes. Bernie didn't think it'd hurt none ta upseat him."

"Oh, you two are the damnedest—"

"Ya ain't ort ta swear, Hester," Lenny said sharply.

"I'll swear if I want to! I'll swear every day for the rest of my life if you don't come in. It's . . . it's only good manners to accept your sister's hospitality."

"If'n yore goin' to make a big to-do about it, I guess we got to. C'mon, Bernie," he said as if he were being led to his hanging.

Mercy opened the door and preceded them into the house. They came in behind her with their peaked hats in their hands, their wild strawlike hair looking very much like sloppy haystacks, and their eyes on the floor.

"Gavin, Eleanor, I want you to meet my brothers. Lenny and Bernie Baxter. These are my friends, Mr. and Mrs. McCourtney."

Gavin stepped forward and offered his hand. "Howdy. It's pleased I am to be knowin' ye." His huge hand swallowed first Bernie's, then Lenny's, and he shook them vigorously.

Both Baxters murmured, "Likewise." But they were eying Eleanor's porcelain, doll-like beauty, as if she were something not quite real. Gavin was used to his wife's effect on men, and his craggy face broke into smiles.

"This little hunk of hair and bone is me wife. She ain't nothin' like what she looks. She's meaner than a dog with his tail in a crack. I keep her in line by whippin' her hinder two, three times a day."

Eleanor held on to her husband's arm with her two hands and smiled sweetly at Mercy's brothers.

"Don't ye be believing the likes a him. He be nothin' but a Scot with an Irish gift a gab," she said, mocking Gavin's Scottish accent to perfection, then gave him a saucy grin.

The brothers looked even more uncomfortable, their eyes going from the big man to his small, beautiful wife. A deep laugh rumbled up out of Gavin.

"I heard Mercy say ye ain't et," Gavin said. "My wife will be fixin' ye somethin'. She not be much ta look at, but she can cook."

"Ah . . . huh . . . no. We don't need nothin'."

"If my big, ugly husband says eat, you'd better eat." Eleanor's tinkling laugh was infectious. The brothers grinned bashfully and followed her to the kitchen.

"I'm going to sit with Daniel, Gavin. Don't let my

brothers leave. They just might disappear without me thanking them. I owe them so much."

"Nora'll be seein' to them. Why don't ye rest, lassie? There be plenty here to sit with Dan'l."

"I'll sit with him while you change your dress. Then I'll put it in a tub of cold water to soak." Tennessee spoke from the doorway.

When Mercy came back down from her room in the loft, she could hear Eleanor talking to her brothers in the kitchen, heard their low, hesitant voices answering, and then Eleanor's laugh.

"You'll have to bring in some firewood, Lenny, if I'm going to heat up this old stove. It's right outside the door. You're not getting by without doing anything, Bernie. Take the lantern and go out to the smokehouse and get a slab of bacon."

Mercy listened long enough to hear Lenny and Bernie scrambling to obey Eleanor's sweet-spoken commands before she went into the room where Daniel lay. She stood beside Tennessee's chair and placed her hand on her friend's shoulder. Tennessee's arm came around her thighs, and Mercy leaned against her.

"Oh, Tenny! We were so happy when we left Evansville this morning. We could hardly wait to get home and tell everyone our news. We were going to stay here tonight, and I was going out to the farm tomorrow. When I think how close those bullets came to—"

"Don't think about it. He's going to need you tomorrow . . . or rather, today. It'll be morning soon. Why don't you lie down beside him and rest? There's plenty of room. I'll be here to call you the minute he wakes up."

"Tenny, I've got so much to tell you, I don't know where to start. It all began to happen after you and Eleanor left to go to Vincennes. Oh, how I wished you were here."

"I know. Mike told us part of it. The rest can wait until you're rested. Lie down. We'll talk tomorrow."

Mercy went to the other side of the bed and stretched out beside her husband. Just that morning she had lain in his arms and they had been so full of life and plans. She reached for his hand, held it in both of hers, and stared at his profile. Until today she had not seen him lying down or sleeping. He was always big, strong, taking care of her. Now she would take care of him.

Mercy closed her eyes, intending to rest them for a moment. Fatigue overtook her and she went to sleep.

CHAPTER EIGHTEEN

Mike and Gavin sat at the table drinking coffee; Eleanor was at the end, busily writing a letter to Farr and Liberty Quill.

"The sooner we get this letter to Farr, the better." Mike watched Tennessee move noiselessly into the room, pick up the brew she had made for Daniel, and leave.

"I wish we be knowin' if Perry had a hand in shootin' Daniel."

"It all happened mighty sudden for him not to have. Who else would have wanted to get inside the mill and kidnap George? If they were just after Negroes to work their damn salt mine, they could have taken any Negro they saw in the fields. They wanted George because it would hurt Farr and Daniel. Poor Turley. There was no reason to kill him. That Perry is a crazy man! He hired someone to kill Daniel because he sent him on a wild-goose chase after Levi Coffin. That's how I see it."

"Ye may be right, but what's it got to do with Knibee? Nora heard Turley say the mon's name."

"What did you find out when you rode out to his place?"

"Nothin'. His woman said he be in Springfield. The looks on his younguns' faces said it was news to them." Gavin drained his cup. "Meanwhile I got no idey where to look for George. I feel like I be lettin' the lad down jist sittin' here."

Eleanor looked up. "Someone's got to run the mill, Gavin. Wait until Farr gets here, or until Daniel is well enough to talk. He may have some idea where Perry would have taken George."

"Nora, me love, tend to yer writin'. I be doin' my own decidin' 'bout what to do." Gavin spoke to his wife with a note of exasperation in his voice, but Eleanor didn't seem to notice. She continued to write.

"I can't tell it all. Oh, won't Liberty be surprised to learn that Mercy and Daniel are married. It's what she hoped for. Not that she ever said . . . exactly. But I could tell—"

"Who did ye say ye would be sendin' to Vandalia with the letter?" Gavin looked up to see Mike's eyes following Tennessee as she moved from Daniel's room to go up the stairs to the loft.

"Quentin Burgess," Mike said absently. After Tennessee disappeared, he added, "That crazy kid of Old Man Burgess's. He'd ride to hell and back for a price. I'll pay him half now, and half when he gets back. That'll keep him honest."

"It's done." Eleanor sprinkled sand on the paper to dry the ink. "I told Farr about Perry coming here, about Daniel and Mercy going to Kentucky, about George and Turley, and about Daniel getting shot. And the wedding."

"Ye was bound ta not forget that, was ye? Weddin's and birthin's is all-fired important, huh, lass?" Gavin laughed at the face Eleanor made at him. She knew to what he was referring. They had not told anyone other than Tennessee that Eleanor was expecting a baby. The news was so wonderful, they were keeping it to themselves to savor for a while.

Eleanor carefully folded the paper, sealed it with wax, and passed it down the table to Mike.

"If I can get Quentin started with this, Farr will have it by late tonight." Mike put the paper in his pocket and got to his feet. "I'll look in on Daniel before I go."

Daniel and Mercy were still sleeping. Tennessee, coming into the room, responded to a touch on her hand and followed Mike out onto the porch.

"What chances does he have?" Mike asked.

"Good, unless fever sets in or the flesh starts to rot."

"You look tired."

"I'll sleep when Mercy wakes up."

Mike took her hand. "Did you see the ring on Mercy's finger?" Tennessee nodded wordlessly. "Someday there'll be ring on your finger like that." He squeezed her hand and hurried away, as if he feared what she would say.

Tennessee stood on the porch in the early-morning light and watched him. What did he mean? A great wave of joy washed over her. Oh, she prayed, let it mean what she hoped it meant. She waited until he was out of sight before she went back into the house.

The day was one of the longest Mercy had ever known. Daniel roused at intervals to drink water or when the warm poultices of slippery elm were applied to his wounds. Bernie had brought a supply of reeds, and Mercy ran her knitting needle through them to hollow them out so that Daniel could drink without raising his head. Eleanor made a broth, and Mercy spooned it into his mouth. He drank cup after cup of the tea Tennessee brewed from her supply of dried, powdered ginseng root.

The townspeople began to appear on the doorstep as soon as the news spread that Daniel had been shot. Eleanor, gracious as usual, thanked them for their concern, accepted the offers of food, refused their offers to sit with the sick, and most of them were smiling when they left the Quill House.

Granny Halpen was not to be put off by one who accepted her honey cake but who refused her the full details of what had happened to the two who left town under darkness of the night.

"Mercy and Daniel took a belated honeymoon to Kentucky, that's all," Eleanor said sweetly. "They were married last Christmas, but Mercy wanted to keep it a secret because of those silly old school people who thought married women shouldn't teach."

"Humph!" Granny snorted. "Why didn't she tell 'em she was proper wed?"

"Pride. Now, Granny, you'd have gotten your back up, too, if you'd been accused of fornicating with your own *husband*. Mercy just made up her mind that if the people here wanted their children to be ignorant, it was their decision. She and Daniel decided to use the time to go visit her *real* family. They are rich plantation owners down in Kentucky, you know. On the way home they were way-laid by robbers. Now isn't that just a cryin' shame?"

"Humph! It ain't what I heard. It ain't what I heard a-tall."

"Well, now you know the truth of it, and we would just be ever so grateful if you'd set folks straight." Eleanor smiled her friendliest smile. "Liberty and Farr will be pleased to know you're concerned for Daniel. They'll be coming home soon, and I shall tell them about this lovely honey cake you brought in our hour of need. 'Bye, Granny."

Eleanor closed the door, leaned against it, and held her hand to her mouth to keep from giggling until after the old lady left the porch. The sight of Eleanor, doubled up with giggles, afforded Mercy her first smile of the day.

Jasper and Gus came from Daniel's farm in the late afternoon. They stood at the back door, their hats in their hands, worried looks on their faces. Mercy went to talk to them to assure them that everything was being done for Daniel that could be done. A big, coal-black woman with a white cloth tied around her head, fat cheeks, and large, intelligent eyes, stood beside them. She listened intently to everything Mercy said. The big wicker basket she carried was loaded.

"My woman comed ta help Mistah Dan."

"Hello, Minnie."

"Yess'm."

"Daniel has told me what a good cook you are. I'll be coming out to the farm to live when he's . . . better. We were married a few days ago."

"Wedded! Lawsy! A wife is jist what dat boy need." Her wide mouth spread into a smile.

"I'm glad you came, Minnie. We can use your help. Thank you for bringing her, Gus. When Daniel wakes up, shall I tell him that things are going well at the farm?"

"Yess'm. Plantin' is done. We help Jeems get his plantin' done, 'n' we make a pen fer Gerrit, like Mistah Dan say."

"I'll tell him. Maybe in a few days you can come back and talk to him."

"Yess'm."

"Come in, Minnie." Mercy went back into the house.

"Ya watch them younguns, Gus," Minnie called. "Make 'em mind. I be home when Mistah Dan don't need me no more."

Minnie put her basket on the table and looked around at the neat kitchen. She liked what she saw and smiled again.

"I brung Mistah Dan vittles what he like—hominy grits, greens with fatback, and sweet-tater pie."

"He's not eating much right now. Jeems put the morning milking in the springhouse, Minnie. I expect it's ready to churn. He'll be bringing the evening milking before long. Before you start something, would you like to say hello to Daniel? He'll be glad to know you came to help us."

"I sure would, missy. Dat boy, he is as close ta my heart as my own younguns."

Mercy sat down in the chair beside the bed and took Daniel's hand. He turned his head carefully and looked at her.

"You're awake again. Are you thirsty?"

"I'm about to float away, honey. I need . . . something . . ."

"I'll get it in just a moment. Look who's come to help us. Minnie is here and she wants to say hello."

"Howdy, Mistah Dan. It do be a shame yo is laid low after ya done got yo-self a wife. Minnie been tellin' ya to do dat. We gots ta get ya on ya feet, so's ya can make us some babies. Ain't dat right, little missy?"

"Everything all right at the farm, Minnie?"

"Farm's fine. Younguns is all fine. Rosie lookin' after 'em while I comed ta take care of ya."

"My wife will appreciate your help."

"Ya got ta pee, does ya, Mistah Dan? Don't ya fret none. I brin' ya somethin' 'n' ya can pee right where yo is at. I be right back."

She flounced from the room, her big hips going up and down beneath the loose shift. Daniel's eyes caught Mercy's to see how she reacted to Minnie's blunt speech.

"Are you worried that I'm shocked? Don't be. I might have been a few weeks ago but not now. Gus and Jasper brought Minnie over. They said to tell you everything is all right out at the farm. The planting is done, they've helped Jeems, and they've built a pen for Gerrit."

"I want them . . . to be careful. Tell them not to leave the farm. We . . . don't know what Perry is up to."

"I'll tell them, and Jeems too."

Minnie bustled in with a jar in her hand, her loose slippers flapping against the floor when she walked.

"Minnie'll take care a Mistah Dan's hind end till he get well," she said firmly, and went to the other side of the bed and flipped up the cover. "After dat, he be wantin' yo sweet little hands on 'em. Ain't dat right, boy?" She laughed, her belly jiggled up and down, and her red mouth opened wide, showing white teeth.

Daniel looked at Mercy and grinned sheepishly. She leaned over and kissed him, then whispered, "I guess you're not wanting my sweet little hands on you now. I'll be back when you're not so busy."

Mercy called on all the reserve strength she possessed as the hours passed. Night came and dragged by slowly, with Mercy and Tennessee taking turns at Daniel's bedside. The morning of a new day arrived, then noon, afternoon, and another long night. Mercy's heart almost stopped each time Tennessee removed the bandages from Daniel's wounds and stooped to smell the puckered flesh. Each time she stood and smiled reassuringly, Mercy's heart thudded with relief.

Daniel gritted his teeth at the pain and endured the discomfort of having his knee boosted on a pile of pillows. His leg felt as if it were being pricked with a thousand needles each time he moved it. He ate what the women brought him to eat, and drank the vile potion Tennessee brewed without complaint.

By the morning of the third day, Gavin took Eleanor

home, and the house settled into a routine. Minnie was capable of doing enormous amounts of work despite her large size. Daniel was comfortable with her and didn't hesitate to ask for her when he had to perform his bodily functions.

Lenny and Bernie came into the bedroom and stood beside Daniel's bed. Mercy was with them.

"Lenny and Bernie want to go home. They've come to tell you good-bye."

"I was hoping you would stay until I'm on my feet. I want to thank you proper for what you did."

"Ain't no more'n what anybody'd done," Lenny said, twisting his hat around in his hand. "Me 'n' Bernie want ya ta know we ain't a bit sorry fer gettin' Cousin Farley ta wed ya up ta Sister. It was somthin' what had ta be did. But we ain't wantin' no hard feelin's over it."

"There's none on my part except for the part about the snake."

"I'da not let it bite Sister. I pulled its fangs, anyhow," Bernie said disgustedly.

"I wish you'd stay and meet Farrway Quill," Mercy said. "He's the one who found me. He's been a father to me all these years. He'd want to meet you."

"We got ta go on home. Hod 'n' Wyatt'll be needin' us. We got whuskey ta tap 'n' sell."

Daniel held out his hand. "You're welcome to our home anytime. I realize the risks you took coming back to help us, and I'm obliged."

"Warn't nothin'," Lenny said.

"Them fellers could back-shoot but didn't have no guts a-tall when they was gettin' shot at." Bernie snorted. "'Spect they got surprised."

"I expect they did," Daniel said, and grinned.

Out on the porch, Mercy put her arms around first one brother and then the other. She kissed them on the cheek, regardless of how they much squirmed. There were tears in her eyes.

"I'm glad you came to get me. I'm glad you were so persistent, too, or I might not have gone with you. I'd have missed out on seeing my mother and knowing my family. You know where I am now if you ever want to come visit. Like Daniel said, you're always welcome."

"Ya'll come if'n ya want to," Bernie said, making a hasty retreat off the porch and jumping up onto his mule.

"'Bye, Hester." Lenny put an arm about her shoulders and gave her a slight squeeze. "We got ya a good man, even if ya didn't want ta wed up with him. Ya treat him right, hear?"

"Lenny Baxter! Where did you get the idea *you* got him for me? I *did* want to marry Daniel." Mercy was talking to Lenny's back. "And another thing, nothing happened before we were married. You can believe it or not, I don't care!" Her brother got on his mule and sat looking at her from under the brim of his peaked hat. "Nothing happened! Do you hear? Damn you, Lenny, answer me."

"Yore man ort ta take a strop ta yore bottom fer swearin', Hester. If'n ya was down on Mud Creek, Hod'd take a switch to yore legs 'n' wash yore mouth out with soap."

"But I'm not down on Mud Creek, Lenny Baxter!" The brothers turned the mules and headed down the drive. "If Hod whipped me, I'd shoot him, or stab him, or something!" Mercy shouted. "And another thing—it's none of your business if I swear. I'll swear *every damm day* if I want to."

The brothers looked at each other. Bernie rolled his eyes toward the sky and flung up his hand in disgust.

"If she ain't a pisser! Shiftfire! Ole Dan'l better put his foot down on her or she'll get outa hand."

"Might be he'll do it when he gets over bein' moon-struck."

"Hester's the feistiest, mouthiest Baxter woman I ever heared of."

"I reckon it ain't her fault. She jist growed up a-spou-tin' off at the mouth when she took a notion."

"What she's needin' is a slap on her butt. Times is she don't 'pear ta have no gumption a-tall."

"Well, it ain't our to-do no more. We got 'er a man. It's on his head now if'n she acts up 'n' shames him. Let's get on home. Looks like them clouds comin' up is bringin' up a real turd-floater."

The sun had gone down, and the birds were settling in the trees for the night when the light coach came up the drive, circled the house, and stopped at the back. Mercy went racing out of the house. "Papa! Mamma!"

Farr Quill, tall and agile, with a physique of a much younger man, jumped down from the carriage. Mercy launched herself at him. He caught her and hugged her.

"Oh, Papa! I'm so glad you're home."

"I'm glad to be here, honey."

"Mamma!" Mercy cried when Farrway helped the slender, blond woman down from the seat. "It seems like it's been years, and it's only been weeks." Mercy went into Liberty's arms, and the two women hugged each other.

"How's Daniel?" Liberty's tired face was anxious.

"He's recovering."

"No fever? No . . . poisoning?"

"Not yet. Tennessee says he's doing all right. I've got a million things to tell you, Mamma."

"Eleanor wrote the most important. You and Daniel are married! Oh, honey, that's wonderful news. You were always close when you were children. I felt Daniel was just waiting for you to grow up."

"You never said anything."

"And ruin the whole thing? My land, Mercy! I'm smarter than that."

"Where's Mary Elizabeth and Zack?"

"Zack left two weeks ago to go to New Orleans with Will Bradford on a diplomatic mission. Farr thought it would be good experience for Zack. Mary Elizabeth is all wrapped up in her music. She's going to sing in the operetta the school is putting on. She'll stay with friends while we're gone. We came just as soon as we could make arrangements. Oh, I've been so worried about Daniel and poor George. Is there any word on him?"

"No, not a word." Mercy looked over her shoulder to see if Farr was coming.

Farr was shaking hands with Jeems, spoke with him for a moment, then turned the tired horses over to him. He followed Mercy and Liberty. The two were walking toward the house with their arms about each other.

Tennessee moved out of the chair beside Daniel's bed.

"Is he awake?" Mercy asked.

"Awake and anxious. He heard the carriage drive in, and his eyes have been on the door."

Liberty had stopped in the outer room to take off her hat and a light cape. She came into the room now, with eyes only for the man on the bed. Memories of a small, serious-faced boy clinging to her, saying, 'Can I call you Mamma?' came rushing at her out of the past, and her eyes filled with tears. She bent over him and kissed his forehead and cheeks.

"I've been so worried, Danny."

"I'll be fine in a few days, Mamma. Hey, don't cry. I can't stand to see my womenfolk cry."

"I can't help it if I cry! I always do when one of my children is sick or hurt."

Farr leaned over her shoulder. "Hello, Son. Your mother's been in a state ever since we got the word about you being hurt. I thought she was going to shoot the messenger bringing the bad news, like they used to do back in the Dark Ages. We wore out three sets of horses getting here."

"I hope you didn't have to leave some important business to come home."

"There's nothing in Vandalia as important as you, Daniel. What's this I hear about you and Mercy? It couldn't have been over a year or two ago that you told me she was a featherhead and dumb as a cow."

"Stop teasing, Farr. That was all of ten years ago. You're just getting so old, you don't remember." She placed another kiss on Daniel's forehead. "I wondered when you two were going to wake up and realize you were made for each other. I could never see you letting another man have her. I only wish I could have been at the wedding."

Daniel's eyes looked past Liberty to Mercy, and they smiled knowingly at each other. Someday they would tell her about their wedding. Someday but not now.

Come here, honey, Daniel mouthed silently. Mercy went to the side of the bed and knelt down. He held out his hand, and she put hers in it.

"As I look back, I think I always knew that someday Mercy would be mine." Daniel looked at Mercy while he spoke to Farr and Liberty. "I remember thinking, while I was growing up, that I wanted my home to be like yours, where there was love and respect. Mercy and I couldn't have had a more loving home than the one you gave us. We had a happy childhood, didn't we, sweetheart? We want our children to be able to say that someday."

"Daniel said it far better than I could," Mercy said, looking up at the two people she loved most in the world, except for the man who lay on the bed.

"Oh, flitter!" Liberty said, sniffing. "I'm going to cry again."

"That's all right, love. You can cry all you want," Farr

said, and gently lifted his wife to her feet. "But please do it in the kitchen, sweetheart. I want to talk to Daniel."

"Well, don't wear him out. Eleanor said he has three bullet holes in him. Lordy! It purely scares me to death to think about it." Liberty turned and saw the Indian girl standing quietly against the wall. "Tennessee! I didn't see you. How are you?" Liberty went to hug the shy girl. "Farr said on the way that I shouldn't worry, that you'd know what to do for Daniel. How are Eleanor and Gavin? Did you know that Amy and Rain are planning to come home at Christmastime? Won't it be wonderful to see them?"

"Libby, love," Farr said patiently, "could you possibly carry on that conversation in the kitchen? You women will talk half the night. Maybe you can get an early start . . . in the kitchen."

With his hands on their backs Farr pushed them gently out the door. They didn't seem to have heard him or felt his hands. They were talking nonstop. He sat down in the chair beside Daniel's bed.

"Are you too tired to talk?"

"Talking doesn't hurt. It's moving that hurts like hell."

"If you can, Son, tell me what's been going on. If you get tired, we'll stop."

"There's a lot to tell. Give me some of that water there on the table and I'll start at the beginning." Daniel drew the water into his mouth through the reed, and Farr placed the glass back on the table. "It started the day Mamma left to go to Vandalia."

Daniel talked off and on for more than half an hour. He rested occasionally and drank water from the glass that Farr held for him. Farr listened intently, his keen mind sorting the details and placing them in order.

"Mercy's brothers left this morning. I wish you could have met them. They were pure hickory. Proud and poor is the only way to describe them. Their word is their bond, and what they think is right, is right. Mercy and I had a hard time understanding them at first. Later we came to like them."

"Hester was her name." Farr sat with his forearms resting on his thighs, his hands clasped, and his eyes on some far-off place outside the window. "Amy named her Mercy the night I walked into Liberty's camp down by the Ohio. I had no idea that she wasn't the child of the people who lived there and were killed."

"You did the only thing you could do."

"Yes, I realize that, but still . . ." Farr shook his head as if to dismiss the problem from his mind. "Now, about this thing with Perry. Do you think he had anything to do with the men attacking you and Mercy?"

"According to what Lenny Baxter said, the men were bent on killing me."

"I need to talk to Gavin and to Mike to find out what they know." Farr got up and paced the room. "I'd not put anything past Hammond Perry. The man has let hate consume him. Hate and revenge is what he lives for."

"I didn't know about George and Turley until this morning. Mike told me. The man I told you about, Edward Ashton, warned me that Hammond Perry was talking of taking George. I had already warned George to be careful. But from what Mike says, they came in under the mill wheel in the middle of the night. Poor Turley just happened to be there." Farr could tell Daniel was tired by his voice.

"You've talked enough, Son. Rest now. We'll talk more tonight when Gavin and Mike get here." Farr stopped his pacing and looked down at Daniel. He couldn't love him more if he were his own flesh and blood. Farr realized now how old Juicy Deverell felt about him when he was a young man. "I want you to know that I couldn't have picked a better man for my daughter to marry. I pray I find one half as good for Mary Elizabeth."

"Thanks, Papa."

Daniel held up his hand, and Farr gripped it hard. Daniel hadn't called him Papa since he had grown to manhood, and it struck a sentimental chord. Farr cleared his throat before he could speak.

"One thing sure, we're not going to let Perry get away with this. I may have to resign my post and work full-time on bringing him to justice."

"I wish it could wait until I'm on my feet so I could go with you."

"I'm afraid for George, Daniel."

"Perry will kill you if he gets half a chance."

"I know that. If I had time, I'd get the militia. But the legal process takes time. By the time they act, it could be too late for George."

"Take Gavin and Mike with you. To hell with the store and the mill. Close them up. God, I wish I was on my feet."

"I know how you feel, but I'm afraid you're going to have to wait this one out."

When Mike came to the house that evening, he had a man with him. Farr took them into Daniel's room and closed the door. Daniel didn't recognize the man until he approached the bed and the lamplight fell on his face. It was Edward Ashton, Levi Coffin's friend.

"Sorry to hear about you gettin' shot, Phelps. It might ease your pain a little to know that those bullet holes cost Hammond Perry five hundred dollars. He paid for them, thinkin' you were dead."

"Where did you hear that?"

"Sickles, the innkeeper. He saw the wagon go by and took it you were dead. He sent word to Perry. Later the ferryman at New Harmony said you were alive. I guess Perry is madder than a stepped-on snake."

"So he was behind it. Who did he pay? The men who shot me are dead."

"He paid James Howell to have you killed. Howell is a middleman. He doesn't do the killing himself—he arranges for someone else to do it."

"Did you find out why?"

"To cross him one time is reason enough for that son of a bitch to have a man killed," Edward said with a look of contempt on his face. "It's a well-known fact that he hates everything connected to Quill's Station."

"Five hundred is a lot of money."

"You pushed him pretty hard in front of his men that day at the mill. And you sent him on that wild-goose chase after Levi. The fact that you're part of Farrway Quill's family would be reason enough."

Farr had been listening quietly. "Do you know where Perry is now?"

Edward Ashton turned to Farrway Quill. He had heard about the man for years. Somehow he had thought he would be older. Quill was a man with an ageless face and only a touch of gray at his temples.

"The last I heard, he was down south at John Crenshaw's place. The reason I came up here was to tell Daniel, if he was still alive, that the young colored boy, George, is at Crenshaw's. He was taken there and put in a cell on the third floor of the house."

"Do you know about that place?" Farr asked.

"I know *all* about that place, Mr. Quill. Crenshaw's mansion is called Hickory Hill. He's a strong Methodist and donates to the church. The man's a bastard and hides behind his religious image. He's wealthy and has great political influence in the southwestern part of the state."

"I'm new in politics, but I've heard of him," Farr said dryly.

"He's a one-legged man," Edward continued. "It's said that while he was whipping some female slaves he was attacked by several males, and they hacked off his leg. He's embittered and cruel. When you go there, the Negroes will smile and wave. You'd think they were all working for wages. That's a pile of horseshit, if you don't mind my saying so. The people are so scared, they'll tell you anything."

"You know for sure that George is there?"

"He's there. He's a nice-looking, light-colored boy with his hair braided Indian-fashion. He's there—unless he's been moved within the past two days."

"Will you go with us to Crenshaw's?"

"I'll go. But if we can manage it, I'd rather not show myself unless it's necessary. I gather a lot of helpful information about the Negro-napping operation for Levi Coffin. If Crenshaw, Perry, or any of the patrollers across the river in Kentucky ever found out that it's me who ruins some of their plans, my life wouldn't be worth the spit it'd take to lick my lips."

"If you lead us there, we'll make every effort to see that you're not recognized. It will help, for you can give us the layout of the place."

"I can do that, Mr. Quill."

"The sooner we leave, the better. Mike?"

"I'm going! Gavin is going too."

"Daniel, if Mike and Gavin go, it will mean leaving the women here by themselves. Eleanor and Tennessee should come over here to stay while we're gone."

"If there's trouble here, Tenny is good with a gun," Mike said with a note of pride in his voice.

"Libby wouldn't hesitate to use a gun if she needed to," Farr added. "With Daniel to tell them what to do, they'd make out all right. Not that I expect any trouble to come here, but it's best to be prepared."

"If we leave here in the morning, how long will it take for us to get to Crenshaw's?"

"Late tomorrow night. We have stations along the way where we can exchange horses."

"I had heard the Underground Railroad was expanding. We would be pleased if you spent the night with us, Mr. Ashton. A meal will be on the table soon."

"If we're going to leave early," Mike said, putting on his hat, "I'd better ride over and tell Gavin. He can bring Eleanor early in the morning. What time, Farr?"

"There's plenty of room if they would rather come tonight. We can leave an hour before dawn."

Daniel lay on his bed after Farr and the others had left the room and cursed Hammond Perry. For the first time in his life he felt useless, and for the first time in his life he felt the need to kill a man.

CHAPTER NINETEEN

A small sound awakened Mercy. She lifted her head from the pillow to peer into Daniel's face.

"Did I wake you, honey?" His voice came softly, his breath on her lips. "I was trying to reach the water."

"I'll get it." Mercy moved carefully off the bed, went around to the other side, and groped on the table for the glass of water she had put there earlier. She held the reed to Daniel's lips, and he drank until she heard the sucking sound that said the glass was empty. "Do you want more?"

"No. That's enough. Come on back to bed." Mercy lay down beside him, keeping a foot of space between them. "I wish I could hold you," he said wistfully.

"I wish you could, too, but we'll have to wait. I'm just so grateful that your wounds are healing and you haven't been out of your head with a fever." She moved her bare foot over to his good leg and rubbed the bottom of her foot caressingly over his instep.

"I kind of remember Lenny pouring that Baxter whiskey on me. It hurt so damn bad, I thought he was trying to kill me. It must have done some good." He found her hand and held it against the flat plain of his stomach.

"Are you wishing you were going with Papa in the morning?" She moved her head to place her cheek against his upper arm.

"It's hard knowing that they're going and I have to stay here."

"I know it is, darling."

"I feel bad about Turley. He was a good man. I wish I knew who it was that struck him down. When I'm on my feet, I aim to find out." His voice vibrated angrily.

Her lips hovered over his, whispering, "Go back to sleep, darling. There's nothing you can do now that's more important than getting well."

"I know, but I can't help thinking about it."

"All this time I thought you were thinking about me," she teased, dotting her words with gentle kisses.

"I do think about you, sweetheart, and our night together. . . ."

"I was awfully dumb!"

"If you'd have been anything else, I would have beat you!"

"Did you really tell Papa I was as dumb as a cow?"

"I don't . . . remember."

"You don't remember?"

"Ouch!" he whispered when she yanked at the hair on his chest. "What did you do that for?"

"That was for not remembering that you *didn't* say it."

Liberty Quill lay curled against her husband's side, her head pillowed in the hollow of his shoulder. She had been awake for the better half of an hour. Farr would be stirring soon. During this time her thoughts had spanned

the years. Tomorrow her husband would go to the Cren-
shaw mansion in the southern part of the state to get
George, the son of their friends, George Washington, the
big black man, and his Shawnee wife, Sugar Tree. That
Hammond Perry was still seeking vengeance against her
and Farr was incredible. Yet, ironically, he was the reason
Liberty, her father, and her sister had come to the Illinois
Territory so many years ago.

Hammond Perry, the brother of Liberty's first husband, gentle, kind Jubal Perry, who had died on their way
out from New York State, had despised Liberty the moment he set eyes on her. Jubal had been old, but he had
married Liberty to save her from the clutches of a man who
would have abused her. At times Liberty felt wicked for
being glad that Jubal had not lived to learn that his brother
was a mean and vicious man. Even then, Hammond had
been jealous of Farr's influence with Governor Bradford
and Zachary Taylor. After his brother's widow married
Farrway Quill, he had become consistently more brazen in
his attempts to seek revenge, for he believed Farr was responsible for the deterioration of his military career.

"What are you thinking about, love?" Farr's hand
began to stroke her arm.

"How did you know I was awake?"

"I'd not be a very observant man if I slept with a
woman every night for twenty years and did not recognize
her breathing when she was awake."

"Nineteen years. And there was that two weeks while
you were in that prison at Fort Knox that we didn't sleep
together."

Farr chuckled and wrapped her in his arms. "Libby,
Libby. I wonder if Hammond Perry knows that if not for
him, I'd not have known the happiness of having your for
my wife."

"I'm sure it hasn't occurred to him. Oh, Farr, I know
you must go, but I'll worry until you get back."

"It isn't a dangerous mission. Perry wouldn't dare to attack me in front of witnesses."

"No, the chinless little sneak is too much of a coward! His way would be to ambush you like he did Daniel. He should have been shot long ago for a mad dog!"

"Are you getting your temper up, Mrs. Quill? Save some of that passion for your husband and give him some sweet loving to take with him tomorrow." He pulled at her gown and spoke with his lips against her mouth.

"I wonder if we'll ever get too old for this?"

"I won't! And if *you* do, I'll just throw you away and get myself a younger woman."

"Ha! You're getting to be like all the rest of the politicians, Farr Quill. You're believing your own lies!"

The arms around her tightened. He kissed her quickly. "When I get back, I'm going to have to take you in hand, Mrs. Quill. You're getting pretty dad-burned lippy."

With the early-morning start, Farr and his party were able to ride fifty miles before they bedded down for the night at a farm that was used as a way station for the Underground Railroad. Edward Ashton had been a tremendous help in getting fresh horses, knowing the out-of-the-way shortcuts and finding a place for them to sleep for a few hours. They left the farm two hours before dawn, and as the sun was coming up over the lush green forest to the east, they came out onto a plateau where they could see Hickory Hill, the end of their journey.

John Crenshaw's mansion was set high on a windswept hill near the village of Equality in Gallatin County. It was only a night's ride from the Ohio River. From the outside the house appeared to be of pseudo–Greek revival design with upper and lower verandas, supported by massive columns extending the width of the house. Double doors and four floor-length windows opened onto the upper, as well as the lower, verandas. The peak of the roof was squared. On the third floor, centered above the large doors, was a single window with small side panes. Not readily apparent was the carriageway that actually entered the house through the large double doors on the north. The immense three-storied house with its massive columns was truly a symbol of the pride of ownership. It had taken the builder from Ohio four years to complete it, using skilled workers and only the finest of materials.

Farrway Quill and his party gathered on their horses behind a screen of cedars and studied the mansion and the terrain around it. Edward Ashton told them as much as he knew about John Crenshaw and the house.

"I have been told that carriages come into the house at night. The slaves are hurried up a narrow flight of stairs to the third floor, where there's a large hallway flanked on either side by narrow doorways leading into small cell-like rooms. There are seven of these rooms on the east and five on the west. All contain double-tiered bunks. The slaves remain in the cells until time for their disposal.

"Does he bring all the slaves to his house?" Farr asked. "I see that he has plenty of outbuildings."

"All perfectly innocent servants' quarters," Edward said. "Only the slaves who are here illegally are brought inside the house. He uses the females for breeding purposes. A pregnant female, or one who already has a child, will bring several hundred dollars more on the southern market than a single slave. He's got a black stud, a giant of a man they call Uncle Bob, in a cell on the third floor. He services the females they steal from here in Illinois, and other states where slavery is illegal."

"I suppose the people who work in the salt mines have quarters there."

"Such as they are. The workers are leased from plantation owners in the South and are here in the state legally.

Crenshaw owns three of the nine furnaces in the state used to reduce salt water to crystals, the mill on the north fork of the Saline river, and thirty thousand acres of land."

Farr whistled through his teeth. "He's more powerful than anyone in Vandalia knows. It may be that no one has taken the trouble to find out."

"Another story I've heard is that a passageway runs from the house to the creek over yonder. The Negronappers bring people up the Ohio by boat, transfer them to a smaller craft on the Saline River, and come up the creek at night and into the house through the passageway."

"The mon be a real sonofabitch!" Gavin exclaimed. "He be gettin' rich on them poor souls."

"And we can't touch him . . . yet," Farr said softly. "We'll get George, if he's there. After that we'll have to work through the courts."

"This is a good time to call," Edward said. "Crenshaw is usually driven to the mines after breakfast. You'll catch him before he leaves."

"Where will you be, Ashton?"

"I'll watch from here. If you come out with George, I'll go on about my business. If not, take the river road; I'll catch up to you and we'll see what else we can do."

Farr extended his hand. "We're grateful for your help. If we don't see you again, let us know if ever there's anything we can do to help you in your work."

"Having the mill on the Wabash as a station for our railroad helps lot. See what you can get done at the State House."

"I will. This has certainly opened my eyes to what's going on down here."

Farr, flanked by Gavin and Mike, rode up the drive to Hickory Hill. As they approached, a colored man in gleaming white pants and shirt came out onto the veranda. As they neared, he motioned with his hand, and another Negro hurried out to stand in the drive that circled the house so that the riders were forced to stop at the hitch rail.

"Welcome to Hickory Hill, gentlemen." The white-clad house servant stood on the steps grinning broadly. "C'mon up on the veranda out of the sun."

Farr, Gavin, and Mike dismounted and tied their horses to the rail. Farr looked directly at the Negro who had come out to take the horses. The man looked down at his bare feet and refused to look at him. The house servant, however, looked him in the eyes, and Farr was sure his smile of welcome was a practiced one.

"I want to see Mr. Crenshaw."

"Yessah. Who shall I say is callin', sah?"

"Farrway Quill, Illinois State Representative."

"Yessah. Come in. Come right on in. I tell Mistah Crenshaw you is here." The man moved silently down the carpeted hall and disappeared through a doorway.

The house was every bit as elegant on the inside as it was on the outside. The ceilings were all twelve feet high, and the walls were papered with a gold-leaf design. The furnishings were finer than those at Grouseland, the Georgian-style home of the Governor of Indiana. The chandeliers were crystal, the carpets imported from India. The place was as quiet as a tomb, except for a few muffled sounds that could be heard coming from a distant part of the house.

"Pretty fancy place," Mike murmured to Gavin.

"Aye. Too quiet to suit me."

The servant came back, still smiling. "Mistah Crenshaw say come back to his office, sah. The gentlemen wait here."

"The *gentlemen* come with me," Farr said, smiling, then added when a look of fright crossed the servant's face,

"I'll tell Mr. Crenshaw it was my idea so you'll not bear the brunt of his displeasure."

"But, sah, Mistah Crenshaw say—"

"Lead the way, or we'll find him ourselves."

"Yessah."

When Farr walked into the room, the heavyset man swiveled around in his chair and looked at him from beneath bushy brows. His hair was combed into a peak on the top of his head, and the face that wore a frown was framed with short whiskers.

"Mr. Crenshaw," Farr said, walking over and extending his hand. "Farrway Quill."

The man shook his hand. "You will have to pardon me for not rising to meet you. I have a slight disability."

"Understandable. Your man insisted that my associates wait in the foyer. They are here at my insistence. We, too, are in business, and I thought it would be good for them to meet a successful businessman such as yourself." Without waiting for him to answer, Farr introduced Gavin and Mike.

Gavin and Mike stepped forward and shook the hand Crenshaw offered, backed away, and sat down when Crenshaw waved them to a seat.

"You're a busy man. My own time is limited, so I'll come right to the point of this visit. A Negro boy who is rather a pet of my wife has wandered down this way. I rather suspect he thought to find work in your mines. My wife has invested time and money in the boy. He paints pictures, and she has the notion to have him paint one on the wall of our parlor. You know how women are. They can get a bug in their bonnet and make your life miserable."

Crenshaw chuckled, but the frown didn't leave his face. Farr had never seen a man frowning and laughing at the same time.

"Women are fanciful creatures. What do you want from me, Mr. Quill?"

"I'm wanting to know if you have a boy here by the name of George. He's a fairly light-skinned, educated, speaks well. His mother was Shawnee, and he usually wears his hair braided, Indian-fashion."

Crenshaw twisted his mouth as if were thinking. Finally he said, "No. We've no one here by the name of George. A few times we have caught runaways and held them for their masters across the river. But we've not had one here who fits that description, or one who calls himself George."

Farr didn't speak for a long moment. He knew his silence was wearing on Crenshaw, so he remained silent for a while longer. Crenshaw swung around in his chair and fiddled with something on his desk, swung back around with his hands clapped together, his thumbs circling each other nervously. It was obvious the man was not going to prolong the conversation with chitchat.

Farr got to his feet. "Well, I guess that's that. We thank you for your time, Crenshaw. I was just thinking it would be a good thing for some of the members of the legislature to come down and see your fine operation before it's time to renew the leases on the public lands. You have a beautiful home here. It might be a good idea if you issued invitations for them to spend some time here."

"I'll give it some thought." Crenshaw's snapping lips reminded Farr of the jaws of a turtle.

"Good morning." Farr strode out the door, followed by Mike and Gavin. They were met by the servant, not smiling now, who led them to the door.

"Good day to ya, sah."

After the door was closed firmly behind them, Farr motioned Mike and Gavin to follow him into the yard. Farr walked over to a rosebush and bent to examine the buds. He began to whistle a loud, shrill birdcall. He picked off a leaf and held it up for Mike and Gavin to see. The birdcall came from his pursed lips again. Gavin stooped to pick up some of the mulch around the rosebush, held it to his finger. All were playing for time and straining their ears.

Finally a faint sound reached them. Farr whistled again. Waited. The echo came back again.

"Where is he?" Farr hissed, and walked slowly toward the horses.

The faint birdcall came again.

"He be back of the house." Gavin stood by his horse. "What to do now?"

"You and Mike wait here."

Farr sprang up the veranda steps and, without knocking, opened the door and walked in. Long strides took him toward Crenshaw's office. The servant was pushing the man out into the hallway.

"Crenshaw!" Farr's voice was as sharp as the crack of a whip.

"What do you want? What do you mean coming back into my house unannounced?"

"My boy, George, is here. Come out onto the veranda." Farr strode ahead and held open the door. The servant pushed the chair over to the veranda railing. "Listen," Farr commanded. He cupped his hand around his mouth and whistled the birdcall, loud and shrill.

Faintly the call was answered.

"What the hell am I supposed to be listening for?" Crenshaw asked. "All I hear is a bird."

"That's no bird. That's George. His father and I used that birdcall to keep track of each other when we were boys. He taught it to his son; I taught it to mine."

"It could be a bird!" Crenshaw insisted, his face growing red with anger.

"Not a *night* bird, Crenshaw!" Farr gritted angrily. "I want that boy. Send your man to get him, or we'll shoot out every window in this house, and you might just accidentally get in the way of one of those shots!"

"There is no one here by that name! Now get off my land. Representative or not, this is my property."

"My advice to you is cooperate. I want the man who answered that call, regardless of what his name is. I warn you, Crenshaw, I fight dirty." Farr called out to Mike and Gavin, "If he doesn't give the order to get that boy by the time I count to three, start shooting. Shoot through the front door, Gavin, and hit that chandelier that came from Italy."

"I'll ruin you!" Crenshaw shouted.

"One . . . two . . ."

"All right, I'll have the boy go get him. We have a runaway locked in the shed behind the house. He's to go back to his owner in Kentucky. Get him!" he snarled to the servant.

Farr whistled the birdcall again. The answer came back.

"That boy better still be whistling after your man gets there, or you'll be whistling from a new hole in your throat."

"Don't you threaten me, you backwoods . . . dolt! I could buy and sell you a hundred times. We'll see who carries weight in this state. I bring in enough revenue every year to pay for that damn courthouse."

The servant came back around the house with a man heavily shackled, his arms tied behind him. At first glance Farr felt his heart sink. The braids, so strongly a part of George's identity, were gone. Shoeless and ragged, he could take only small hopping steps.

"Mistah Farr!" The cry was a weak whimper.

"Good God! George!" Farr hurried to him, pushed the servant away, and folded George in his arms. He held the sobbing boy. "God damn you, Crenshaw," Farr said over George's head. "I ought to kill you!"

"Mistah Farr, Mistah Farr. . ." It was all George could say.

Gavin poked the servant with the end of his gun. "Get them irons off him."

The servant looked at Crenshaw. Crenshaw nodded, and the servant went into the house. He returned almost immediately with a ring of keys, then knelt and unlocked the chains that bound George's legs.

"He doesn't have braids. He's not Indian. He's a nigger," Crenshaw said. "Not that there's a mite of difference between them. How in the hell was I to know who he was? He was brought here for safekeeping, is all."

"You stick to that story, Crenshaw. It's the only thing that's keeping me from putting a bullet in you. We're leaving. This boy is half starved, and the sores from the chains are festering." He led George over to Mike. "Take him up with you, Mike, and ride on out. Gavin and I will be behind you."

Farr and Gavin mounted when Mike and George were a distance down the road.

"I'd think a smart man like you, Crenshaw, would be more careful with whom he does business. Tell your associate, Hammond Perry, that my son lives in spite of three bullet holes in him. The men Perry hired are dead."

"Tell him yourself if you want him to know something."

John Crenshaw sat on the porch for a long while after the riders were out of sight. Farrway Quill was a man to be reckoned with. He felt fortunate that he had gotten out of this situation as easily as he had, considering the influence the man had in Vandalia.

"Raymond!" he shouted, although the servant was

right behind him. "Get your black ass over to Hammond Perry's and tell him to get up here."

Crenshaw was in the office when Hammond came hurrying in. The sight of him walking on two legs, when he only had one, always irritated Crenshaw.

"What's going on, John? Raymond said to hurry, and I did."

"It's a goddamn good thing too. The longer I sit here, the madder I get. You're the stupidest damn fool this side of the Ohio. If, by your stupidity, you have blown my whole operation here, I'll have you killed."

"What . . . what's happened?"

"I'll tell you what's happened, you blundering idiot! Why didn't you tell me that boy you brought here to stud was a pet of Farrway Quill?"

"Well, I . . . what difference does it make?"

"A hell of a lot of difference! Quill was here looking for him and found him! How is that going to set with the state officials when he goes back to Vandalia and tells it?"

"Found him? How?"

"He used a birdcall. The boy answered. Cutting his hair wasn't enough, fool! You should have cut out his whistle!"

"He would've made us some money." Hammond began to get his courage back.

"You chinless bastard!" Crenshaw shouted. "I don't think you've got the brains you were born with. I've no use for a man who can't think. Get out! Come around here again, and I'll have the dogs put on you."

"You . . . can't mean that!" Hammond gasped and stepped back a step, coming up against the arm of a chair. "I've brought you some of your best people."

"You've brought me trouble I can't afford, Perry. I'll manage somehow to make my peace with Quill. I don't need you around with your petty little grievances to mess up my operation. You have bleated to everyone who will listen about how Quill has wronged you and that you intend to even the score. You'll not do it at my expense. Get out! I've said it twice, and I'd better not have to say it again."

Hammond went to the door. His legs were not quite steady, his eyes not quite seeing. He looked over his shoulder. Crenshaw swung himself around in the chair, presenting his back to him. Scarcely knowing where he was going, Hammond left the house. He climbed up on his horse as a black rage started deep inside him and spread, until he was trembling and saliva was running from the corner of his mouth.

He gigged the horse cruelly. The animal took off on the run, his hoofs digging up and throwing chunks of the carefully tended lawn. In the woods, Hammond threw himself off the horse; rolled on the ground, his hands pressed to his temples; and cried out his rage like small boy having a temper tantrum. Finally he turned on his stomach, pillowed his head on his arm, and cried real tears. They ran down his face into his beard.

"God damn Quill! And God damn the whole world!"

All his dreams of being someone important had been washed away again, by Quill. This time he would get to Quill in a way it would hurt him the most. He'd take that bitch he had married, rape her, give her to his men, then kill her, leaving the body for Quill to find. After that he would go downriver to New Orleans and take a boat to come foreign port and start anew.

Hammond sat up and dried his tears on the sleeve of his shirt. The son of a bitch would not win this time.

CHAPTER TWENTY

Daniel sat on the edge of the bed shaving with his right hand while his left arm lay in a sling against his chest. Mercy held the mirror.

"I don't know how you do that so easily. Do you ever cut yourself?"

Daniel dipped the razor in the pan of water and swished it back and forth before he answered.

"Sometimes." He brought his upper lip down and held it between his teeth so that he could shave beneath his nose.

"Will you ever grow a mustache?"

"Do you want me to?"

"No. You're handsome enough as it is. I don't want to have to fight the women off."

He looked at her quickly and saw a serious look on her face, but he also saw that she was holding her lips between her teeth to keep from laughing. Daniel laid the razor down beside the wash dish and picked up the cloth to wipe away the soap he had used to soften his whiskers.

"Some women like to kiss a man with a mustache. They say it tickles."

"Humph!" She snorted. "And where did you pick up this valuable information?"

"Here and there."

"If you couldn't use your right arm, would you let me shave you?"

"And have you ruin my handsome face?" He looked at her with mock alarm. "Sweetheart! That shot merely grazed my head. It did nothing to addle my brains!"

"Conceited creature!" She turned the mirror facedown on the bed. "You've looked at yourself enough for today. Now that you're on the road to recovery, I'll have to stop spoiling you." She lifted her chin and looked down her nose at him, as if she were talking to one of her students.

"You're the one who told me I was handsome," he said teasingly, his eyes full of bewilderment.

Suddenly Mercy remembered the serious-faced boy of long ago. This Daniel was smiling; his eyes glowed. Her heart sang. Because of her, Daniel was happy. A feeling of supreme happiness washed over her. She turned her mind back to the teasing.

"To me you *are* handsome, because you're mine. To someone else you may be as ugly as a mud fence."

"A mud fence!" He spoke as if he were talking to some unseen person in the room. "I can't believe she's saying these things to me."

"And there is more, my love. I made it clear to Belinda's mother when she was here yesterday that you are no longer an eligible man. I told her to say hello to Belinda for *us*, and to tell her that *we* want her to come visit us as soon as you've recovered and we've moved out to *our* farm."

"We're back to that, are we?" He grinned at her, his eyes shining.

"No, we are not back to that. Your prowling days are over. You are a married man with a very jealous wife. Now get back in the bed before I kick your sore leg."

"What a mean and vicious wife I have," Daniel said to the ceiling. "Does Mamma know how you're treating me?"

"She and Eleanor are upstairs looking at Mary Elizabeth's baby clothes. Eleanor was going to wait until Gavin came back to tell the news, but she let something slip, and Mamma pried it out of her. I hope we don't have to wait ten years to start our family."

"I'll do my part," he said innocently. "I'll work on it day and night. Put that washdish down and kiss me."

Mercy bent over him. His hand came up to the back of her neck, pressing when she would have moved back after a light, feathery kiss.

"Hmmm . . . you smell and taste good."

Mercy rubbed her slim nose against his. "I love you," she whispered, as if there were ears to overhear.

"I love you. I wish you were in bed with me," he whispered back. His hand moved down and fumbled with the buttons on her dress. Her hand caressed his smooth cheek, then dropped to his hand to hold it still.

"You're a lot better . . . if you're thinking of *that*!" She straightened and looked down at him, with bright, twinkling eyes. "You are the light and the love of my life, Daniel Phelps, but behave yourself."

"But, honey, it's hard to behave when you're leaning over me and your soft breasts—"

"Being the only man in this house for the past few days has gone to your head! We've all spoiled you— Mamma, me, Tenny, and Eleanor, not to mention Minnie, who thinks you're the stars and the moon."

"I'm a very lovable man," he admitted.

"Tomorrow or the next day, or whenever Papa gets back, you'll have to share our attention; you might as well get used to the idea," she said in her stern, schoolteacher voice.

"I'll not share your attention, Mrs. Phelps." His hand slid along her spine. His eyes teased her. "A husband has rights. You promised Cousin Farley to obey me. So kiss me again."

"Lie down and rest." She snapped her teeth at him. "If you're good, we'll let you get up and sit on the side of the bed to eat your supper."

"What are you going to do?"

"I'm going to take this washdish out to the kitchen, and I'm going to take the clothes off the line. I don't know what I'll do after that, but I won't be in here, so rest." Mercy picked up the washdish, the razor, and the towels.

"I wonder if Belinda would have been so mean to me!"

"You'll never know, will you?" Mercy retorted, and grinned impishly.

She left the room with a smile on her face. Her heart was light. Daniel was better, so much better. When she had lifted his leg back onto the pillow, he had not even grimaced. She saw in her mind's eye the bedeviling slant of his smile when she left him. Oh, how she loved that man!

The morning had been bright and sunny, but shortly after the noon meal, dark rain clouds banked in the west and moved steadily toward the east. Now, as evening approached, lightning flashed against the dark clouds.

The wind picked up, whipping the dry clothes around Mercy as she lifted them from the line. She buried her face in Daniel's shirt and laughed with pure happiness at her foolishness. When she was growing up and had to take his shirts off the line, she had grumbled and complained.

"Meow!" The cry of the cat brought Mercy's head around. "Meow!" Blackbird sat beside the barn door. He was not the slick, fat cat they had left when they went to Kentucky. He was thin, and it appeared that part of his long, proud tail was missing. "Meow," he cried again, but didn't move to come toward her.

"Blackbird! For heaven's sake! What's happened to you? You look half starved." Mercy walked toward him, her arms full of clothes. "Oh, dear. I'll have to take these in. You stay right there, I'll be right back." She spoke to the cat as if he understood what she was saying. He licked first one side of his mouth and then the other and stared at her with huge amber eyes.

Mercy hurried into the house, dumped the dry clothes on the kitchen table, picked up a few scraps of bread, and headed back to the door.

"What yo doin', child?" Minnie, her hands in a mass of bread dough, asked her from her work at the counter.

"These are all the clothes, Minnie. I'm going to see about Mary Elizabeth's cat. He looks half starved, and I think he's been hurt."

"It goin' ta rain. Yo get wet, 'n' yo'll come down with the coughin' fever."

"I won't get wet. If I do, I won't melt." Mercy smiled as she left the kitchen. Minnie, with her bossy ways and loving concern, was becoming very much a part of her life with Daniel.

"Yo mind me, chile. Yo get in here if'n the rain comes," Minnie called, then seconds later lifted her voice in song. "Good news! The char-i-ot is a-comin'. Good news! The char-i-ot is a-comin'. . ." Minnie usually sang while she worked. It was a happy sound.

The wind, becoming increasingly stronger, wrapped Mercy's skirts about her legs as she hurried to the barn where she had last seen the cat. Blackbird wasn't in sight, but he could not have gone far in such a short time.

"Blackbird! Where are you?"

The barn doors were closed. Mercy opened one of them, stuck her head inside, and called again.

"I've got something for you." There was no answering meow from the cat, so she closed the door and walked along the rail enclosure where they sometimes kept the cow. She called, stopped, and listened. At the end of the rail fence and behind the barn was a thick growth of sumac. Something black fluttered in the grass.

"Blackbird," she called. "Come, kitty, kitty." She almost laughed at the sound of her voice. If Blackbird could understand, she was sure that he would be insulted to be called kitty.

"Meow!" The loud screech came from the sumac. "Meow!" It was an angry cry.

Mercy went around the barn, hurrying toward the sound. The cat seemed to materialize out of nowhere. He leapt past her, screeching, and bounded toward the woods.

"Blackbird!"

Mercy made a half turn to go after the cat and came up against two men who stepped out from behind the bushes. Each grabbed one of her arms. She was so startled, she was struck dumb for an instant. When her senses returned, she opened her mouth to scream. Before she could make a sound, a rough hand was clamped over her mouth. She struggled wildly, but her strength was no match for the men holding her.

"This is her. Ain't we in luck? She come right to us. We was figgerin' on havin' to go in ta get 'er."

"She's a fine-bodied woman. I ain't goin' ta mind havin' 'er a-tall."

Mercy was more frightened than she had ever been in her life. She lashed out with her feet, her fear giving her strength. Her foot struck a shin.

"Bitch!" The man holding her mouth dug his fingers into her cheek and shook her head viciously. "Stop that or I'll pinch your head off!"

Mercy's fear had carried her beyond reason. She flayed them with hands and feet as they lifted her and carried her behind a screen of bushes. Her eyes were wide as she looked at first one man, then at the other. One had front teeth missing and wore the cap of a riverman. His face was scarred and his breath putrid. The other man was whiskered, his eyes red and watery. She was sure that she had never seen them before. Into her dull mind drifted the thought that they were going to kill her, and she'd not be with Daniel. . . ."

The riverman roughly swung her around. The instant his hand left her mouth, Mercy drew in a long breath to scream. The man's fist shot forward. Lights flashed before her eyes in a bright blast of pain. Then, just as quickly, she dropped into a pit of darkness.

The whiskered man caught Mercy as she fell. "What'd ya do that fer? I likes 'em fightin' and scratchin'. I ain't likin' to hump no limp woman."

"Ya can't do nothin' here, nohow. The boss says brin' her to the woods out back a that shack where the nigger lives."

Rough fingers fondled Mercy's breasts. "She shore do have fine titties."

"They ain't no different 'n a whore's titties. Let me get on my horse, then boost 'er up."

"Let's go. Hit looks like them clouds is goin' to open up 'n' piss all over us."

"Ain't ya ever been wet, Melcher?"

"Oncet when I fell in the river." He laughed a hoarse laugh, as if his throat were full of sandburs.

"The little prick'll be waitin'. He shore don't take no risk."

"He don't have ta take no risk. He's got the money ta pay *us* ta take the risk."

They moved the horses out of the sumac, taking care to keep out of sight of the house, and rose toward the woods. A low rumble of thunder came from the west. The man who held Mercy facedown across his thighs patted her bottom and chuckled. This was the easiest fifty dollars he had ever made, and a bonus was also attached. He ran his palm over Mercy's hips at the thought of the treat that awaited him. His flesh hardened suddenly; he pushed it tightly against the soft hip that moved in response to the motion of the horse. He was going to get in the drawers of a quality woman. It would be something to brag about when he shipped out again.

Hammond Perry watched the men approach with the woman across the saddle. Her blond hair had come loose from the pins and was hanging down over her face. He felt a flush of satisfaction. At long last he had something of Farrway Quill's in his possession, to do with as he saw fit. And he had plans for the bitch!

"We got 'er, Mr. Perry," the whiskered man called. "It warn't no trouble a-tall."

"Shut up, ya fool," the riverman hissed. "Let 'em think it was hard 'n' risky."

"I mean it warn' no hard job fer *us*."

"Anyone see you?" Hammond asked.

"Not nary a soul excepts fer a cat. I put my foot in his ass. He's crossed the Wabash by now."

Hammond turned his horse and looked back toward the house. The bent figure of an old man was walking slowly toward them.

"Get in the woods," Hammond hissed, and gigged his horse. The others followed, moving out of sight behind a stand of cedars. "That's the old nigger who lives in the shack. When he gets here," he said to the whiskered man, "knock him in the head."

"That won't be no chore a-tall." The man drew the pistol from his belt and grasped the barrel end.

Lightning cracked overhead, followed by a loud clap

of thunder. Hammond Perry cursed when a few drops of rain began to fall.

Jeems walked slowly, his head down. When he reached the end of the cedars growing along the path, he looked up in time to see three men on horseback. A blond-haired woman lay across the lap of one of them. Seconds later, one of the men charged him, and even as he lifted his arm to protect his head, a gun butt came crashing down. Pain exploded in his head and he dropped.

"Did you kill him?" Hammond asked.

"He dead, Mr. Perry," the man bragged. "I knows where to hit 'em. Thar behind the ear's the place."

"Good. We can take the woman on down to his shack outa the rain. It'll be dark soon. She'll not be missed till it's too late to look for her. I figure there's no men at the house except the one that's shot. After we take care of her we just might go back up there and finish the job."

"I can do it, Mr. Perry," the whiskered man said eagerly. "But . . . it'd cost ya extra."

"I figured it would," Hammond said dryly. He put his horse into a fast walk and hurried him toward Jeems's cabin.

Thunder and lightning came together now. Large drops of rain began to fall as they reached the shack. They tied the horses beneath a lean-to shed, and with Mercy throw over the shoulder of one of the men, they went inside.

"Jesus! This place stinks worser than a hog pen."

"Never mind, we'll not be here long. Put her down and light a couple of torches so we can see." Hammond's voice shook with excitement.

The riverman dropped Mercy on the shelf built into the wall where Jeems slept. A flame was coaxed from the embers in the fireplace, and soon a blaze flared, fed by handfuls of kindling. As light filled the room, Hammond moved inside. Across one corner of the room, stout bars had been erected, and sitting quietly behind them on a stool was the largest Negro Hammond had ever seen. The man looked at them without any expression on his face, his forearms on his knees, his hands clasped together. He didn't seem to be curious about them, merely accepted their presence.

"Jesus! What's that?" The men moved up to get a closer look. What they saw was a big, bushy-headed, filthy Negro in ragged pants and shirt.

"It's a hog pen!" Melcher said. "Niggers is strange. They don't go fer whippin's. His paw's locked him up fer somethin'. He smells like he shit on hisself."

"It's a fitting place for you to die, you slut! We'll let the nigger have ya when we're through, and then they'll hang him." Hammond chortled happily. He grabbed a handful of blond hair and lifted Mercy's head. When he glimpsed the young face, he stared in disbelief. "This isn't the one," he screamed. "You fools, idiots, sons of bitches!" He threw Mercy's head down and turned on the two men as if he would kill them. His eyes blazed, his hands shook, his lips quivered. "This isn't the one I told you to get! Shitheads! Bastards!" He called the men every filthy name he could think of, while they looked at him in stunned silence.

"But ya said light hair, thin—"

"S-sightly, she is," the riverman said, stammering.

"This is not Liberty Quill!" Hammond was gradually losing control and continued to scream. "This is not Liberty Quill! This is not Liberty Quill!"

"Who is it?" one of the men dared to ask.

"It's the brat that lives with them. Oh, God! Why am I always surrounded with incompetent fools?" Hammond sank down on a stool and put his hands to his face.

The men stood uncertainly. The riverman eyed Mercy's legs. They were hanging over the bunk, and her dress was up around her thighs. "I don't give a shit who she is. I got a thin' in my britches what wants a woman."

"Ya better wait—"

"Shut your goddamn mouths!" Hammond snarled like a vicious animal.

As the men looked at each other one of them made a slash across his throat with his finger. The other one nodded in agreement. The rain poured down on the roof, and water began to drip onto the earthen floor. Long minutes passed into a half an hour. They waited for Perry to speak. He sat as still as a stone, his eyes on some distance place. The men moved restlessly. They were uneasy about the way Perry was acting.

The big Negro watched too. He stood up, his head reaching almost to the roof. He came to the bars and looked at them with flat, black eyes.

Mercy slowly began to regain consciousness. Memory came back to her in a rush. Her jaw hurt, her head whirled, and her stomach churned. She was afraid to move. Her face was pressed against something that smelled foul.

"Mr. Perry? What ya want us to do?"

The words sank into Mercy's mind like a stone. She moved her head cautiously, but she couldn't see. Her hair was over her eyes. Then she felt her skirt being lifted and a hand probing between her legs. She reared up. Her vision was blurred, but she could see the face of the man close to hers, his front teeth missing.

"She come to, Mr. Perry."

The pain in Mercy's head was almost unbearable. Her eyes finally focused on Hammond Perry, sitting on a stool. He stared at her. She tried to get to her feet, but the man jerked her arm and she fell back down.

"Please . . ." she whimpered.

"Do you remember me?" Hammond asked.

Dazed with pain, Mercy could scarcely understand what he was saying. The faces that looked down on her were grotesque and, to her, no longer human. She felt a scream building in her throat and choked it back.

"Do you, slut? Answer me," Hammond shouted.

"Yes."

"Say my name."

"Ham . . . mond Perry," she whispered fearfully.

"That's right. *Major* Hammond Perry." A snide smile curved his lips.

"Are ya wantin' us ta go get the other'n, Mr. Perry?"

"Not yet. We got time. All the time in the world." Hammond laughed as if he had said something terribly funny. His mouth opened wide. "Haw! Haw! Haw!" He slapped his hand against his knee as he doubled over with laughter.

Into Mercy's mind came the thought that these men were going to do unspeakably cruel things to her. Her mind cleared enough so that she wondered where she was, and if there was anyone who would come to help her. The thought was followed by utterly black despair.

Hammond continued to laugh, but it was now a giggle, high and girlish. His eyes began to glow and his nostrils flared. He got to his feet and reared back with his arms folded across his chest.

"Men," he said as if he were addressing a troop. "The nigger can have her!"

The two men looked at him as if he had gone insane. They stared openmouthed. The riverman began to protest.

"The nigger? Ya promised me—"

"I promised you Liberty Quill."

"By God! I ain't goin' ta stand fer it!"

"You obey my orders, or by God, you'll get no money from me. Get the nigger out here."

"Have ya gone loony? I ain't puttin' my pecker where no nigger's been, by God!"

Hammond's shoulders reared back even more, and his head slanted back.

"I give the orders. Hump her, screw her, board her, I don't give a goddamn what you do to her, but bring that nigger out and let him watch. He'll be so horny by the time you're through, he'll split her in two." A mad gleam glowed in Hammond's eyes. "Lay back, Miss Quill, and spread yourself for the pleasure of my . . . associates. My moment of revenge has arrived."

"No, please!" Mercy sobbed frantically. "Please . . . please . . . no!" She twisted and turned, trying desperately to break loose from the hands holding her.

"Beg, you slut!" he shouted. "I only wish Farr Quill was here to see it." Hammond reached out yanked down the front of her dress, found the nipple of her breast, and squeezed viciously. A shrill scream tore from Mercy's throat. Hammond laughed. "Get the nigger."

Mercy's frantic eyes turned to the cage. The whiskered man lifted the bar and opened the door.

"Come on out 'n' see the show nigger boy. Yore goin' ta get ya some a that pussy when we is done. I jist bet ya've got a stick as big as a fence post in yore britches right now."

"Gerrit! Please . . . Gerrit!" Mercy sobbed. The big Negro looked at her, blinked his eyes several times, and moved slowly out into the room. "Gerrit, help me!"

The riverman wrapped her hair around his hand and, twisting it up tight, held her head tilted up to him.

"He ain't goin' ta help ya. Ain't nobody goin' ta."

As soon as as he slammed her down on the bunk, she struggled to get up. Hammond laughed shrilly. He put his foot on her hair and held her. Almost out of her mind with terror, she screamed and screamed.

"Shut up, ya uppity slut!" Hammond drew back his arm and slapped her across the face with such force, it knocked her head against the wall. Her screaming stopped and was replaced by a moan of pain. She felt something heavy drop on her. Her eyes flew open to see the whiskered man's face just inches from hers. The tip of his tongue was running over loose lips that were spread in a wolfish grin.

"Danny," she whimpered. "Danny, Danny..." Something snapped in her mind, and she screamed again and again and again.

Mercy never heard the guttural sounds that came from Gerrit's throat, as if the low rumblings had started deep within him before errupting in a roar that she heard over her own screams. Vaguely she felt the weight lifted from her when Gerrit plucked the man off her and flung him to the floor.

Hammond Perry looked up into the face of a madman. He had never seen such a terrifying sight and was momentarily stunned. The Negro's eyes were wild, his mouth an open red cavern. Earsplitting shouts of high fury filled the small cabin, and the air fairly crackled with his rage. The hands that reached to encircle Hammond's neck were as large as a washpan. Hammond knew one moment of intense terror before he was lifted from the floor by the neck like a chicken. Gerrit shook the small man until his neck snapped and his tongue came out. Then he threw him against the wall, where he lay twisted, broken, and lifeless.

Mercy saw what was happening as if she were living a nightmare. She was mad. She had to be. Nothing like this had ever happened. Her mind whirled through a black void, spinning her dizzily into oblivion.

The whiskered man recovered from his terror and drew the gun from his belt. He took aim and fired as Gerrit's hamlike fist swung. The bullet struck, Gerrit stumbled back a step. Then he charged the man, roaring like a mad bull. The terrified man tried to fight him off with the butt of the pistol, but it was a puny effort. The maddened strength of the beast increased. Gerrit picked him up bodily and slammed his head against the stone chimney. It split like a melon.

Gerrit stopped suddenly and stood swaying. A blank look came over his face, his rage leaving him as quickly as it had come. He held his hand to his side, where blood seeped through his fingers and dripped to the earthen floor. He turned his eyes to the woman who lay on he bunk as still as death. Her face was ghostly white amid the masses of gleaming blond hair that spread across her bared breast. Gerrit turned his head this way and that and mumbled, "Purty, purty."

Melcher cowered in the far corner, his gun in his hand. His life depended on one shot. Slowly he eased himself to his feet, his eyes on the Negro, who looked more animal than man.

"Ya bloody beast!" He snarled. He held the gun at arm's length and aimed it at Gerrit's heart.

The door flew open. A woman stood there. Wet hair hung in strings about her face, her wet skirt wrapped about her legs. The rifle in her hands was unwavering. Which of the two were the greatest threat, the woman or the beast? Melcher made an instant decision. He fired his gun. As Gerrit fell, he flung the empty gun at the woman in the doorway and drew his knife. He took one step before the blast from the rifle threw him back against the wall. He hung there. His mouth was wide-open, his hands clawing at his chest where blood was spurting.

"Ya . . . kilt me." He sagged slowly down the wall to the floor and sat there, his eyes open and staring.

Mercy fought her way to consciousness, moaning and sobbing in terror. She screamed for Daniel, for her papa and her mamma.

"I'm here, darling. I'm here." Arms were around her, her mother's reassuring voice in her ear. "Don't be afraid. It's over, darling. You're safe now."

Mercy sobbed uncontrollably and clung to Liberty, who held her and stroked her hair. It was agonizing minutes before the terrified girl grew quiet. Mercy raised her tearstained face and glanced around fearfully.

"Are they gone?" she whispered.

"They're still here, but they're dead. All of them," Liberty added coldly. "Tennessee and I came as soon as poor Jeems dragged himself to the house."

"They let Gerrit out . . . he killed Hammond Perry. I was glad! Mamma! I was so afraid—"

"Did they . . . hurt you?" Liberty asked, and pulled Mercy's dress over her bare breast.

"They brought Gerrit out to watch. He . . . went crazy all of a sudden—"

"Gerrit's dead." Tennessee came and knelt down beside the bunk where Liberty sat holding Mercy. "He lived for a few minutes. I held his hand and soothed his forehead. He seemed to be in his right mind. He called me . . . Mamma." Huge tears trickled down Tennessee's cheeks. "Poor boy."

Liberty clucked her tongue sadly. "Jeems will be lost without him."

"Did they hurt Jeems?"

"He saw your light hair hanging down just before the man struck him down. He didn't know if it was you or I. The poor old man, as badly hurt as he was, staggered all the way to the house."

"Did Gerrit kill all of them?" Mercy avoided looking at the bodies on the floor.

"We'll talk about it when we get home. Daniel will be out of his mind with worry. He was worried because you were not in the house when it started to rain. I was just going out to look for you when Jeems came staggering up to the door."

"Liberty got the guns. We left Eleanor to cope with

Daniel, and Minnie with Jeems." Tennessee found an old coat and covered Gerrit's face.

"I thank God Farr taught me to use the rifle." Liberty helped her daughter to her feet.

"I was sure I'd never see any of you again. Hammond Perry wanted to make sure that I knew who he was. He said he wished Papa was there to see what he was going to do. Hammond said . . . that they would leave me here with Gerrit, and that Gerrit would be hung—"

"Gerrit saved you. That will be a comfort to Jeems."

Liberty looked down at the man who had dealt her and her loved ones so much misery over the past twenty years. He lay there, like a small poisonous snake, looking even smaller in death.

"This was a fitting end for you, Hammond Perry. The world would have been a better place if you never had been born."

Liberty Quill took her daughter's hand, and they walked out into the dark, wet night.

Minnie was waiting on the stoop with a lantern when the three wet, tired women approached the house.

"Dat you? Dat you?" Minnie called. "If dat not Miz Quill, I goin' ta shoot."

"It's us, Minnie. Don't shoot.," Liberty called, and then added to Mercy and Tennessee, "She doesn't even have a gun."

"Ya bringin' dat chile back?"

"Yes, and she's all right."

"Praise de Lord! Hal-le-lu-jah!" Minnie shouted. "Mistah Dan, she a-comin! Miz Quill done found dat chile! Hurry on up in here," she said, scolding. "Mistah Dan 'bout fit ta be tied, he so worried."

Minnie's arms crushed Mercy against her voluptuous softness.

"I'm all right, Minnie. Just wet."

"Just wet? Den what yo dress a-doin' all tore up?" she demanded.

"We'll tell you about it later, Minnie," Liberty said, and held open the door.

The first thing Mercy saw when they all crowded into the house was Daniel, sitting in a chair right in the middle of the kitchen with a rifle across his lap.

"Thank God you're here," Eleanor exclaimed. "He was going outside to look for you."

"Danny!" Mercy ran to him, knelt down, and buried her face against his side. The rifle was lifted from his lap, and his hand cupped her head and held it to him.

"Sweetheart, love! Oh, God, I was so worried."

"Danny, I thought I'd never see you again."

"What happened to her?" Daniel's eyes were as cold as steel as he looked into Liberty's.

"Hammond Perry," Liberty said quietly. "Hammond Perry took her to Jeem's cabin. Nothing happened. Gerrit saved her."

"And . . . Perry?"

"He's dead."

"The men with him?"

"Dead too. We'll tell you everything, but first I've something to tell Jeems."

Some of the tenseness went out of Daniel's shoulders. He hugged his wife to him and kissed the top of her head.

Liberty went to kneel down beside Jeems, who had never in his life remained seated in the presence of white people. He sat now at the table because Daniel had insisted that he sit there and eat the food Minnie had prepared.

"Jeems," Liberty said gently, "Gerrit is dead."

"Lordy, Lordy!"

"He died saving Mercy from being raped and killed

by the men who hurt you. I'm so sorry." She patted the old man's arm. "Gerrit was very brave. We're proud and grateful for what both of you did for us. I'm sorry I couldn't keep the man from shooting him."

"Gerrit dead. Oh, Lordy. I gots ta go ta him."

"No. Stay here with us tonight. Tomorrow we'll see that Gerrit has a burial. He wasn't alone when he died. Tennessee held his hand. And, Jeems, he called her . . . Mamma. Wherever he is, he'll not have to be locked up or afraid. He's with someone who loves him."

"Lordy. Oh, Lordy, Miz Quill . . ." Tears streamed down the old man's face. Minnie came to put her arms around him, and Liberty stood to wipe her eyes.

Eleanor and Tennessee wiped away tears, and Mercy, her head against Daniel, suddenly looked up into his drawn face. Sweat was beaded on his forehead, and he was clenching his jaws so tightly together that the muscles jumped.

"How did you get out here to the kitchen?" Mercy asked.

"He hopped on one foot and used the rifle for a crutch," Eleanor said. "Gavin is the stubbornest man in the world, and Daniel is right behind him."

"You've got to get back in the bed," Mercy exclaimed, suddenly realizing the effort it must have taken for him just to get out of bed, much less come into the kitchen. Dark spots of blood were on his shirt. "Your shoulder is bleeding again!"

"Tenny and I will take care of him, Mercy," Liberty said. "Get out of those wet clothes, honey. You're as exhausted as he is."

Farr was in Liberty's thoughts, as he had been since the morning he'd left to look for George, as he always was when he was away from her. He would be angry with himself for not having been there when Hammond Perry had come. Farr had not expected him to come to Quill's Station, but as always, Perry had done the unexpected, and Mercy had almost been lost to them forever. Hammond had met his end by two whom he considered less than human: Jeems and his demented son, Gerrit. Who would have thought, Liberty mused, that Gerrit, unmanageable for most of his life, would have a lucid moment and see the wrong being done to Mercy?

Farr, darling, hurry home, I miss you so! Liberty worked to help change the bandage on Daniel shoulder and to settle him comfortably in bed. Oh, how she loved these two, who had been orphan waifs so long ago. They were as precious to her as her own flesh and blood. Hester Baxter, whom Amy had named Mercy, and Daniel, the serious little boy, had grown up to be in love and married—to each other. How fast the time had gone by.

Hurry home, Farr, I've so much to tell you!

They were finally alone. The door was closed, and Mercy snuggled close to Daniel's side, her head resting on his uninjured shoulder, her face tilted to his. They talked and talked, between soft kisses. Mercy told him every detail that she could remember about her ordeal. He told her that he had died a thousand deaths while she was gone.

"I never thought when I went out to find the cat that so much would happen. If not for Gerrit, and Jeems coming to get Mamma—" She felt a chill and shuddered.

"I'll see that Jeems is taken care of for the rest of his life." He hugged her to him and tried to push away the chilling thought that he had almost lost her.

"I'll hurt you," she whispered, and moved away slightly.

"Come back—you'll not hurt me! Sweetheart, I hope never again to feel the pain that I felt in my heart when you couldn't be found. They tried to keep it from me that

Mamma and Tenny had gone out looking for you, but I knew in my heart something was wrong. I have never felt so helpless, or had so much fury. If something had happened to you . . ." he whispered in an agonized voice, and buried his face in her hair like a child seeking comfort. "I just want to kiss you and kiss you and hold you. But I know that bastard hit you and you're bruised and sore." He moved his head to kiss her lips, his mouth so tender on hers, so reverent, that it almost brought tears.

"We're a battered pair, Danny. I find new sore spots all the time, and you— That slimy little toad that hired someone to shoot you is dead. I'm glad Gerrit killed him!"

"We're rid of him. Don't talk about it. Talk about something pleasant."

"Like our wedding night, the one we had in Evansville."

"Our next wedding night will be in our own bedroom, in our own house, with our own door shut!"

"What's wrong with this bedroom, this bed? The door is shut." Her hand trailed down his chest, and her finger burrowed into his navel. His hand cupped her buttocks and pulled them tightly against him.

"I'm so hungry for you. I wish we could—" he whispered.

"I wish we could too."

"I could turn on my side if you fixed the pillows for my leg. If I break it open, Tenny will have to stitch it again."

Mercy jumped out of bed and went around to the other side. She carefully piled the pillows between his knees to keep his wounded leg off the bed. She hastily slipped off her nightgown and hurried back to snuggle against him.

"Ah . . . you feel so good. Oh, sweetheart, come here, come here. I want to touch you everywhere," he murmured, running his free hand over her. "Don't ever leave me, not for one day, one hour."

"Hold me, Danny."

"I'm going to hold you every night for the rest of our lives."

He made love to her slowly, with melting tenderness and whispered erotic words that thrilled her. They were so intense in their pleasure of each other, the little stabs of pain they felt occasionally melted away like snow on a warm day. The entry he made was long, slow, and gentle; the plunges and withdrawals exquisitely tender. His lips traveled across her face; his hands teased her breasts.

"I love you, sweetheart," he whispered.

The rain fell softly on the roof while they gently rode the crest of their passion to fulfillment, knowing that for now it was enough to be together, to be joined.

And then, totally exhausted, they slept in each other's arms.

AUTHOR'S NOTE

Quill's Station on the Wabash River, as well as the characters in this story, are imaginary, with the exception of Levi Coffin and John Crenshaw.

Levi Coffin, abolitionist, known as the President of the Underground Railway, assisted thousands of runaway slaves on their flight to freedom. He lived in the area at the time and may have acted as I have portrayed him.

John Crenshaw built his mansion, Hickory Hill, in 1834. I took the liberty of moving the date forward five years in order to include him and his home in this story. After more than one hundred and fifty years, Hickory Hill, known as the Old Slave House, still stands overlooking the rolling Shawnee Hills in Southern Illinois.

In 1847, the Illinois lease system ended, and the salt wells were purchased by school trustees. Crenshaw farmed his land, and it is believed he continued his slave operation until the beginning of the Civil War. He died at Hickory Hill in 1875.

Uncle Bob, the Negro Crenshaw used to beget strong and healthy offspring, fought in the Civil War and died in 1940 at the age of 114. He was of African descent and is said to have fathered more than three hundred children.

I would very much like to thank Rita Farney, of Evansville, Indiana, for the material about Hickory Hill, the area along the Wabash River, and Evansville. *The Cavern of Crime*, by Judy Magee, and the history, *The Old Slave House*, provided by its present owner, Mr. George M. Sisk Jr. were most helpful.

For the readers who may be interested in the death crown mentioned in my story, the information came from my aunt, Orah Delle Colson, of Kingston, Oklahoma. She has in her possession a mysterious clump of feathers known as a death crown. It was found in her dead father's pillow and is as I have described it in this book.

Dorothy Garlock

Dear Reader,

This is the last book of the Wabash River Trilogy. I hope my characters have given you a few hours of enjoyment, while allowing you a peek into the lives of our pioneer ancestors. While writing the books I became increasingly aware of the hardships endured by the people who colonized our country, and now have a greater appreciation for their stamina, courage, and perseverance.

The setting for my next book will be Southwest Wyoming in the year 1872. The story will be about an Irish colleen and the Irishman who loved her. She is an educated, refined young lady, and he a teamster who earns extra money bare-knuckle fighting. Look for *Midnight Blue* to be released in the summer of 1989.

Your letters are appreciated, your ideas recorded. In answer to the many of you who have asked for the other books—The Wabash Trilogy, the Colorado Trilogy, as well as *Annie Lash* and *Wild Sweet Wilderness*—write Warner Books, Box 690, New York, NY 10019.

My address is Warner Books, 666 Fifth Avenue, New York, NY 10103.

Until next time,
Dorothy Garlock